Gallivanting in the Gem City

Other books by Steve Sporleder

- *A Fouled Nest*
- *In the Corner of the Cats* (coming in 2010)

Steve also contributed to:
Saratoga Fire: A Century of Volunteer Firefighting in Saratoga, California, by April Halberstadt

"Los Gatos, the Gem City of the foothills,
is in the most delightful part of the
most delightful California county."

Eugene Sawyer,
History of Santa Clara County, 1922

Gallivanting in the Gem City

Stories of
LOS GATOS, CALIFORNIA

STEVE SPORLEDER

Gallivanting in the Gem City

ISBN: 978-1-935125-57-0

Library of Congress Control Number: 2009939417

Cover design and illustrations by: Letty Samonte
Cats on the Top Cat Tavern section break by: Kim Conley

This is a book of fiction. Most of the characters, names, incidents, organizations, and dialogue in this novel are either products of the author's imagination or are used fictitiously.

Second Printing: February 2010

Printed in the United States of America on acid-free paper

For additional copies of this book go to:
www.rp–author.com/Sporleder

Robertson Publishing
59 N. Santa Cruz Avenue, Suite B
Los Gatos, California 95030 USA
(888) 354-5957 • www.RobertsonPublishing.com

For my parents, Louis and Virginia Sporleder

Table of Contents

Acknowledgments

First, I must thank my dear companion and confidant, Mary Wolf. She always hears my stories first and her feedback is critical. When she laughs when she's supposed to or cries when she's supposed to, I know I'm on the right track. If she scrunches her nose and purses her lips, I know I need to do better.

To my best girl friend Susie Kankel, who corrects my writing, grammar, and spelling. Reading what I give her must seem like fingernails on a chalkboard. I am an academic underachiever, but she forgives me and I'm always grateful and forever in her debt.

To Jennifer L. Carson, my good friend and editor, she makes my dull words and scenes vibrant. I take undo credit for her expertise. I truly learn to be a better writer because of Jennifer.

To Peggy Conaway, Los Gatos librarian, a wonderful author and resource. She and the library staff are extremely knowledgeable and freely share the history archives, an absolutely wonderful resource.

To my dear friend, Kim Conley, for her artistic inspiration and talent.

To Letty Samonte, a wonderful artist and friend. She designed the cover and did the story illustrations; her drawings alone tell a story. Thank you so much.

To Jonathan and Alicia Robertson of Robertson Publishing in Los Gatos, for all their hand-holding and insight into the publishing and marketing world. The product they gave me was absolutely awesome.

To Marnya Campbell, whose words always inspire me: "You can write."

To my parents, Louis and Virginia Sporleder, for sharing their remembrances of the "olden days." But mostly for a sense of home, family, and love of Los Gatos.

And last, but most important, to my children, Lou and Jessica, who have given me the most precious gifts of all: four beautiful and perfect grandchildren!

Just how lucky can a guy be?

Dirty Boys of Boo-Gang

Los Gatos, California, 1933

The sounds of laughter echoed off boulders that surrounded the swimming hole. The boys playing in the water were on the threshold of manhood and the squeak of a changing voice piped every so often. A mossy aroma wafted from damp leaves and debris that were trapped from the current between rocks next to the bank.

The feel of the bottom of the swimming hole was just a bit more than silt. In places large rocks, worn flat from years of erosion, were smooth to the touch. Over the years, most of the stones that were troublesome to footing and could be easily removed were placed under trees along the bank. Most of the bottom where the boys played was gravel that felt good on their feet.

Sunlight dappled through the canopy of trees that hung over the cool water. The sun cast diamonds on the ripples caused by four boys roughhousing in the water.

Gooseflesh adorned the naked chests and arms of the teenagers, and whoops of mock bravado and laughter crossed their lips often. It was another perfect day in the little California town. These four friends had no idea that their lives would change irreparably that summer afternoon in 1933.

The game they were playing was one they played every time they went swimming at Boo-Gang. Boo-Gang was a favorite spot along the Los Gatos Creek for the local youth. A small waterfall rimmed with large boulders splashed down into a swimming hole dug out by cascading water and a lot of time. Huge sycamore and oak trees provided shade on warm summer days. The creek flowed through the town of Los Gatos and emptied into the south end of the San Francisco Bay near Alviso. Downstream, a half a mile from Boo-Gang, sat the town park and municipal swimming pool where most of the young people learned to swim. Adolescence gave access to the swimming hole, leaving the public pool to children and families. The creek continued northward behind homes and businesses toward a gravel quarry on the edge of town, which also served as a hobo jungle after dark. The Southern Pacific Railroad tracks crossed the creek at several locations and ran parallel to the creek most of the way into the cities of Campbell and San Jose. Prune and apricot ranches dotted the landscape along its banks as the creek ran between cities.

Nobody really knows who gave Boo-Gang its name or even how it got the name, not for certain. It was just passed down from generation to generation. The story goes that older boys would hide above the falls and scare younger boys swimming below. The older ones would let out banshee-like wails and "boo, boo, boo!" sending the young ones hightailing it back down the trail toward town. At times, love-struck couples would skinny-dip and make love under the trees. If an article of clothing were hanging from a bush on the trail that led to Boo-Gang, privacy was the implied request.

Today, the four friends were wrestling in the water. Two boys each had another boy on his shoulders. The ones atop grappled with their counterparts and tried to knock the other off—bragging rights were at stake.

"Jesus, Georgie, quit kicking, you're killing my sides," the boy under Georgie said.

"C'mon, John, get me in closer," Georgie urged the boy whose shoulders he sat on.

John's foe down in the water was Arnold Webb. Arnold's brother, Wendell, faced off with Georgie from atop Arnold's shoulders.

"Let 'em have it, Wendell," Arnold screamed to his brother.

The Webb brothers and John Spencer were lifelong friends and classmates from Los Gatos High School. Of the brothers, Wendell was the elder by nearly two years. His dark blond hair was kept short and neat, which accented his chiseled, tan face. Arnold wasn't much like his older brother. He had a rounder face and brunette hair that had hung in his eyes all summer because he couldn't waste time on such vanities when places like Boo-Gang called. The Webb brothers and

John were in the same class. Wendell had repeated the first grade, putting him and Arnold together all through school. Most schoolmates thought they were twins, a notion that both boys resented.

John had been their friend for as long as they could remember. The Spencers lived down the street from the Webbs. When he was younger, John's short red hair and ruddy complexion had reminded more than a few people of a circus clown, but he'd grown out of that awkward stage. His round face had given way to stronger features like a square jaw and hawk-like nose that girls were starting to notice.

Their friend Georgie Hollis lived in nearby Campbell. Georgie was slighter than the others, though he made up for his size with a tremendous sense of humor, and a loyalty that was hard to beat. He was treated like a mascot when he first started to come around, but he soon proved himself to be daring, and he didn't swagger like other rich kids sometimes did. He had told the other three one night while drinking beer that being with them was the best life could offer. "You are my best friends, forever."

"I feel the same about you, Georgie Hollis," John replied in a drunken slur. "You are a man among men." John looked around to Arnold, and Arnold nodded his head. "Whadda say, Wendell?" John asked.

"Yeah, you betcha," Wendell said.

"Goll dern, Georgie! I've had enough of your kickin'!" John whined as he propelled Georgie off his shoulders. At the same time, Wendell made his attack and shoved Georgie forward. The impact changed the direction of Georgie's fall; he crashed into a boulder, head first. The horrible splat was a sound that none of the boys would ever forget. Blood clouded the water.

"Georgie!" the three boys cried with one voice.

John was there first and pulled Georgie to the bank. Wendell fell off Arnold as he tried to leap to aid John. The brothers splashed their way frantically up behind John as he knelt over Georgie. They were all breathing rapidly. All except Georgie.

"Is he breathing?" asked Wendell.

"I don't know," John's voice was high. "I—I don't think…" He leaned over and put his ear to Georgie's mouth. He heard not a whisper of air, felt not a wisp of breath. John bit his lip against the welling in his eyes. He shook his head and whispered, "Georgie's dead."

"We better run to town for help!" Arnold said.

His brother grabbed Arnold's upper arm with an iron grip. "Are you nuts?" Wendell's demeanor startled Arnold.

"What do ya mean, Wendell?"

Nervously he replied, "The cops'll think we killed him!"

Arnold shook his arm to break his brother's bruising grasp. "We did," said Arnold. The brothers turned to look at their friend John.

"He was kicking me in the ribs. It was an accident." John's chin began to tremble. "Oh, God, what have I done?"

"Let's not panic. It was an accident," Wendell said.

Arnold exclaimed, "All the more reason to call the cops."

"Jesus, Arnold, will you think! Pa works for Georgie's dad. If Mr. Hollis finds out we had anything to do with his only son's death, Pa won't work again. Things are tough enough already."

John was shivering as he knelt beside the body of his friend. With a monotone voice and a blank stare he said, "Blood's coming from his ears."

Wendell and Arnold looked at the dead boy. His hairless chest, dripping wet, was motionless.

"What do we do, Wendell?" Arnold asked.

Wendell took a deep breath and crossed his arms. "We have to get rid of him," he answered back with authority.

"No, Wendell! We gotta tell the cops," John replied between sobs. "His folks need to know."

Wendell ignored John and said to Arnold, "Go ask Pa if you can borrow the truck. Meet us under the Main Street Bridge at ten sharp."

"What do I do between now and ten?"

"Find a dame, have a good time—I don't care, just meet us at ten. Jesus. It ain't difficult, Arnold."

"What're you gonna do?"

"We're going to get Georgie ready for his burial."

John swiftly rose to his feet. He got in between Arnold and Wendell and shoved them.

"This isn't happening. We just can't get rid of him. We need to tell Georgie's folks. Please."

Arnold and Wendell looked at one another, searching the other's face for an indication of what the other was thinking. Wendell saw Arnold's shoulders slump and exclaimed, "Oh my God! Arnie, we have to do it this way. You see that, don't you?"

Arnold bobbed his head up and down slowly and turned and headed for town.

Wendell watched as his brother walked away and thought to himself, *Would Pa see it this way?* Their father was a good and sturdy man with morals hard to beat. He always told his sons: "Be accountable for your actions, clean up your own shit, and be a man." *Yeah, this is what Pa would do. I saved the family name and Pa's job*, Wendell told himself.

Lights were beginning to come on in the houses in Los Gatos. Mothers could be heard calling their children to wash up for supper. Shopkeepers were putting sidewalk displays inside for the night. Traffic was light at the intersection of Main Street and Santa Cruz Avenue. Arnold noticed the lights from the baseball diamond at the rear of the high school. He told himself that he would see a ball game and then meet his brother and John.

Old Man Matthews, the police chief, stopped his car for him at a crosswalk. Arnold nodded. The chief raised his right index finger from his grip on the steering wheel in acknowledgment and stared at him through the windshield all the way to the sidewalk across the street. He wondered if the chief noticed he was sweating more than the heat of the day would account for. It was all Arnold could do to keep putting one foot in front of the other. With each step, Arnold was tempted to jump into the car and tell the police chief everything.

But the lean times his family had faced and his father's hard-won job with Mr. Hollis kept Arnold on the sidewalk toward home. *We are nesting on a slippery slope*, he thought to himself. *I hope Wendell knows what he is doing.*

And as he walked along the street with neat little houses, he also wondered, when had his older brother become so self-assured. "Hell, he can't decide what flavor of ice cream he wants, and he's making life-changing decisions," he mumbled as he walked onto the porch of his house.

5

Wendell was drying Georgie's body. Mockingbirds were chirping, almost as if they were scolding. "C'mon, John, you gonna help?" But John just rocked back and forth on his knees as he just stared at the waterfall. With shaking hands, Wendell started to dress the corpse of Georgie Hollis. He lifted the torso to put the shirt back on, and as he lowered the body back down, an audible sound emitted from Georgie's chest. Startled, Wendell sat back on his haunches, his face draining of color.

"Did he say something? Is he still alive?" John Spencer asked with hope in his voice as he crawled on all fours over to where Wendell and Georgie were.

"I dunno," Wendell replied as he moved his face closer to Georgie's. At the same time, John shook the body and cried out, "Be alive! Please be alive!" The movement caused another gurgle, and an air pocket that smelled like vomit blew into Wendell's face. He fell back and wretched and gagged. His body wracked with dry heaves for several minutes, and then his stomach finally started to settle down.

At 9:55 PM Arnold eased his father's stake-side flatbed truck into the creek. He crossed the water behind the high school and drove the Ford up the opposite side. As he approached the Main Street Bridge, he cut the headlamps. Moonlight and the baseball field lights gave him enough illumination to navigate the bank. Wendell was standing next to a cement abutment, and John cradled the corpse, crying. Tenderly John smoothed Georgie's hair, like a mother nurturing a baby. The two brothers waited. Finally they nodded to each other. Arnold went over to John and said, "It's time to go."

"No!" John hissed. The word ricocheted like a bullet off the bridge arch they were standing under.

"John, please, we need to do this," Arnold whispered softly in John's ear.

"That's right, John," Wendell added. "This is the best thing to do."

"Really?" John shot an angry glance stained with tears at the older boy. "You honestly think this is the right thing?"

Arnold dropped his gaze to the ground, while Wendell looked away. But after a long moment, Wendell met John's stare. John could see the steel set into Wendell's grey-blue eyes. Wendell nodded once, slowly. "It's what a man does, John. He cleans up his own shit." He stooped and slid his arms under Georgie's cold body. "C'mon, Arnold. Time to be a man."

Both brothers lifted the body into the bed of the truck. They helped John up off the ground by his shoulders and got into the truck cab. John just stared at the dirty oil-canvas pile that hid Georgie's body. As Wendell cranked the old truck to life, John whispered into the gentle night air, "What about his Ma?"

Wendell drove them along the creek to the quarry. Water lapped at the pilings of a small dock. A diversion channel allowed water into the gravel pit. The quarry workers were long gone, and the hobos were at their campsites. Several campfires could be seen on the hills surrounding the gravel pit when they drove in. The smell of smoke hung over the quarry like an eerie fog. Their actions should go unnoticed because the small dock was behind large piles of gravel and enormous yellow earthmoving vehicles.

The three boys carried the body to the small dock. As Arnold straightened up from laying Georgie on the weathered planks, he glanced at his brother with a look that said, *What now?*

"Before we go any farther," Wendell whispered, "we need to swear that we will never, ever speak of this again." He put his right hand, palm down in front of him. It hung in the air over Georgie.

Arnold quickly put his right hand on top of his brother's.

"This is not some kid's club thing," John said, uncertainly.

"No, it isn't, John. It's more serious than that," Wendell said. "Our futures—all of our futures—depend on this oath."

John looked to Arnold. Arnold pursed his lips, but then nodded agreement. Exhaustion lined John's face, and his shoulders slumped reluctantly. Hesitantly, John placed his hand on top of the two brother's hands.

"That's it then," said Wendell. "Now we better finish up. The oath won't be worth much if we're caught here with him." Wendell looked around. "We need to anchor him somehow."

"Rock and rope," John said with a control that surprised them all.

"Rock and rope it is," Arnold replied.

They put rocks into a burlap sack they found and tied it to Georgie's waist with wire. Arnold found cement pier blocks on the bank near the dock and tied one to each of Georgie's feet. The brothers lowered the body into the creek with unanticipated tenderness. The current from Los Gatos Creek carried the body for a few feet then it rolled. The lifeless face looked back at the trio on the small dock. Small bubbles broke to the surface as the body turned over once again and disappeared under water, leaving nothing but a few ripples where Georgie had just been.

"God, please take our dear friend unto your house," John whispered. "And forgive us our sins."

Arnold stared at the water as it smoothed back to glass. When he spoke, his voice was thin and strained. "What have we done?"

"Saved our butts," Wendell shot back. "Where do you think he'll end up?"

"Probably out into the bay, if he don't get hung up on a snag or something," Arnold supposed.

John doubled over and moaned.

"Come on, John," Wendell said and stepped up to put a hand on John's shoulder. "We did the right thing."

John snapped upright and slapped Wendell's hand off of him. "Goddamn it, Wendell, if you don't shut up I'll knock your block off."

"Yeah, yeah. Tell me about it."

Arnold went over to John to give him a hug.

John started to accept the solace Arnold offered then stiffened and backed away with a small huff, "Don't, Arnie, my ribs are really hurting."

"From what?"

"Georgie was kicking me in the ribs." John clutched at his side. "I think some are broken."

"It was just supposed to be a game," Arnold said.

"Yes, it was, Arnold. A game gone very bad," John replied. The three stood stock-still for several minutes.

Finally Wendell whispered, "Let's beat feet and remember your oaths—not a word to anybody."

The pickup stopped a block from John's house to let him off. He stood on the sidewalk and watched his friends drive away. He didn't move, even after the taillights of the old Ford had faded and disappeared round a corner. *God, please let me get beyond this,* he whispered under his breath. The block-long walk to his home was agony.

Back in the well-worn cab of the old truck, Arnold was surprised when his brother started to whistle a tune. Arnold gave him a sideways glance as he shifted gears.

"What?" Wendell asked Arnold.

Arnold kept his eyes on the road, and his hands gripped tightly on the wood steering wheel. "You're acting as if nothing out of the ordinary happened today, Wendell."

"Oh, it happened, Arnold, but the sooner we put it behind us and get back to normal, the better off we'll all be."

Arnold wasn't sure he should say the next thought plaguing his mind, but finally he couldn't hold it in any longer. "I'm not sure Dad would approve…You know what he always says, 'Be accountable for your own actions, boys.'"

"That's just what I did!" Wendell snarled so vehemently that Arnold half jumped in his seat. "I held us together, I cleaned up the mess, I acted like the man Dad says we should be." Wendell slumped back in his seat and turned to look out the side window before adding softly, "Don't ever forget that."

When John opened the front door his mother started to chew him out: "Where have you been, John Spencer! Your supper was ready hours…" She stopped midsentence when she saw him holding his side and grimacing with each step. "Oh, dear. What happened to you?"

His mother drove him to O'Connor Hospital emergency room. He had a broken rib and numerous bruises on each side of his torso. He told the nurse and doctor that he was in a fistfight and was kicked on the ground. They taped him up and gave him pain medicine.

That night, the brothers lay in their beds, neither sleeping nor whispering as they so often did. Not until after their parents had gone to bed and the house was long quiet did Arnold finally speak. "Did we really do the right thing, Wendell?"

"Yeah, Arnie. I think we did." Wendell shifted and the sheets whispered as he turned over on his side. "Now go to sleep."

But Wendell could not follow his own advice. He tossed and turned all night with two warring thoughts on his mind: *On one hand I saved us—on the other, if we get found out, I'm going to be blamed.*

San Jose, California, 1933

Holden Mawson walked along a cement path in St. James Park in downtown San Jose. He approached his friend, Sterling Kress, sitting on the park bench beneath a Modesto ash tree, the same bench where he had made friends with Holden almost a year ago. Holden, thirty-two, lived in an apartment several blocks from the park. His handsome face, jet black hair combed straight back, and his friendly, outgoing manner made him very popular with the ladies.

He reached his friend and sat down. "You look tired, Sterling. Were you out late last night?"

Sterling nodded his head, but said nothing. At thirty years old he still lived with his widowed mother in one side of a duplex in Willow Glen, a suburb of San Jose. He was a slow-witted man, nearly six feet tall, who had dropped out of school in the seventh grade. He had short brown hair with a high forehead, which made his face appear long and not a little mulish. A lazy eye made it difficult for people to tell which eye to look at while talking to him, but Holden was used to it.

"Well, did you have a date or something?" Holden inquired, leaning back and spreading his arms along the top of the bench. An inquisitive squirrel hopped a zigzag line toward them, eager to see if any morsels might get tossed his way.

"Nah, nothing like that, Maws. My ma got robbed last night when she walked home from her job. Somebody pulled a knife on her."

Holden jerked forward, "Is she okay?" The squirrel darted up the tree at the sudden movement and chided them from a low branch.

"Yeah," said Sterling, just sitting, unmoving, with his head hanging and his elbows propped on his knees. "I just spent most of the night at the police station while they questioned her. God, that place gives me the creeps."

No wonder Sterling looks so hangdog, thought Holden. "Yeah, I know what ya mean. I'm glad your ma is okay."

They sat on the park bench for several minutes looking across the wide expanse of lawn. The summer sun warmed the mown grass, perfuming the air with a sweet earthy smell. The breeze tousled their hair, tiny birds flitted about, and the squirrel decided he had better things to do than scold two sorry men on an old park bench.

Finally Holden broke the silence. "Say, did you read the *San Jose Herald* this morning?" Then he felt bad for asking because he knew his friend couldn't read.

Sterling just shook his head.

"Some rich kid's gone missing. His parents are offering a reward."

That seemed to get Sterling's attention. He sat up and turned toward Holden. "Yeah? How much?"

"Five g's."

"Whew!" Sterling replied and stared blankly at his companion. "That's sure a lotta dough!"

Holden smiled and arched an eyebrow. "Me thinks me smells a payday."

"How so, Holden?"

"If his folks think he's kidnapped," he said lowering his voice as he continued, "we could ask for ransom."

Sterling's eyes lit up as if a light had gone on in his head. "Yeah, just like Lindy's kid, huh?"

"That's right, brother," Holden said nodding and leaning back again. "Just like it."

"How?"

Holden looked over his shoulders and motioned Sterling closer in a conspiratorial manner. He put a hand on Sterling's shoulder and whispered past his ear, "We send 'em a note, tell 'em to put the five g's in a suitcase, and drop it off. Then we say that once we have the money, we'll tell 'em where their kid is."

"Think it'll work?"

"Sure. Why wouldn't it?"

Sterling shrugged his shoulders. "Where is the kid, Holden?"

Holden stretched out his arms across the back of the bench again. "Just let me worry about the details, okay?"

Sterling sat back, too, and nodded. "Okay, Holden."

———◆———

The day that Holden and Sterling had met was one of those foggy mornings so common to the area. Holden had sat down next to Sterling and they exchanged nods. No words were spoken for several minutes until a shabbily dressed hobo approached the two and asked for spare change. Each shook their heads *no* and the hobo shuffled off.

"Why should I give that bum anything?" Holden said.

"I don't know," Sterling responded.

"What's your story, brother?"

"Who, me?"

"Nobody else sitting here but me and thee."

"I got fired from my job at a department store." Sterling told him how he had been out of work for months. Still, every day, his mother packed him a lunch because he couldn't tell her he got fired. She would be disappointed with him, again. So he left the house each morning, brown bag in hand, and hitched a ride into downtown San Jose. He sat on the same bench in St. James Park for eight hours, until it was time to head back home.

Holden nodded understanding. "Why'd they can ya? What did ya do?"

"The boss said I was stupid."

"Being stupid ain't a sin, brother," Holden said, making Sterling smile. They introduced themselves and sat back.

"What about you, do you have a job?"

"A good job," said Holden sitting up proudly. "At a filling station." But then he scowled. "Or I had one. My boss gave my job to an Okie. He took ten cents an hour less than me." Holden slumped against the slats on the back of the dark green bench. "Shoot, I would have taken less money. The bastard just gave my job away. I bet your boss fired you because he could pay somebody less."

"You think so?"

"Hell, yes, Sterling."

"Goddamn that bastard!" Sterling yelled.

Sterling shared his lunch with Holden each day after that. Their friendship grew, and then one evening they entered into a life of petty crime.

—————

It was 11:00 PM and the filling station attendant was putting the oil jars away, getting ready to lock up. The cash drawer was sitting on the desk in the sales room.

Holden and Sterling, dressed in black, sprang from their hiding place behind a stack of used tires. The duo knocked the attendant to the ground, then blindfolded and tied him up.

They got away with seventy-five dollars.

The next caper was a little more daring—a breaking and entering job at the department store where Sterling used to work. They were on the roof of the building removing a turbine vent cover. Holden was surprised at the skill Sterling had with ropes and knots. Sterling lowered himself into the office on the upper floor of the store. Before Holden could lower himself down Sterling was back at the rope with the money. He was smiling up at Holden, hoisting the bank deposit bag in his right hand. The day's receipts, six hundred in cash and several checks, were in the bag.

In his whole life, Sterling had never seen that much money at one time. Holden knew if he gave Sterling his share all at one time he would spend it all right away, so Holden kept the money and gave Sterling just what he was getting when he was earning a paycheck. He did the same for himself. He didn't want to draw suspicion. He kept the rest of the money in a hidey-hole in his apartment.

Los Gatos, California, Present

"There you go, Venice, hon," the waitress said as she placed a cup of hot coffee in front of me. I was sitting with my sister, Lydia, in the café of the El Gato Hotel, just like I do most mornings. This daily ritual is one of my greatest pleasures. She's the manager of the hotel and oftentimes must leave the table to handle some detail that needs her attention.

On this particular morning, Charlie, the desk clerk, approached our table. My sister got that *what-now?* look.

"Not you this time, Lydia. Venice is wanted on the phone."

"Take it in my office, Sweetie," my sister said.

"This is Venice Webb," I said into the receiver expecting it to be my boss in Seattle. Until last year I lived in Blue Port, Washington. My employer is Resorts International Insurance. I am a fire cause investigator and fire safety specialist for hotels worldwide. An injury during my employment in the fire service put me out to pasture with a disability retirement. I came back to Los Gatos, my hometown, last year to assist my sister with funeral and estate arrangements after our dad died, and I just never left. I moved into my childhood home, which my sister owns, and set up an office. She didn't want to charge me rent, but I insisted; my company would be paying it anyway. It is a good situation for all: I live rent free, and my company pays my sister and gets inexpensive office space in return.

"Good morning, Venice, this is Chris at CB Hannegan's." He told me that my old friend, the Professor, was at the bar asking for me.

"Is he drinking, Chris?"

"Like a fish, Venice."

"Don't give him any more. I'm on my way over." Hanging up the phone, I sighed. This could ruin a morning.

———•———

Upon my arrival at CB's, Chris Benson was hosing off the sidewalk. He had a bewildered look on his face. He turned the nozzle off, dried his hands on his apron, and then smoothed his gray beard around his mouth.

"Sorry to bother you with this, Venice." He said as he extended a hand for me to shake. "The prof was sitting in a cab waiting for me when I got here to open. He was pretty well plowed already. When I told him I wasn't going to serve him, he got obnoxious and was raising a scene out here on the sidewalk. I was going to call the cops but thought better of it and called you instead."

I was glad he had decided to do that. John Spencer was a lifelong family friend. My father, uncle, and John went to grammar school and high school together. What's more, John and I had something in common: we were recovering alcoholics. We have both slipped from time to time, though it had been quite some time since I fell. John, however, was a regular returnee to AA meetings. "Thanks for calling me instead of the police."

Chris nodded. "Sure, but could you please get him out of here before the lunch crowd starts to arrive, Venice?"

"No worries, Chris. He'll be gone in a few minutes."

Chris went back to hosing off the sidewalk as I went into his place.

John Spencer was a retired professor of California history at San Jose State University. His classes were well attended. He was one of the most popular instructors during his tenure. Lectures were informative, interesting, and animated—though you couldn't tell it to look at him now.

He sat hunched on a barstool in a dim corner. His once red hair was almost stark white. His bloodshot eyes were starting to mist over. A creased and ruddy face needed shaving and told a tale of better days. Food and booze stains decorated the front of his white polo shirt, urine spotted the front of his pale blue casual slacks, and dock shoes, sans socks, completed the ensemble. He probably looked pretty dapper when he started this episode. Not so now. The cheap whiskey smell and body odor kept Johnny Hannegan, Chris's business partner, stocking booze bottles away from John and at the other end of the bar. Hannegan nodded to me with a bemused look.

"What's happening, John?"

"Hey, Venice. Glad to see you. Can I buy you one?"

I sat on the edge of the stool next to him. "No, thanks. I don't drink."

"Yeah, me neither," he said weakly.

"What do you want to do, John?"

"Have a toddy, goddamn it."

"Do you really think that's a good idea?"

John slapped his hand on the counter and sat up a little straighter. "Sure I do, Venice."

"You can't drink in here today. They cut you off."

"Cut me off? To hell with them!" he shouted.

"That's right, John, they cut you off, and no other place in town is going to serve you either."

"How sad," he said slumping back onto the barstool. "Well, then, just take me home, please, Venice," he slurred.

As I was securing the seat belt around his waist, John exhaled, making me gag.

"If you feel like you're going to puke, let me know so I can pull over," I said, exiting the parking lot.

When we arrived at John's condo in Campbell, he was mumbling under his breath.

Opening the passenger side door, John sobbed, "I have lived with this too long."

"That's how it is, my friend, alcohol doesn't ever leave you be."

John shook his head as he gave me his front door key with trembling hands. "Too long," he repeated.

Opening the door caused me to gasp. Stale booze stench permeated the room. Dirty dishes were piled in the sink and on the counters and table. Four empty Old Crow quart bottles lay next to his bed. His bedroom smelled of sweaty socks. I opened the window to let fresh air in.

While the bath water was running, I gave the toilet and sink a quick scour. When the tub was half full, I went to get John. He was snoring softly. The bath could wait.

A couple of hours later the dishes were done, the trash taken out, the furniture dusted, and the floors swept and vacuumed. John's pad was pretty clean. I was sitting in the spare bedroom that John used as an office. Certificates, diplomas, and photographs lined the wall. One of the photos, a black and white one, showed a group of teenagers at an outside dance pavilion. My father, Uncle Arnold, and John were evident in the crowd. White letters on the bottom of the photo said SARATOGA SPRINGS—1932. Another picture from a newspaper showed a mob of men ramming a telephone pole into the door of a building. The caption under the picture said LYNCH MOB STORMS JAIL. The photo was dated 1933. There were X marks over several of the thirty or so men holding onto or standing around the pole. The hair prickled on my neck. *What did those Xs represent?* I chewed over. The photo was from an incident that took place in San Jose when my father was in high school. One of his friends was kidnapped and found dead several weeks after his abduction.

I knew that the name of the abducted boy was Georgie Hollis, and my father had considered him a dear friend. I recalled a stag barbeque my father hosted in our yard after hunting season. Ducks were on the grill and men were standing around talking, some sober, a few drunk. My dad was ordering me to get this and do that. I wasn't bothered by this; in fact I was happy to be finally included. Sometime after dinner a scuffle broke out between John and my Uncle Arnold. My father intervened, but before they parted my father stood toe to toe with John Spencer and said vehemently, "Georgie was my friend, too, John." And he spun on his heels and walked back to the picnic table, removing his apron and throwing it on the ground in disgust.

———————

I had been in John's condo about three hours when the retching started. John was on his knees hugging the porcelain. I stood over him and flushed the mess away.

"Get me a cola, Venice, please, in the refrigerator."

With trembling hands he took the can of cola and gulped down half. He belched and leaned back over the commode. Nothing came up. Another swig and another belch.

"Whew, that's better."

"You look terrible, John."

"Thanks."

"Want a bath?"

He ran fingers through his dirty hair, "No, a shower sounds better."

I continued tidying as he showered. About the time the water turned off, I sat down with a soda myself. As John was toweling himself off in the other room, I yelled in from the living room, "How you doing, partner?"

"A little rough around the edges, but okay. Thanks for helping me, Venice."

No reply was needed. Every recovering drunk knows that helping a soul in distress is therapeutic for both parties. He would do it for me in a heartbeat.

He was buttoning his blue oxford shirt as he entered the living room.

"Feel like talking, John?"

He shrugged. "Suppose so."

"Do you feel like you want another drink?"

"Oh, God, yes."

"If I left, would you get another quart?"

"I would have the liquor store deliver several bottles and start all over again." He sank down in an armchair canted off to the right of mine. "So don't leave."

I nodded. "Maybe you better figure out why you called the liquor store instead of me when you had the urge."

He just sat with his head down. I can become a little preachy at times when it comes to recovery. The silence was palpable. "Do you want a suggestion, John?"

"What do you have in mind?"

"Get into a rehab center."

He reached for the soda can he'd left on a dated Danish-style end table and took several sips before answering. "How and where do I do that?"

"John, first, you have to believe your life is unmanageable because of alcohol."

John barked a disgusted laugh. "You have a gift for stating the obvious, Mr. Webb."

"Don't talk to me like a delinquent student."

"Then you quit treating me like a patient."

"If you want to get loaded, hey, great, go for it. But if you want to get sober, I'll help. Either way, I'm your friend. Just let me know."

He just sat there staring out the window, can dangling from his right hand as his arm rested across the arm of the chair. Nothing was said for what seemed like years. It was probably only two minutes.

Finally I broke the silence. "There is a place in the Santa Cruz Mountains called the Camp. I know the director." I stood up and put my own soda can in the trash. Before I turned to go, I said, "If you want to give it a try call me."

I hadn't reached the door when John asked me to call the Camp.

Santa Cruz County, California, Present

As I drove John over the summit from Santa Clara County into Santa Cruz County, John rode in silence. He was taking a giant step toward recovery. He told me that his first entry into sobriety was court ordered because of drunken driving charges. It felt fitting to let him talk. Listening is just as important as talking among drunks trying to get sober. *Take the cotton out of your ears and put it into your mouth*—that's what they say at meetings. Good advice, but hard to do.

I gave John a hug in the administration building.

"Tell Lydia I won't be in for lunch for awhile. If you want, you can tell her where I'll be." He looked so small and alone as he was led through the door to the treatment area; my heart went out to him. He wouldn't be able to have visitors for ten days.

My friend Florence, the director, assured me John would be fine. "Don't worry," she said. I told her before leaving that his bill would be covered if his insurance didn't pay all costs.

The Camp is located just a few miles from Santa Cruz and the Pacific Ocean. I really loved the water and decided it had been too long since I'd enjoyed a walk along the ocean. After parking my car across the street from the Boardwalk, I entered the arcade. The bells, buzzes, and clinks from the video machines were deafening. The smell of popcorn, cotton candy, and candy apples made my mouth water.

Strolling down the Boardwalk, eating a bag of popcorn, my mind went back to high school and the Easter vacations spent in Santa Cruz. Not a care in the world; five days of sitting on the beach looking at the girls in two-piece bathing suits, followed by five nights of drinking and chasing after those girls.

The click-clack of the roller coaster climbing the first hill of its ride brought me back to the present. I watched the cars of the coaster reach the top and plummet down the other side. The yells and screams are the same from generation to generation.

I was standing in front of a building that used to house an indoor swimming pool called the Plunge. It was now an annex of the Santa Cruz County Historical Society History Museum. A museum didn't quite seem to fit in this atmosphere, so I went inside to check it out. Maybe John would enjoy visiting it on one of his days away from the Camp.

The young blonde behind a desk greeted me with a warm smile and hello.

"How's business?"

"Pretty slow."

The room seemed dim after being out in the sun. I blinked and looked around at the cases and counters housing exhibits. "How long has this annex been here?"

"Almost a year. It's a pilot program that started because of low attendance at the downtown location. The directors thought the foot traffic on the Boardwalk would generate business." She looked embarrassed about the explanation. She told me her name was Blair and that she had been a docent for two months. I asked her if she ever wished she could be on the beach rather than working. She got a glazed look in her eyes and nodded yes. She was a very typical beach girl.

"What qualifies you as a docent?"

"I am in my senior year at UC Santa Cruz majoring in history. My senior project is on California seaside communities. This job was a natural for me. My boyfriend works here too. Are you from around here?"

"I was born and raised back over the hill in Los Gatos. I remember when this used to be the Plunge," I said, sweeping my hand around me.

"You remember the Plunge? Wow."

Suddenly I felt ancient. She saw the look on my face.

"I didn't mean to say it like that. I apologize. Would you like a guided tour or do you want to go around by yourself?"

"Do you have time to give me a tour?" She looked around and nodded her head in a *yeah-I-think-so* manner.

She got up from behind the desk. She was wearing a pair of faded Levis that fit low on her hips. Her sweater rode above her navel. As she walked away from me toward the displays she automatically hiked her pants up and started talking about the first display.

It displayed the geology of Northern California, a very detailed dimensional map that started at the summit, stretched down into Santa Cruz County and over to the Monterey County coastline to the south, and reached to the San Mateo County coast to the north. There was a cutaway that showed layers from topsoil to the earth's core.

The next exhibit displayed skeletons and drawings of prehistoric animals. It depicted photographs of archeological digs in Davenport, just up the coast north of Santa Cruz. She started to explain about the

Loma Prieta earthquake. I had heard enough about this, but not wanting to interrupt her delivery, I let her go.

The phone started to ring. She looked at me, and I nodded for her to go and get it. I was relieved that she was gone. I quickly went through the next displays. I had seen enough photos in my lifetime of the Coastal Indians, the missions, and the fruit and lumber industry to last, well, a lifetime. The fishing and fish canning display was very well done. I knew that some of the Stagnaro family, a pioneer fishing family, had to have helped with this display. The Italian fishermen and their many boats would off-load their catch at canneries in Santa Cruz. When those canneries went out of business the fishermen would then take their catch to Monterey. After fifty or sixty years the bay was fished out as far as commercial fishing was concerned. Most commercial fishermen now charter to weekend hobbyists. The canneries in Santa Cruz gave way to homes; Monterey's gave way to boutiques and restaurants.

I skipped the housing boom and urban sprawl that hit postwar California. I lived that era and could lecture on the subject.

The public safety display was done expertly. A placard thanked the firefighters of the Santa Cruz City Fire Department and the Santa Cruz County Fire Department for their help in setting up the exhibit. Glass cases of firefighting equipment and old helmets and badges were neatly displayed. Some pictures of past devastating fires hung on a wall. Group photos of firefighters from the past standing in front of old fire stations on ancient fire apparatus are part of any fire department's archives. I lingered here, half daydreaming about my former life as a firefighter.

Blair rejoined me as I was entering the police department section of the public safety display. "Sorry I had to leave. Do you have any questions?"

I told her I didn't and continued to look at pictures of old crime scenes. One picture caught my eye. It was the same picture I observed earlier at John's house, except it was clearer and there were no *X*s over any of the figures. The placard for this photo display said that the Santa Cruz County Sheriff's Department offered aid to their counterparts in Santa Clara County to stop a riot and lynch mob. They obviously weren't very successful at stopping the mob since the next picture showed two men hanging in St. James Park in downtown San Jose. She noticed me gazing at the representation. I was reading a newspaper article that indicated that the men arrested for the kidnapping swore over and over to their dying breaths that they didn't kidnap or kill anybody. After reading about the missing kid, they had just thought up a scheme to try and get ransom.

Blair started talking about the photo. "People don't think that vigilantism can happen in the twentieth century. Most think it was only in the wild west. That happened in San Jose in 1933," she said pointing at the picture.

"I know about that incident."

"You weren't there for it. C'mon, you're not that old," she said grinning.

I laughed.

"Well, did you know that one of the men lynched had an alibi?" Blair asked.

"No, I didn't know that," I answered, perplexed.

"Yeah. Sterling Kress was at the police station at the time Georgie Hollis was kidnapped."

"Are you kidding me? How come the police didn't tell people that?"

Blair stood staring at me with wide eyes shaking her head in an *I-don't-know* fashion. I realized that my voice went up an octave or two. "Sorry. It's just that I was surprised by that revelation."

"A lot of people are surprised by this incident."

I told Blair that the displays were expertly done and complete. She thanked me as I started to leave. I slipped a twenty into the donation jar on the desk, and she thanked me again.

Los Gatos, California, Present

On the way back into Los Gatos I stopped at the El Gato to let my sister know what was going on with the Professor. She frowned as her face registered her concern. "Just a minor setback, Sis. He's in the best spot he can be at this time."

"I suppose so," she said, then invited me for supper. I told her that my friend Kate and I were supposed to have dinner that night. Kate was my high school sweetheart, and we'd become reacquainted since I'd come home.

"Already covered," Lydia said with a twinkle in her eye and a one-sided smile. "She'll be at your house at five o'clock." While we continued to talk, Lydia's partner, Helen Gray, walked over to us. Her hair was well coiffed, and she always smelled like a strawberry popsicle. Lydia and Helen had been together for over twenty years. Helen owned the El Gato Hotel. Both women wore business suits while at work and never showed overt affection toward one another in front of the hotel staff. When I was with these two women, the term *unconditional love* always came to mind. They were my family, and I loved them unconditionally right back.

At my home office there was a fax from my boss telling me about an important staff meeting in Seattle next week that I needed to attend. I still owned a small house in Blue Port near Lake Washington so I always had a place to stay. I marveled again how my arrangement with Resorts International was really pretty sweet. Telecommuting was the way to go. Faxes, e-mail, and laptops were my tools, and I could take them anywhere. The only downside was that when I moved to Los Gatos, my beat became the Western United States, which caused me to lose travel to more exotic locations such as the tropics and Europe. But in the end, being home again was the best perk—that and Kate Wilson.

After finishing a fax to the office, I heard the back door open. Kate entered the kitchen, dressed in a pair of blue jeans and a black knit pullover. She looked stunning. Every time I see her, my heart skips a beat. Every single time.

"What are you doing, Venice?"

"Waiting for the one I love."

"You say all the right things."

We embraced and kissed. We needed to leave for Lydia's. Kate gave me a *wait-until-later* look. I offered her my arm and we walked the few blocks to my sister's house.

Lydia had prepared a pitcher of martinis for the girls; I had a tonic with lime. We were sitting in the living room. My sister's house is one of the most comfortable places I have ever been in. Berber beige carpets and a couch of pale green brocade with matching love seat made up one side of a conversation area. Across a large oval cherry coffee table were two tan upholstered easy chairs making up the other side of the conversation area. The open drapes shifted lazily in a gentle breeze, and the picture window revealed the pleasant tree-lined street outside. A vanilla candle was emitting its aroma from somewhere within the dwelling. Every so often a hint of garlic introduced itself. I took a deep breath and sank back happily into the overstuffed couch.

"Sorry to hear about John, Venice," Helen said.

I shot Lydia a disappointed look. She just shrugged her shoulders. I stopped myself from rolling my eyes; trying to protect John's anonymity was useless. Then again, he probably wouldn't be upset that his friends were talking about him. With a sober voice, I told them all about John's stay in treatment. We toasted him with our drinks—John would appreciate the irony.

After a dinner of roasted chicken, green beans, and oven potatoes, we went back into the living room for coffee. I told them about my walk along the Boardwalk. They were intrigued by my account of the museum and the demise of the Plunge. I mentioned the photographs at the museum and the one on John's wall.

"I remember Dad talking about that," said Lydia. "Don't you remember, Venice?"

I nodded yes.

"Are you talking about the lynching in St. James Park?" Kate asked.

"Yes, some boy, a friend of our dad's, was kidnapped and murdered. The men who did it were caught red-handed trying to extort the ransom money. A lynch mob stormed the jail and hung them in the park."

Helen sat shaking her head and tsking.

Kate knew quite a lot about the event because of a class she took from John at San Jose State.

"The two men were jailed because of the kidnapping. The boy was from a prominent farming family."

"Hollis." Lydia and I said simultaneously.

"Yes, that's the name. He was in his late teens and didn't come home one evening. The guys who took him thought they covered their tracks. But the local sheriff caught one of them talking on the phone to the family trying to get them to bring money. They nabbed him, and he gave up his friend. They were in jail the day the body was found."

"That sounds like a movie," Helen said.

"When John was talking in class," Kate continued, "he was very animated and threw his hands all over with herky-jerky movements." Kate stopped and lowered her voice as if she wasn't sure she should say such things about John. "You know he got so into it, spittle formed on the corners of his mouth. It was really rather strange and not a little unnerving. One student asked him if he was there. He said simply yes and moved on in the lecture, didn't say much about what he was doing there."

We all exchanged looks. If John Spencer was at the lynching, that meant that Wendell and Arnold might have been there also. The *Xs* in the picture crashed back into my psyche.

I'll have to ask John about the people in the picture, I thought to myself. Then I told them what Blair had said at the museum. "Did you know that one of the men lynched had an alibi, and the police never told anybody about it?" They were all tsking now.

Santa Cruz County, California, Present

John was at the Camp for ten days when he called and asked me if I would come to a group meeting that night. "We're supposed to have family members attend. Florence said it would be fine if you came, Venice. You and Lydia are the only family I really have."

When John greeted me in the reception area, he gave a sincere hug.

"How are you doing, John?"

"Mostly good, Venice. I still have some things to work out."

"This is the best place for that," I told him.

We took seats in the meeting area of the main building. Florence asked if there were any visitors. I stood up and said, "My name is Venice, and I am an alcoholic." The group answered back in unison, "Hello, Venice." Several people stood up and introduced themselves. Some were family members or loved ones, others were just people in need of serenity.

Florence stated, "The topic for the meeting tonight is *choices*. Would anybody like to start off?"

A boy about eighteen stood up and said, "My name is Tony, and I am an addict and an alcoholic."

"Hello, Tony," the group answered in unison.

"In my short life I have had to make many choices. One choice was to use drugs and drink. My most recent choice was to not drink and use drugs." He received a round of applause. Several people stood with similar stories. I was looking at John to see if he would say anything. He looked at me and stood up just before Florence was going to close the meeting. "I want to thank my friend Venice for bringing me to the Camp." John was clearly the oldest person in the room by at least thirty-five years.

"I'll be eighty-three years old on my next birthday." The crowd started to clap. He stopped them by raising his hands. "I never thought I'd live this long. I retired from teaching ten years ago. Making the choice to go into teaching was easy. To retire was not. I've made other choices in life where I didn't do quite as well as when I picked my career—choices I'll regret all my remaining days. Some of those choices were made with friends no longer living."

His voice was chilling, and he was staring right at me. In a split second the teaching instincts took over, and he had the attention of the group. They soaked in his wisdom, laughed at his jokes, and really liked him. He needed that. I was uneasy, however. Was he referencing the photo with the *Xs*?

Florence announced the meeting was over. The group stood up, held hands, and recited the Lord's Prayer.

John showed me to his room—a single twin bed with a green plaid bed spread and matching window curtain. The headboard, nightstand, dresser, and chair consisted of mismatched wooden material. The tan carpet was a well-worn low pile. Shower and restroom facilities could be found down the hall

"Did it feel good to get up in front of a group again, John?" I asked as I sat on a wooden desk chair. John was sitting on the edge of his bed.

"Yeah, the old feelings come back now and then. But this is somehow a different motivation than teaching."

My stare stopped him.

"What?" he asked.

"John, when you were teaching, you were making a living."

After a moment he replied, "Yes. So what's your point, Venice."

"Now you are in treatment so you can keep *on* living. Do you see?"

A slow smile spread across John's face. "Thank you, Venice. I need to get grounded from time to time. I will think about that for a long time."

Florence stopped by and announced that next Saturday John could leave the premises for a few hours. John didn't say anything. I told him to be ready to go to lunch next Saturday at eleven o'clock. With a wide grin, he said that was fine.

At the end of the porch that led to the parking lot, John thanked me for coming and supporting him.

All the way home my mind was thinking about what he'd said: *I have made choices with friends no longer living.*

———◆———

I tossed and turned all night long. I gave up trying to sleep at six and walked up the creek trail to Boo-Gang. I always found the creek trail to be a place of solitude and Boo-Gang a sanctuary for figuring things out. The early morning chill made my breath visible. A man and his dog jogged toward me. The man's face was pained as he nodded a greeting. His dog, on the other hand, had a huge smirk on his mug.

I sat on a rock along the bank near the waterfall. The sycamore trees overhead let in early morning sunlight, and the lightly churning water masked any sounds of the town.

Choices, choices, choices. What did John mean?

Los Gatos, California, Present

I was pulling weeds out of the pea gravel on the driveway when a throaty-sounding muffler roared up behind me. My friend Gil Morales stopped in front of the house in a restored 1949 Mercury convertible. Gil was in his late sixties but looked like he was still living in the 1950s. Except for his hair, that is. He still styled it in a DA, or as might be more politely described, a duck's tail. It was more silver than the shiny jet black of his younger years. Levis and a white T-shirt finished off his look. He turned off the engine and the relative peace of the street returned.

"Hola, amigo. What are you up to?"

"Nada, Gilberto. Just doing gardening chores." I said straightening up and stretching my back. "Como esta, compadre?"

"Hey, your Spanish is getting better, Venice."

"Thank you. Hey. How is your mama getting along?"

"She's good. Every day she thanks the Lord for you and asks Him to bless you."

"That's nice. Tell her thanks for the prayers. I need them."

My uncle left me his house when he died and Gil's mother now lived there. She had a tough life and deserved a break.

"Where are you off to, Gil?"

"Downtown San Jose, to the courthouse. Do you want to ride along?"

"Anything beats pulling weeds. Let me wash up."

Cruising down Bascom Avenue the wind blowing our hair, Gil said, "I remember when there was nothing but apricot and prune orchards as far as the eye could see."

"Do you miss the orchards?"

"Yeah, now I do. But back when my family was picking fruit, my sister, Connie, my brother, Javier, and me would wish that a fire would rage through where we were working so we could take the day off. Stupid when you think about it. No picky, no tickey."

Gil parked in front of the courthouse in a passenger-loading zone. "I'll leave the keys if the fuzz comes by and you have to move."

I looked at the push-button starter and the gearshift, confident that driving it would be within my capabilities.

Pedestrians slowed down and admired Gil's car. Feeling funny about sitting in the passenger seat, I got out and sat on a cement planter on the sidewalk next to the car. I was staring at St. James Park across the street. A cold chill went through me. Could I be looking at the same tree where the lynching took place?

I was so lost in my thoughts that I didn't notice Gil's arrival till he was right in front of me.

"You look like you've seen a ghost, Venice," he said.

"Do you remember hearing about the lynching that happened across the street?" I asked, motioning my head toward the park.

"Mama worked for the family of the kid who got killed."

"The Hollises?"

"Yeah, that's their name. They were a rich family. Most of my relatives worked for them from time to time, either in the house or in the orchards."

"Do you think your mama would answer some questions about them?"

"Probably. Why such an interest in that, amigo?"

Telling him that seeing a picture piqued my curiosity was a good enough explanation for Gil.

Entering Gil's mother's kitchen, the smell of simmering onions, garlic, and cilantro made me salivate.

"Mama, Venice Webb is here to see you."

Yolanda Morales spun around and gave me a huge hug. In broken English she told me how happy she was that I came to visit, and told us to sit and she would fix us something to eat. Warmed over tamales and beans satisfied my hunger.

Gil's younger sister, Connie, came in the front door. She smiled warmly at me. "Hola, Venice." She wore a pair of tight jeans and a sleeveless white blouse that added to her allure.

I smiled back and said "Hola, Connie," as we gave each other a hug. The two of us had spent time together at a school dance after a football game. I remember our first dance together; it was to a song called "Sleepwalk" by Santo and Johnny. Every song that played, we danced to. Guys would try to cut in, and she would tell them no.

Connie sat down at the table and joined us as we chatted. After about thirty minutes, Gil told his mother that I had questions about the Hollis family. When she heard the name she crossed herself. "Those poor souls," she said under her breath.

"What did you do for them, Yolanda?"

"Cook and clean."

"Where do they live now?"

"Jane, the girl, lives in the farmhouse by herself. She never married."

She went on to explain that Mr. and Mrs. Hollis were very good to work for. The boy's name was Georgie, and when he died Mr. Hollis never really recovered.

"Mrs. Hollis hardly ever got out of bed after that." She crossed herself again and her eyes teared up. Connie reached over and squeezed her mother's hand. No doubt she was thinking about Javier, her own son who had died a teen. My heart went out to her.

"Georgie and Jane were nice children. They always had friends over. That is where I met Senor Wendell, and Tio Arnold." Yolanda tapped a finger to her mouth. "You know, I might still have it…Wait here, Senor." She stood up with a noisy scrape of the chair across the linoleum floor. When she came back, she loaned me a folder of news articles about the kidnapping, murder, and lynching.

Campbell, California, Present

Miss Jane Hollis was sitting on the front porch of the Victorian farmhouse when I walked up the brick path.

"You must be young Webb."

"That I am, Miss Hollis."

She was a slender woman with a thin face and strong chin. Her hair was gray and nicely coiffed. She wore a dress with flower prints on it. We shook hands; her grip was firm and her hand was warm.

"Please have a seat." She gestured with her head to a white wicker chair. It was part of a set that included a chaise, a rocker which she was seated in, and a coffee table.

"I was surprised by your call, what did you say your first name was?"

"Venice, Venice Webb."

"Yes. Venice. When you called, I was baffled. Nobody has asked me about Georgie in a long, long while. Why are you interested?"

I told her about the photo of the lynch mob and that my curiosity wouldn't let me forget about it.

"Well, some things are best not dredged up. Don't you have a job?"

"Yes, I do. I am a fire investigator for an insurance company. Before that, I was in the fire department in Washington state."

"Fire department and insurance? It fits that you would follow after your father and uncle."

"You knew my father and uncle?"

"Hell, yes, I knew them. Georgie and I were their friends. Did you know that your grandfather worked for my father?"

"No, I never knew. When was that?"

"Mr. Webb and his sons built our tractor shed in the summer of either '31 or '32." She sighed as she rocked. "Can't remember for sure, that was a lot of years ago."

Campbell, California, 1931

"It's gonna to be hot today. Did you boys bring water?"

"They got water there, Pa," Arnold answered.

Wendell sat sulking in the bed of the truck as it rattled down the road. Today it was Arnold's turn in the cab. Conrad Webb pulled the flatbed to a stop next to a rose garden that lined the driveway next to the house. Wendell and Arnold took their canvas tool aprons and headed for the tractor barn.

George Hollis, Sr., came out onto the porch to talk with Conrad Webb. "Hiya, boys."

Wendell and Arnold waved to Mr. Hollis and continued to the barn. This was a morning ritual. The men would converse about the construction, weather, crops, and politics. Same thing every morning. But during that conversation Mr. Hollis would let Conrad Webb know what he expected to have completed that day. It was a good system, and Conrad liked it.

"I expect you'll finish today, Conrad."

"Lord willing, Mr. Hollis."

"Fine. I'll be here at five to pay you and your boys off. See you then."

"Sounds good to me, sir."

George Hollis nodded to the other man and turned to go into the house. Conrad Webb could see that Mr. Hollis had a big wet sweat stain on the back of his dress shirt. *It is going to be hot today,* he thought to himself.

The depression hit everybody hard. Work was taken where it was found. Conrad Webb was a carpenter by trade, but there just weren't any jobs to be had. So when Mr. Hollis contacted him to build a tractor barn on the Hollis Ranch he jumped at the opportunity. He was told that it needed to be completed by the first of September, and

Conrad Webb committed himself and his sons for the job. Everybody knew that Conrad Webb was honest and did fine work. If he said he would do something, he did it.

———————

"Goll dern sum bitchin' jackin' bastard!" Conrad Webb yowled after hitting his thumb with his framing hammer.

"What happened, Pa?"

"Nothing. Keep working."

Wendell and Arnold were putting the last of the shingles on the roof of the tractor barn. "Hey, Wendell, what is a jackin' bastard?" Arnold did a perfect impression of his father. Every time one of the brothers mimicked their father the other couldn't keep from laughing. Today was no exception. In spite of the extreme heat on the roof, the boys were in hysterics.

"What's so goll dern funny?"

"Nothing, Pa. The heat is getting to Arnold. We're coming down."

The interior of the barn was at least fifteen degrees cooler than the roof. It smelled of freshly sawn wood and body odor. The boys were leaning on a wooden half-wall that would be a parking stall for equipment. Their father worked at stringing together the knob-and-tube wiring. When he moved the ladder, the nails clanked against the porcelain knobs and tubes in the pocket of his apron.

"You ready for some water, Pa?" Wendell asked.

"Yes, I am."

Arnold took an old pickle crock to the garden faucet outside and filled it with cool water. He handed the ladle to his father first. Then he handed it to Wendell and finally took refreshment for himself. Oldest to youngest. That is how it was with the Webbs.

"Don't drink too much, boys. You don't want to get sluggish."

"We got about a square left to do, Pa, and we're finished," Arnold exclaimed.

"After you finish the roof, you come down and help me with the wiring, Arnold.

"Wendell, you clean all the debris off the roof and rake up around the ground. Put all the trash in the truck. Do you understand?" Both boys nodded.

Back on the roof, Wendell, started stomping around, kicking trash off the roof. Wendell knew Arnold was making an effort to keep out of his way, but he didn't care.

"You want to switch jobs, Wendell?" Arnold finally asked.

"No. I'll do the grunt work today," Wendell huffed. "It don't matter."

But of course, it did matter. He was the oldest son. He felt he should be working by his father's side, and Arnold should be doing the menial chores. Maybe his father thought Arnold was smarter. Arnold telling his father that there was only a square left to do on the roof as they drank water was a quote from Wendell.

As he was raking up around the perimeter of the barn's exterior Wendell could hear his father giving instruction to Arnold on the phases of electricity. Every once in a while he heard the words *ohms*, *watts*, and *fuses blown*.

Maybe Pa thinks I can't make up my mind, Wendell thought to himself.

"They'll see."

At four forty-five, Georgie Hollis, Jr., his mother, and his sister drove up to the tractor barn in a beige Chrysler convertible. The huge chrome grill reflected the bright sun. They exited the car with a pitcher of lemonade, cubed ice, and glass tumblers.

"Hey, Wendell. Hey, Arnold," Georgie Hollis said as a greeting.

"Come, have a cool drink of lemonade. Yolanda made it for you," Mrs. Hollis said. When Mrs. Hollis looked at the sweaty dirty faces of the boys, she exclaimed, "Good heavens, Conrad, you shouldn't be working these boys so hard. They're just children."

"Hard work won't hurt 'em none," he said as he took a glass from Jane. "Thank you, Miss."

"You boys going to the dance Friday night?' Georgie asked.

"You bet," Arnold declared.

"Isn't that nice, Jane? Maybe you will have somebody to dance with," Georgie said snidely.

"Don't be a brat to your sister, George Hollis, Jr.," said his mother.

Jane's cheeks pinked up and Georgie snickered.

"You bet, I'll dance with you," Arnold said.

"Thank you, Arnold. I accept," she said as she gave her brother a dirty look.

Mrs. Hollis told Mr. Webb that her husband would be home any minute. Conrad said that would give him the time he needed to hook up the fuse box, and the barn would be complete. She acted interested, but wasn't.

When Mr. Hollis drove up to the barn in his black Pontiac sedan, Mr. Webb turned the barn lights on. Mr. Hollis got out of the car smiling from ear to ear. "It is a fine barn, Conrad. You and your boys did a bang-up job. Thank you very much," Mr. Hollis exclaimed with his hands on his hips.

"I'm glad you like it. Thanks for the work," Conrad said grinning from ear to ear.

Hollis gave him an envelope fat with money. "This should cover materials and labor, Conrad. If it doesn't, let me know."

"I am sure it is just fine, Mr. Hollis," he said as he slipped the envelope into his coverall pocket without counting it.

"Will we see the Webbs at the dance?"

"We'll all be there," Arnold said looking at Jane Hollis. Her cheeks turned pink again.

After a final walk-through and cleanup, the Webb clan climbed into the truck and drove home. Though it was Wendell's turn to ride in the cab, he chose to get in back. Arnold shrugged and just climbed in the cab next to his pa. No reason he had to suffer along with Wendell just because Wendell was in a stew. After jostling along the road a minute or two, Pa asked, "Why did you tell them we would be at the dance, Arnold?"

"Don't get your water hot, Pa. The man just paid you for work done. His feelings might get hurt if we didn't accept his invitation."

"I suppose you're right."

"Besides," said Arnold, "might be nice to dance with Jane Hollis. She's a real peach." Pa nodded once, which Arnold took to mean he accepted the explanation. Nothing more was said on the ride home.

Los Gatos, California, 1931

Back at their house, they washed off in an outside shower Mr. Webb had rigged up in an enclosed space between the house and garage next to the back door. Each of them had a robe hanging on a hook. When finished showering and drying off, they would each don their respective robe and go inside to change. On the way in they would discard dirty clothes in a laundry basket. The workman's shower was a godsend. There was less mess in the house, and the only cleanup was to take the robes back out to the shower stall. Mrs. Webb usually did that chore.

In the kitchen, Clara Webb was preparing dinner. She was standing at the sideboard getting silverware ready to set the table.

"How did it go today, dear?" She asked her husband as he came in the kitchen in a clean pair of overalls and a clean blue work shirt.

"It went just fine. We finished and got paid."

"Oh, how nice."

Pa went up behind her and put his arms around her waist. "Say, would you like to go to a dance Friday night?"

Clara turned around within the circle of his arms. "Are you asking me out on a date, Conrad Webb?"

"You bet I am. You know you're my best girl, you sugarplum," he said and kissed her forehead.

"Conrad, stop it! The boys will see."

"Let 'em. Their combs are red anyway. You should see 'em bowing and scraping over Miss Jane Hollis."

"She is a lovely girl. She would be a nice catch for one of my boys," she mused as she set the table.

To have money in the cookie jar during tough economic times was a feeling of security and accomplishment. Times were good around the Webb household for now. During this depression, people were migrating by the droves into the valley looking for work. Jobs were few and far between.

After dinner each boy was given fifty dollars for their summer labor of building the Hollis tractor barn.

"What are you going to do now, Conrad?" his wife asked him.

"Well, I don't rightly know. Use that flatbed truck to haul materials, I guess. They're starting to build the Southern Pacific Depot in San Jose. You boys up for it?"

"Conrad, there's only two weeks before school starts. Let them have a break."

"I suppose so, but they can work around here."

"There will be plenty of chores to do," she said with a smile.

Wendell and Arnold sat at the kitchen table saying nothing, just listening and looking at their parents. After the dishes were done the two boys went out on the lawn and played catch.

"What are you going to do with your money, Arnold?"

"I don't know. Probably buy school clothes."

"Yeah, me too. Hey, you were sure flirting with Jane this afternoon. What gives, you sweet on her?"

"I don't know. She's a swell kid. Besides, Georgie really embarrassed her. I had to say something."

"The dance should be fun," Wendell said as he tossed the ball back to his brother.

Campbell, California, 1931

As the Webb family entered the Grange Hall on Friday evening, a few couples were already dancing to a western swing band called the Skillet Lickers.

Mr. Hollis was holding court in a far corner by a door that led to the kitchen. Men stood in front of him talking. A big cigar was shoved in his mouth. He was nodding his head vigorously. Tobacco smoke hung above the crowd of men like a winter fog.

Tables were loaded with dried and fresh fruit. Cupcakes, pies, and cookies sat on a pass-through counter to tempt those with a sweet tooth.

Mrs. Hollis and her daughter, Jane, served punch and coffee at a card table in the corner. Jane handed Arnold a Dixie cup of punch. They exchanged smiles. "Don't forget you promised to dance with me, Arnold."

"I didn't forget," Arnold said with a grin he couldn't contain. "I've been thinking about that all day."

Arnold found his brother, and they stood together. John Spencer came up to them and said, "Where've you boys been all summer?"

Wendell told him they were building a barn with their father.

"What've you been doing, John?" Arnold asked.

"I've been delivering ice for Union Ice Company. The job finished today. They don't need any more summer help. Who'd you build the barn for?"

"The Hollises," the Webb brothers replied simultaneously.

"Did I hear my name?" Georgie Hollis said as he approached the group. The four boys stood talking and joking, watching the pretty girls wander by.

That is how most dances started. Males on one side of the room and females on the other. Wives sitting at tables talking about children. Husbands talking about politics and the economy. Boys watching the girls, and the girls pretending not to notice.

Jane was standing at the punch bowl with her friend Veronica Cooke. "Who are the boys talking with your brother, Jane?"

"The one with the slicked back brown hair is Arnold Webb. The blond with the buzz cut is his older brother, Wendell. The redhead is John Spencer. They all go to Los Gatos High."

"He is cute, Jane," whispered Veronica with a short giggle.

"Which one?"

"Wendell. I hope he asks me to dance."

Jane said she had an idea; she would have the band announce a ladies' choice, and off she trotted to the bandleader. The bandleader did as requested, and both girls headed for the Webb brothers.

Jane asked Arnold for that dance he had promised, and Veronica Cooke asked Wendell a little more shyly. He was a little unsure of himself because he had only danced at dance lessons. The way Veronica hesitantly took his hand bolstered his courage.

Veronica introduced herself as she slipped into his arms for a fox trot. Halfway through the dance the bandleader yelled to change partners. Arnold danced with Veronica and Wendell with Jane.

"She likes you, you know," Jane announced to Wendell.

"Who?"

"Veronica. She likes you. She is a great gal."

Wendell lost his breath and felt his cheeks redden.

"What do you mean, Jane? She likes me?"

"Good Lord, simmer down. She said she wanted to dance with you. She thinks you're cute."

Wendell smiled with a self-assured smirk on his face.

"Hold on, tiger, you're cute, kinda. But don't get a swelled head."

As Veronica and Arnold danced, an electric-like jolt coursed through Veronica. The way he held her did something to her; she just tingled all the way down her spine.

At the end of the dance, Arnold and Wendell exchanged partners again.

Jane and Arnold walked over to the punch bowl. Veronica and Wendell followed. Veronica kept sneaking looks at Arnold, and he winked at her. Veronica quickly turned away, blushing.

As they reached the table, John Spencer crashed backwards through the rear door and landed on his backside. He sat up rubbing his jaw. The crowd parted, and a lanky fair-haired man, about twenty, in work clothes, came charging toward John. "Take it outside!" somebody yelled.

The Webb boys dashed toward John. "What happened?" Arnold asked as John got to his feet and charged back outside.

Georgie held his hands out wide, his chest heaving as he gulped air. "John told somebody outside that Okies were no better than rats. I guess that guy took the remarks personal," he said between breaths.

By the time Wendell, Arnold, and Georgie got outside, the guy in work clothes was straddling John's chest and pummeling his face. John wasn't fighting back, and his eyes looked glazed. Blood was being splattered all over the concrete patio from John's nose.

"He's had enough!" Wendell yelled.

"Let him know he's been in a fight, Leonard!" another man hollered.

Arnold, Wendell, and Georgie charged into the melee to pull the guy off of John.

"Hey, those guys are ganging up on Leonard!"

Three other men rushed the Webbs and one went for Georgie.

Wendell pasted a guy in the nose and flattened him. Arnold was fending off two when Wendell joined him. Arms encircled Wendell from behind in a bear-like hug. A whiskey-breathed voice said to Leonard, "I got this one, Son, let 'em have it!"

As Leonard was squaring off, a voice from the door way boomed, "That's my son. I suggest you let him go, mister," Conrad Webb said as he stepped onto the patio.

"Yeah?" he sneered, "You and what army is gonna make me?"

"I don't want to fight you, mister. Just let him go, and we can all get back to the party."

"Who do you think you are, you son of a bitch?"

All the fighting stopped as the two men faced each other.

Conrad Webb said in a flat voice, "Only my mother and father can call me that. They aren't here to verify what you say. So I suggest you apologize."

"Up yours, you son of a bitch!"

Mr. Webb turned and said to Mr. Hollis, "I am very sorry about the party."

"You do what you have to do, Conrad." Hollis replied with quickened breath.

As the two men circled one another, Conrad asked the man, "Who are you anyway?"

"I am Leonard Wood, Senior. Those boys over there," he gestured with his head, "are my sons."

As soon as he said *sons,* he lunged and faked a jab with his left while his right hit Webb square on the jaw. Webb's head snapped back, but he recovered quickly. Wood senior came at him again with an evil snarl on his face. When Wood threw his punch, Webb was waiting. He blocked the punch and hit Wood with a combination: two left jabs, each stunning Wood, and a right to the jaw that sent him to his knees, then face down on the ground.

Arnold and Wendell shot glances to each other. The swiftness of the combination punches startled them. They knew their father had a rawboned toughness about him, but they never expected him to pack a punch like that.

The fray was over almost before it started. The Woods helped their father to his feet and left the dance.

Conrad was greeted with pats on the back and murmurs of "attaboy."

He was upset, and it showed. He walked up to George Hollis, Sr., and his wife and apologized. "I am sorry the party was ruined, Mr. Hollis. We will leave now."

"It's not your fault, Conrad, please stay."

"No," he said patting the corner of his mouth with the flat of his fingers. A little blood came away onto his hand. "I think we better go."

On the way home Mr. Webb apologized to his wife and said he was ashamed of himself.

"Why are you ashamed, Pa? You whipped him!" Arnold said excitedly.

"Your father doesn't like to fight. It solves nothing," Mrs. Webb said.

"You looked like Gentleman Jim Braddock, Pa."

"Knock if off, Wendell!" Mr. Webb said heatedly as his fists clinched the steering wheel.

"What was the fight about, anyhow?" Mrs. Webb asked.

"John said that Okies were no better than rats," Arnold explained.

"He deserved to get a licking," Conrad said.

"I don't want you boys seeing him again. He is a bad influence."

"Jeez, mom. He's just repeating what everybody's saying since the Okies started to arrive!" Wendell whined.

"You heard your mother. Stay away from him."

Campbell, California, Present

Miss Hollis showed me the barn that my family had built for her family. It was old and dusty. The interior smelled like diesel fuel and rubber tires, and a faint odor of insecticide could be detected. Over the years, she told me, her family had upgraded a few things. Wiring, new windows, and workbenches made up most of the new touches. But the basic shell was all Webb.

"Come over here with me for a minute, Mr. Webb."

I followed her to the far side of the barn to a huge double door that led to an orchard. She swung the doors open with surprising speed and strength. I stood in the open space and looked out at the orchard.

"Not out there. Look down. That is what you should see," she said pointing at my feet. I squatted down and dusted off a spot on the cement floor. The initials *C.W., W.W.,* and *A.W.* and *AUGUST 1931* were carved in the cement.

"How about that," I exclaimed. "Conrad Webb, Wendell Webb, and Arnold Webb, August 1931. Well, I'll be." Touching each initial gave me a sense of my family and an arc to the past.

"Thank you for showing me this, Miss Hollis."

"You are welcome, Venice. Most memories of the 1930s are bad. The summer of 1931, however, was special. Georgie and I met your family. Your mother and father met. Two years later poor Georgie was murdered." Her voice choked and her eyes welled with tears. Putting my arm around her shoulders seemed like the appropriate thing to do at the time. She became rigid for a second then leaned into me. As quick as that happened, it ended.

"If we don't get some rain soon we'll all be in trouble," she declared as she stepped away from me and strode off toward the house. I caught up to her and got in step alongside. If she felt embarrassed, it didn't show. Softness showed through her tough-as-nails facade. I grinned to myself as we marched to the porch. Her stride reminded me of Douglas MacArthur wading toward the beach.

Before leaving, Miss Hollis asked me if I was going to continue my search into her brother's death.

I replied, "This inkling of mystery has me intrigued, and the investigative instinct tells me there is more to the story."

"I wish you would leave it alone. Delving into the past will solve nothing. Just let it be."

As I drove down the driveway of the Hollis Ranch, I found myself turning over her last words in my mind: *Just let it be.*

Santa Cruz County, California, Present

The Professor was waiting for me on the porch of the Camp. He looked thin and appeared delicate, like an ocean breeze could blow him away. His hair was wet from a recent bath. As he got into my car he exhaled an audible sigh.

"How you feeling, John?"

He nodded his head several times before he answered. "Pretty good, Venice. Thanks for picking me up. Where are we going?"

"Where would you like to go, John?"

"Home. But I signed out saying I was going to Santa Cruz. Is that alright?"

As I drove south on Highway 17 toward the coast, I asked John if he felt some serenity after ten days in rehab. He gave a very noncommittal "Yeah."

He talked about the weather, mostly the lack of rain. When I pushed him about the Camp, he replied, "Can we talk about anything other than program and recovery? Tell me what is happening in your life, please."

"I met an old friend of yours yesterday."

"Yeah, who is that?"

"Jane Hollis."

He shot me a sideways look so quickly that I thought he would pull a neck muscle.

"Jane Hollis! Is she still alive?" he said half jokingly. "Where did you see her?"

I told him about my meeting with her and how nice she was.

As the truck wended its way along the road, John seemed to relax and took on a casual air as we talked. But I could tell John knew her more than he let on. After years of investigating, a person gets a feel for such things, a radar that lets you know something just isn't right, so I pushed a little more, "How well did you know her, John?"

His cheeks reddened, but he didn't say anything.

"You stag! You knew her well, didn't you?"

"Your Honor, I never touched that woman!" He said in a funny pleading voice. He was trying to pass it off as a joke, but he hadn't quite succeeded—and then he changed subjects too quickly. He started talking about what he needed to do when he got back to his home in Campbell. I let him ramble on about that while my mind turned over what had just happened. Why was John avoiding talking about Jane Hollis? Why did he have a picture of the mob executing the men who purportedly killed Georgie Hollis? Just what were those Xs for? And the question that most nagged me, how did my family fit into it all?

We were sitting in a coffee shop across the street from the Boardwalk in Santa Cruz when John asked, "What caused you and Jane to cross paths, Venice?"

I told him about my curiosity about her brother's case. "Seeing that picture at your house, you know the lynching? That started it."

He didn't say anything. He just stared at me and stirred his coffee. The screech of tires and a honking horn interrupted his thoughts. He turned his eyes to the two cars that almost collided on the street. I noticed his hand trembling as he held the spoon.

"Why do you have that picture, John?"

"Georgie Hollis was a friend of mine."

"Were you at the lynching?"

He hung his head and nodded almost imperceptibly.

"My father and uncle were there too?"

"Right next to me. We were all good friends," he murmured.

"Please tell me about it."

"That was so long ago, Venice. Life is for the living. Let it alone."

"Where were you when…?"

"Give it a rest," John hissed.

His reaction made me think: *Why are two people, maybe the only two people I know that were alive when the kidnapping and lynching took place, telling me to let it alone?*

We walked along the beach just at the water line for several hundred yards. Neither one of us said a word the whole time. Seagulls were squawking, and the scent of cinnamon used for candy apples drifted from the Boardwalk down to the sand. John turned and walked toward the Boardwalk. He stopped and watched college-age students playing beach volleyball. The guys were athletic and well tanned in their baggy swim shorts. The girls were in bikini bottoms and sports halters. They, too, were tanned and dived just as quickly for the ball as the guys did.

As we stood and watched in silence, I got the impression that John would rather be at the Camp than with me. "Do you want to go back, John?"

"No, I don't. I can be out until three. The beach looks good, doesn't it?"

I was thankful that a dialogue finally started. We began walking toward the museum. "Yes, it sure does."

"There are a couple of surfers in the Camp. All they can talk about is the waves, parties, and sunshine and what they are going to do when they get out. They never talk about recovery. Just about surfing, parties, and girls."

"What about you, John. What are you going to do when you get out?"

"Taking it one day at a time, Venice. I'll worry about getting out the day it happens. I can't worry about the future or the past."

His veiled message was clear to me: *Let it go.*

John didn't seem very enthused about the museum, and hesitated before entering. "You go in if you want to, Venice. I'll be on the bench over there next to the wall."

Having been there just a few weeks prior was enough for me so, I asked, "What do you want to do?"

"Well," he said running his hand across his head. "If I'm going to turn over a new leaf, I need some new clothes and a haircut."

I smiled. "Come on, then."

We drove to the Capitola Mall where there were department stores and a barbershop. I was sitting on a bench in the center of the mall waiting while John got his haircut. I watched people go by, thought about the day, thought about my family, and about Kate. After sitting a while, I got up to look in the salon; John was no longer in the barber chair, nor even in the shop. It had never occurred to me that John would try to give me the slip. I asked the female barber where the man who was just in her chair went. She nodded to the Macy's across the mall.

In the men's section a sales clerk told me that a man fitting John's description purchased some items and left about ten minutes ago.

I started back down the mall where I had been sitting hoping the Professor would be there. He wasn't. What was I going to tell Florence? A check of the parking lot and the car was to no avail. I was getting mad. Then rationalization started. He's an adult. He can take care of himself. Not my job to watch him.

"You looking for me?" John yelled from a shoe store.

Despite telling myself that it was not my job to watch John, I was relieved to find him. "You should have told me where you were going, John," I said in a stern voice.

"Jesus Christ, Venice, you were looking straight at me when I left Macy's. I thought you saw me." Then a look of understanding raised his eyebrows a little. "You thought I took off, didn't you?"

"Yeah, I did, John," I said sheepishly.

"Where would I go?"

I just shrugged my shoulders. John laughed. I felt my cheeks flush, which made John laugh even harder. "God, that was great. I haven't laughed like that in some time."

Well, at least I was amusing him on his one day out.

Los Gatos, California, Present

Ironically, I was sitting in the cocktail lounge of the El Gato Hotel. There were no other patrons in the bar, just the bartender Bert, a veteran mixologist, and me. I was beating myself up for not trusting John Spencer. The swizzle stick in my tonic and lime was getting a workout. Part of me felt the need to take care of John. At the same time, I knew he should take care of himself. "Jesus, Venice, you can't save the world. Quit trying," I said aloud to myself.

"You talking to me, Venice?"

"No, Bert, just thinking out loud."

"That happens a lot in here," he said, moving to the other end of the bar.

The door from the lobby opened and a block of light spilled into the darkened bar room.

"Hello, Sweetie," my sister, Lydia, said as she walked up behind me.

"What's up, Sis?"

"Not much, just another day in paradise. What are you doing sitting in a bar on a beautiful day like today?"

I told her about my experience with John and how bad I felt.

"What would John think if he knew you were sitting in a barroom stewing about some comment you made?"

"Wondering the same thing myself, Lydia."

"Have you ever tried worrying about your side of the street, Venice? It sounds to me that you might have overreacted."

"Sis, he was my responsibility. He signed out into my care, goddamn it!"

"John Spencer is a grown man. Let it be, Venice."

"If another person tells me to let it be, I'm going to blow a gasket!"

"What are you talking about?"

I staved off her question with a wave of my hand. "Some other time, Lydia."

She nodded and went behind the bar to get the cash register receipts for the morning and afternoon shifts and laid them out on the bar top next to me. She stopped separating the beverage and meal tags. I sensed her looking at me. I stared at my glass of tonic for as long as possible before I looked up at her. Her head was tilted faintly, and she had a little smile on her face.

"Sweetie, you can't save the world," she whispered.

"I know that, Sis. It's the alcoholic in me that keeps trying."

I decided to use John's earlier tactic and change the subject to the first thing that came to mind, Jane Hollis. Fortunately, Lydia was interested enough not to notice, or sister enough not let on. I told her about my visit with Jane, and she said that she would like to meet her sometime.

Campbell, California, Present

That next week we visited Jane Hollis. After introducing Lydia and Miss Hollis at the front door, we were let inside. The front room was neat as a pin, as I am sure the rest of the house was. The hardwood floors were buffed to a shine and the Persian throw rugs immaculate. Tiffany lampshades sparkled in the sunlight. A huge stone fireplace with smoke stains up its face was flanked with bookshelves full of books taking up the whole wall of the living room.

"What a lovely room," Lydia announced.

"Why, thank you, dear. Would you like to see the rest of the house?"

We both nodded that we would, and Miss Hollis looked pleased. As she led the way, Lydia and I exchanged grins.

"Have you lived in this house all of your life?" I asked as we entered the kitchen.

She looked at me sternly and said, "I was born on that kitchen table right over there." She pointed to an old pine harvest table sitting in the middle of the room.

"Doctors came to the houses in those days. Hospitals were too far sometimes. I was supposed to be delivered at O'Connor Sanitarium, but I couldn't wait, and the doctor was notified. He was paid with two twenty-dollar gold coins."

"Was your brother born at home?" I asked.

"Yes, he was fifteen months after me. His birth was more civilized. Mama had him in bed," she said with a chuckle. "Daddy and Mama were good parents to Georgie and me. They are all dead now. It's just me left."

Lydia asked her if she had any other family, and Jane Hollis told her that she was the only one.

"And you never married?"

"Good heavens, no, Lydia. Why would I want to burden myself with a husband?"

Lydia gave her a look of understanding.

"Oh, I had suitors from time to time, but nothing serious."

"I saw John Spencer the other day, and he wanted to be remembered to you."

Jane stiffened, momentarily, then softened, and replied, "How is that rascal?"

"He is just fine." I looked to see if her cheeks were pink. They weren't.

She led us into a dark wood-paneled room. "This was Daddy's office. It's just the same as it was when he ran the business, except, of course, for the computer, fax machine, and such."

Adorning an old brown leather couch was a white throw with a large red *S* on it.

"I see you're a Stanford fan."

"Alumni, class of '34. Georgie was supposed to enter in the fall. But he…" Her voice trailed off. "I don't know why I support them. They changed the mascot from the Indian to the Cardinal. Indians were getting upset. They said it was demeaning. I don't see it. Anyhow, if you ever want football tickets, I have them. Let me know."

Photographs adorned every wall and surface. Lydia was perusing the photos, and I was sitting with Miss Hollis in the living room.

"I've made a fresh batch of lemonade. Would you care for some?"

We sat at the kitchen table while Miss Hollis brought tall tumblers and a pitcher of lemonade on a shiny black plastic tray to the table. A plate of oatmeal cookies sat in the middle.

Tapping her finger on the sugar bowl, she said, "I tend to make it a little sour. If you want to add sugar, feel free."

"Miss Hollis, when I was here the other day to talk to you about your brother, you told me to let it be. I find it interesting that John Spencer said the same thing."

She slowly put her glass down, picked up a napkin, and wiped imaginary crumbs from her mouth. I glanced at Lydia, and her expression said, *don't mess up a good afternoon.*

Miss Hollis's eyes glistened as she slowly measured her words. "If and when I want to talk about that horrid incident, I will let you know. But don't hold your breath."

I regretted my question, and was about to say so, when Jane Hollis broke the silence.

"Lydia, would you like to see my Wedgwood collection? It is really quite extensive."

The two of them walked through a swinging wooden door into the dining room and left me alone at the kitchen table.

On the way home Lydia gave me a good reaming. "Venice, you have a knack for screwing up a nice thing. You don't do it very often, but when you do it's a doozy." Her comments were accentuated with periodic finger jabs at my face. She was silent for a few miles, and I was glad. When I stopped in front of the El Gato, Lydia said before she got out, "I know what you meant when you said if you heard another person say 'let it be,' you were going to blow your gasket. Well, don't forget to wipe up the oil—let it be, Venice. They don't want to talk about it."

San Jose, California, 1933

Holden Mawson and Sterling Kress were seated at a table in the Italian Gardens Restaurant. Holden had just arrived from making a phone call to the kidnapped kid's father. "What did he say, Holden?" Sterling asked at full volume.

"Shush! Sterling! Not so loud. I told him to get five g's ready by noon tomorrow, and that someone will call him then. He said he wanted some proof that the kid is okay. I hung up then."

"Do you think it'll work, Holden?"

"Yeah, I do. Why wouldn't it?"

Sterling just shrugged his shoulders.

What Sterling and Holden didn't know was that the FBI had been called in when the Hollises received the ransom note. Phones were tapped that afternoon. The first phone call Holden made was untraceable because the line went dead before a location could be determined. The officers were certain they would find the kidnappers—it was just a matter of time.

At noon the next day Sterling phoned the Hollis home and spoke to Mr. Hollis. He told Hollis to drive south on Union Avenue toward Los Gatos. Mr. Hollis had been instructed by the FBI agent to keep the caller on the line as long as possible. He did his best to stall for time, and he'd succeeded by keeping the kidnapper on the line for quite some time.

"Hold on a sec, where did you say to turn left?"

"I said turn left on Dry Creek and then right on San Jose–Los Gatos Road."

"Okay then I'll be going toward San Jose. Right?"

"No! jeez, you thick or somethin'," the kidnapper puffed an exasperated breath into the phone. "Drive to Los Gatos!"

"Los Gatos? I live in Campbell. What? I didn't get that." Mr. Hollis turned to the agent and said, "Something is going on there. I hear scuffling and yelling."

"Good the agent replied. The cops must—"

Mr. Hollis held up his hand and said, "Yes, yes I'm here! It's Captain Axelroth of the San Jose Police Department," Hollis exclaimed excitedly as he handed the phone over to the FBI agent.

The caller was taken into custody in the DeAnza Hotel garage. Mr. Hollis did a dance and then went and hugged his wife and daughter. "My boy is coming home!" he screamed in jubilation.

In an interview room in the police station, Sterling sat with his head down on the table.

He was moaning and saying he didn't kidnap anybody.

"That ain't what your partner said, Sterling," the interrogator said as he flipped through blank pages of a pocket notepad.

"Let's see. Ah, here it is; 'It was Sterling's idea.'"

"Mawson said that? That rat!"

"Yeah, Mawson. Is that his name?" the officer asked.

"It's his last name," Sterling replied dejectedly.

"I was wondering. He said his first name was Larry. I didn't believe him."

"You shouldn't. His first name is Holden."

The officer scribbled into his pad. "Where were you supposed to meet him?"

"At O'Brien's Candy Store."

Smugly the interrogator smiled, as he realized that his ruse had worked easily on Sterling Kress.

"Yep, that's right where he was. Having a hamburger and shake."

The cop looked at Axelroth who motioned to another detective to leave.

At O'Brien's, Holden Mawson was taken into custody without incident.

They were arraigned on kidnapping and extortion and were placed in the Santa Clara county jail. They professed the whole time that they kidnapped no one.

———————

Two members of the prestigious Alviso Yacht Club were boating back into the harbor when one of the men spotted a clump of clothing on a mud flat. After securing the boat in the slip, they walked to the end of the dock and down the ladder into the mud. It was knee deep but they sloshed out to the debris and turned it over. The soapy white face of a young man stared back at them. The men plowed back to the yacht club as fast as the mud let them move and phoned the police.

Arnold caught up with John Spencer as John was walking home. "Wait up, John. Where're you going in such a hurry?"

"Hey, Arnie. Going in to take a pain pill."

"Are you feeling any better?" Arnold could smell booze on John's breath.

"Yeah, okay most of the time." As they were talking, the horn from a truck blasted. The two turned and saw Wendell driving his father's truck. He screeched to a halt in front of the Spencer home. "Get in, guys. They caught the kidnappers!" he announced. "A mob is forming at the jail. C'mon get in." Arnold started for the truck, but John stood his ground. "I'm not going. You fellers go ahead."

But the Webb brothers wouldn't leave him alone and after several minutes of cajoling, John gave up and climbed into the truck.

Word that Georgie Hollis's dead body was discovered spread like wildfire. By three that same afternoon a small crowd gathered in front of the jail. They were mingling around, murmuring, "Georgie, Georgie." By five the throng had swelled to over one hundred, and they were now chanting, "Georgie, Georgie." Radio station KXRX reported that the body had been discovered and that a mob was forming at the jail. This radio report sent hundreds more into the area of the jail. The police and county sheriff were understaffed for such a mob, so they sent to neighboring cities and counties for mutual aid. The boxing team from San Jose State was called to help keep the peace, but what they did, however, was to help keep the police from doing their jobs.

At seven o'clock the mob brought a telephone pole from a construction site across the street and used it as a battering ram to break down the door of the jailhouse. The jailer tried, to no avail, to keep the keys from the mob. He was beaten and shoved into a closet.

———

"Sounds like someone's coming up the stairs, Holden. I hope it's supper," Sterling said.

The two were unaware of the goings-on outside. There were no windows to the exterior, and the thick cement walls rendered the interior sound proof. Holden thought to himself, *Jesus Christ, Sterling is hungry. He has no idea how much trouble we are in, the poor sap.*

The door at the cellblock crashed open, and the mob started down the interior corridor. Chants of "Get 'em," "String the bastards up," and "Georgie, Georgie," resonated off the cement walls.

"It ain't supper, Sterling. That's for sure," Holden said with a catch in his throat.

Sterling started whimpering and sat quickly on his cot, and as quickly as he sat, he stood up, repeating this motion several times before the mob stood menacingly outside their cells.

When the angry men opened Holden's cell and dragged him out, Sterling climbed up on piping overhead in an attempt to hide. He clung to the pipe as the mob pulled on his torso. One of the men saw a pair of hard soled shoes on the floor of the cell and started thumping on the clenched fists around the pipe.

With a loud scream of "Mama!" Sterling joined Holden on the floor next to their cells.

Holden yelled, "You sonsabitches, you can't do this!"

The mob dragged the two down the stairs. Holden was knocked unconscious.

He came to when the rope was pulled over his head. He looked up and saw Sterling Kress swinging from the tree. Sterling's tongue was bulging out, as were his eyes. His legs were flailing and urine was making a spot on his pants front.

"For the love of God, we didn't kill anyone!" Holden screamed. Those were his last words. He was knocked out again when he was hit in the head with the butt of a shotgun.

The police, unable to stop the crowd, stood on the fringe of the park watching the undulating mass of humanity. The crowd was frenzied and screamed "Georgie! Georgie!" Some of them, police and crowd, were jovial. Others were stoic.

Wendell Webb stood next to the men pulling the rope. Arnold was a few feet behind him, and John Spencer was kneeling next to a hawthorn bush, vomiting and crying between heaves.

He moaned over and over, "Why did I come? Why did I let them talk me into this?"

After the whole chaotic affair was over, Arnold Webb and John Spencer met at Mr. Webb's truck at the same time. "Did you see Wendell?" Arnold asked John. The three had driven over together and parked in front of a pool hall adjacent to the park. The crowd in the pool hall was rowdy and kept toasting Georgie Hollis.

Wendell arrived about ten minutes after the other two. His cheeks were beet red. "Did you guys get questioned by the cops?" he asked as he came trotting up to the vehicle.

Both said they hadn't. "What did they ask you, Wendell?" John wanted to know.

"My name. Where I was from, and what was I doing there." As he caught his breath, his color returned to a normal tone.

John's eyes were as round as saucers, "What'd you tell 'em?"

"I told them I was John Spencer."

John's mouth dropped, "You what?"

"Just joking with you, John."

"Very funny," John said faintly.

Despite Wendell's attempt to lighten the mood, the drive home was a silent and heavy one. As they drove down Main Street on the way to drop John at home, Arnold sighed heavily. "I guess we're in the clear now."

Wendell looked at Arnie and nodded his head.

"I just wish I could get clear of it up here," John said pointing to his head.

"Put it behind you," Wendell told him. "It's over and done."

"Over and done," John echoed.

Los Gatos, California, 1933

Wendell Webb and his father were in a heated discussion in the kitchen.

"I can't be wrong all the time, Pa," Wendell whined to his father.

"Well, you are about this, boy. What do you think you're gonna do if you quit school?"

"Go to work with you!"

"With me? There isn't enough work to keep me busy."

"Then I'll find something else."

"You're not using your head. Everybody is scrambling for jobs. The best place for you is in school. End of discussion."

Wendell stormed out of the kitchen. Opening his bedroom door, he had the feeling of defeat. Every time he had an idea, somebody always shot him down or discouraged him. It wasn't fair. "I can make good decisions," he said aloud. Hadn't he saved Arnold's and John's skins as well as his own in dealing with Georgie's accident?

"Why so hangdog?" Arnold wanted to know.

"The old man is so wet he drips, if it's any of your concern."

"What are you talking about, Wendell?"

He flopped down on the bed. "I just told him I was quitting school and going to work."

"He told you no, right?"

"Yeah. He did."

"What did you expect him to say? Hell, even if he said yes, Mom would say no."

"Maybe you're right, Arnold. All I know is I'm wrong at home. I'm wrong at school. Hell, even a broken clock is right twice a day."

"You're babbling, Wendell."

"Forget it. I'm going out."

Wendell entered the Eat More Creamery and joined John Spencer in a booth. John's eyes were bloodshot and his complexion pale.

"What gives, John?"

"Not so loud, Wendell. I have a hangover."

"Again? That's the third this week. You better be careful or your insides will fall out."

"Yeah, yeah. You're starting to sound like my mom. What've you been up to?"

"Nothing. Hey, did you ever find a job, John?"

"There aren't any jobs, besides school starts next week. Where did this lousy summer go?"

They both stared across the table and said nothing about the accident. They each knew the other's thoughts.

Wendell broke the silence when he told John about his plan to quit school and go to work.

"That's stupid. Didn't you just hear me? There is no work, Wendell. Graduate high school, go to college, or join the army. Just don't quit anything. Quitting is a trap. Once you quit one thing, the next will be easier and the next easier than the one before. All of a sudden you are a dog chasing his tail.

Saratoga, California, 1933

Wendell Webb called Veronica Cooke and asked her to a dance at Saratoga Springs. She accepted. Veronica thought to herself, *He would be upset if he knew I had been with Arnold.* But Arnold had quit calling for some reason. Over the last several weeks, girlfriends had reported seeing Arnold Webb with a succession of girls on his arm. "He only calls me when he can't find a date," she found herself saying out loud. "I'll show him."

They walked onto the outdoor pavilion of the Saratoga Springs. Japanese lanterns of blue, green, yellow, and red crisscrossed over the dance floor. A dance band, The Royal Cadets, played a swing tune.

Wendell and Veronica joined Arnold and Jane Hollis and John Spencer next to the refreshment counter. Arnold started to lead Jane out on the floor, when John stopped him and said it was his turn to dance with Jane.

"Stop it, boys. There's no need to fight," she said in a perfect imitation of Mae West. Arnold stepped aside to allow John to escort Jane to the dance floor as a foxtrot tune played.

Veronica was swaying to the music. Arnold noticed her and said to Wendell, "Man, if you aren't gonna ask her to dance, I will."

Wendell took Veronica's arm and led her to the dance floor. She looked back at Arnold. He smiled back and winked. She turned her head in an effort to snub him.

They had danced several dances when Veronica asked Wendell to take a walk along the creek. They sat on a large rock alongside the stream. Water cascading over rocks muted the band. With arms around each other and heads touching, they gazed at the roiling current. Sometimes they looked at the stars through the treetops, and sometimes they looked at each other.

"Do you want to kiss me, Arno—I mean, Wendell. God, I am sorry. Wendell."

"Arnold? Why did you start to say Arnold?"

"It was just a slip," she said quickly. Then she lifted her face until it was bathed in moonlight. "Well, do you want to?"

Wendell smiled and said softly, "Yes, I do."

She leaned forward, just a little more. "Then do it."

The kiss lasted a long time. Veronica was glad that Wendell could not hear her thoughts—she couldn't stop thinking of Arnold even as they embraced.

When they came back to the dance floor, Jane asked them where they had been. Veronica told her they were on a walk by the creek as she grabbed Wendell's hand and led him to the middle of the floor. A slow song was playing, and they held each other close. She was trying not to think about Arnold.

After the dance Veronica Cooke of Campbell and Wendell Webb of Los Gatos were an item. What Veronica didn't know was that Arnold had only stopped calling her because he couldn't bring himself to entangle her in the mess he'd made of this summer. He needed to get his head together and his emotions settled before he could face her again. He'd been hoping that once school started, he could get past it, then he could pick up with Veronica again. But she hadn't waited, and Wendell hadn't backed off.

So now Arnold didn't call on Veronica any more.

Los Gatos, California, Present

I was helping John Spencer get settled back into his house. I had stocked his shelves and refrigerator with basic food and supplies. John would need to do a more in-depth shopping later. After the tenth *thank you*, I told him to shut up. He was glad to be home; it showed on his face.

"What are you going to do, John?"

"Work on the steps of AA. I'm having trouble with one of them, though, and I think if I can get beyond it I'll be okay, I hope."

"Which step is that, John?"

"Making amends to any people that have been hurt by my actions. I just need to begin. There have been so many people and so many indiscretions. Most of my friends are dead. I have you and Lydia, some colleagues. I just need to get thoughts together."

I sat and listened to John, and felt I was in the presence of a man on the precipice. I waited for him to start talking and all he said was, "I need to start a grocery list."

Driving away from John's condo I was weighed down with disappointment. John was on the run emotionally, and it appeared he was working on the problem rather than the solution. Every time I called John his goddamned answering machine squawked the same recorded message. Finally the machine said "mail box full." I quit calling. I drove by his place several times and felt like a jealous suitor. I quit that too.

"Aren't you concerned if he is alive?" Lydia asked as we sat on the veranda of the El Gato.

"I know he's alive. I put feelers out, and he's been to after-care at the Camp. One of my other guys I sponsor drives him."

"He'll call when he's ready, Sweetie. Don't worry. See? I didn't say let it go."

I smiled as my sister walked across the porch and entered the lobby.

"Hey, pal. How ya doin?" John Spencer asked as he approached my chair. Startled, I looked up. Frustration, resentment, and finally relief fought for a station in my mind.

"Can I sit with you?"

I motioned to the chair Lydia had just vacated.

"I got all your calls, Venice. Don't think they weren't appreciated. I've been trying to work things out, and I was isolating, which I know is dangerous."

"You could have picked up, or returned a call. Just to let me know you were okay, John."

"I do apologize. But the upside is I didn't drink, and I am here. I want to tell you something."

I just sat and looked at John. His leg was crossed, the top leg bounced incessantly. He appeared faltering, as if he was anxious that somebody might overhear. "Can we go inside, Venice? I'd feel more comfortable."

At an ancient, felt-covered game table in the lobby, John sat against the wall. He was able to see in all directions and could moderate his voice if somebody approached.

The anticipation of what I thought he was about to reveal had me breathing a little more rapidly.

He started to speak and stopped several times. Finally he shook his head, like he was getting the cobwebs out and said, "I want to have a luncheon at my house. You and Lydia and maybe Jane Hollis. Get some cold cuts, sodas, and salads. Have a nice tea party. What do you think?"

"What do *I* think? What for? That's what I think!"

"To honor you folks, my friends," John replied slightly taken aback by my attitude. His eyes failed to meet mine. I was certain a luncheon was not what was on his mind when we left the veranda and came inside.

Pulling my horns in, I said, "It sounds like a great idea. What can I do to help?"

"If you called Jane Hollis for me that would be a huge help, Venice."

We chatted for another half hour, and we got up to leave. Crossing the lobby we could hear the blender in the lounge crunching ice for a frozen drink and the rattle of bar dice hitting the wooden bar. John stopped momentarily. We looked at each other and smiled. John pointed to the exit door and said, "It looks much nicer out there, doesn't it, Venice?"

———

Jane Hollis insisted that the party be at her house. She stated that she didn't want to leave her property because she was too immobile. I explained this to John, and he told me he thought it was the antics of a rich woman wanting to control everything.

"It will be your show, John. Just the venue is different," I said into the phone.

"I don't know, Venice. I have to think about it. I'll let you know."

As John hung up the phone, he started to feel the edema of resentment course through his bearing, almost smothering him. "Son of a bitch!" he yelled in his living room causing the door bell chimes to emit an echo. His hand hovered over the phone. *All I gotta do is phone the liquor store, and they'll bring me a bottle...*

His hand stayed over the phone until it was almost numb. He flexed his fingers and shook life back into them. He decided to take a walk around his complex. At the gate of his fenced-in courtyard, his neighbor's calico cat meowed from her perch on the fence. John reached up and scratched behind her ears. The cat closed her eyes and smiled as the sun rayed down on her. "All we need is a little sunshine and someone to scratch our ears, isn't that right, Molly?" John clucked aloud. Molly purred her concurrence and was upset when John slammed the gate shut, shocking her world. At the community pool, he stopped at the fence to observe the swimmers. Several elderly women were wading in the shallow end doing some sort of isometric exercise. He noticed a walker near the steps of the pool and was grateful that during times of sobriety he played tennis. For his age he had good balance and mechanical aids weren't necessary. *Maybe I should go get my swimming trunks on and take a dip.* He thought to himself. As soon as that thought was done, a sense of foreboding swathed over him; he had not been swimming since 1933.

John insisted that he bring all the food to Jane Hollis's house. It was his party, and it was going to have to be that way.

On a pleasant Thursday afternoon, Lydia and I, along with Jane Hollis, sat on the porch of the Hollis house waiting for John to arrive. He was thirty minutes late, and I was beginning to think that John had flaked out. Lydia and Jane chatted like two women content with who they were, while I squirmed. "Give him a call, Ven," Lydia said. "Maybe he got lost."

I was standing at my car starting to dial John from my cell phone when a red Toyota drove up the drive and stopped behind me. John got out and announced that he was sorry for being tardy. He was dressed in a light brown suit with a pale blue shirt, opened at the collar. "There is a picnic basket with munchies, Venice. Would you please bring it? It's in the trunk. I need to say hello to an old acquaintance."

Jane Hollis stood on the porch and said, "Hello, old friend. How have you been keeping yourself?" John ignored her extended hand and embraced Jane. In the beginning the hug was awkward but quickly became familiar and natural.

I noticed that John's eyes were misty and saw Jane's back shudder with an audible intake of air.

Lydia and I sat and listened to John and Jane as they brought each other up to date on their lives. It was extremely nostalgic, and I missed my parents at that moment. I looked in Lydia's eyes and knew she felt the same.

Paper plates and other debris from the picnic were strewn over the wicker table and on the gray-enameled wooden porch floor. Lydia started to chase a paper napkin that scudded around the table leg. "Just leave it, dear. It will be okay," Jane said.

"I'll just take some things inside," Lydia replied. And Jane gave her a *suit-yourself* nod.

After a lull in the conversation, John announced in an authoritative voice, "Lydia and Venice know about my troubles with booze. I'm not sure that you know, Jane."

In a kindly voice, Jane said, "Your trouble with the bottle is no secret, John. But I do admire you bringing it up and your valiant endeavor to control it. Keep up the good work."

"My drinking, disease drinking that is, started in 1933 and has been unrelenting. I've had stints of sobriety, but I always start again. When the war broke out, Wendell and I enlisted. Arnold tried to go too, but he ended up with some sort of deferment. Wendell went overseas and saw combat, and I stayed in the states. I was the only one in my outfit that didn't go over there." He said with a nod toward the south. "Why? Because I was the only SOB that could type. And the major I worked for was a drinking buddy. He kept me with him. We played tennis every afternoon and went golfing on most weekends. The others fought the war, and I battled the bottle on the social scene."

At an appropriate interval, Jane Hollis asked John what started him drinking. John's shoulders sank and his pink complexion paled. He crossed and uncrossed his leg several times.

"Maybe I pried. It's probably none of my business. Forgive me, John."

I sat quietly listening to the dialogue thinking that John was starting to weaken, when he announced, "No, Jane, your question is very germane."

With a shuddering gasp, John started to talk, and then stopped several times. I noticed that his hands were trembling, and his breathing was labored. He looked at me, and I just nodded, faintly, with encouragement. Jane sat with her head slightly tilted and her hands primly in her lap gazing at John.

Lydia said, "Go ahead, John. You're with friends."

John quickly snapped his head in Lydia's direction, which startled her. As quick as he had looked at Lydia, he softened and said, "Thanks, honey. I know you are my friends."

John gulped air and said, "In a flash in time, lives were changed forever. God, we were such good friends…" All the while he was speaking, John continuously rubbed his fingers over his lips, cheeks, and chin leaving brighter pink streaks on his face. "That summer in 1933, we were inseparable. It was nothing short of bucolic. And in the blink of an eye, our childhoods ended."

John looked to each of us and our puzzling expressions. He looked hardest at Jane and blurted out, "Oh, God, Jane it was just a game! Georgie hit the rock and was dead when we pulled him out of the water." John wailed.

"Georgie? We?" Jane leaned forward and said, "Who is 'we'?" Then she turned to me with a look that said, *Stop him, please, I don't want to talk about this.*

But all I could do was give her a sheepish downturn of my mouth and a slight shrug.

"Arnold, Wendell, and me," he replied weakly.

Lydia and I sat straight up in our chairs and looked at one another. Jane was gently shaking her head.

"No, John, don't," she whispered. "It was so long ago, a lifetime ago…"

A tear slid down John's cheek, but he kept it together. "I have to, Jane, I don't want to hurt you, the good Lord knows that, but I have to."

Jane smoothed out the unwrinkled skirt of her floral-print dress. She sat up rod straight and set her chin up just a little higher. "Then tell me all of it, John," Jane Hollis said in a harsh voice, but whether it was sternness or a brave front, I couldn't tell.

My heart was pounding as John revealed to us the circumstances surrounding Georgie Hollis' death. I felt uneasiness because of my father's and uncle's involvement. Lydia reached over and held my hand tightly. I thought of the *Xs* over the men in the photograph.

"I am so sorry, Jane. It was an accident."

"Why didn't you tell the police if it was an accident?"

"Because, Jane, Wendell and Arnold's father worked for your family and Wendell thought Mr. Webb would get fired. We made an oath that we would never talk. Arnie and Wendell took it to their graves, and here I am," he said extending his hands out with palms upward.

"I think my father would understand that his son's death was accidental. I don't think he would comprehend two innocent men being hanged," she hissed as she pointed a rigid index finger in the air as an exclamation point. John grabbed her hand, which Jane removed as if she received an electrical jolt.

With this gesture, John broke down and sobbed. He tried to get her hand back, but Jane kept it at a distance from John.

"Do I know how to ruin a party or what?" he said between sniffles.

Jane sat, shaking her head.

"It was an accident, Jane. Can you forgive me?"

"Like I said earlier, John Spencer, it may have been an accident, but the fact remains that two innocent men were killed because of your cowardice and deceit," Jane said in a whisper.

"I think of that every day, Jane," John sighed.

"I always thought that justice was too swift," Jane Hollis declared. John started to get up. "Sit down, John Spencer. You need to listen to what *I've* got to say. And you may not like it."

Jane Hollis continued. "The county sheriff, Emory, I think was his name, and my father were friends. I think Emory felt pressure to solve the case, and the men that got lynched took that pressure off. I was in the room when daddy was on the phone. When he heard that the man was arrested, my father did a pirouette. Can you imagine?"

"One of the men, Sterling, had an alibi. He was in the police station most of the night Georgie went missing."

John raised his head quickly, and Jane gave him a smug smile and a curt nod of her head. "That's right, he had an alibi."

Remembering an article I read from the file Yolanda Morales loaned me, I said, "Two days later they found Georgie's corpse out in the bay." Jane Hollis shot me a look that said, *I know that, Buster, and if you want me to continue, be still.*

"For whatever reason, the police decided to keep the information about Sterling's alibi from the public. In many ways they were as guilty as you and the others, John." Jane Hollis took a sip from her water glass, cleared her throat, and continued. "It was agony for us. One day we were thinking about cooking Georgie's favorite meatloaf and wondering why he wasn't home yet, and then the next day, one of my father's friends from the Alviso Yacht Club and the sheriff are standing in our parlor telling us that Georgie was dead."

Turning to John Spencer, Jane Hollis murmured, "My mother never got out of bed after that. The only times she left the house was when they took her to the mortuary for Georgie's funeral and then again when she died. Daddy was never the same either. They blamed themselves for not looking after him closely enough! He was a zombie in a suit after that. You, John, and the Webb brothers might have been able to ease that if you had come forward." Jane fetched a kerchief from her sleeve and wiped her eyes. "My God, the three of you were pallbearers. We loved you boys as much as Georgie did."

We were all silent, each with our own thoughts. For a moment, the only sound was the slight rustle of the paper napkin stuck on the table leg as the breeze tried to tug it loose.

But then Jane went on, "Instead of sitting here trying to make things right with me, you ought to find the survivors of Sterling Kress and Holden Mawson and make amends to them." With those final words, Jane Hollis stood and walked into her house, slamming the huge front door. It had the finality of a coffin lid slamming shut.

John stood up and looked at Lydia and me, still seated and stunned by the events of the afternoon. He was able to get in his car and speed down the Hollis driveway in a cloud of dust before either Lydia or I found enough of our wits to move or even speak.

"Go after him, Venice," Lydia urged.

"I'll take his picnic stuff to him," I said weakly. "That'll give him time to settle down."

"Just make sure you do it, Venice. He is in turmoil and might need you now. He'd be there for you."

"I know, Sis. I'm just thinking about Dad and Uncle Arnold and their involvement."

"Are you surprised?"

"Sort of."

"Why are you surprised? They were flawed characters. Do you forget some of the things they did?" Lydia said in disgust.

If John was home, he wasn't answering the door. I left his picnic basket on the door step. A calico cat sniffed curiously at the basket, and I urged her away gently with my foot. She gave me a snarl that said, *Who in the hell do think you are?*

I went to several of John's old haunts, and they all said they hadn't seen him in quite some time. One of the barkeeps, in a joking manner, at least he thought it was a joke, said as he wiped the mahogany bar, "If you do see him tell him to come back. I need the income. I gotta kid startin' college soon." Those sitting in the barroom laughed.

Very funny, I thought to myself.

With a glimmer of hope, I called Florence, the administrator of the Camp, where John went through rehab.

"He called me this afternoon, Venice. I wasn't here. He just left his name on my answering machine. He sounded kind of shaky. Is he okay?"

"I'll let you know when I know," I told her before I hung up.

I walked into the lobby of the El Gato hoping he was sitting in the coffee shop or on the veranda and not in the bar. He wasn't anywhere there.

I was driving across the bridge over Los Gatos Creek when I suddenly stopped my car and got out. I hurriedly walked down the path off of Main Street and started up the creek trail—toward Boo-Gang. The late afternoon sunshine was filtered by the sycamore trees along the creek. The gurgling of the current muted any sounds from town. About twenty yards from the falls, a flash of light blue caught my eye. On a bush was the shirt John wore to the picnic earlier. As I emerged into the clearing surrounding Boo-Gang, I saw John sitting naked on the shore with his legs in the water. His back bristled as he heard my foot snap a twig. When he turned to me, I noticed a bottle of Jim Beam next to him.

"Back in the day, a shirt hanging on the bush meant privacy. I guess nobody knows that," he said disgustedly.

"Do you want to be alone, John?"

When he didn't answer, I continued toward him. The seal on the bottle wasn't broken. I was relieved.

"What are you doing, John?"

"I'm thinking about getting shit-faced. Do you wanna join me?"

"No, not today."

When I looked in his face I saw tear streaks glistening on his cheeks and his eyes were swollen and red, as was his odd-shaped nose, which was runny. He sat child-like. He dipped his hands in the water and wiped off his face, then dipped them again and ran his fingers through his hair.

"Those people were saints." I knew he meant Jane and her folks. "They didn't deserve to have the lives they ended up with. You know?" He stood up. His spindle legs were alabaster white, and every few inches blue and red veins marked up his legs making them look like a road map. "Georgie was a cute little boy, and he grew up to be our friend, and we killed him," he whined as he waded into the water.

"Do you know that I haven't been here since that day? As a matter of fact, I haven't been swimming anywhere."

He lifted the bottle above his head as he eased in the water doing a sort of back stroke and said, "It would have all been okay, if there hadn't been a mess."

"John, you faced up to it. You were a man today, and cleaned up your shit."

John snorted. "You sound like your old man, and your uncle, too. They always said that. Said it that night, in fact."

For a moment, I thought I could hear the ghosts of the past reaching out in the lengthening shadows of sunset. Even though the sky was still light, trees huddled around the hollow shielded the water with wind-tossed leaves, bringing dusk early to Boo-Gang. Was it in my mind or on the breeze that I heard my father recite those words?

John chased away the voice when his own broke the silence: "Don't you think it was a little too late?"

Was it? The program was my lifeline, had been for a while. I believed it, believed *in* it. Hell, I lived it…but what if they were wrong? What if there were things you could not atone for? I shook my head to clear it of what felt like thick cobwebs. *No,* I told myself, *no, I refuse to accept that. That is not what I believe, not what I've taught others. There has to be a way, even for John, even out of this. And I am his sponsor!*

"Maybe so, John. But you did it."

"Is that your way of letting me off the hook, Venice? Better late than never? Is that what you're saying to me?" He stood up next to the waterfall, water cascading down his time-withered body, and pointed to a large rock. "That's the rock that Georgie died on." He waded to the rock, and the cascading water splashed off his shoulder. He reached out to touch the rock but his hand kept moving as if the rock were hot to the touch. His shaking fingers finally came to rest on top of the rock.

"Right there." John choked up a little. He reached out his arms and tried to circle the rock. The whiskey bottle clanked and John stepped back.

"His blood swirled in the current for several yards downstream," he said pointing with the bottle.

"Are you going to drink that, John?"

He stood and moved back toward the rock and stopped suddenly—and opened the bottle. The sound of the paper seal cracking as he twisted the cap was like an acute report from a rifle. I cringed, then stared at him and wondered what I would do. I know what the AA program says, and what therapists say, but in reality I did not know.

He sniffed the contents of the bottle and closed his eyes and sighed. I wanted to blurt out *Don't!*

I stayed silent.

I saw his shoulders sag, and his head touch the spot where his friend Georgie had hit in 1933. With a sob so loud that birds and squirrels vacated the area, John poured the bourbon over the spot and used water from the pool as if washing it off. His wail became louder. He splashed and scrubbed at the rock furiously, as if he might never stop. I ran into the water, clothes and all, splashing my way to John. I pulled him to me and held him as the last of the whiskey spilled out into the water and swirled downstream. The bottle floated for a while, turned over several times, and, finally, went under.

John raised his arms and with hands outstretched above his head, reaching upward to the heavens, he cried, "God forgive me!"

I pulled his arms down and continued to hold him. The cold water, numbing my legs. John collapsed against me, shaking like the leaves overhead and sobbing. I stroked his hair. "God can forgive all things, John," I whispered in his ear, "Now it is time to forgive yourself."

I pulled him back to arm's length, and he looked at me with the wonder of a child, as if I had just revealed the greatest of secrets. For a moment, I thought I saw the teenage boy he had been, the happy-go-lucky person he must have been until that terrible day.

"Come on, John, let's go home. You still have work to do on this earth. It is time to do it."

John nodded, and together, we made our way to shore and back into the present, leaving the ghosts of 1933 there at Boo-Gang.

Sheen on the Water

Road Trip

David "Devil" Devlin, thirty-six years old, sat on the threadbare couch in the living room of the old farmhouse he called home. Flecks of dust danced in the shaft of light that slashed through the slit where the curtains met. A typed letter was on his lap. He picked it up and read it again for the fifth time. It was from an attorney in Detroit, Michigan, informing him that his father died in prison just weeks before his sentence was over. The crux of the letter was that David's father left him all his possessions. He ran his fingers through his long blond hair, then over his acne-scarred face.

The whistle from a teapot roused David from his thoughts. He untangled his six-foot frame from the blanket he had slept in and headed for the kitchen. He still held the letter as he poured hot water into a coffee mug. He forgot how many spoonfuls of instant coffee he scooped into the cup. He put the letter on the counter, shrugged and began to stir.

The pounding on the back door startled him. His eyes narrowed as he said, "Come in."

Frankie Fellowes, his best friend, entered the kitchen, nodded to David, and mixed himself a cup of coffee. Frankie, also thirty-six, was short of stature but held himself tall. He was sporting short red hair and a red goatee.

"So, are we going on a road trip?" Frankie asked.

"Yeah, we're going to Detroit, Frankie."

"How long do you think we'll be gone?"

David said, "Hard to tell. A week. Maybe ten days at the most. He's already buried in the prison cemetery, so there are no services to attend."

Steve Sporleder

"The guys put together a little fund so you won't be out of pocket for your expenses. That's nice of them, don't you think, Devil?"

"Yeah, that's real decent of 'em, Frankie. Thanks"

David Devlin was the president of the Gem City Gypsys Motorcycle Gang. The residents in town called them the Gem City Galoots, but not to their face. The Gypsys detested the nickname and beat people up for making fun of the gang.

"Do you think the boys can take care of the collections while we're gone?" David asked Frankie. Frankie pulled on his red goatee and said, "They're more than capable," nodding his head the whole time.

"Leave them a list of places that are due for collection; I don't wanna miss any product deliveries or funding."

Frankie nodded his head again.

———◆———

On the flight to Detroit, David and Frankie received suspicious looks from the other passengers. They were used to the looks. They went with the lifestyle of outlaw bikers. The clothes they wore—blue jeans, leather jackets, and engineer boots—were clean but not your typical travel attire.

Both men were required to get a travel permit from their respective probation officers. The permits allowed Santa Clara County the right to extradite them if they happened to be arrested in the jurisdiction they visited. David's and Frankie's criminal records were extensive. Their offenses ranged from assaults and extortion to grand theft, narcotics trafficking, and attempted murder. They were products of the juvenile judicial system and had graduated to the adult criminal system.

Frankie waited until David awoke from a midflight nap to ask him about the plan when they landed in Detroit.

"Well, when we get on the ground we need to rent a car. I think it'll be a Cadillac. Yep, I am sure it'll be a Caddy."

"Why're you so sure it'll be a Caddy?"

"Well, sir, because the last time my old man got arrested, he was driving a Caddy. Yeah, it will be a Caddy in honor of Daddy." They were both laughing when the flight attendant's voice came over the intercom telling the passengers to put their food trays up and get ready to land.

70

Just before landing, Frankie exclaimed, "That's the most I ever heard you talk about your father." The statement just hung in the air. David looked at his friend and shrugged.

"Not much to tell, amigo. He was in and out of prisons all of my life. I vaguely remember one Christmas when he was home. Right after that, my mother and I moved to California, and he stayed in Detroit. I saw him once after that at my grandmother's funeral. We weren't close." The last statement was said with a slap to his thigh. Frankie knew this as a signal to change the subject.

The maroon Cadillac pulled into the ten-story parking structure of a downtown Detroit office building. The attorney's office was comfortable and had a wonderful view of the city skyline.

Frankie waited in the lobby while David Devlin met with the lawyer.

"Your father had a handwritten will. It is legal and binding. The prison secretary notarized it. Everything your father possessed is yours. There are only a few dollars in debt left. What there is will be taken care of with the money your father earned in the prison woodshop. If there are any funds left over, I'll forward them to you at your address in Los Gatos, California. Is that all right with you, Mr. Devlin?" the lawyer asked taking a deep breath.

David stared at the attorney for a second too long, making the attorney nervous. He then stared at a Boston fern sitting near the window that had seen better days, and said, "Yes, Counselor, that's fine."

"Now, about the dwelling on Third Avenue. It's owned free and clear. However, the city redevelopment agency has condemned the property..."

"So, it isn't owned free and clear," David stated.

"Well, no, not technically, but the city is willing to give you fair market value for the property. This house is the only one left to be dealt with. Your father kept telling the city that he would let them know when he was ready to sell. He didn't understand the condemnation process."

"Oh, I think he understood the process," David said to the lawyer.

"Maybe you're right, Mr. Devlin. Even so, he was quite a thorn in the city fathers' sides."

David smiled as he asked what the offer was.

"Thirty-eight thousand dollars. Not a lot of money but a fair offer."

He was told that the figure was the average for the dwellings in the neighborhood.

"Well, sir, it is money found, so I'll take it."

At the Detroit City Hall complex, David was talking with a planning clerk from the redevelopment agency. Ammonia smell filled the room and off in the distance a phone was ringing. The clerk was relieved to be finally moving ahead with this project. David looked at a map of the area with a proposed park, school, and low-income multifamily dwellings. A yellow highlighter designated the boyhood home of David Devlin, right in the middle of the proposed development. The clerk droned on about the benefits of the project. David could not care less. In midsentence, he interrupted the clerk and asked, "How long before the place is demolished?"

"Thirty days."

David and Frankie slid through the cyclone fence surrounding the property. "Are we gonna get in trouble for this?" Frankie asked.

"Nah, the lawyer and the goon at city hall said that I'm still the owner and that I have thirty days to get any personal belongings out that I want."

As they entered the back door through the laundry room, David became very quiet. Frankie was chatting away about the smell of a house left vacant too long, when he realized that his friend was not with him. He retraced his steps and found his friend in the living room. David's cheeks were wet with tears. Frankie stepped toward his friend, but David put his hand up in a halt motion. Frankie went to tour the rest of the house, avoiding David.

Twenty minutes later Frankie heard the floor squeak in the laundry room. David was looking out the screen door at the backyard.

"I used to have an old tire swing on that elm tree out there. I spent a lot of time on that swing. Hey, Frankie, let's get out of here. There isn't anything here to take."

"Are you kidding? There's a fortune in the lumber; it's all solid redwood. Let's salvage what we can before they take it down. The copper fittings are worth something too."

"You think so?"

"I know so! All we need are a few basic tools."

——◆——

On the second day of dismantling, David was pulling up the floor in the laundry room. Some of the boards came up very easily; others were difficult. Two five-foot pieces came up together. "No wonder this floor squeaks," David said to himself. As the dust settled, David peered into the space between the floor joists. He could not quite comprehend what he was looking at. He felt with his hand and determined that a burlap sack lay under the floor. He lifted the sack out. It weighed about fifteen pounds. The contents were hard, like metal. David opened the sack. Inside, a cardboard sheath surrounded a pillowcase. "What have we here?" He realized that his heart was beating faster and that he was talking to himself.

"Hey, Frankie! Get over here a second!"

"What's up, Boss?"

"Help me with these, will ya?"

"What are they?"

"Can't say, but let's have a look."

David peeled the burlap off and slipped the cardboard sheath away. The pillowcase was old and dirty. The contents inside were plates for paper money. Five, ten and twenty, dollar bills. A distinct odor of oil filled the room. The two looked at each other with eyes as wide as manhole covers. They both looked around as if somebody might be watching them.

Frankie started to say something, but David shushed him with a finger to his mouth, got up, and shut the back door.

"What should we do?" Frankie whispered.

"Let me think," David hissed.

"Was your old man a counterfeiter?"

"Yeah. Among other things."

"I say we catch the next plane out of Detroit," Frankie said.

"Yeah, security will let these pass. Think Frankie, come on. No, we buy a car and drive back to California. Take our time, real cool like," David said confidently.

To Los Gatos

On a westbound plane, Bishop McKeever, thirteen, and his father, Hank, sat silently. Bishop was looking out the window at the dark landscape. Every few miles the lights from a small town could be seen. Bishop was tall for his age. His brown hair was cut short, and he had a smattering of freckles on his nose and cheeks. His father was taller and had an angular face set off by gray around his temples. Mrs. McKeever used to say that he looked like the actor James Stewart. Father and son favored one another.

"Man, this is a long flight," Mr. McKeever said aloud.

"It sure is, Dad. I hope Choppy's okay."

"He'll be fine, Son. Dogs have a way of adapting in adverse situations."

"Tell me again about Los Gatos."

"I've told you so many times, you could tell me about it, Bish."

Hank McKeever looked at his son and realized that he had hurt his feelings. He knew that this move was the most difficult. Bishop liked Pensacola and was happy with the middle school he was attending. Ever since his wife died in a boating accident two years ago, the McKeever men had been on the move. Staying in Cape Cod after his wife's death was not an option. Six months in Chicago, two months in Green Bay, ten months in Delaware, and the last period of time in Florida.

"You'll like my aunt's house in Los Gatos. I used to spend summers there when I was your age. It's a wonderful town. There is a creek behind the house. We can get a canoe or a row boat and float down stream to Campbell. I don't know if the swimming hole is still there, but I spent many summer afternoons in that creek." The telling of Los Gatos always started the same way. It was like the dialogue from *Of Mice and Men*, except neither of the McKeevers was a half-wit.

"Tell me about your job again, Dad."

"I'll be working for the Santa Clara County Water District. I will manage the control of water pollution for lakes, streams, and small bodies of water."

"Is it a good job?"

"It seems so, Bishop. The pay is okay, and they like my marine biology degree. So, it seems ready made."

"Tell me about your friend, Venice."

"When I would visit your Great Aunt Hildy each summer, I would see Venice Webb. He lived just a few blocks away. We hung out all summer together. He lives in the same house where he grew up. He was a fireman in Washington before he retired and moved back to Los Gatos."

"Is he your age, Dad?"

"He is. He was hurt as a firefighter and went out on a disability. Now he's a fire cause investigator for an insurance company."

"Tell me more about the town."

"It's called the Gem City of the Foothills. It sits in a natural amphi-theater formed by the Santa Cruz Mountains. Wildcats used to roam those hills. Spanish land grant owners named the town Los Gatos—*The Cats* in Spanish."

Undercover Ops

Late at night, a man in dirty jeans and an old army coat sat behind some huge rocks along the banks of Los Gatos Creek. He was looking at the rear deck of a restaurant and cocktail lounge on the other side of the creek. The establishment at one time had been a farmhouse. The quartz vapor light over the back door illuminated the area as if it were daylight.

He had a notebook to make entries in if anything out of the ordi-nary should happen.

What could happen? he thought to himself. *I've been on this assign-ment for weeks, and I have nothing to report.*

As he was getting ready to leave his vantage point, the back door from the kitchen flew open. Music, voices, and laughter from inside followed a man out. The door slammed shut, and the noise stopped. It was the cook stepping outside for a smoke.

"Just like he's done every night this week," the man behind the rocks said to himself in a whisper.

<hr>

During the day the Waterside Bar and Grill was a decent lunch-room. The cocktail lounge had good lighting and an airy feeling; it was a place town residents could feel comfortable. The dinner hour was always crowded, and the steaks were very good. However, after 8:00 at night the Waterside turned into a rough and tumble place. Gem City Gypsys took over the place. Rumor had it that the motorcycle gang conducted illegal dealings there. If town people wanted to imbibe after dark and not be bothered, they went to the lounge at the El Gato Hotel or the Top Cat Tavern.

Finally Home?

Choppy, a tricolored boarder collie, was so happy to see Bishop, he was wiggling all over the floor in the baggage claim area of Mineta International Airport in San Jose, California. Bishop was hugging the dog every time he got near. Mr. McKeever was smiling at the display of affection.

To think, I was about to suggest we give Choppy to a neighbor before the move, he thought to himself. *What was I thinking?*

<hr>

"Welcome home, pal."

Hank McKeever wheeled around and saw his childhood friend, Venice Webb. The two men embraced for a long time. "You are where you belong, Hank."

"I think you're right, Venice. Come over and meet my son."

Venice Webb was fifty-three years, stood about 5'10", and wore clothes that hid the fact that he was slightly overweight. His brown hair was receding and graying around his temples.

<hr>

Bishop and Choppy sat in the back seat of Venice Webb's car. Bishop was barely aware that the two men were talking in the front seat, he was so tired. His father was shaking him awake. He was startled, and then realized he fell asleep on the way from the airport. He watched from the backseat as Choppy became familiar with the yard.

221 Water Street, Los Gatos, California

Table lamps in the living room illuminated the interior of the single story Craftsman-style home. A female greeted them as they stepped onto the front porch. Both McKeevers were startled.

"Hank and Bishop, this is my friend Kate Wilson," Venice announced. "She's responsible for setting up the household with your belongings."

"I am pleased to meet you, Kate. I am also overwhelmed. Thank you so much," Hank McKeever gushed. Bishop was very quiet. His father gave him a nod and a look that required him to speak. "Thank you very much," Bishop said looking down.

Choppy whined at the screen door. Bishop started to go let him in, then stopped and looked at his dad. "Go ahead, Son, let your dog in the house." As quickly as Choppy wanted to enter, he wanted to go outside; his recon of the interior was brief. The yard was more intriguing and held more possibilities.

Bishop and Choppy stayed in the yard until Kate and Venice left.

"Are you coming in, Bishop?" Hank asked as he held the screen door open. When Bishop and his dog entered the house it wasn't with the bluster of a wagging tail and running feet. Bishop avoided eye contact with his father as he walked down the hallway to the bedrooms. In one of the bedrooms he recognized his furniture and entered and shut the door. Choppy stood at the closed door and whined once, then looked forlornly at Hank who was still standing in the living room. Choppy gave his tail a hopeful twitch, and then whined again.

Hank knocked gently on Bishop's bedroom door before he entered. "Are you okay, Son?" The sad look on his face broke Hank's heart. Bishop was on the bed gripping a basketball. A framed picture of him and his mother was lying next to him.

Bishop looked at his father and started to speak several times but stopped. Hank could see the tremble of his son's chin and sensed a breakdown. "I just didn't expect to see a lady come out of the house. It reminded me of Mom."

The basketball hit the floor and bounced, scaring Choppy. Bishop's hands went to his face, and he started to sob. Hank sat on the edge of the bed and raised Bishop's upper body up and embraced him tightly. The two wept in each others arms.

The next morning Hank McKeever sat in a wicker rocking chair on the front porch of his new home. The coffee mug he held was steaming. From the porch, he looked out on a wide paved street. Various species of trees in grass parking strips lined both sides and provided a dense canopy over Water Street.

Hank was mentally checking off the list of things he needed to do. First, and foremost, was to get Bishop registered in the Oak Meadow Middle School.

Bishop was lying in bed gazing up at the ceiling of his bedroom. He had the urge to get up and explore his new house and yard. However, he was thinking of his mother and the last time he saw her alive. She was sitting in a powerboat holding a line around a cleat to keep the boat aligned with the dock. She was waving to her husband and son who were walking down the dock toward her, carrying bags of sandwiches, chips, and sodas. The last thing Bishop saw her do was brush her wind-blown hair back from her face as she turned her head toward the sound.

The knock on his bedroom door brought him back to the present. "You awake, Son?"

"Come on in, Dad."

"I want to show you something," Hank said to his son. "Get dressed and meet me in the living room."

Bishop walked into the living room. His father was standing and looking out through the screened door. "What's up, Dad?"

"Bishop, we've lived in rented places for a long time. This house is ours. It belonged to my aunt, and it is now ours. I promise you we will stay here."

Bishop was smiling and nodding as he listened to his father. He glanced at a framed photograph of his mother on the mantle over the fireplace.

The screen door squeaked. "Do you hear that, Bishop?" Hank asked as he opened and shut the door.

"Yes, Dad, I do."

"There is nothing more comforting than listening to the squeak of a screen door on your own home. Hank kept opening and closing the door. You'll remember this squeak wherever you are. And it'll give you a warm feeling."

Bishop knew what his father meant. His thought was not about a noise, but about his mother touching his neck every time she walked behind him while he sat at the kitchen table in their home in Hyannis. At the most opportune times he would remember that playful caress, and comfort, calmness, and serenity enveloped him.

———————

The McKeevers stood at the front door. The rattle of a skateboard on the cement sidewalk shook them back to the present. A group of kids Bishop's age were going by. Boys rode on skateboards or bikes. Girls walked in groups. Some of the kids talked on cell phones. All wore backpacks or carried their books.

The boys wore sweatshirts and baggy blue jeans and tennis shoes. The ball caps they wore were on backwards. Those on bikes wore brightly colored helmets. The girls were attired in blue jeans and sweaters or skirts and light coats. This was a change from the last school Bishop attended; there he had to wear a uniform. He liked this better; his dad's military training about keeping a clean uniform was, at times, annoying.

Bishop gazed down at the group as they passed. His heart rate increased and his mouth became dry. Choppy yipped at the group causing several of the kids to look up at the porch. One of the boys made eye contact with Bishop, but neither acknowledged the other.

Bishop stood on the sidewalk looking back at his house. Horizontal wooden siding went from grade to under the windowsills. Shingle siding extended from the windowsills to the eaves. The house was painted ivory with gray trim around the windows and on the doors. A porch spanned the front and wrapped around the right side where there was a set of French doors. The pink cement walkway went straight from the sidewalk to brick steps, dividing a well-tended lawn. The porch was terra cotta tile and had white wicker furniture scattered across it.

He walked around the left side to a gravel pathway that led to the backyard. On each side of the paths were rose gardens.

The backyard was almost all lawn. A brick patio across the back wrapped around the other side and met up with the porch with the French doors. Stepping-stones led down to the peacefully flowing Los Gatos Creek.

A public dirt pathway crossed the rear of all properties along the water. About a hundred yards downstream from the McKeever's new home was a footbridge spanning the creek that led to another path on the opposite shore. A boat rental yard, Verducci's, was to the right of the footbridge and a footpath led into downtown Los Gatos. To the left of the footbridge was the Waterside Bar.

Hank McKeever was watching his son from the window above the kitchen sink. Bishop was picking up rocks and throwing them into the creek in an over-the-head basketball shot. Choppy was trying to herd ducks from the water, to no avail.

Hank knew that these moves were extremely hard for Bishop. *He never complains*, Hank thought.

Oak Meadow Middle School

Bishop and his father sat in the office of Mr. Victor Cruz, principal of Oak Meadow Middle School. Cruz sat behind a huge oak desk. Bishop and Hank sat in matching straight-back chairs in front of him. Cruz had an olive complexion with a fringe of dark black hair around a shiny bald head. His short sleeve blue oxford cloth shirt had a recent ink stain on the pocket.

With a slight Spanish accent, Cruz acknowledged the ink stain with a shrug and said, "My wife gave me this pen for my birthday, and it has leaked since I got it. Anyhow, I received the transcripts from your school in Pensacola, Bishop." Bishop nodded and smiled at the man across the desk. "Your GPA is very impressive." Hank looked proudly at his son.

"I think you will find Oak Meadow a challenging and rewarding experience."

Hank and Bishop looked at each other and smiled. This was a private joke between father and son. In every school over the last two years, they heard the same boilerplate description about the excellent academic achievements of the student body and the success of the athletic teams. Hank learned the parents association was very active, and they hoped he joined.

Bishop told Mr. Cruz that he was anxious to settle in.

"Based on the curriculum from Pensacola, I had the counselor, Miss Hobson, create a schedule for you," Cruz explained, as he rearranged some papers. "These classes are somewhat advanced, but judging from your transcripts, you shouldn't have any problems. However, if you do, please contact Miss Hobson. And remember, my door is always open to any student."

Cruz stood up and shook hands with Hank and with Bishop. "Do either of you have any questions?" Hank told him no. Bishop asked about the basketball team. He was told the team was already practicing, but he would contact the coach and tell him that Bishop would meet him for a tryout. This pleased Bishop.

As Hank left his son in the attendance office, he heard Cruz ask his secretary to send a volunteer student escort for Bishop.

<hr />

Spring Tanaka, thirteen years old, with long, jet black hair and dark brown, almond-shaped eyes, entered the office. She was dressed in a blue plaid skirt and a white cashmere sweater. Bishop and Spring looked at each other and smiled, and then both averted their eyes quickly.

"Bishop, this is Spring Tanaka. She will be your escort today. Spring, meet Bishop McKeever. He is a transfer from Florida." Spring extended her hand and Bishop shook it.

As the two students left the office, Mr. Cruz said, "Take good care of him, Spring."

Outside in the hall, Spring rolled her eyes and smiled. Bishop liked her immediately.

"Florida is such a long ways away. What brings you to California?"

Bishop told her, "My father's new job."

"What does your father do?"

"He's a marine biologist. He's going to work for the county water department."

"You mean like for pollution?"

"Yes, and water tables and conservation."

"Well then, you might be interested in the student volunteer group, Friends of the Creek."

Before Bishop could ask what the group did, the change-of-class bell pealed and startled Bishop. Instantly a throng of students mobbed the corridors, all talking at once. Bishop and Spring plastered themselves against the wall as the horde passed.

Spring said they had five minutes between classes. "And if you show up late three times, you get detention." She held out her hand. "So if you let me see your schedule, Bishop, I can help you make it on time."

He handed her his paperwork and as she studied his classes, he studied her pretty face. She looked up suddenly, and his face turned red.

"Okay, it's third period now. You have English. I'll take you to your classroom and introduce you to the teacher. After each class, I'll meet you, and we'll go to the next one. How does that sound?"

"Good." That was all Bishop could say. His embarrassment was still evident. This time Spring smiled, but just a little.

In every class Bishop sat in, some of the students acknowledged him, and others ignored him. He didn't care. He just wanted the class to end so he could see Spring again.

She probably has a boyfriend, he thought to himself.

Sure enough after the last class of the day, Spring was standing with a boy, waiting for Bishop. His heart sank.

Spring said, "Bishop, this is my friend, Dewey Leighton. Dewey, this is Bishop McKeever."

"I'm happy to meet you, Bithop," Dewey lisped.

"Yeah, me too," Bishop said as he shook Dewey's hand.

"We were hoping we could talk you into coming to the Friends of the Creek meeting after school," Spring said.

"I am supposed to meet the basketball coach at practice."

"Don't worry about that," Spring told him that after school sports started forty five minutes after the last class to accommodate community projects for students.

"Come on, dude, the meetingth are only thirty minuteth long," Dewey added.

"Lead the way," Bishop proclaimed with a sweep of his hand.

Friends of the Creek

In a meeting room off the cafeteria, a few students were mingling around and laughing. It got quiet as Bishop entered. "Everyone, this is Bishop McKeever, a new student. Bishop, this is everyone," Spring announced, waving her hand from wall to wall. Hellos were exchanged, welcomes were voiced, and the talking and laughter resumed.

Bishop was surprised to see Venice Webb enter the room. "That is our coordinator for the group," Spring told Bishop.

"Well, hello, Bishop," Venice said aloud. That stopped the chatter again. Spring cocked her head and looked curiously at Bishop.

"Bishop's father and I are old friends," Venice explained to the group. "Maybe, just maybe, we can have Bishop bring his dad to one of our meetings. He works for the water department and is in charge of monitoring pollution in streams, creeks, and small bodies of water in the county. Part of his responsibility is Los Gatos Creek."

Bishop sensed the group looking at him with a little more respect. He hoped Spring felt that way too.

"Speaking of the creek, let's talk about the cleanup this Saturday," Venice declared.

Every student sat down and paid attention.

Just before the meeting was over Venice said, "Okay, then it's all set. We'll meet here at the school Saturday at 8:30 AM." There were groans and half-hearted sighs, and good-natured comments about wanting to sleep in and get more beauty rest.

Bishop liked the group and felt comfortable and welcome.

Spring and Dewey left the meeting with Bishop. They stopped by Bishop's locker to get his gym bag and continued in the direction of the gymnasium. Just before arriving at the gym, Dewey took a turn and said he was going home.

Oak Meadow Mavericks

The bouncing of basketballs and the squeak of sneakers on the hardwood floor could be heard from outside. The basketball coach, Mr. Fisher, stood by the sideline watching his team warm up. He was dressed in khaki pants and a white polo shirt. A chrome whistle on a blue cord hung around his neck.

"Coach, my name is Bishop McKeever, and I want to try out for the team."

Fisher shook Bishop's hand and said, "So you're the Florida Flash" with a friendly grin. He told him that the starting lineup was pretty much set, but he was welcome to practice with the team. Bishop had heard the same story in every school he attended. He always made the team, became the first substitute for the beginning of the season, and was a starter midway through. Bishop was changing into his athletic attire and heard the tweet-tweet from the coach's whistle.

"Start your layups! A row of shooters and a row of rebounders!" Bishop stood next to the coach. Fisher looked at him and said, "I don't need an assistant! If you want to make this team, show me what ya got!"

Bishop got in line, took a rebound, and passed it to the next shooter. As he trotted back to the end of the shooter line, a foot came out and tried to trip him. Bishop avoided the foot and glared at the jokester. Bishop received a *what-are-you-going-to-do-about-it* look. He continued to the back. When it was Bishop's turn to receive a pass from the rebounder, the ball was thrown purposely wide so he had no chance of catching it. Bishop stood there helplessly and heard a sarcastic "oops" from the person who made the bad toss. The bad thrower high-fived the tripper as they passed each other.

So, that is how it is going to be, Bishop thought to himself.

The coach brought the team together at center court.

"Awright, listen up. We have a new student here today. His name is Bishop McKeever." There were snickers and snorts. "Knock it off, or you can start doing wind sprints until the end of practice." Bishop was standing apart from the rest of the team. "He's a transfer from Florida and was a starter at the last school he attended. He wants to join our team."

"Not bloody likely," someone said under his breath.

Bishop was surprised to see Spring waiting for him after practice. "How did it go?"

"Pretty bad, Spring."

"They gave you a hard time, huh?"

Bishop stared at her for a moment and then grinned. "It's nothing new. It's been the same at every school since I left Cape Cod."

"Cape Cod? I thought you were from Florida."

"I am. I was born in…just forget it."

"Okay," Spring said as she hugged her books closer to her chest.

At the bridge on Main Street, Spring and Bishop stopped. "This is my street, Water Street."

"I live a couple of blocks on the other side of the creek, up the hill," Spring said with a nod toward her neighborhood.

"Okay then," Bishop said, "I'll see you tomorrow."

Spring started to walk away. "Hey, Spring, thanks for everything."

"You're welcome, Bishop. Why don't you meet me here in the morning and I can help you with your first couple of classes."

"That'll be great. See you then."

As Spring reached the other side of the bridge, she turned to see if Bishop was still standing there. He was, and she waved. *Yes!* she thought as she turned. She ran right into a man with a scruffy growth of beard wearing an army fatigue jacket. They excused themselves and continued walking in opposite directions.

The Carlyle Place

In a renovated farmhouse along the Los Gatos Creek, about a mile from downtown Los Gatos, Erin Carlyle was carrying her two-year-old daughter, Faye, across the dirt driveway toward an old barn. Erin was in her late twenties, had auburn hair and a tanned face. "This is such a nice place," she said to Faye. "It would be perfect if those motorcycle guys didn't live next door." Her daughter gurgled and cooed. The mid-morning sun warmed the two.

The Gem City Gypsys shared a driveway with the Carlyle family. The driveway dropped down about five hundred yards from the road above and split off, the Gypsys' clubhouse to the left and the Carlyle family on the right. At the split in the driveway, a large hedge divided the lots. The hedge continued all the way to the creek. The foliage was thick enough to provide privacy. Still, at times the rumble of the motorcycles was deafening. Fortunately, during the day the Gypsys were gone to their jobs, or whatever they did. On the other hand, they did respect their neighbors and would always inform them if there were going to be a party at the club headquarters. David Devlin harped on the gang to stay out of the neighbor's yard.

Erin and Monty Carlyle had purchased the property in an as-is condition just a month before. Canning jars and other farm kitchen gadgets remained as if the farmer and his wife had just gone for the day. Even the farm wife's plaid apron still hung on a hook by the back door.

The tracks for the barn door, rusted from the lack of maintenance, made it difficult to slide open. "You're daddy told me the day we moved in that he would show me to the barn," Erin cooed to Faye. "He's just so busy, baby. You and I are going to go on an adventure. Aren't we?" With some effort, Erin got the door open, and the smell of fertilizers and motor fuel wafted from the interior of the old barn. Behind the barn were twelve acres of apricot and prune trees. Monty Carlyle hired a man and his son to work the land and tend to the trees. They shared any profit from the fruit. There wasn't much. Monty had a good job as an engineer for a large civil engineering firm in nearby Palo Alto. Not making money from the fruit was no big deal. On the other hand, the place looked great. When disking was completed and the tree trunks were painted white, the old farm displayed a very peaceful and rural atmosphere. When the Carlyle's realtor showed them the property, the apricots were being dried and the smell of freshly worked ground sold them immediately.

"Can't you just see it, Faye? We can rewire the place, put up sheet rock, and have a nice guest room for Grandma and Grandpa. We can have parties out here, too. Won't that be fun?"

An old Ford wheel tractor sat in a horse stall. Other stalls had hoes, shovels, scythes, and various other farm implements hanging from hooks or just propped up against the walls or each other. The top boards of the stalls showed chew marks in spots where horses, over the years, had gnawed on the wood. All of the stalls contained Dutch doors—the kind of doors that split across the middle so the bottom could stay shut and the top open—that led to paddocks. Erin opened all the doors to let in fresh air and light and then looked up from the floor to the loft.

She stepped onto the first rung of the steep ladder. The rung wobbled slightly causing Erin to step back to the ground. "We'll go up there another day, Honey. Okay?" She walked around the tractor and saw a door that led to some kind of storeroom. The door opened with a creak. Erin started to walk in, but a mask of cobwebs stopped her. Sputtering and spewing she cleared away the mess and put Faye down to check for spiders. She cleaned the doorway, found a string, and pulled. A bare light bulb hung from an overhead beam. When the light filled the room, a creature of some sort darted behind sacks of fertilizer.

"Eeew!" Erin shrieked.

"Eeew," Faye said.

"We better have Daddy set some traps, huh, Honey?"

As Erin was herding her daughter out of the room, a wooden box on a shelf caught her eye. Stenciled in large letters were the words *Danger Dynamite*.

Emergency Operations

Within ten minutes of the call to 9-1-1, the street above the Carlyle property was full of emergency vehicles. Three fire engines, a ladder truck, a HAZMAT rig, and an ambulance staged in strategic locations. Police patrol cars blocked the road from both ends. The county sheriff's bomb squad was en route. All the emergency vehicles had their rotating red light beacons flashing. Their rays provided an eerie presence on what had been a serene morning. The squelching and squawking of emergency radio traffic on the apparatus added to the confusion of the situation for the citizens. "What did they say?" and "What does that mean?" echoed throughout the crowd.

Police evacuated the Carlyle property and the Gypsys' headquarters. Neighbors in all directions for one thousand yards received the order to evacuate. Television news vans were jockeying for position.

About fifty residents, and as many emergency personnel, gathered at or around the command post. Erin was talking to her husband on her cell phone. He was speeding south on freeway 280 toward home. Erin kept assuring him that she and Faye were all right.

Some of the Gypsys were milling around, not really taking it too seriously. One of the gang members was eating a doughnut. When he was done, he blew air in to the white paper bag and popped it on his knee. All present screamed and ducked at the same time. His cohorts laughed and pointed. A police officer escorted them away from the crowd, reading them the riot act the whole way.

Linc Collins, the chief of police for Los Gatos, arrived on the scene. He met with his officer in charge, Garnett Maddox. Garnett was forty-two, with black hair streaked with gray. His face was square and tan. He had rugged features with deep blue eyes. It was evident he was in good shape.

The police and fire departments shared command on incidents of this magnitude. Any thing larger in scale, the police and fire department chiefs would share command of the emergency from the Emergency Operations Center at city hall.

Garnett and the battalion chief from the fire department were discussing tactical options when the police chief interrupted.

"Whadda we got, G.M.?" Chief Collins asked Garnett.

"The reporting party, Erin Carlyle, was in her barn when she discovered an old wooden box of dynamite." Garnett pulled over a parcel map of the tract of land. He was pointing to the Carlyle property on the map when he realized the chief was not even listening to him. Collins was posturing for the media and not paying attention. Garnett could have said that the chief was an idiot and the chief would have just kept nodding his head up and down looking serious for the cameras.

He's a bobble head, Garnett thought.

The bomb squad removed the box, put it into a hole they had dug, and lit it on fire. If there were no blasting caps or other ways to detonate the explosive, burning the stuff was the safest way to dispose of it. About thirty minutes after the dynamite was torched, the emergency was over.

The bomb squad commander was giving an interview to the local television station. He was saying that the sticks of dynamite were sweating nitro glycerin and that was when the material was least stable.

Chief Linc Collins was giving a statement, which Garnett Maddox had prepared, imploring the public, especially those on agricultural property, to check for any blasting materials. If any were found, he admonished the public to not move them, but to call 9-1-1 immediately. He further explained that the dynamite was used for blasting tree stumps, a common practice on agricultural properties in past years.

Later that evening the TV crews were interviewing the Carlyles in front of their barn. Had the interviewers been a little quicker, they would have seen Chief Collins joking with several Gypsys in front of their headquarters.

———•◦•———

At the Waterside Bar and Grill, Maggie Mendez, the restaurant hostess, was watching a newscast of the emergency on the television over the bar. She started to make a call on her cell phone, when a patron interrupted her and requested seating in the dining room.

First Alternate

At Bishop's first scrimmage with the Mavericks, Coach Fisher put him on defense against Tommy Myers, the boy that tripped Bishop at his first practice. Tommy was dribbling down court, alternating his direction to get across center court. Bishop's defense was frustrating Tommy. Tommy tried to fake a move to his right. When he did this, he lost a step, and Bishop picked the ball clean and drove to the opposite hoop. Fisher blew his whistle to stop the action. Fisher picked up a ball to demonstrate a maneuver to use in a situation like the one Tommy just tried. Tommy Myers was not listening. He stood with his hands on his hips breathing hard and glaring angrily at Bishop. Bishop was following the coach's instructions intently. He held the basketball to his hip as if he had just won a trophy. He could feel Tommy's stare. *This is going to lead to trouble,* he thought to himself. *Bring it on.*

For the remainder of the practice no incidents occurred. Bishop was the recipient of hard checks a couple of times, but there were no cheap shots. Bishop felt good about his performance; he would make the team.

————◦•◦————

At the next practice, the same type of scenario was set up. This time, however, Bishop was on offense. As he brought the ball up court, Tommy consistently fouled him. Still he drove toward the basket, all the while waiting for the whistle to blow for a foul.

Bishop drove for a layup and while in the air, Tommy Myers slammed him hard. He landed on his back with Tommy standing over him. Tommy was grinning and extending his hand down to Bishop to help him up. Bishop took the hand. Then Tom kneed him in the stomach knocking him to the ground again. Mr. Fisher watched the exchange between the two boys.

Bishop was on his feet in a nanosecond and squared off with Tommy Myers. Tommy took the first swing, which Bishop avoided. The next swing landed on Bishop's cheek. The crowd was cheering Tommy on. His confidence was up because of the landed punch. The two combatants continued to circle one another. Tommy took another swing. Bishop blocked it and gave Tommy a hard punch to his belly. Tommy doubled over in pain. He was gasping for the air that was knocked out of him. The fight was over almost as quickly as it started.

Bishop was walking toward the locker room when the coach yelled, "McKeever, get back here! Myers, you get over here too!"

Bishop shuffled up and stood in front of the coach, his head down. "I will not tolerate fighting on my team!" Fisher yelled at him. The hair on the back of Bishop's neck started to prickle as he pointed to Tommy, who, by now, was being helped to the bench by his teammates. The coach put up his hand to stop Bishop from talking. "Do I make myself clear?"

Bishop nodded his head.

"You hear me, Myers? Fine, now get back out on the court!" He yelled as he gave his whistle a long bleat.

Tommy Myers was sitting on the bench. He stared at Bishop as he made his way to the floor. "You'll get yours, Florida," Tommy hissed. Bishop stopped in his tracks, looked at Tommy, and shrugged his shoulders in a gesture that said *If you want to go again, Dude, I'll be ready.* Outwardly Bishop was doing a good job of showing bravado, but inwardly he was messed up. He wanted to make the team, he wanted to be liked, and he knew fighting was an avenue to not making the team and not being liked. The bleat from the coach's whistle stopped the posturing.

Friends of the Creek Cleanup

On Saturday, the Friends of the Creek assembled at the school. Some complained about the early hour. Others looked half asleep. Spring and Dewey arrived together.

Venice Webb announced he had plenty of burlap sacks and gloves for all to use, then opened the tailgate of his pickup to reveal the pile.

"We'll start at the rear of the school and go to the footbridge, then cross and go to Boo-Gang for a picnic. We'll pick up sandwiches and sodas at my place on the way there, then come back down the other side and finish back at the school." Venice stuck his hands in his pockets and rocked back on his heels a moment. "How does that sound?" he said with a big smile.

A few half-hearted okays could be heard.

"Come on, ladies and gentlemen, a little more enthusiasm, or it might be liver and onion subs for lunch!"

A laugh rolled through the crowd of kids as they crowded up to the back of the pickup for their supplies.

When they were strolling the banks of the creek, Bishop asked Spring, "What's Boo-Gang?"

She told him that it was a small waterfall upstream, where kids from town used to swim. She told him several stories of older kids hiding above the falls and scaring the younger ones by yelling like banshees.

Sounds familiar, Bishop thought, searching his memory. "Oh, I think my dad told me some stories about that place, too," he told Spring and launched into his dad's tale of the local swimming hole. He

91

was mostly through the tale and a half full sack of trash when suddenly Bishop stopped short.

"What's the matter, Bishop?" Spring asked.

"That's my house! There, across the creek!"

"I know."

"I'm surprised, that's all. I need to learn how to get around town." Spring said, "I'll teach you."

"Hey, wait a sec, you know that that's my house?"

Spring's cheeks reddened.

Bishop didn't want her to be embarrassed so he gave her a smile and headed for an errant bit of newspaper while Spring found a crushed Coke can to add to her sack.

When they crossed the bridge, Choppy ran up to the group. Bishop was pleased and proud to tell them that this was his dog and that was his house. The Friends of the Creek emptied their accumulated trash in the McKeever's garbage tote and used the facilities to freshen up.

They ate sandwiches and drank sodas under the sycamore trees that rimmed Boo-Gang. Bishop finished his tuna sandwich and looked around. Boo-Gang was a very peaceful and beautiful spot. The smell of moss, the chirping of birds, and the sound of cascading water hitting rocks were mesmerizing. He almost dozed off before they started back to work. They crossed the falls to head back down the other side. As they walked along, he said to Spring, "I'd like to go there again."

"Sure, me too," Spring chimed in, but then she reigned in her voice and said a bit hesitantly, "Did you mean with me?"

"Well, I guess that would be okay," Bishop said teasingly.

She punched him lightly on his upper arm.

Bishop was hard-pressed to remember ever having a better day. He was truly glad to be in Los Gatos.

Maverick Victory

The foul buzzer on the scoreboard in the gym jarred the crowd as if being zapped with an electrical jolt. Bishop was kneeling at the scorer's table ready to substitute for Tommy Myers. The entire student body knew about the altercation between the two and watched with anticipation as the two passed. They exchanged half-hearted high fives in an obligatory show of good sportsmanship as they changed positions. Off court, they were adversaries and had no use for each other.

As Bishop took up his place on the court, he caught a quick glance of Spring sitting next to Dewey. Over the hum of the crowd, he heard her yell his name. At the same time, he saw his father turn to look in that direction.

The referee's whistle brought Bishop back to the moment.

The Mavericks tossed the ball crisply and performed their plays with ease while on offense. Their defense, on the other hand, needed help. The game was back and forth. Each team answered with a score. The Mavericks, with a surge of aggression, swiped the ball and headed down court. Bishop received the ball at half court and faked a drive to the basket then abruptly stopped, hoping to be fouled. When the whistle didn't blow he looked right and passed left to a teammate standing under the basket who tossed it in at the final buzzer. The Mavs won thirty-four to thirty-two.

Everyone had spilled onto the court and was milling around center after the game. Several people slapped Bishop on the back, congratulating him.

Spring ran up and hugged him just as his dad arrived. "You played wonderfully, Bishop," Spring gushed. One side of his dad's mouth twitched into a quick smile. Bishop would have blushed if he weren't still flushed from playing.

"Dude, you rebounded theven and made eight pointh. Good going!" Dewey told him.

"Thank you," Bishop told both of them at the same time, then introduced them to his dad.

After hands were shaken and his dad was talking to Dewey, Spring leaned over and whispered, "Are you going to stay for the dance?"

Shall We Dance?

The lights in the gym were low, and rock music played from a portable jukebox. Some students were dancing, but most were standing in groups. Bishop, Spring, and Dewey were near the center of the floor reliving some of the finer points of the game, when all of a sudden a water balloon exploded across Dewey's chest. Water splashed over Spring's face and hair and down Bishop's right arm. Dewey froze and looked down at his soaked clothes. Bishop whipped around and saw Tommy Myers and some of his cronies sniggering as they hightailed it from the area where the water balloon had come from.

"Those jerks," Bishop said with clenched teeth. He started toward them, "I'll—"

"Bithop, no," Dewey cried out. "Can't we go, pleath?" His eyes pleading with Bishop.

He looked at Spring. She nodded. "Let's just go."

The trio passed the chaperones table. A pinched-face woman called out that they would not be able to reenter once they left; it didn't even slow them down.

Dewey's house was in the general direction of Spring's home. As they walked along Dewey said, to no one in particular, "I don't understhand Tommy Myerth. We were betht friendth in grade thcool. When we hit junior high, he dropped me."

"Yeah," said Spring, "Tommy, Dewey, and I started first grade together. We were always together, until the sixth grade, and Tom changed. He made new friends and dumped us like we were embarrassments to him."

"You guys are really lucky, you know," Bishop said. "I couldn't name one person I went to first grade with." He wondered what it must be like to have friends for so long. They walked in silence for several blocks. "Don't fret about Tom Myers, dude. You have Spring and me. Who needs any more than that?" Bishop said, slapping Dewey on the back.

By the time they said their goodbyes at Dewey's house, he was smiling. Bishop and Spring continued toward her house. In the distance the blare from an air horn on a fire engine echoed through the night air as it responded up the canyon into the foothills, the sirens lessening the farther up the engine got. As they strolled along the sidewalk, there were areas of illumination where street lights stood then several yards of darkness. In one of the unlit areas their hands came in contact awkwardly. When it happened again, Bishop took hold of Spring's hand, and they continued on, hand in hand. At an old rock wall, the two stood and looked down into town. The Main Street Bridge that spanned Los Gatos Creek was sparse of traffic. Spring pointed at the bridge and said, "Where Main Street and Santa Cruz Avenue meet? That intersection is called the *elbow*."

"Where? I don't see where you mean," Bishop said. Spring stood closer to him and pointed again, wondering how he couldn't see what she was talking about. She realized he was playing, and wanted her to stand closer to him, and she did.

———◆———

Bishop was floating on air as he crossed the footbridge toward his house. As he reached the center rise of the bridge and started down the slight incline, the footbridge began to undulate, shaking his reverie. He grabbed the handrail to steady himself. "Is this an earthquake!" he said aloud. The next thing he knew, "Oomph!" he was on the seat of his pants, the wind knocked out of him. A large man in a plaid woolen coat and a ball cap had barreled into him and knocked him down. The stranger stopped and glared at Bishop. Bishop stared at the man, but could not see his face. The bill of his cap shadowed his features. The man smelled like beer. Bishop swiveled around and watched the man as he ran to the opposite side. The bridge continued to sway long after he was gone. Bishop sat stunned, until he heard the back door of the Waterside Bar slam shut. Then he picked himself up, took a deep breath, and dusted off his seat. The incident faded from his memory as he continued his walk home in the crisp late fall evening; his mind was on Spring.

Crime Scene

The next morning Bishop got up a little late. His father let him sleep in on the weekends. He couldn't find his father in the house, but noticed the back door ajar. He pushed it open further and went outside. Choppy was walking back toward the house; when he saw Bishop, he broke into a run. With a tousle of Choppy's ears, Bishop said, "Come on, boy, let's find Dad."

At the water, he looked down stream and saw his father, Venice Webb, and a uniformed police officer standing on the footbridge talking. Bishop couldn't hear what they were saying but noticed steam from their breath as they conversed.

As Bishop stepped onto the footbridge, a flash of yellow caught his eye. He looked left to see crime scene tape strung around an outcropping of boulders. Several men and women wearing blue coveralls were milling around the rocks inside the taped area. Choppy ran toward Hank and the others, his tail wagging as he urged Bishop to hurry. All three felt the bridge sway as Bishop approached.

"What happened?" Bishop asked as he nodded his head toward the group on the other side of the yellow tape.

His father motioned him closer and told him that a man's body was found behind the rocks. "Is he dead?" Bishop asked in a shocked whisper. The group looked to the officer, and he nodded curtly. "Was he murdered?" he asked in an almost whine. The cop said that it appeared like it, but he wasn't sure and no one should jump to conclusions. "That's what those folks are gonna tell us," he said as he pointed to the taped area by the rocks.

The news stunned Bishop, and it must have showed. All he could do was look down and shake his head.

———◆———

Garnett Maddox, the man in uniform, had a cop's instinct that told him Bishop knew something about the incident.

"Where do you live, son?" Garnett asked Bishop.

Bishop just stood there and said nothing, like he didn't hear the question.

"This policeman asked you a question, Bish," his father said

Venice Webb, spoke up first and said to Bishop, "Bishop, this is Lieutenant Garnett Maddox of the Los Gatos Police Department."

They shook hands, and an awkward moment passed.

"Do you know anything about this?" Garnett asked Bishop.

"I can't be sure. Last night as I was walking home, a man came running toward me. He ran into me and knocked me down."

Hank bristled, and he gripped the railings on each side of the bridge turning his knuckles white as Bishop spoke.

"What did this man look like, Bishop?"

"He was big, tall, you know, and wide."

"Had you ever seen him before?"

Bishop shook his head from side to side.

"Do you think you could recognize him if you saw him again?"

"I don't think so. He was by me in a flash."

"What type of clothing did he have on?"

"A black and red checked wool jacket. Like a lumber jack would wear."

"Anything else?"

"He wore a baseball cap and smelled like beer, ya know?"

All four looked over at the Waterside Bar.

"Did you see what direction he was headed?"

Bishop nodded. "He went left when he got to the other side."

———— • ————

As Bishop, his father, and Venice Webb walked up the lawn to the McKeever's home, Hank said, "I wish you would have told me about this last night, Son"

Bishop hung his head and mumbled, "I didn't think it was a big deal, Dad."

"Not a big deal? Holy moly, Son, a man is dead!"

Hank felt chaos bubbling and brewing in his gut. *He loses his mother; I keep him on the move. Running from what? I don't know. He can never get settled to really grow any roots, any friendships, and now this. Bishop could very well be the one person that saw the murderer—if it was a murder. Of course it was a murder. Bishop just doesn't need this. It was supposed to be different here; it was supposed to be safe; it was supposed to be a place to heal.* Hank kept a tight lid on the turmoil he felt, so his voice came out flat and strained when he asked Venice, "What if the guy finds out where Bishop lives?"

Venice reached out and put a hand on Hank's shoulder, giving it a brief squeeze. "I wouldn't waste time worrying about that, Hank. I mean, how will he find out?"

"I don't know. Maybe his name could end up in the newspaper."

Venice pulled out his cell phone and punched in some numbers.

"Hey, Garnett, it's Venice. There won't be any info given to the press about Bishop seeing this suspect will there? Great."

Venice closed his phone and nodded to Hank as if to say *That's that.*

Hank reached out and clasped Venice's hand firmly between both of his. "Thank you, Ven. Thanks a lot."

Later that afternoon Dewey and Bishop stood at the creek in Bishop's backyard.

"No kidding? You thaw the guy. The murderer? Wow!"

The news was all over town about the dead body, and the police confirmed it was a homicide.

"I am not sure the guy I saw is the murderer. It's no big deal, Dewey. I don't know what the guy looked like."

"It ith thtill eckthighting."

Dewey told Bishop that he wanted to be a CSI detective.

"I love forenthicth. It'th my pathion, tho I notith thingth. I have to, you know, if I'm gonna be a detective." Dewey looked around carefully, making quite a show of looking back over his shoulders before he leaned in and whispered, "And I can tell you, there are funny thingth happening at that creek, Bithop."

"Yeah," said Bishop as he nodded, "like a murder."

"Not only that," said Dewey as they approached the little footbridge, "Haven't you notithed anything weird going on around here?"

Bishop shook his head this time, "Other than last night? I don't think so."

Dewey lifted his chin and gave a smug little smile. "Well, two dayth ago, I wath—"

"Hey!" one of the police volunteers yelled as the two set foot on the bridge. "Get off the bridge!"

Dewey and Bishop both stopped as the man came up to them. "Sorry, boys, you will have to take the long way around. The crime scene has expanded to the bridge. Technicians are collecting evidence. We can't have you contaminating the scene now, can we?"

"No, thir!" Dewey agreed enthusiastically.

Bishop was a little less excited about a long walk around, so when he was out of earshot of the bridge, he said, "Come on, Dewey, when we were out collecting trash, I saw a place we can get across, probably won't even get our shoes wet, not much anyway!"

"Okay," said Dewey.

Just before they turned off the path to head along the bank, a woman who had come out from the back of the Waterside Bar and

Grill strode by. "Hey, Maggie," said Dewey. But she passed by without so much as a *hi there*. The fierce look of concentration in her eyes made Bishop curious, and he slowed down. She started talking to the man who had turned them away from the bridge, offering to get the volunteers sodas or ice teas. Then she was asking questions about what was happening with the investigation.

Bishop didn't hear too many answers because by that point the running water became louder than the voices. All he could notice was the police volunteer shaking his head and shrugging his shoulders. "So, Dewey, tell me about all the spy stuff you've been doing."

"Detecting," Dewey corrected. And with that, he started telling Bishop all manner of stories to prove that Dewey had finely honed detecting skills. When Dewey mentioned about chemicals leeching into the water, Bishop peppered him with questions.

"Where does it come from?" He asked.

"Any number of platheth. There could be an old pipe that may drain in there. I'm not thertain. But I'm working on it. Dewey ith on the job!"

Gypsys in Trouble

David Devlin was talking heatedly into a portable phone. His pacing was an indication to Frankie Fellowes that something was wrong.

"I told you he was out-of-town talent! How many times I gotta tell ya? Nothing can be traced to us. Relax, okay?" He slammed the phone down into its holder.

"He's more trouble than he's worth," he said aloud.

Frankie knew, from experience, that you do not talk to Devil Devlin unless he talks to you directly when he is in a foul mood. So he sat silently watching Devil pace back and forth.

David looked directly at Frankie and said with narrow eyes, "Get rid of that guy from Oakland."

"He's already gone, Devil."

David stopped in his tracks and whirled around. Before he could say anything, Frankie put up his hands in a placating gesture that said, *it's done.*

Back at Headquarters

Garnett Maddox pulled his police car into the parking lot of the town hall complex. He noticed a four door Chevy with government plates parked in a visitor's space. He stepped into his office and read a note from the chief: *G.M., see me ASAP, L.C.* The note was left ten minutes prior to Maddox's return. The chief's clerk buzzed Collins that Lieutenant Maddox was here. Garnett heard his reply through the door and over the intercom: "Send him in."

A man in a navy blue suit was sitting in the police chief's office.

"Lieutenant Maddox, this is Agent Jerry Webster from the Secret Service." Garnett and Webster shook hands and sat in wooden chairs in front of the chief's desk. Garnett took sideways glances at Webster and wondered what he was doing in Los Gatos. The wall behind Collins was loaded with diplomas, certificates, and plaques. One of the officers on the force called it the ego wall. Garnett thought it was the mark of a man who had his brains hanging on the wall. A glass pitcher of water and clear plastic cups sat at the side of Collin's desk. Condensation was dribbling down the pitcher onto a paper towel under it. As if on cue, Collins poured himself a glass and didn't offer any to his guests.

"It seems," Collins said pointedly, as he sipped, "that undercover ops have been going on for a while."

Garnett cocked his head, and Collins continued, "Oh, I know. I told him that the locals should have been notified, Garnett." Collins was hoping to get Lieutenant Maddox to jump in on the locals-versus-Feds bandwagon. Garnett just kept looking from the chief to Webster.

"There was no need to contact you until now. We believe that the man killed in your town was our agent.

"Garnett is the lead on this investigation; he will cooperate with you fully. I have a press conference to give, so, if you will excuse me."

"Hold up a minute, Chief. I must tell you that to mention the operation will jeopardize months of hard work, and if that was our agent, he would have died in vain."

"Well, don't you think I know that? Do you think we're a bunch of hicks?"

Garnett winced to himself and thought, *Chief, you really don't want to know the answer to that question*, because he was sure that the agent was indeed thinking to himself that this police chief was an enormous hick.

In Garnett Maddox's cubicle, Webster confirmed that the morgue photos were definitely the agent.

"What do we do from here, Jerry?"

"I'll keep you posted on developments on our end and you keep doing the investigation on your end, see?" He replied. "Also the more you tell your chief, the more info he's going to give the press. I don't know him at all, but I get the impression he is a self-made man who is going to die in the arms of his maker."

"Care to explain that?"

"He's a press hound, Garnett. I've seen his kind before."

Garnett raised his hand up and Webster stopped talking. "He is what he is. Nothing more. But in this building, please don't talk about him like that, okay?"

"Sure, sure, Garnett."

When Jerry Webster shut the door, Maddox sat behind his desk and wondered how Webster got such a spot-on read of Collins.

<hr>

At the same time, the police chief was telling the media the slain man was a transient.

Maggie Mendez was alone in her apartment crying.

Learning the Town

"Thith," said Dewey as they stood at the intersection of Santa Cruz Avenue and Main Street, "is the town."

"Spring told me this intersection is called the *elbow*."

"Yeth, thath what they call it alright," Dewey said with a slight grin. "It'th a unique town. All boutique-type ethtablithmenth." Dewey sounded like a tourist brochure. "No chain thtoreth. The thity counthil don't want 'em"

"Where is your house, Dewey?"

He pointed to the other side of the Main Street Bridge. "Up above Main."

"You live near Spring?"

Dewey nodded and smiled.

"What are you grinning at?" Bishop asked him.

"Oh, nothing. Thpring really liketh you, you know."

Bishop's heart started to beat faster. "Yeah? How do you know?"

Dewey told him, "Dude, I have known Mith Tanaka for a long time. I probably know her better than anybody doeth. When I thay she liketh you, take it to the bank."

The two boys moved on in this town tour until they were standing on the front lawn of the town offices watching the media interview with the police chief. News camera lenses glinted in the sunlight.

"I met a police officer this morning. Maddox was his last name. He seems cool."

Dewey said, "He ith way cool. He ith the go-between."

"What's a go-between?"

"Between the thchool and the poleeth," Dewey told Bishop.

Dewey said that Garnett Maddox handled all police incidents at the school. He also talked to the parents and students on crime prevention and safety. "He wath in the Poleeth and Fire Olympicth. He won a gold medal in martial arth. Everybody at thchool liketh him, he'th eathy to talk to."

The ice cream parlor was the next and last stop on the Dewey town tour. Bishop and Dewey sat in a booth finishing their sundaes when Tommy Myers and his group walked in.

Tommy said over his shoulder to those following him, "Check it out. Geek alert! Geek alert!"

Bishop and Tommy glared at each other.

"Oh, great," Dewey said under his breath and studiously focused on eating his sundae.

Tommy and his crowd sat down for their ice cream, being loud and disruptive and rude the whole time.

"Let's leave, Dewey. What do you say?"

Even though his sundae wasn't quite finished, Dewey nodded and got out of the booth.

"Hey, Dewey, anymore water balloon accidents?" Tommy asked as Dewey walked by.

The boys at the table were laughing. Dewey kept walking for the door.

Bishop stopped at the table and was about to say something when Dewey took his arm and said, "Leth go, Bithop."

"Bithop? Oh man, that is priceless!" Tommy said aloud with a noisy laugh.

Bishop was steaming as he walked through the door. He heard, "Thee you, Bithop," as the door closed. Dewey was standing on the sidewalk.

"They're just punks, Dewey. Don't let it get you down."

Dewey just nodded. Bishop could see tears starting in Dewey's eyes even though Dewey turned away to try to hide it.

Why do people need to be cruel to one another? Bishop was thinking as he walked home. His head was down, and he walked right into Chief Collins.

"Hey, boy, better watch where you're going."

"Excuse me, Chief. Sorry."

"It's all right son. Got a lot on your mind?"

"You might say that. Why do people have to treat others so bad?"

"Are you talking about the murder?"

Bishop said, "Yes, and other things."

"Are you new in town? I don't think I've seen you around."

"My father and I just moved here from Florida."

"Are you the lad that saw the man on the bridge last night?"

Bishop sucked his lower lip between his teeth and then nodded.

"Don't be too concerned about the guy that got whacked last night. He was just a bum. What is your name?"

Bishop told him his name, and the chief introduced himself.

"You live over on…?"

"221 Water Street."

"Yeah, right, Water Street. Your dad and Venice Webb are friends, right?"

"Yes, sir."

"Well be a good lad and get on home. Get your school work done."

"Yes, sir," he said again.

As Bishop continued on his way, he thought about what the chief had said: *He was just a bum…What a weird thing to say*, he thought. *The bum must have a family. Somebody is going to miss him, eventually.*

Getting to Know You

The next morning after church, Bishop was sitting on the picnic table in his backyard. The creek was burbling serenely. Overhead, he watched a jet vapor dissipate.

His father called down to him. "Bishop, there's somebody here to see you."

Bishop turned around and saw Spring walking toward him. Bishop's heart skipped a beat. Spring was smiling at him. Bishop looked past her at his father standing at the back door. His dad gave him a thumbs-up and shut the door.

"Mind if I join you?" Spring asked when she got closer.

"Not at all, please sit," he said as he gestured toward the table.

"Dewey told me about the trouble you had with Tommy Myers yesterday. Thanks for sticking up for Dewey. He is such a sweet boy."

Bishop said to Spring, "You and Dewey are the only friends I have in this town. If you can't stand behind your friends, then you're not worthy of their friendship." Bishop's head slumped.

"What's the matter?" Spring asked.

"Nothing."

After a few minutes Bishop said, "My mother used to say that without friends you had nothing. I was just thinking about her."

"What was she like, your mom?"

Bishop stared at her for a couple of seconds, then said, "She was beautiful."

"Go on, Bishop."

"We lived on Cape Cod. It is, or should I say was, a good place. We lived in a cape-type house, like just about everybody. There was a fantastic view of the ocean. We had a lawn that sloped down to the lane in front of our house. The seashore was just across the street. We had our own pier, and in the summer, my friends hung out there, and we did cannon balls off the end to see who could make the biggest splash. Mom and Dad took me boating all the time."

Spring kept nodding, urging Bishop on. He hesitated as if he was trying to gather the nerve to continue.

Choppy was asleep under the table and when a squirrel started to yak he raised up his head and yipped. The squirrel stopped and got up on its hind legs and twitched its nose. Choppy sat up and started to move for the chase. The squirrel romped away and scurried up a sycamore tree. Spring and Bishop watched it disappear in the canopy of leaves.

A cool breeze wafted through the yard and caused ripples in the meandering water in the creek. "Anyhow," Bishop went on, "it was a beautiful late summer morning. My mother, dad, and I were in our sailboat cruising around Hyannis Port—my dad is an excellent sailor," Bishop boasted, sitting up a little straighter. "And he was teaching me to sail." Bishop sighed at the memory of the wind and the sun and the water. "Man, I really loved it. There's something about the salt air that, I wish I could show you…

"Anyhow, my mother wanted to head for the dock to go in, and my dad headed for shore. 'Let's stay out longer,' I whined. But Mom said it was time for lunch so we went to get sandwiches at the deli next to the harbor master's office.

"She was holding the line around a cleat. My Dad and I were walking down the dock with paper bags full of chips and sodas and sandwiches. My mother waved to us. She had a big smile on her face."

He stopped talking, and Bishop's lip trembled. Spring took his hand and squeezed it. He knew she was telling him that it was okay to stop.

"No, that's okay; this is the most I have talked about it since it happened. It feels good to tell someone about it—to tell you, Spring."

"Okay, Bishop, I'm listening."

"My father and I were about fifty yards from our boat. A very loud outboard motor boat screamed into the 5-mph zone. The man claimed that the throttle stuck, but he was drunk and pushed the lever forward instead of pulling back, making that throttle wide open." Bishop took a moment to chew his lip so that tears wouldn't come. "He hit our boat midship. Mom never knew what hit her. The boat landed on top of her. My dad ran to her. They tell me his adrenalin must have been pumping, because he picked the bow of the boat up and off her. He was holding her in his arms. I was frozen. I stood there with the sack of sandwiches in my arms. I couldn't move."

He had to stop a moment. It was getting harder to fight the tears, and his voice was betraying him. After a few moments, he continued. "But Dad says it doesn't matter, that he's glad I didn't see her like that, but…Anyway, she died before she got to the hospital." This time he couldn't hold back and a tear started down his cheek. "My last image of her is sitting in a boat on Lewis Bay waving."

He was silent for a long time. He looked at Spring and smiled. His cheeks were wet now from tears. Spring's eyes welled up also.

"You know, sometimes I forget what she looked like. I have to concentrate very hard to bring her face to mind. It's weird. There's a picture of her on the mantle that keeps me grounded. Sometimes I need to get up in the middle of the night to go look at that picture. Sitting here by the creek, thinking of her, keeps me on solid footing."

Spring rubbed his hand, and they sat in silence for a while, listening to the birds, the breeze, the distant trickle of water, just holding hands.

Finally Hank interrupted with a yell from the back porch, "Hey you two! I have lunch ready. You want me to bring it down to you?"

Bishop made sure his eyes were dry and waved his hand to bring it on down.

Flows to the Bay

The three of them sat at the picnic table looking at the water. Choppy sat waiting for a scrap of fallen food or a benevolent handout.

Just as they were finishing up their meal Spring pointed upstream and said, "Look!"

Hank and Bishop followed her pointing finger to a cloud of milky white water meandering downstream.

Hank shook his head in disgust.

"What do you think it is, Dad?"

His father was silent as he stood on the creek's edge and looked upstream. From side to side and for as far as the eye could see, the water was white.

"Hard to say what it is without taking some samples. Could be somebody cleaning up after painting. Folks think they can just hose off their painting equipment and let the water go into the storm drain. They don't realize the harm they cause."

"Last year the Friends of the Creek group spent many weekends stenciling FLOWS TO THE BAY at the drains in the gutters," Spring announced. Bishop and his father both nodded to let her know they understood what she was saying.

Hank McKeever made the call to the police department about the white substance in the creek. Twenty minutes later the County Fire Department Hazardous Materials team was standing in the McKeever's backyard. The captain in charge of the HAZMAT team was talking on her two-way radio. She had short black hair and angular features. When she was done, she came over to Hank and said, "My dispatcher told me that you are with the Santa Clara County Water District. Is that true?"

"Yes. I started recently." They introduced themselves. Hank learned that her name was Gina Carlin.

She replied, "Great! How do you want to handle this?"

"I've already started by collecting some samples for the water district," Hank said.

"Good. That is our standing operating procedure in situations like this. I'll have my guys collect a few more for the city. Why don't you—" Before she could finish her sentence, her radio started talking again.

Spring and Bishop were sitting at the table watching the incident unfold. Bishop enjoyed watching his father at work.

"10-4, Dispatch," Captain Carlin replied into her handheld radio.

When she got off the radio, she told her two firefighters to take samples of the water in two different spots. Then she turned back to Hank. "P.D. caught a homeowner washing out paint rollers in the gutter in front of his house. We're going to take samples for evidence."

"Sounds like some public education needs to be done," Hank said.

The fire captain's eyes glistened with emotion. She took a deep breath before she spoke. "Many budgetary dollars are spent on public education for fire prevention programs. About the only education citizens get about water pollution is in the punitive damages the guilty person receives after an illegal discharge. And the possibility of having their name plastered in the newspaper seems to deter others for a while."

Hank smiled. "You seem passionate about this, Captain, I like that. I'm guessing you've told that story before, haven't you?"

"Yes, I have, at every budget planning session since the HAZMAT team was formed."

Hank agreed with her and told her that in other jurisdictions he'd found the press to be an important ally. "Positive articles are a great source for good publicity for the department, and it spreads the word about the perils of pollution and what the laws are. I can help you with that."

"I'm going to hold you to that," said Gina Carlin. Then she thanked him for his assistance and advice before she returned to her engine.

———

Several hours later the creek was running clear. A fire hydrant at the Main Street Bridge was turned on full blast and spilled into an outfall putting thousands of gallons of clean water in the creek and allowing the polluted water to be diluted as it flowed to the San Francisco Bay.

A Nice Meal

Hank and Bishop were having dinner with Venice Webb and his friend Kate Wilson at the Waterside Bar and Grill. The place was starting to fill up and the noise level increased. A busboy filled the water glasses. When he turned from the table he ran into a waiter, almost causing him to drop his tray of plates with food. As table talk took place, Hank became more and more distracted every time the hostess entered the dining room. He had trouble taking his eyes off her pretty face, her dark hair, and especially her long legs.

"Hey, pal! So which is it, Florida or Delaware?"

"What?" he said, trying to search his brain and the faces around him for a clue to what the question was.

"Dad, what is it? You seem like you're in La La Land," Bishop exclaimed.

He just shook his head with a sheepish look. When he focused on the others at the table, they were all smiling at him.

"How's your steak, Bishop?" he asked in a change-the-subject statement.

Bishop made some noise that Hank took for a positive answer, and then he tried harder to track the talk at the table. When Bishop went to the restroom, Kate asked Hank, "Would you like to meet her?"

"Who do you mean?" Hank asked innocently.

"Her," Kate said as she nodded toward the hostess.

Before Hank could answer, Kate waved her over to their table. Hank was mortified and miffed.

"Hi, Kate," the hostess said. "How was the meal?"

"Hello, Maggie. The food was delicious. I want you to meet a longtime friend of Venice's."

Maggie nodded to Venice, smiled at Hank, and extended her hand. Kate said that she and Maggie were in Pilates class together.

Maggie's proximity ripped Hank with emotion. It was one thing to look from afar, another to meet someone, talk to her, and think about her as a woman he could like. His wife's memory kept creeping into his psyche creating conflict.

Bishop returned to the table and Hank introduced him to Maggie.

"Oh, yeah, I saw you at the bridge the other day," Bishop told her. She gave him an odd look and then smiled. When Maggie walked away, Kate told Hank she was sorry if she caused him any discomfort. Hank just smiled weakly and nodded his head.

"Dad, she seems real nice, and she is pretty," Bishop said. Hank and his son grinned at one another.

The Investigation Continues

One brisk Saturday morning, Bishop and his father walked up the street toward their home. In front of the house sat an LGPD patrol car. As they approached the walkway, Garnett Maddox and a tall blond-haired man in a navy blue suit got out of the car.

Garnett introduced the man as Jerry Webster. Webster asked if they could go inside and talk.

Around the kitchen table, Garnett explained that Webster was an agent with the government. Hank and Bishop looked at one another with confusion.

"My visit here is confidential. Do you both understand?"

Garnett could see that they were intimidated, and he attempted to lessen the impact of this visit.

"Agent Webster wants to ask some questions about the man killed the other night and if Bishop remembers anything about the man he saw on the bridge. The man murdered was an agent working undercover."

Bishop said aloud, "An agent? The police chief said he was a hobo."

Garnett and Webster looked at each other with some distain.

"No, Bishop, he was not a hobo. He was working on a case."

"What case?" Bishop asked excitedly.

"I can't divulge that information," Agent Webster stated flatly.

"Any information you can offer would be helpful, Bishop," Garnett said.

Bishop thought about what Dewey had told him about the pollution leeching, but thought that it couldn't matter.

Agent Webster asked Bishop to retrace his steps back to the footbridge.

The three of them went down to the water's edge. The agent asked Hank and Garnett to stay back, then he and Bishop walked onto the old wooden planks of the bridge and up the incline. As Bishop and Webster stood midspan on the footbridge, he suddenly felt the hair on the back of his neck go up. He looked around and found the reason why—people were watching them. A pair of ladies walking by slowed down and kept glancing in their direction. One even pointed. A man on the back porch of the Waterside Bar and Grill sat with an open newspaper, but it was collapsed in his lap, and he made no effort to hide his stare. From a restaurant window, he saw the waitress his dad seemed to like, Maggie Mendez—she watched too, but she kept looking between the man with the newspaper and Bishop. Bishop looked away, shifting his weight and partially turning his back on the observers. "I can't remember anything more than what I have already told you. Sorry." He couldn't resist a quick glance over his shoulder. "Can—can we go back now?"

Amateur Sleuthing

Bishop was in his room getting ready for bed when he heard knocking on his bedroom window. He stepped between the twin beds and moved the lamp to the side. He grunted as he pushed open the old window. A breeze blew the curtains in and rustled the poster of Kobe Bryant hanging on the wall above the old oak library table he used as a desk.

Outside on his back lawn stood Dewey—in full camouflage gear.

"What in the heck are you doing, Dewey?" Bishop hissed.

"Night thirveilanth."

"Dude, are you nuts?"

"Maybe. Come on, I have a theory on the murder."

"No way. If my father caught me, he would skin me alive."

"We won't get caught. I have been thirveiling every night thinth the murder.

"I think I know why the guy got hit."

"Really?" Bishop looked at the clock by his nightstand—nine o'clock. He might be able to sneak out in an hour and meet up with Dewey. "Maybe if—" He heard the old floor boards in the hall squeak, and then footsteps. "No, never mind. Please, Dewey, go before my father hears you."

"Okay, I'll thee you tomorrow."

Bishop just nodded as he closed his window as quickly as he could.

Somewhere Bishop heard a bell ringing. He awakened momentarily and then thought it was a dream. Just before he fell back to sleep his father opened his bedroom door. The light in the hallway made him squint.

"Mr. Leighton is here, Bishop. Come out into the living room."

Dewey's father was sitting on the couch and rubbing his bald head nervously with his right hand.

"Son, Mr. Leighton tells me that Dewey is not at home. Do you know anything about that?" Hank fixed Bishop with an unwavering gaze.

Bishop fidgeted, he didn't mean to drop his eyes for that moment, but it was noticed; Bishop's hesitation made Mr. Leighton sit up rod straight.

"I am very concerned, Bishop. Please, if you know where my son is tell me."

The clock on the wall chimed—one, two, three—what should he say? What could he say? He didn't want to turn in his friend. And he didn't really know where Dewey was—five, six—still, the way his dad pinned him with his stare, the way Mr. Leighton leaned forward, holding his breath—nine, ten—Bishop took a deep breath as the clock struck the eleventh and final time.

"About 9:00 tonight, Dewey came to my bedroom window."

Mr. McKeever and Mr. Leighton exchanged looks.

"He said he was doing some surveillance…"

"Of what?" Mr. Leighton asked.

"I don't know what he was looking at. But I know it has to do with the murder."

Mr. Leighton put his elbows on his knees and hung his head between his hands. "Damnation," he muttered. "I don't know how many times I've told that boy to stay out of other people's business. Dewey considers himself a detective, you know."

"Where did he go, do you know, Son?" Hank asked.

Bishop sucked in his lower lip. "Maybe down the creek?"

The three headed downstream along the creek trail, Hank wielding a flashlight. Moonlight glistened off the ripples of water. The smell of moss was heavy in the night air. Just after passing the footbridge, mockingbirds stopped serenading as the trio approached an outcropping of boulders, where, ten days earlier, a murder had taken place.

Mr. Leighton gave a sudden sigh of relief. "Dewey!" Bishop looked where he was rushing to. There was Dewey, leaning up against one of the rocks, sound asleep. Hank, a little behind them, came out from behind the stump he was investigating and headed toward them.

Even as everyone converged on Dewey, something gnawed at the back of Bishop's mind. *The rocks where the murder took place, isn't that kind of an odd place to hide and observe?*

Mr. Leighton tapped him on the shoulder. Dewey didn't stir. "Come on, Son," he said, shaking him by the shoulder now.

Dewey fell over.

Hank caught up and shined his flashlight on Dewey. Everyone gasped. The right side of his head was crushed. Dried blood was crusted on his temple and cheek. His face was a death mask, mouth slack and eyes staring lifelessly.

Mr. Leighton clutched his son to his chest and rocked over the body, sobbing and chanting, "Oh no, my boy Dewey, oh no."

Hank had summoned the police with his cell phone. Within twenty minutes, the generators that ran the portable lighting for the crime scene investigators woke the people in the houses along the creek. Interior lights in windows came on. Residents were standing in their yards watching real-life CSI.

Bishop had been sent back to the house. He crawled up on the picnic table in his backyard and sat with his arms wrapped around his tucked legs and his head on his knees. Occasionally he looked up to see medics, police, and lookers-on milling and swarming on and by the bridge. Mostly he just rocked back and forth, not looking. The snap of a twig under Hank's foot roused Bishop. He stared at his father as he approached from the creek trail.

His father stood in front of him. "Oh, Dad!" Bishop cried out as he launched himself at him. He clung to his father around the waist and sobbed.

Hank was crying, also.

A Farewell to Dewey

The funeral for Dewey Reginald Leighton was held on a mostly sunny Saturday morning.

Almost the entire student body of Oak Meadow Middle School was present. There was standing room only. Bishop sat between his father and Venice Webb. The sweet aroma of fresh flowers permeated the chapel.

Dewey was lying in a dark oak casket. A white lace veil draped the head of the casket to conceal Dewey's fatal wound. His features could be discerned but the trauma to the head was concealed.

The priest started his sermon by saying that sometimes events that take place on this earth have no explanations. "Why should a son be taken from his parents? A classmate taken from fellow classmates? A friend taken from his friends? These questions can't be answered this side of heaven," he announced with solemn emotion. "When an older person dies, the past is lost, and when a middle-aged person dies the present is gone." He looked out over the sea of young faces in the crowd. "But when a young person dies, we lose the future."

Mrs. Leighton sobbed uncontrollably. Her sister and husband both held her to them at the same time, but could not console her.

The priest implored the congregation to pray for the repose of Dewey's soul and for his acceptance into heaven.

The next speaker was Mr. Victor Cruz, principal of Oak Meadow Middle School.

He addressed his comments to Dewey's mother and father, extolling Dewey's character and saying how delightful he was to be around. That he was well liked by students and faculty alike was an understatement. "You are living every parent's nightmare," he told the Leightons. Every mother wept for Mrs. Leighton. Parents sat a little closer to their children in the chapel that day. There could not be too much protection for the children of Los Gatos.

Just before the casket closed, Mr. Leighton stood looking at his beautiful child for the last time. Hank took Bishop's hand and crushed it between both of his own. And though they were squeezed shut tightly, tears welled in the lines pinched up around his eyes.

He wasn't the only father crying and holding on to his son.

They buried Dewey beneath a huge deodar tree. The school choir sang "Just a Closer Walk With Thee" as the casket was lowered into the grave.

When the song was over, Bishop left his father's side, and walked up to the Leightons.

He had no idea what he was going to say. As it turned out, he did not need to say anything.

The Leightons wrapped their arms around him. Mrs. Leighton whispered in Bishop's ear that Dewey cherished his friendship.

This brought Bishop to his knees. He held his head as he sobbed. Hank saw this unfolding, rushed to his son's side, and cradled him in his arms as he cried.

Over his father's shoulder he saw Spring watching him. Her face, too, was glistening in the weak sunlight.

Bishop stood next to Spring with his hands in his pocket watching the black limousine drive away. They were silent; neither had said anything since the service, but they didn't need to. When they turned around, they were face to face with Tommy Myers. To Bishop's surprise, Tommy's eyes were puffy and red.

"Dewey was the first friend I can ever remember having." As he talked, he seemed to shrink. He was silent for several moments and then said, "I treated him so bad…"

Bishop could see Tommy's chin tremble, saw the slumping shoulders and knew that his collapse was near.

Bishop took his hands out of his pockets and grabbed Tommy's shoulders. They stood like that for five or ten seconds, then came together in a crushing hug, both weeping. Spring put her arms around them both.

Town Meeting

In the town hall chambers, a standing-room-only crowd was listening to the mayor speaking about the recent murders and the progress of the investigations. At an appropriate interval, the mayor called on the police chief to speak.

Chief Collins started out by saying that two murders in the same area in a short period was a rarity. In the past five years, only two other murders had occurred in Los Gatos, and they were solved immediately.

Whispers buzzed throughout the chambers.

Venice Webb told Hank McKeever that those two previous slayings were crimes of passion, and that the persons doing the killing confessed, and in fact had called the police.

"Collins is making it sound as if he solved them single-handedly," Venice said under his breath. Garnett Maddox gave Venice a knowing nod, and then quickly gave him a knitted-brow look of chastisement. Venice grinned.

Linc Collins' next statement sent a shock through the crowd. "Many of you may not know it, but the FBI is assisting us in these investigations."

Garnett did a double take. "FBI?" he muttered. *What FBI? What was Collins up to? Hadn't Webster said to keep their involvement hush-hush?* Venice looked at him curiously but Garnett just shook his head. In every strategy meeting he had with Webster, he was told to keep the Feds' involvement quiet, and now this.

The crowd took several minutes to quiet down. The mayor was pounding his gavel in an attempt to gain control.

Jerry Webster exited the meeting out a side door. Several minutes later Garnett Maddox's cell phone vibrated on his hip. With an exasperated sideways glance to Venice, he, too, exited the meeting.

He found Jerry Webster pacing back and forth angrily on the bricks of the town plaza.

"I cannot believe how inept that jerk is."

Garnett just nodded his head in agreement.

"What the hell is Collins doing? We told him we don't want our presence getting around town—he could ruin everything!" Webster paced back and forth, swiping his hair back from his down-turned face. "And he has the FBI doing the investigation! What an idiot. I can't believe he has the wrong agency," Webster vented. "We are the Secret Service, for Chrissakes."

"He's not as stupid as you might think, Jerry."

Webster stopped pacing and looked up. "What do you mean?"

"He is sly like a fox. I have seen this ploy too many times. Citizens think he is smart. The officers and mayor know differently."

"Why doesn't somebody blow the whistle on him?"

"Jerry, you know as well as I, the code of silence applies in all police agencies. Even yours. Nobody is going to rat out another officer. So let's quit griping and figure out how we are going to solve these murders."

Webster crossed his arms. "Yeah, I guess you're right." He seemed to be thinking, so Garnett waited. "I have a question for you Garnett. If you were the chief, what would you do next?"

"That's easy. I would try and find out why the Feds were in my town. But I am not the chief, so let's get back to reality."

"Reality, you say? Okay. Why do you think the Feds are here?"

"I think you are investigating the Gem City Gypsys for narcotics."

"You are half right, Garnett. But think. When was the last time you heard about the secret service investigating drugs?"

"I guess I hadn't thought it through. You guys do protection for big wigs and—" Garnett Maddox stared open mouthed at Webster as he realized what he was telling him.

— • —

Inside the town meeting, the police chief was taking questions from the audience. Most present wanted to know if the population was safe and if more officers should be hired.

Collins was doing a good job appeasing the folks until Venice Webb spoke up. "Chief, do you think the killings are related?"

Collins stood speechless for several seconds. He appeared to not understand the question. He winced as if the noon sun were blinding him.

Finally, he replied, "There is nothing to link these killings."

This brought a swell of murmuring from the crowd.

"How could they not be linked?" somebody asked. "They happened in the same spot."

"The Gypsys are involved!" someone else chimed in.

Collins stood mute until the crowd quieted down. "I can tell you with certainty that the Gem City Gypsys had nothing to do with the crimes in question." With that said, he abruptly thanked everyone in attendance and walked away from the podium.

As Collins exited, the mayor assured everyone they were safe; they just needed to take a few precautions and buddy up on the streets. He trusted the police and said the town could take comfort that the FBI was on the job, too.

Some Semblance of Normalcy

Several weeks passed since Dewey's funeral. On a Saturday morning a number of members of the basketball team, Tommy Myers and Bishop included, assembled at the Leighton home to do yard work. Three hours later the chores were finished. Bishop was on the porch and was ready to ring the bell to announce their completion when the front door opened. Mrs. Leighton asked Bishop in. As he stood inside, he glanced back over his shoulder and saw Tommy wave so long as he left with the rest of the team. The interior of the Leighton's home was neat but smelled like moth balls. On the mantle were three framed photographs of Dewey; a baby picture, a grade school picture and his latest school picture. Bishop got a lump in his throat.

"Bishop, Dewey's father and I need to clean out Dewey's room. We just can't seem to bring ourselves to do it. Do you think you could help?"

"Absolutely. I'll go call the guys back," he said as he went for the door.

"No! Wait," Mr. Leighton exclaimed. "We don't want a huge crowd. Just you. Please? I don't think the other boys will be respectful of Dewey's things."

Bishop said, "Fine, I'll get started right away."

The color drained from the Leightons' faces. They wanted the job done, but clearly not just yet. Bishop offered a plan. "Er, um, how about if I come over after church tomorrow? My father could help me maybe."

"What will you do with his things?" Mrs. Leighton asked.

"Do you want to save anything?" Dewey's parents just stood there saying nothing.

"What about giving his clothing to the needy? Dewey would like that."

His father grinned and said that was a good idea. Mrs. Leighton walked away mumbling to herself. Her husband told Bishop that she was not doing too well. Bishop said he understood and thought to himself, *Neither are you, sir.*

"I'll see if I can bring boxes to package up his personal items. You can store them until you and your wife are ready. How does that sound?"

"I have a few, too, I can pull out of the garage," Mr. Leighton tousled Bishop's hair. He thought he was too old for such a gesture, but he stood still anyway. "You are a very understanding young man. Thanks." Just as he was leaving, Mrs. Leighton came over to him and gave him a hug. She started to cry as Bishop hugged her back. As Bishop walked down the street, he was wiping tears from his cheeks.

The next afternoon Hank, Bishop, and Venice Webb were packing Dewey's clothes in boxes to give to charity. The bedroom was neat and tidy with a single bed covered in a yellow bedspread. The headboard, nightstand, dresser, and desk all matched. There was a poster of J. Edgar Hoover on one wall.

Mr. and Mrs. Leighton left when the trio arrived. They were going to the cemetery and on to relatives for the remainder of the afternoon.

The boxes of clothes were being stacked in the back of Venice's pickup truck ready to be deposited at a collection center for the needy.

As Hank took out the last of the clothes and Venice followed dragging the twin mattress, Bishop was going through Dewey's desk, where he came across a leather bound journal. The first page said *Investigation Journal of Dewey Reginald Leighton.*

A brief perusal of several pages showed dates, times, and entries. On one of the pages, Bishop saw his name written down. The last page was the date Dewey was murdered. *This may be interesting*, Bishop thought as he slipped it into his back pocket wondering how the police missed this when they searched Dewey's room after the murder.

Bishop finished boxing up Dewey's belongings and took them to the Leighton's garage. Three boxes—they were a sad summation of a short lifetime.

———•———

Later that afternoon, Bishop stood midspan on the footbridge reading some of Dewey's entries in the journal. He looked up from time to time and glanced at the Waterside Bar and then to the rock formation where two people died. He walked over to the rocks and looked at the bar. He had learned that Dewey was watching late night activity in and around the Waterside. Some sort of machinery could be heard, usually after three in the morning. On the following mornings, rainbow sheen could be seen on the water.

As Bishop read the journal, he kept thinking back to something Dewey said one time: "There are funny thingth happening at that creek."

Over at the Waterside Bar, the same man sat reading his newspaper, but Bishop wasn't sure that the man's eyes were always on the paper. Sometimes he thought he caught him looking over the paper's edge, watching his every move.

Sick as a Dog

Bishop was feeling very low after dinner. Cleaning out Dewey's room bothered him more than he thought it would. Dewey's room was just so empty now—it all seemed so final. He strolled to the creek and tossed rocks in the water when he realized that Choppy was not around. "Choppy!" he yelled, "Here boy!" Bishop paused and cocked his ear. Usually he would hear the jingle from his dog's collar as soon as he summoned Choppy.

Bishop went and found his father raking up leaves from among the tree roses in front of the house. "Dad have you seen Choppy?"

"I thought he was with you."

Hank propped the rake up against the porch. He and Bishop scoured the neighborhood searching for Choppy. He was nowhere to be found.

Bishop was worried as he went back out in the yard to take one last look for his pet. Just before Bishop was going into the house to make posters announcing a lost dog, movement under a camellia bush next to the house caught his eye. Choppy was whining when Bishop approached. He lazily wagged his tail, as if to say, *Sorry, buddy, I couldn't come when you called.*

"Dad! Come quick, I found Choppy! He looks like he's half dead!"

———•———

The inside of the animal hospital smelled like disinfectant. Try as he might, Bishop could not sit still. His father was trying to read a golf magazine but kept going over the same paragraph.

"I wonder what's taking 'em so long. Oh God, I hope he makes it," Bishop whined for the umpteenth time.

The veterinarian explained that Choppy was suffering from poisoning. He stated further that the type of poison was unknown. More tests were needed.

"Will he live?" Bishop asked pleadingly.

"He should be back to normal in about a week," the vet explained.

Bishop sagged with relief. Internally, so did Hank.

— ·—

"Yeah, it was awful, but the vet said he thought Choppy would make it," Bishop said to Spring as they stood on the footbridge gazing downstream.

"Did you find what he got into?"

Bishop shook his head. "Nothing on our property. Dad and I searched inside and out all afternoon yesterday."

"Well, at least he's okay," Spring said for not the first time.

"Yeah," Bishop nodded. Then the two of them just stood in silence for a time, lost in thought.

A flash of silver near a bridge piling pulled Bishop from his reverie as it caught his eye.

The two scrambled down the bank to investigate. Their closer inspection showed two dead fish bobbing in the current. "Keep an eye on them!" Bishop told Spring as he clambered up top again. He dashed across the bridge with noisy footsteps.

Five minutes later, Bishop returned with a plastic bucket and a length of rope. Spring watched as Bishop tied a knot around the bail and lowered the bucket into the water. After several tries, Bishop brought two dead blue gills up to the bridge.

As he was looking into the bucket at the rainbow sheen swirling lazily about the floating fish when Spring leaned over and whispered, "Did you see that guy?"

"What guy?" asked Bishop starting to look around.

"No, no! Don't look now," she said. "There's a guy watching us from the back of the Waterside."

Bishop glanced over, but more covertly so as not to alarm Spring more.

"He gives me the creeps," Spring said with a shudder.

Bishop nodded, "I've seen him before. He gives me the creeps too."

— ·—

121

"Dad? It's Bishop. Call me at home." He gave Spring her cell phone back and said, "I wonder if the dead fish have anything to do with Choppy being poisoned."

Before Spring could comment the phone rang inside the house.

Bishop dashed in the house so fast he was out of breath when he answered his father's return call.

"Spring and I found some…"

"Whoa. Whoa, Bishop. You know you are not to have anybody in the house when I am not home.

"Dad, Spring is outside. I know the rules."

"Okay, Son. Sorry to jump to conclusions. Tell me what you found."

After hearing about the dead fish and congratulating his son on retrieving them, Hank told his son to get another sample of creek water from a different location.

So Bishop and Spring went back to the stream, but they stayed on the same side of the creek as his home. No need to get closer to the creepy guy.

Bishop chose a spot across the creek from the back patio of the Waterside Bar and Grill. A bunch of guys were hanging out there now, and Bishop wasn't sure which, if any, was the guy that had been watching them. He tried to ignore them as he tossed his bucket into the current, and let it fill, then pulled it to shore.

Even though he tried not to watch the men, he knew they were pointing at him and laughing.

"Hey boy!" Bishop looked up. A particularly scruffy looking man was standing at the edge of the bar's back porch with a mug in one hand. "That's a funny way to fish!" he yelled. More laughter erupted through the man's buddies. Spring grabbed Bishop's elbow. "Come on, Bishop," she said in a shrill whisper, "let's get out of here, I don't like those jerks."

Bishop nodded as he grabbed the bucket and headed home.

Test Results

"Bishop, I just got off the phone with the vet. He says that Choppy was poisoned with antifreeze," Hank said.

"Antifreeze? How could he get antifreeze?" Bishop wondered aloud.

Upon hearing his name, Choppy was squirming around the kitchen chair Bishop sat in.

"What about the fish? Did he tell you how the fish died, Dad?"

"No, son. The lab at work is testing the fish. It appears they died from a petroleum-based product."

"You mean the fish dying and Choppy being poisoned are unrelated?" Bishop asked.

"Seems so, Son. The lab techs did say there were other cases of dead fish near the percolating ponds in Campbell. They died from petroleum products also."

Bishop looked at his father as if to say, *Well, what are you going to do about it?*

Hank raised his hands in surrender and said, "I'll add it to my list of things to do."

Dewey's Work in Progress

Over the next several weeks Bishop could be seen on the footbridge at sun up. Six days out of fourteen he noticed sheen on the water. In Dewey's ledger, he made notes of the dates and times.

Ramon Sepulveda, a Gem City Gypsy wannabe, reported to David Devlin each time he saw the McKeever kid on the bridge. There seemed to be some importance in that—though what, Sepulveda did not know.

Sepulveda, a thirty-five-year-old construction worker, stopped every afternoon at the Waterside for beer and two wishes: one, to get in good with any Gem City Gypsy; and two, maybe to get a date with the hostess, Maggie Mendez.

"Maggie, darlin', do you know that boy on the bridge?" Ramon asked her one evening as she brought him another beer.

She looked over at Bishop, "Nah, just another town kid. I don't keep track of the little urchins."

Ramon narrowed his eyes when she answered. He could have sworn that she had been talking to that boy and his father in the restaurant on several occasions.

A Minor Tiff

"Don't you see, Spring? Dewey was onto something."

Bishop and Spring were sitting at a lunch table in the school yard. Spring was nodding, but not commenting as she nibbled away on her sandwich. "Every few days there is a sheen on the water, and sometimes there are dead fish. It is always from the bridge toward downstream."

"Really?" she said after pausing to swallow. "You've taken samples upstream, too?"

Bishop looked at her, started to say something, and stopped for a beat.

"No, I just never saw the sheen up there, but maybe I should, just to eliminate that area as a source for sure."

"Source of what?"

"You don't get it, Spring?"

She had finished the last bit of lunch and wadded up the plastic wrap and napkin before tossing the ball into a paper bag. "Well, why don't you explain it to me."

But before Bishop could answer, the break bell rang, summoning students back to class.

"Hmph, saved by the bell," Spring said as she turned and flounced off. If he couldn't guess from the edge in her voice that she was mad at him, he could still see it in her walk as she left him.

Confused, he went to his next class. The rest of the afternoon was a blur to him. Spring being upset and his wondering about the cause of petroleum in the creek made it hard to concentrate.

After school, Spring told Bishop she had some student government meeting to attend. As she spoke, she averted her eyes.

I guess she's still not speaking to me, Bishop thought unhappily.

———

Bishop lowered his bucket from the Main Street Bridge into the swift current. Several pedestrians stopped to watch as he dipped test tubes his father gave him into the bucket. He explained to those that asked, "I'm doing a science project."

———

"Isn't that Bishop?" Mrs. Tanaka asked her daughter as they drove home.

"U'huh," was all that Spring said in reply.

Her mother gave her a knowing look and said "Do you want me to honk?"

"Mother! Absolutely not!"

Her mother made a gesture to honk.

Spring gave her a pleading look.

"Okay, okay, relax, I was just joking."

Spring was happy when they were finally past Bishop.

———————

Bishop sat at his bedroom desk and put chemicals into a test tube filled with the water retrieved from the Main Street Bridge. The test results were inconclusive.

He wanted to call Spring and let her know about this but knew there was no good end in that. So he went to the living room to talk with his father about his test samples.

"What are you trying to determine, Bish?"

"Dewey kept a journal with his observations of the creek and his surveillance at night."

Bishop's father interrupted him and said, "Did you ever think that what he was doing got him killed?"

"Yes, Dad, I do, all the time. I think he was zeroing in on activity in or around the Waterside."

"It sounds like a police matter. That frightens me, Bishop. Drop this. I'll have some of the people I work with look into it. The fish and game people and the police can take over. Let me handle it. Okay?"

Bishop didn't answer. He wanted to comply with his father's wishes, but did not think he could just drop it—not after what happened to Dewey. He owed Dewey at least this much. He also didn't think the police were interested in his or Dewey's findings.

"Did you hear me, Son?"

"Yes, I heard you."

Night Skies Lit Up

Sirens woke Bishop. He looked out his bedroom window and saw an orange glow in the sky. The acrid smell of wood burning and smoke hung in the air like a blanket. From his window he could see the orange glow from a fire across the creek.

He dashed into his father's room. "Are you awake, Dad?"

"Yeah, what's up?"

"The Waterside Bar is on fire."

The two threw on the clothes they'd worn the day before and dashed outside. Hank and Bishop stood looking across the creek toward the bar. They could see that the building was intact, but a dumpster and a wooden enclosure adjacent to the bar were engulfed in flame. The lights from a fire engine and steam from the water applied to burning materials cast eerie shadows across the scene. Figures of firefighters were distorted as they sifted through the debris.

Later they would learn from the morning paper that the preliminary investigation determined the fire was accidental. It was caused by discarded charcoal from a barbeque held for the men's softball league. A cook told investigators that he thought the coals were dead out.

<hr>

Venice Webb was on scene the next morning with Garnett Maddox looking at the burned mess. Venice had been asked by the fire chief to assist in the investigation. The fire department did not have a designated fire-cause investigator so from time to time Venice offered his service and expertise as an investigator.

"I believe the report, Garnett," Venice said to Maddox, "It was an accident. However, the glow in the sky last night was not from ordinary combustibles."

"How so, Venice?"

"Too bright," Venice replied.

Garnett added, "The officer on the first-due engine stated that the first hose on the fire was ineffective."

"I wonder if some sort of chemical was put into the dumpster," Venice opined.

Venice went to his car and put on a pair of overalls, boots, and gloves. Once inside the dumpster he sifted through debris with a short handled shovel.

The smell of burned, wet garbage nauseated Garnett, so he busied himself away from the dumpster.

Most of the burned articles were items normally related to bar and restaurant work. He was looking for anything out of the ordinary.

He pulled out two one-gallon metal cans. The heat from the fire and the water from extinguishment oxidized the cans, rendering the writing on the containers unreadable. The caps were missing and the tops were expanded. This meant that the lids were affixed when the fire started, and the cans expanded from heat, causing the lids to blow.

Other than the cans, there was nothing out of the ordinary.

Just as Venice was about to climb out of the dumpster, he noticed a piece of torn white paper. It was different from other restaurant papers. All of the papers except for this one were food orders taken by servers in the dinning room and newspapers patrons left behind. The paper that caught Venice's eye was a partially-burned receipt or invoice on regular white printer paper. Across the top was the word *Distributors* and a partial address in nearby Campbell. Flames had destroyed all other information. Venice put the cans and the paper in a cardboard box in the trunk of his car.

He left the cans at the fire station and took the paper home. He was looking on the Internet and the telephone yellow pages for any enterprise in Campbell that had *distributors* in its name. If he was lucky, there might be a place that sold petroleum products, and they might be able to help find out who put the cans in the dumpster. After an hour of looking, he came up with a dozen places in the city of Campbell with *distributors* in their name.

The last place on the list was an outfit called Globe Distributors. The man answering the phone explained that Globe Distributors sold work gloves.

"You don't sell petroleum products?" he asked the man on the phone.

"No, we don't. What is this about, anyway?"

Venice explained what he was doing and that he was having no luck.

The man asked Venice, "Does the sales slip have an invoice number?"

"It's hard to tell because the paper is burned so badly. I don't know if this number is partial or whole. 2278. Does that ring a bell?" Venice asked.

"It sure does. Our invoices are four digits in the 2200s. Let me look up that number."

Venice's spirits were starting to lift.

"2278 was a cash sale on February 20 of this year."

"Cash sales don't give a name, do they?" Venice asked.

"No, but I remember this one. We are primarily a wholesale type of place. Every once in a while, we get walk-in trade. This guy was a Gem City Gypsy."

"What did he buy?"

"A pair of 12-inch, PVC-coated gloves for chemical handling," the man replied.

Venice thanked the guy and then dialed Maddox. "Garnett? It's Venice. Call me as soon as you get this message."

"How do you know the guy didn't buy the gloves to work on his Harley, Venice," Garnett said in a devil's advocate tone of voice.

"I don't, Garnett."

"The district attorney will need more evidence before a search warrant is issued."

"Then I'll just get more evidence," Venice said passionately.

"Now, hold on a minute, Amigo. Don't go taking the law into your own hands."

Venice just gave a sheepish grin as he headed to the door. Before he walked out, he turned to Garnett, shrugged his shoulders, and said, "I don't need a search warrant."

"You be careful."

Back in Good Graces

Spring had been in a depressed mood since her tiff with Bishop. As she walked through the kitchen of her home, she said aloud, "I wonder why he won't call."

"Then why don't you call him?" Her mother's voice startled Spring.

"How do you know what I am thinking, Mom?"

"Honey, I don't know what you are thinking, but when you speak to yourself aloud, well, there is no mystery."

"Huh? I was talking out loud?"

"Yes, and you have been wearing your heart on your sleeve for a week. Give him a call. And give your father and I a break!" she said under her breath just loud enough for Spring to hear. Then she looked shocked and held her hand innocently to her chest, "Did I say that out loud?" She winked at her daughter with a broad grin spread across her face.

Spring went to another room to make the call—hoping it was out of earshot of her mother. She picked up and put down the phone without dialing five times. Just as she reached for the phone a sixth time, it rang. On the caller ID window, she saw that the call was from the McKeever's. Before she let it ring again, she snatched it up and said, "Hello?"

Bishop and Spring were sitting in a two-seat glider on the Tanaka's patio overlooking downtown Los Gatos. Both were glad to be there.

Bishop was showing Dewey Leighton's journal to Spring.

"He documented everything," Bishop said, "and I mean everything! Here, just look at all this stuff."

He opened the book and showed Spring page after page with Dewey's neat handwriting chronicling dead fish info: dates, times, and numbers of fish. The journal also tracked the sheen on the water.

Spring leaned in close and then she took the book and flipped the pages herself. "Hey, look at this, there's a pattern to sheen on the water!" Spring exclaimed.

"I have taken samples from the creek near all businesses where sources of petroleum products are used. Nothing shows up. It all seems to be from the footbridge down past the bar."

Spring looked at him and said, "That is good investigating, Bishop. Dewey would be proud."

"Thanks to you, Spring, I learned to be patient and eliminate all other possibilities for pollution. I'm sorry we had to fight about it."

"I am sorry too, Bishop." They looked at each other for a moment. Bishop started to lean in toward Spring, and she responded by coming closer. Just as she was tilting her head, Spring's mother came to the sliding patio door and asked if they wanted sodas. Spring was beet red.

Summer Is Coming

Throughout the remainder of the school semester, Bishop continued observing the creek and making entries in Dewey's journal whenever dead fish or a sheen on the water appeared. He knew that whatever was polluting the creek was a human's doing and that it was probably coming from the Waterside Bar and Grill.

———•—•———

The distinct aroma of a barbeque fire greeted Bishop and Hank McKeever as they walked up the front walkway of Kate Wilson's house in Saratoga. Kate and Venice greeted them at the front door and showed them to the backyard.

In the backyard, Maggie Mendez was sitting on the edge of the swimming pool dangling her feet in the water. The cool clear water lapped around her tanned legs.

Hank stopped short in the sliding glass door that led out back. Maggie waved and beckoned them over.

Kate said to Bishop, "You brought your swimming suit didn't you?"

Dejectedly, Bishop said no.

"Not to worry, we have plenty of extras in the pool bathroom. Help yourself."

When Bishop came out to the pool, he saw his father sitting next to Maggie. His feet were in the water also. He had his pants rolled up, and he looked comfortable.

Bishop tested the water with his right big toe then dove in. The water was refreshing.

As Bishop did a lap underwater, he realized he hadn't been swimming since the day his mother died. An odd feeling came over him when he thought about his mom. What he felt was not sadness, but nostalgia. He knew from time to time he would feel sad. However, today, nostalgia was good.

———•—•———

Venice and Kate were in the house putting the final touches on dinner. Maggie, having been shooed from the kitchen when she asked if she could help, sat back down next to Hank. She put her hand on Hank's shoulder as she lowered herself.

"Dinner will be ready in about twenty minutes," Kate announced from the kitchen.

Bishop hoisted himself out of the pool and Maggie tossed him a towel. He was chilled and the baked aggregate pool decking on his bare feet warmed him.

It wasn't long before the group sat around the picnic table savoring steaks, corn on the cob, and green salad. Maggie asked Bishop what plans he had for the summer.

His usual answer was to say he was working on a science project when anybody asked him about his creek water observation. He figured that his summer would be doing just that—observing the creek. That was his answer to Maggie.

With narrowed eyes she asked, "What do you expect to find?"

"Maybe why fish are dying."

Hank gave Bishop a hard stare. "He thinks his old man doesn't know that he is playing supersleuth, trying to find Dewey's killer."

Maggie and Venice exchanged looks. "That probably isn't the best way to spend your summer, there, kiddo," Maggie said, her tone overly cautious in its neutrality.

Bishop rolled his eyes. "I'm just testing creek water." Everyone continued to stare at him. "Really, that's all. Dad does that kind of thing all the time for work." Hank and Venice drifted back into other conversation, but Maggie seemed withdrawn. Was she watching him more now? Did she know more than she was saying?

After dinner, the guests insisted on helping with cleanup. The table was cleared, the grill scraped down, and the condiments and leftover food put away. Just as the last dish was rinsed and the start button on the dishwasher was pushed, Maggie said her farewells.

Hank seemed disappointed she was leaving, but smiled as he walked her to her car.

Bishop stole that moment to ask Kate his question. "Did I say something wrong?"

"No, honey, of course not. Why do you ask?"

"She didn't say two words after I mentioned the creek," he said.

"I wouldn't worry about that. But maybe you should think about going and getting dressed. The sun is going down, and I think you are starting to shiver a bit. Bishop nodded and ducked out to the pool bathroom.

As he was changing into his clothes, his father and Venice came out back and sat in deck chairs under the bathroom window.

"One of the Gypsys bought a pair of rubber gloves for chemical handling," Venice said. "I am telling you something is going on, Hank."

"Maybe so, Ven. It scares me that Bishop is so passionate about this. Passion is what killed Dewey."

"I've seen him on that bridge often," Venice said.

Bishop heard a really big sigh. "It's too bad that bridge doesn't fall down," his dad said.

"Talk to the town engineer. Tell him you think the bridge is unsafe. He will have to post it as dangerous, and then an investigation has to be done before foot traffic will be allowed again."

Hank gave half a laugh. "Tempting, Venice, tempting."

Bishop steamed as he heard this conversation. He flushed the toilet to signal that he was coming out.

The sound seemed to do the trick because Hank and Venice were quiet when Bishop joined them.

<hr>

"What's eating at you, Son?"

Bishop just shook his head from side to side.

They drove on in silence for several blocks. "I am not going to stop investigating the creek, Dad. You said you would look into it. Are you going to have the engineer say the bridge is unsafe? Is that how you will handle it, Dad? You can dynamite that bridge. I don't care. I will find out why Dewey died."

"Is that so? Well, guess what? You are not to be on or near that creek after dark. No exceptions. Am I clear on that, Bishop?" Hank's jugular was throbbing.

Bishop nodded his head.

"Nodding your head is not good enough. You need to say to me you understand."

"I understand you don't want me on or near the creek after dark."
The rest of the drive was silent.

As hard as Bishop tried, he found he could not abide by his father's order. It took him several days to come up with a justification for his actions if caught.

Bishop and Spring were watching a movie at the Gatos Theater. Bishop could not sit still. Spring asked him if he were all right. He told her he wanted to leave and she agreed.

The two were sitting in the ice cream parlor when Spring said, "My parents didn't tell me I couldn't go to the creek after dark. I will make the observations and report to you."

"Gee, Spring, that sounds great. But I am worried for your safety."

<hr/>

For several days after that, Bishop received reports from Spring. This was a good alternative, but Bishop became restless. He could not stay away. He started to stand on the bank of the creek directing Spring.

A Devil's Act

"I don't care what you have to do!" David Devlin fumed to his motorcycle gang. Get those kids to stop watching. They are as bad as cops. Worse than cops."

Frankie Fellowes nodded and said, "Consider it done, Devil."

<hr/>

It was very late at night when Bishop met Spring at Verducci's Boat Works dressed in dark clothes.

"I feel bad sneaking out, Bishop. What if my parents find out?"

"I don't know, Spring," he snapped—as if he didn't have his own Dad to worry about. But then he saw the wounded look in her eyes, and he was sorry that he made her unhappy. He took both of her hands in his. "I'm sorry, I feel bad too. I hate disobeying. However, I can't get this out of my mind. So are you with me?" She gave him a slight smile and nodded.

They dashed from shadow to shadow along the creek bed. Every few yards they needed to go more on shore to find trees to cover their advancement. A feral cat scampered in front of them with a low wail frightening them and causing them to a standstill in the open. The late hour made the cat noise reverberate in the night air. Bishop motioned for Spring to crouch down. The grass was damp and their knees were becoming soaked.

The bar had been closed for two hours as they approached the patio of the Waterside. The entrance was dark, and all interior lights were off except for a neon Coors sign behind the bar. In the far corner of the parking lot, a quartz vapor light on a pole cast an eerie glow.

The sweet aroma from a night-blooming jasmine filled the air. A screech owl shocked the two as they neared the building. Spring's eyes were as wide as saucers, and Bishop's heart was thumping in his chest.

Bishop grabbed Spring's hand, and crept through the parking lot to the building. All was quiet—he didn't hear the sounds of machinery that Dewey had written in his log.

"Do you hear anything?" he whispered ever so quietly to Spring. She shook her head.

"Neither do I."

"But the pattern in Dewey's book says something should be happening tonight." Spring whispered back.

Bishop didn't know what to do or what to think. Maybe Spring was wrong about the pattern; maybe Dewey was wrong; maybe he, himself, was wrong to even be here. *It doesn't matter,* he told himself. *If I'm wrong, there's no reason not to finish checking out the place, but if I'm right... This is for you Dewey.*

"Come on, then." Bishop led Spring up to the east side of the building where the path sloped down toward the water and the patio.

Bishop put his finger to his lips, and Spring stopped. She looked at Bishop with a tilt of her head as if to say, *I've barely said a word since we started the adventure.*

Bishop gave her a sheepish grin and shrugged his shoulders. He stopped again and cocked his head. This time he thought he heard something. He inched down the path a few feet and pointed to the ground next to the building. He mouthed the word *basement* to Spring.

An audible hum came from the basement, and light was visible from an old ground level window. The clanking from some type of machine punctuated the hum in an otherwise quiet night.

Bishop and Spring exchanged looks.

Bishop quietly tramped down the weeds and bushes by the window and lay down to have a look.

A thick layer of dust coated the glass. Inside a bare light bulb hung from an extension cord attached to the ceiling. The basement looked like an old sepia-toned picture from years gone by. Men were milling around. Through a doorway, Bishop could see others moving items from the machine making all the noise in the far room to a side table along the opposite wall from the window. One man was washing a flat metal object with a liquid from a one-gallon can. The rinse waste was going down the drain of an old cement laundry sink.

An older man was working with the group, giving instructions of some sort. He was older by decades than the others and was obviously not an outlaw biker. He limped to the sink and started to mix materials in a jar. He continued talking to the other men, but Bishop could not hear what he was saying.

Bishop slid back along the ground until he was clear of the window. He stood up and tried to slap the dirt and weedy seed pods from the front of his jacket. Then he motioned for Spring to go round the side of the building and wait for him there. After she turned the corner, he snuck down the length of the building toward the water. Under the deck, he found the strong smell of a petroleum product. Bishop crawled farther under and discovered a three-quarter-inch rusted pipe dripping the toxic waste from the laundry sink.

Jubilant, Bishop hurried back to Spring. She was nowhere in sight. He ran to the entrance, but could not find her. "Spring," he called out in the loudest whisper he could muster. Still no answer. After he circled the building, he found himself back at the window. He lay down again and looked in.

A man was shoving Spring into a wooden chair. She said something, and the man raised his hand and slapped her across the cheek.

Bishop tensed and in an instant jumped feet first through the basement window.

Glass was sparkling on the cement floor of the basement. The men in the room were startled for a moment then regained their composure.

"Well, well, well, what have we here?" Frankie Fellowes said to no one in particular.

Bishop was getting to his feet when another Gem City Gypsy grabbed him.

"Came to save his girlfriend, I guess," said another member.

Frankie Fellowes said, "This will be a nice gift for Devil."

As Bishop was being lifted off his feet and tossed into a chair, he noticed stacks of currency neatly piled on the side table. The hum was emanating from a printing press.

Counterfeiting! Bishop thought to himself. *They're cleaning the printing plates with gasoline or something else, and it is draining into the creek.*

———— ⋅•⋅ ————

Bishop and Spring were in the trunk of a car. Bishop could hear the men in the passenger compartment talking but couldn't understand their words. He felt something hard and metallic under his torso. He figured it was a tire jack. *I need to grab the tire iron when they lift me up, but my hands are tied behind my back.* He told Spring he was so sorry he got her in this jam. Before she could answer, the car left the asphalt. There was a change in tire sound and the sensation of going downhill. Spring groaned.

"Are you okay, though?"

"Shut up, you two, or I'll stove in your heads!" a gruff voice yelled from the passenger compartment of the car.

———— ⋅•⋅ ————

"What'd you bring them here for, Frankie?" David Devlin growled.

"Where was I supposed to take 'em, Devil? I had no place else to go."

Bishop and Spring were tied in wooden kitchen chairs watching the dialogue between David Devlin and Frank Fellowes.

Bishop noticed that the kitchen had dishes and meal remnants stacked in the sink, and the old O'Keefe and Merritt gas stove needed cleaning. The dingy yellowed wainscoted walls were scarred from years of nicking and roughhousing. The clock on the wall said 2:50.

A man standing on a chair was putting stacks of the bogus money in a cupboard. Another man sat atop a stepladder looking from Bishop to Spring. Bishop felt a momentary smile tug at his lips at the irony.

"What're ya smirking at, boy?" the man seated on the stepladder asked.

Bishop started to explain, but stopped and shook his head.

"Tell me or I'll smack you, punk."

"Nothing, really," Bishop said. "It's just that you're sitting on a ladder, and he's standing on a chair. That's all."

One of the Gypsys approached Spring. Bishop recognized him as the one who hit her. The man ran the back of his hand over Spring's cheek. She recoiled at his touch. Remorse cascaded into Bishop like a dam breaking. He noticed the welt under Spring's left eye and winced, increasing his guilt.

"Leave her alone," Bishop hissed

"Wow. Big brave man protecting his China doll. Heh, heh."

"She's Japanese, you moron," Bishop answered back with a snarl and look of disgust.

For his comment, Bishop received his own welt on the face.

Get Up Lazy Bones

Hank McKeever knocked on Bishop's bedroom door. When his son did not answer, Hank opened the door and went in. Bishop's bed was made. Hank thought for a moment that Bishop was up and out of the house already.

Then his eyes narrowed as he realized that Bishop was not at home last night.

He spun on his heels and went to his car. "I can't believe he disobeyed me," he said aloud.

Hank stepped on to the Tanaka's porch, not really certain what he was going to say. He gave the brass knocker a good rap and stepped back. "Mr. Tanaka? I'm Hank McKeever, Bishop's father," he said when Lee Tanaka opened the door. "I was wondering if I could talk to Spring."

Mr. Tanaka told him that Spring spent last night at a friend's house, and he assured Hank that when she returned, he'd have her call him. A shudder coursed through Hank as he thought about the night Mr. Leighton came looking for Dewey. Mr. Tanaka could read the alarm in Hank's face and invited him in. Mrs. Tanaka offered him a cup of coffee as they seated themselves in the neatly kept kitchen.

"I'm going to call Spring's friend and talk to her." She left the table and sat at a stool next to a wall-hung phone. Hank could only hear Mrs. Tanaka's side of the conversation, and it worried him. When she stole a look at him and her brow knitted slightly, he panicked. He sat drumming his fingers on the oak table and his knee bounced incessantly. Mr. Tanaka hadn't stopped stirring his coffee.

Garnett Maddox sat in the Tanakas' living room. Hank McKeever sat on the couch next to him. Mr. and Mrs. Tanaka were in matching easy chairs. Mr. Tanaka sat forward, wringing his hands.

"So, we know that Bishop was last seen going into his room, presumably to go to sleep. What time was that, Hank?" Garnett asked.

"Around 10:15."

Garnett was writing in a pocket-sized notebook.

They established that Spring left her home at 6:30 PM. Where she went, nobody knew. All agreed that they thought Spring and Bishop were together and that both children would call if they could. Mrs. Tanaka was crying. Mr. Tanaka stood next to her chair. His hands were in his pockets nervously jingling his loose change.

"Lee, will you please stop that!" Mrs. Tanaka scolded. Mr. Tanaka embarrassedly sat back down.

It wasn't long after that that the four of them parted. When Hank McKeever rushed home, he hoped to find Bishop eating cookies and drinking milk. He wasn't. Hank picked up the picture of his wife and said, "Baby, you left him in my care, and I did a lousy job. I hope you can forgive me." He replaced the picture on the mantel and stood looking at it and then swiftly covered his flooding eyes and in a sob said, "What am I gonna do if I lose him, too?"

He called Maggie Mendez, but there was no answer.

His next call was to Venice Webb.

At that moment a glass pane was being replaced in the basement window of the Waterside Bar and Grill. One of the Gem City Gypsys was a glazier by trade and completed the task. By noon, no trace remained of a broken window; even the dust had been emulated with a thick soaping, making the window as milky as it had been before.

Still Bound

It was noon, and Bishop and Spring were still tied to chairs. Sometime during the early morning hours, duct tape was put over their mouths.

Spring, her face streaked with tears, looked exhausted. Bishop was wracked with guilt because of the dangerous spot he placed Spring in. He knew his father was worrying frantically about him. *If I survive this, I will never disobey again,* he promised.

———

Spring was thinking about something her father told her a long time ago when they were discussing people getting into trouble. "Daughter, when a kid gets into trouble it is because they are doing something they are not supposed to be doing, in a place they are not supposed to be, with a person or persons they are not supposed to be with. Remember that fact and you will stay out of trouble."

Sorry, Dad, she thought.

———

David Devlin stood in front of the two captives.

"Take the boy to the garage, Frankie. Leave the girl where she is."

Bishop started to rock in his chair and was shaking his head back and forth.

"Get him out, now!" David yelled.

Spring tried to relay to him, through her eyes, that she would be all right.

———

The garage was actually an old barn located about thirty yards from the house. The interior smelled of gasoline, oil, and dust.

A young Hispanic man in a Gem City Gypsys jacket tied Bishop to a leg of a workbench. Bishop noticed a plastic container of anti-freeze. The man noticed Bishop looking at the antifreeze and said, "By the way, how's yer mutt?"

The vein on Bishop's neck was protruding and his breathing was coming in pants through his nose.

The man laughed as he turned off the light in the barn and walked back to the house with long strides. Bishop's eyes adjusted to the early morning darkness. Sunlight was starting to brighten the dirty garage, and Bishop had another opportunity to survey his dungeon and think about his and Spring's predicament. Dread invaded his being. Images of his mother flashed before him, and he started to cry.

Reporting to HQ

Garnett Maddox entered the police station through the glass front doors. He bypassed the chief's secretary and went right in to Linc Collins's office.

Collins looked up from his stack of papers, evidently startled to see somebody at his desk unannounced.

"What's shaking, G.M.?" he asked in a friendly tone.

Before Garnett answered he thought, *This guy tries so hard to be one of the guys. It just is futile for him to keep trying. He always talks about his exploits as a patrol officer in Southern California. What a sparkling career he had as lieutenant and how he solved the most horrific crimes single-handedly.*

During a weeklong seminar in Reno, Garnett met some of the members of his chief's previous department. Their comments differed from what Collins was saying to his new force. At that seminar, Garnett learned that Collins was the most disliked cop on patrol. His coworkers hated working with him because he couldn't be counted on for backup. They swore he was promoted to keep him out of the way. They were happy to see him go.

Garnett was on the hiring committee that looked into Collins's resume.

He told the group from Southern California that he contacted that department about Collins and was told he was the best, and they hated to see him go.

The men just shrugged their shoulders with a look that said, *We had him, now you got him.*

That the department Collins came from gave a less than truthful recommendation was a fact that Garnett kept to himself for years; however, he thought of it every day.

For these reasons, Garnett never felt like perpetuating small talk with Collins, so he got straight to the point. "Chief, we have two children that have gone missing."

Collins put his pen down and folded his fingers in front of him. "Yeah. Who?"

"Bishop McKeever and Spring Tanaka."

"They are probably mad at their folks and took off for a couple of hours, G.M. They'll come back. Just wait."

"They don't seem like the type."

"They're teenagers. They are the type, all right," Collins looked down at his desktop and started shuffling papers.

After a moment, he looked up at Garnett Maddox with a look that said, *Are you still here?*

Garnett ignored the look. "I am going to contact the FBI, Chief."

"Not without my approval!"

"May I have your approval, then?"

"You may not."

Dumbfounded, Garnett asked why.

"I don't have to give you an explanation, Maddox! I suggest you get back to work!" he said as he stood and pointed to the door.

Garnett went back to his office fuming. He flopped into his chair and pulled up a letter of resignation he kept in a file on his computer. He composed it seven years ago, two months after Linc Collins became police chief in Los Gatos. He changed the date on the letter to the present date and saved the document.

Chief to the Rescue

The sound of a car door slamming shut aroused Bishop from his half-waking stupor. The late afternoon sun was an indication of how long they had been held captive. He had wet his pants several times; after the second time he didn't care anymore. He was worried about Spring and her discomfort. He craned his neck to look out the door. He saw a white sports car. His heart rate jumped and he was fully alert in an instant. Bishop tried to signal the person in the car. He was rocking the workbench back and forth, pounding up and down.

A man wearing a tropical shirt stepped out of the car. He fiddled with something in his hand, and Bishop heard a chirp from the car. As the man was about to pocket his keys, he paused. Bishop tried harder to rock and buck, he thought he was going to bust a gut. He tried to yell but the tape over his mouth did an effective job of muffling him. Still the man cocked his head then looked around. His gaze came to focus on the garage where Bishop was held. Bishop felt the rush of elation as the man stepped inside to investigate.

As he stood looking at the inside of the garage, Bishop tried to focus on the person standing just inside the doorway. The setting sun back-lit the figure. Then the man sauntered into the room, and Bishop recognized him. *Chief Collins, thank God!* Bishop thought.

Collins and Bishop locked eyes.

Bishop, with relief in his eyes, relaxed.

Collins came over, his sandals slapping against the concrete floor and bent down next to Bishop. The chief's aftershave was a refreshing aroma compared to the foul-smelling garage. Collins quickly removed the duct tape from Bishop's mouth. The first layer of tissue on his lips came off with the tape.

"Thank God you are here, Chief. Spring is in the house! Go rescue her, please!"

Collins didn't say anything and, in a surprise move, reapplied the tape to Bishop's mouth.

Bishop heard a noise from the Gypsys' house. He twisted against his bonds as he panicked even more. His wide eyes tried to implore Chief Collins to hurry and set him free. His mind didn't want to accept what it already knew. Then Bishop slumped as he realized the chief was not there to rescue them.

Spring, still tied to a chair, kept busy trying to loosen the rope around her wrist. Her eyes darted around the room. The movement of her hands aroused the suspicion of an ugly, scarred orange cat. The cat started to nuzzle Spring's hands. To thwart the curious cat, she stopped her movements. The cat came close and started to purr and rub her snout on Spring's hand. After several seconds of this, Spring flicked the cat in the face. The cat hissed and moved away.

But the cat came by several more times. Each time she flicked it away until finally, the cat retaliated with several deep scratches to Spring's tied hands.

Not long after that, the front door opened, and Spring saw the police chief standing in the entry. *We're rescued!* she thought and her heart skipped a beat. Then anguish crept into her psyche; David Devlin said to the chief of the Los Gatos Police Department, "I thought I told you to never come here!"

Spring was shocked. She could feel the tape holding up her slackened jaw, and she stared, wide-eyed, at Chief Collins.

"I know, Devil. But I heard about this complication you have here. What are you thinking? Kidnapping is too risky."

David looked straight at her, a gleam in his eyes. Spring felt like her heart had stopped. She tore her gaze from his and leaned forward trying desperately to make contact with the chief. *Chief, you have to help us!* she screamed in her mind.

"Too late, Chief. There're gonna to be a few more funerals in town. And, if you don't get out of here, one of them might be yours."

Rescue or Recovery

Garnett Maddox followed Maggie Mendez as she drove slowly in front of the driveway to the Gypsys' house. He shut off his headlights when she pulled over about five hundred yards beyond the property. He parked his sedan in a turnout and headed off the road in an effort to come in behind where he had watched Maggie scale up the embankment through a row of oleanders across from the Gypsy's driveway. He wondered what a waitress was doing observing a motorcycle gang's haunt. Garnett kept feeling his way along in the dark. In the thicket of trees dotting the field above the road, it was difficult to see.

As Garnett Maddox approached Maggie's observation point, a twig snapped under his foot and in an instant Garnett was knocked off his feet and straddled by Maggie Mendez. She had removed his revolver from its holster and held it to his head.

Garnett's heart was pounding as he looked up at Maggie.

"You sure aren't a waitress, Maggie," he said in a whisper. "Who do you work for?"

Relaxing, Maggie said, "I work for the Waterside Bar and Grill."

"My foot you do. Moves like you just pulled on me are taught in police academies."

Maggie got off Garnett, but kept the gun on him.

"Look, I think we are on the same team. Please put the gun down," he said as he got on his knees.

"Just take it easy," Maggie said as if she were talking to a frisky colt. "How do I know you aren't as dirty as your chief?"

Garnett narrowed his eyes and said, "If you think I am crooked, cuff me now. You have cuffs, don't you? Here, use mine," he said as he reached behind him to his handcuff case.

Maggie stiffened as she watched Garnett move. He slowed down so as not to make her nervous when he pulled out the handcuffs.

In the distant darkness, they heard a sports car start up. Maggie knelt down and crawled to look through the bushes to the point where the driveway met the road. Garnett, still on his knees, followed her.

"That's Collins's car," Garnett whispered as the headlights momentarily shone on them. Maggie said aloud after looking at her wrist watch, "21:50."

Garnett stood up and started to brush the dirt and leaves off his street clothes.

Maggie relaxed and gave Garnett his revolver. Over the next several minutes, Maggie told Garnett that she worked for the Secret Service and was undercover investigating a counterfeit operation. The leader of the Gem City Gypsys was the son of a recently deceased master counterfeiter. She explained that her partner, the "bum" killed by the creek, was close to cracking the case. Her eyes welled with tears as she spoke. "He was a good officer, father, and friend." She wiped at her eyes with the back of her hand, rolling her eyes as if she were exasperated with herself. "Jerry Webster wanted to pull me out. Then the Leighton kid got killed, and that changed everything."

Garnett sat listening to Agent Mendez explain. Things were starting to make sense. When Maggie paused for a moment, Garnett said, "The chief got a memo from the FBI. It said that Whitey Devlin died, that the plates he used were never recovered, and that his only known relative lived in Los Gatos. Collins made a visit to the Gypsys to tell David Devlin he was aware of his father's death and about his trip to Detroit."

Maggie interrupted him and said, "That memo was from us. It only hinted that the FBI was involved. How did you see it?"

"Any communications not marked as *confidential* are copied and put in my file," Garnett told her.

"Collins never said another word about Devlin, and any of the crimes surrounding the Gypsys were covered up. We all guessed it was under the shroud that the Feds would handle it."

"Because your chief didn't do his job, two people are dead and two are missing," Maggie said as they both got on their stomachs and looked at the house down below them.

"You must think the same as me. Bishop and Spring are down in that house. Right?" Garnett asked.

"Yes, I do think they are there."

"Let me muster the SWAT team."

She shook her head vigorously. "Collins will see what's going on and tip off the Gypsys," Maggie said in disgust.

"I know people on the county task force that can operate without notifying their department heads. I could have them on scene in less than an hour."

"That's not good enough, Garnett. We're already into this for over twenty-four hours. Every minute is crucial. Webster is waiting for my phone call. He's close by."

It wasn't long before Maggie, Garnett, and Jerry Webster were looking down on the house. Gypsys were coming and going on motorcycles making it difficult to tell how many were inside.

"I kind of feel like the Alamo in reverse," Garnett said.

Jerry and Maggie looked at him oddly.

"You know. Like Travis and Crockett and a band of few storming the Alamo with Santana's army inside."

They stared blankly.

Garnett shook his hand in a *never mind* fashion.

After more observation, the three of them decided that Maggie would make her way down the hill and approach from the front. Webster would enter through the hedgerow that separated the Gypsys' property from the Carlyle property. And because Garnett knew the territory best, he would make his approach from the creek side.

The fastest way for Garnett to do that was by car.

As he was driving to the other side of town to get on the other creek bank, he received a call from Venice Webb. "I can't talk, Ven, call me later," he said and flipped his cell shut.

The phone rang again instantly. "Ven, I told you—"

"Garnett, I am right behind you. Where are you going so fast?"

Garnett thought a moment and then pulled over and waited for Venice to come to his car.

"Get in."

As they drove on, Maddox explained to Venice what was going down. Venice sat wide-eyed as he listened. Then said under his breath, "Maggie Mendez works for the Secret Service?" Garnet nodded as they drove to the other side of the creek. "She seems so quiet."

"Still waters run deep, my friend," he said as he remembered her taking him down and disarming him in one motion. He was embarrassed because he was a medal winner in karate at the Police Olympics.

His eyes got even wider when Garnett handed him the key for the shotgun rack. Venice could hardly get his hands to stop shaking as he tried to unlock the shotgun.

"How you doing with that, pal?" Garnett asked.

———•———

Via text messaging, Garnett explained to Jerry and Maggie that Venice Webb had been recruited by him to assist. The two federal agents messaged back objections, but then dropped them in the interest of brevity—time was of the essence.

Garnett told Venice to stand at the rear of the property and detain anybody trying to escape. Their shoes and pant legs were wet and muddy from crossing the creek.

Venice's mouth was dry and his stomach was churning as he watched Garnett approach the side door of the house. He saw Jerry on the other side ready to break through a window of the living room. He couldn't see Maggie Mendez's assault from the front.

———•———

Maggie announced her presence by swinging the front door open forcefully and plunging into the room with an evasive crouching tactic and swinging her revolver in a sweeping motion.

Simultaneously, Garnett dashed into the kitchen from the side door, and Jerry crashed through the side widow. The Gem City Gypsys were caught off guard and didn't have time to pull out sidearms. In no time, all the outlaws present were sitting on the floor with their hands behind them and their weapons on the messy counters amid the dirty dishes.

Maggie released Spring and asked her where Bishop was.

———◆———

From inside the garage, Bishop heard the commotion from the house.

He saw a figure in the moonlight and recognized Venice Webb. He was holding a rifle.

As things quieted down in the house, another man approached Venice from behind a stack of lumber.

Bishop never felt so helpless as when he saw the man knock Venice to the ground. Venice got up in an instant and traded blows with the man. The two were evenly matched—for a while. Both were tiring fast. In a flurry, Venice shoved the man down. When the man got up, he had a four foot piece of lumber in his hand. Bishop sucked in air; he wanted to yell, get someone's attention to help Venice. He screamed with all his might as the man clubbed Venice on the side of his head, and Venice went down. It wasn't enough; no one could hear his muffled cries as he watched the man march Venice to the house while pointing the shotgun at his back and every so often pushing him along with the barrel.

———◆———

Ramon Sepulveda, the Gem City Gypsy follower, shoved Venice Webb to the floor of the house startling everybody. He aimed the shotgun at Venice's head and hollered, "Drop 'em!" He was surprised and disappointed to see Maggie the waitress.

The three officials knew that the collateral damage would be massive if they tried a shoot-out, but on the other hand, the upper hand could be regained if all the stars and the moon aligned. That scenario fizzled after one of the gang picked up a weapon and held it to Spring's temple.

"Ramon! My man!" David Devlin yelled in triumph as he got up.

Jerry and Maggie exchanged looks then glared at Garnett.

———◆———

Bishop was rocking the workbench up and down. Several times the bench leg he was tied to came off the ground. He realized that the bench was lifting off the floor, and thought he could somehow coordinate the lifting with moving the rope to the bottom of the leg and off. It took him several tries, but the rope moved down, and he could feel his hands getting looser. He was free! He looked around the garage for a weapon. He saw no firearms, just tools. He picked up a 14-inch pipe wrench and a claw hammer and sneaked off toward the house. His lips stung as he licked them. *I should go for help,* but he knew there was no time.

His first thought was to barge in and make a scene. But that hadn't worked out quite as well as he'd hoped last time, so he thought he'd better see what the situation was. He looked covertly through the kitchen door, then around to the broken living room window. Everyone was in the kitchen. Somehow, he needed to get a weapon other than what he had; he felt a gun was what he needed. He shook his head and was confused. *Is that what I'm really thinking? I need a gun? Am I going to shoot somebody? Me?*

"There are officers on their way, Devlin," Garnett said in an authoritative voice.

"Collins is in custody," he lied. "He ratted you out."

"He don't matter, Cop. He's a fool, and you're bluffing."

Bishop crept through the broken front window, tentatively placing his weight carefully with each step; he didn't want a loose floorboard to give him away. When he reached the kitchen door, he realized he'd been holding his breath. He exhaled slowly and listened.

"He protected us for a time. Then he began to get greedy. And when the agent got whacked, he got afraid. Greed and fright are a bad combination."

Because he had an audience, David Devlin continued. "Man, it was beautiful. We were making the money in the basement of the bar, after hours. We sent people all over the United States with fake tens and twenties. The money rolled in. We did it right under your noses. Daddy's plates are works of art. We brought in one of Daddy's old pals, and he helped us with the ink and coloring. New guys make fake dough with laser printers. Not us. We did it old-school style. Daddy would be proud. Then the geek caught on to us, and he had to go."

Dewey! That jerk killed Dewey! Bishop rushed into the room and swung his pipe wrench at Sepulveda's arm with all his might. Three sounds pierced the air almost at once: Sepulveda's scream, the breaking of bone, and then the deafening report of the gun. Oh, no! The gun… Bishop frantically looked around to see if anyone had been hit, but the room had erupted into a melee.

Maggie put judo moves on Devlin, rendering him useless, and she retrieved his weapon. As some of the Gypsys ran for the doors, Maggie ordered them to halt. "Line up against the wall, and don't do anything stupid!" she yelled. Jerry scrambled to grab the shotgun that Sepulveda had loosened his grip on; the motion caused the gun to discharge into the ceiling, hitting the overhead light making the scene dark. All movement stopped momentarily.

In a moment of clarity, Spring realized the severity of the situation, and in a swift step to the refrigerator, she opened the door illuminating the room enough so that the officers could maintain control. Garnett reached the counter before any of the outlaws, and in a heavy swipe of his forearm cleared the counter of guns and dishes; the raucous clatter was muted because of the earlier shot gun blast.

Jerry and Maggie had each outlaw sit on the floor and secured plastic tie temporary handcuffs to them.

Bishop eyed the menacing gang, heads hanging down, like errant school boys waiting to go to the principal's office. He could read their minds, thinking about their alibis.

Garnett secured the other weapons and went to check Venice, Spring, and Bishop.

All the phone calls the Tanakas made to Garnett Maddox went unanswered. Each time they left a message, the exasperation in their voices was evident. Mr. Tanaka even tried to telephone the chief of police and the mayor. Nobody seemed to be interested in the missing children.

APB For the Chief of Police

"Confirm, again, please," the dispatcher asked Garnett Maddox over the police frequency. "You want the chief of police taken into custody?"

"That is affirmative, Dispatch. Notify all transportation facilities with his description."

"What will the charges be?"

In a penal-code format, he rattled off the numbers for suspicion of murder, kidnapping, child endangerment, and racketeering into the microphone.

A long silence met him on the radio. Then it crackled to life. "10-4."

Inside one of the interrogation rooms in police headquarters, David Devlin sat fidgeting. He knew this was his third strike and that he was going to jail for the rest of his life. *I ain't taking this alone,* he thought to himself. He was ready to sing, until Garnett Maddox walked in. The criminal mentality took over and he said in as tough a voice as he could muster; "I want my lawyer, cop."

"No problem, Devlin. Frankie Fellowes is in the lobby ready to post bail, and your attorney is on his way."

Devlin rocked back in his chair with a smug smile on his face. "Frankie always has my back. Get me out of these cuffs."

Garnett took out keys from his pocket. They weren't really the handcuff keys, but his ring of personal keys made a more impressive jingling sound when he shook them. He approached Devlin, leaned over with the keys. "Oh, wait," he said standing up and dangling the key ring, "I almost forgot, Devlin. Frankie is about to be arrested." He pocketed his keys with a flourish. "And just in case you might manufacture some ideas about the chief coming to your rescue, Linc Collins is under arrest and being held at the county jail. And let me tell you, can that man sing; he's singing like crazy. Based on what he's saying, I wouldn't expect any bail. But don't worry, that lawyer you asked for is on the way from the public defender's office. He can hold your hand… if he's not too busy with the slew of other cases their office always seems to be swamped with. I thought you hot-shot bad guys were always lawyered up. I guess you forgot about that part, huh, Devlin? Like father like son, I suppose."

Shaken, David Devlin slumped in his chair.

Garnett moved in. He sat on the table in the middle of the interrogation room.

"Come on, you really want to depend on some overworked, underpaid public employee? How'd that work for you last time?"

Devlin looked up at him. "You got any alternatives?" His voice was carefully neutral…too neutral. Garnett knew he had kindled a tiny flame of hope.

"Sure, who do you think the system wants more, a counterfeiter or a corrupt public official who had betrayed every person in this town by being involved with counterfeiting, kidnapping, and murder?" Garnett wasn't sure the Feds would see it that way, but Devlin didn't have to know that.

"Give us the final nail for the chief's coffin, and I'll talk to the district attorney's office and tell them how helpful you can be."

Devlin chewed his bottom lip for some time. Finally he said. "What do you want?"

"You waive your right to an attorney?"

Devlin nodded. "For now."

"Fair enough," Garnett said, "Let's start with how did you get Collins into this?"

Devlin just looked at him for thirty seconds, shook his head, and said, "I didn't. He came to me at the house. Said he knew my father was dead and that the plates used were never found. When I got back from Detroit, I put the plates in the basement of the Waterside. No one ever went down there. We were up and operating several weeks before Collins notified me."

"Why do you think he notified you?"

Devlin shrugged. "Good question. He said that there would be no bogus money manufactured in his town. If any of the funny money showed up, he would take me down. It was several weeks before we started to distribute the bills to other states. We got sloppy. Some of the bills landed in the Feds hands. They notified Collins, and he came to shut us down. We offered him a salary, and he took it."

"How much you offer him, Devlin?"

"Three G's a week. All he had to do was look the other way. Do you remember the chop shop that you busted several months ago?"

"Yeah, I remember that, Devlin."

"That was a setup. We sacrificed some of our members to throw the cops off. Collins knew about it. It was his idea."

Garnett caught his jaw just as it was about to drop open. He took a moment to recover from his surprise, and then asked as casually as he could, "You sacrificed members?"

"Yeah. Their families were given a lot of loot for their incarcerations."

This time Garnett gave in to his reactions, and whistled a low note. "Unbelievable."

"Listen, that money the families receive is more than those jerks could make on the outside."

Garnett held both his hands up, "Fine, a guy's gotta do what he can for his family."

"Damn straight," Devlin said.

"So, tell me when the Feds entered the picture." Garnett said.

"I ain't sure. I figured the first guy killed was an agent. He had a bunch of notes about the operation, so he had to go," Devlin said with bravado.

"Who did him?"

"I don't know. It was out-of-town talent from Oakland. He won't be around."

"What does that mean?"

Devlin shrugged one shoulder and cocked his head. "I can't really say. He might have been eliminated before he got back to Oakland."

"By who?"

Devlin squinted, shook his head and grinned, and put on a go-to-hell face.

Garnett was becoming irritated by Devlin's attitude.

"We made over a million the first two months. It was better than dope money. The more we made, the more we delivered. We couldn't stop. Then, those kids started to investigate. I thought if we killed McKeever's dog that would scare them off."

Garnett's friendly tone changed and a severe look came across his face, and he said, "Man, you tried to kill that kid's dog. How low is that?"

Devlin seemed to relax a bit. He figured that Maddox wasn't going to grill him about the geek, so he started to ask for things. "Can I get a soda?"

Garnett put an unopened can of cola in front of Devlin. Devlin glared at Garnett and asked to have the cuffs taken off so he could take a swig. Garnett had been a cop long enough to know when a guy in custody was trying to gain control. He stood and opened the can and held it for Devlin as he sipped awkwardly, some of the soda dribbling on his chin. Garnett watched as Devlin disgustedly moved his shoulder and chin closer to wipe the drip. He got real close to David Devlin's ear and hissed, "You did more than try to kill the dog, you killed Dewey." Devlin started to look around and Garnett said, "Devlin, don't look for somebody to blame. You're in it by yourself." And spun on his heels and exited the room.

He entered the room next to the one he just left and met Maggie and Jerry. Through the one way glass, they saw David Devlin's head slump and his chin tremble.

Homecoming

"Dad?" The moment Hank heard the voice, he lost his breath. His knees gave out from under him, and he sank down into the couch. "It's Bishop. I'm okay, Dad."

"Thank God!" Hank couldn't keep a sob from choking out of him. But he got his voice under control, or mostly. It was still a little husky when he asked, "Uh, are you okay? Where are you?"

"We're at Community Hospital."

"I'll be right there, Son." When Hank found out his son disobeyed him and sneaked out at night, his first thought was to punish him— now all he wanted to do was hug him forever.

"Dad?"

"Yes, Son?"

The line was quiet for a moment. "Please hurry."

"I'm on my way." He hung up the phone then squeezed his eyes tight. A tear spilled out.

He made it to the emergency room in what he was sure was record time. There he found Mr. and Mrs. Tanaka. He didn't know what type of reception he would receive. But he needn't have worried; the Tanakas hugged him. They felt the same relief he did.

Hank noticed Venice Webb sitting down holding a cold pack to his head.

He grinned as Hank approached and said "You should see the other guy. He has a broken arm."

"How did you break his arm, Venice?"

"Not me, buddy. I didn't break his arm. Your kid did. With a pipe wrench."

"Bishop hit somebody with a pipe wrench?" Hank's jaw just about hit the floor.

"You bet he did. He's a real hero."

A million questions crowded Hank's mind, but they had to wait. He knew they would eventually be answered, but right now he wanted to see his son.

When Hank entered the curtained exam room, Bishop was sitting on the edge of the examining table buttoning his shirt. Bishop's whole face brightened. Hank grabbed him and father and son held each other and cried. Bishop kept saying over and over how sorry he was. Hank kept telling him it would be all right, Bishop was safe now.

Spring's reunion with her family was as joyous as Bishop's was with his father.

When Bishop saw Spring, he went to her, and the two hugged and wept. Their ordeal was over, and they had survived.

Crime Comes to an End

The county task force served a search warrant on the Waterside Bar and Grill. In the basement, they discovered a printing press stored in a defunct walk-in freezer. They determined that the money was being printed between the hours of 2:00 AM and 6:30 AM. The freezer muffled the noise. The seclusion of the cellar made detection practically impossible.

Jerry Webster was on the evening news giving a press conference. On the screen were mug shots of Linc Collins, David Devlin, and David's father, Whitey Devlin.

Next to Jerry was Maggie Mendez and acting police chief, Garnett Maddox.

A reporter asked Garnett to comment on the report that a civilian was injured in the melee.

"Yes, that is correct. Mr. Venice Webb was recruited by me to assist in this operation. And he did an excellent job." Garnett explained to the press that several factors led to the arrests of the counterfeiters. "Dewey Leighton's interest in police procedures coupled with his curiosity about the sheen on the water were instrumental in solving the murders and breaking the counterfeiting ring. After Dewey's death, Bishop McKeever and Spring Tanaka took over the investigation and helped in apprehending the guilty parties. This town owes a great deal to these brave kids."

When the news people started asking questions about Linc Collins, Garnett turned the podium over to the mayor.

Venice Webb was embarrassed that he was touted as a citizen avenger.

"I got my butt kicked by a young punk. Bishop McKeever is the real hero, not me," he exclaimed to Kate as she was changing the bandage that covered the stitches on the side of his head. "You're my hero," she said soothingly.

Several days after their rescue, her mother dropped off Spring at Bishop's house. She would not let Spring go anywhere by herself.

Bishop greeted her on the porch. Hank gave Spring a hug and asked her to come in. She hesitated and looked to Bishop.

"Dad, we're going to go to Boo-Gang and create a shrine for Dewey. Why don't you come with us?"

"No thanks, you kids run along. I may come up later."

"We have to get a couple of things from my room first, is it okay if…"

Hank opened the door wide, "Go on then."

Bishop and Spring emerged just as Maggie pulled away in her beige rental sedan, her arm out the window waving as she went.

"You ready there, son?"

Bishop nodded. "I got what we want in here," he said hefting a knapsack on his back. "Come on, Spring," Bishop said as he started to head for the creek.

Spring hesitated and then said, "Do you mind if we go to Boo-Gang off of the Main Street Bridge?" And with a point to the rear of the house, she said, "I've seen enough of that part of the creek to last me awhile."

Bishop gave her a knowing smile and led her to the sidewalk. A few doors away, Bishop reached for her hand. Hank stood on the porch and watched as his son and girlfriend walked hand in hand down the street. Choppy ran alongside.

Hank watched them stroll out of sight, and then he turned and opened the screen door. It squeaked. He smiled and opened and closed once more, just to hear the sound. Hank looked down the street and saw Bishop turn back and cup his ear, letting Hank know he heard. Hank gave him a thumbs-up gesture.

The image of his son walking down the street holding hands with his first girlfriend with his dog jumping along beside them was one of the sweetest things he ever witnessed. Hank breathed the freest breath he'd breathed in years. *We're finally really home.*

Tales from the Top Cat Tavern

Tilson and Milky

Milky Tolliver sat under the back porch overhang of the bar fidgeting. The sun was just starting to show itself on the back alley behind the buildings that faced Santa Cruz Avenue. Traffic on the alley was light this early. The grocer was unloading his purchases from the fruit and vegetable wholesaler. The baker, whom Milky heard arrive at 3:00 AM, was hosing down the garbage area behind his shop.

"Come on, Tilly, where are ya?" he said under his breath. An orange cat approached the stoop where Milky sat. When the cat started to step up to scrounge for something to eat, he saw that somebody was occupying his haunt. The cat meowed and Milky grunted. Realizing there was no future on the porch, the cat padded away.

Milky, twenty-six years old, was just over six feet tall. His prewar weight was 185 pounds. Now he weighed 160, and, quite frankly, he looked like a refugee. His red hair was cut short and his features were gaunt. He bunched his olive green army coat up around his neck. He was shivering, but he wasn't cold. *I can't believe I slept here last night.* Every bone in his body ached. Every move was a chore.

Spring days were pleasant in Los Gatos, California, but the nights could be terribly cold. A wicked wind swept out of the Santa Cruz Mountains right down Santa Cruz Avenue; it usually lasted into the midmorning hours.

Milky watched his feet whenever he walked or his knees whenever he sat; it was a habit that helped him avoid catching the eyes of others. Today, he sat between cardboard boxes and concentrated on blowing warmth into his laced fingers, trying to ignore the kids walking to school. He willed himself impervious to their stares and snickering, but it was no use.

"That's Milky Tolliver," one of the kids whispered to another, his breath visible with each word. "He was in a Jap concentration camp. My old man says he ain't right." The boy made a gesture like he was drinking. Milky saw that and his posture stiffened. The boy and his companion laughed and ran off toward the school yard, hiding behind the huge trunk of an ancient pepper tree before running to the corridors of the parochial school across the alley.

Milky's real first name was Harry. He earned the nickname Milky because he became the local milkman when he graduated from grammar school. He started out with a horse-drawn wagon. When he turned thirteen, he got an agriculture driver's license and drove the dairy's Diamond T truck. But when he wasn't at school or delivering milk, he played baseball. He was popular with his classmates, and always had dates. Even during the depression, he had walking-around money; not much, but more than his companions. He was a soft touch if somebody needed a loan.

He played softball on various teams throughout the Santa Clara Valley. In high school Milky was a star football, baseball, and basketball player. His favorite, though, was baseball. It was rumored that the San Francisco Seals were willing to give him a tryout, until the war interrupted any chance of playing professional ball.

Milky enlisted in the army the week after Pearl Harbor was bombed. He hadn't fought for his country long when he was captured. After the Japanese surrendered, he was liberated and shipped to a veterans' hospital where he stayed for six months. Just over a year ago, he had come home, home to Los Gatos. The former milkman, baseball star, and POW was now a drunk, and his old friends avoided him.

Tilson Mandrake, thirty-two, unlocked the huge front door to the Top Cat Tavern, just like he did every morning. Always at 8:30 AM. And always with the morning edition of the *Mercury Herald* under his arm. He closed the door, which had a round window with dark blue glass, and locked it. The smell of stale cigarettes and spilled booze greeted him, just like every morning. "God, I am grateful that I don't drink anymore," he said aloud. Just like every morning.

Once inside he turned on the interior lights. He set about cleaning the bathrooms. The women's room was hardly ever used and was easier to clean. But the men's room…that was another story. *At least there were no pukers last night,* he thought to himself this morning. The pukers did not always make it to the commode. Most of the time the men using the wall-hung toilet were less than specific with their streams. He often wondered when he was cleaning the men's bathroom just what these guys' homes looked like—and then would quickly add that he would not care to see them!

Tilson hated cleaning the restrooms, so he did that chore first every morning. His uncle always said, "A clean restroom is the true indication that this place is an establishment and not a joint." His uncle told him to clean the toilets in the morning, at midday, and after dinner. The bartenders in the afternoon and evening had the responsibility of cleaning the restrooms, usually parceling the job out for a free drink or two to one of the regulars.

He started a pot of coffee, and while it was brewing, he vacuumed the carpeted areas of the barroom and mopped the hardwood floors under the bar stools and in front of the Wurlitzer juke box. He emptied the amber-colored ashtrays and washed them and set them back in strategic locations throughout the barroom. Finished with his tasks, he sat at the end of the bar with a mug of black coffee to read the newspaper. Tilson ran his hands over his tanned face, chin to forehead, then through his curly brown hair, forehead to nape—it was something of a habit with him. Then he picked up his pencil and opened the paper to the crossword. To Tilson Mandrake, this was the best part of the day. After the crossword, he counted the money from the night shift and readied the bank deposit. Every other day he inventoried the booze and ordered more if needed.

At 11:20 AM, he plugged in the juke box and the pinball machine, turned on the light over the shuffleboard, and sprinkled powdered shuffleboard wax the length of the playing surface. He raised the shade and turned on the neon SCHLITZ sign hung in the front window. Then, with the unlocking of the front door, the Top Cat Tavern was open for business.

Before he had the keys back in his pocket, someone rattled the doorknob on the back entrance. "Jesus, Tilly, open the door I gotta take a leak." The voice was Harry Tolliver's.

Tilson rolled his eyes. "Oh man, Milky. Did you stay in my shed last night?"

"If I had known it was available, I woulda slept inside."

Tilson fished the keys out of his pocket and unlocked the back door.

"Well, if you didn't sleep in the shed, where did you sleep?" Tilson asked after Milky came out of the restroom.

"On the back stoop." Milky made his way to the coffeepot and helped himself before sliding onto one of the stools at the bar.

Tilson watched Milky as he struggled with the cup. His face was ashy and his eyes were bloodshot. Looking at him affirmed again that he was glad he chose not to drink yesterday. "Aren't you staying up at the Abbey Inn?"

"Got evicted two days ago. I had a misunderstanding with the landlady. Apparently she didn't like it when I tried to put the make on her daughter."

"Me thinks alcohol was involved, Milky," Tilson replied jokingly.

"Maybe so, Tilly."

The back door of the bar slammed shut, startling the two men. "Hey, you guys want some doughnuts?" Ray Robertson, the owner of Polly Prim Bakery, tossed a white bag with chocolate cake dunkers inside onto the bar. Milky dived into the bag and finished his in two bites. Tilson and Ray gave each other a knowing stare.

Ray nodded at the baseball trophies above the bar and asked, "How'd your team do last night?"

"We lost. By the hangdog looks on their yaps, they musta got slaughtered. Luckily, it was just a practice game."

"You ever go to those games?" Ray asked.

Tilson shook his head. "Not since I became proprietor of this fine establishment. Games are all during business hours."

"You should get out there once and a while to watch your team," said Ray.

"Someday." It was the same answer he always gave.

"Maybe you ought to suit up old Milky, here," he said with a nod of his head in Milky's direction.

Tilson smiled. Milky seemed unaware of the conversation or that he was the topic.

"What's in that shed anyway, Tilly?"

Ray turned to leave and said, "Nice talking to you, Milky, enjoy the dunkers."

"Oh yeah," Milky replied. "Thanks, Ray."

———◆———

Tilson Mandrake's uncle, Carl Gabriel, opened the Top Cat Tavern in 1928. Then the place had a full kitchen that served lunch and dinner seven days a week. It was a good business and provided Carl and his sister, Blanche, Tilson's mother, an adequate income. Tilson's father was killed in a trucking accident at the Permanente Cement plant when Tilson was seven years old. Since that time, Carl took on the responsibility of caring for his sister and nephew.

Summers and after school for Tilson were in the bar at his uncle's side. By age fifteen, Tilson was doing the liquor orders and running the kitchen. "He was born to it," his uncle often said with pride.

In 1938, Carl Gabriel died of a heart attack. He was found face down, behind the bar. One of the regulars discovered him and called the ambulance. Tilson would never forget that day. He had walked to work that morning. A black and white police motorcycle and the light gray Cadillac ambulance from Place's Funeral Home sat askew at the curb on Santa Cruz Avenue just outside the door of the tavern. At first he thought, *There must have been a fight.* Then in an instant he knew something was wrong with his beloved uncle. He ran the last two blocks. Digby, the cop, was standing at the door in his uniform. As Tilson charged up to push through, he put a hand on Tilson's chest. "It ain't good, Tilly. Your uncle is dead. Looks like a heart attack." Digby dropped his hand and stood aside for Tilson to go in.

All the energy that had carried him so quickly the last two blocks suddenly failed him, causing Tilson to pause before taking the final pace into the tavern. When he did, it was with slow and heavy steps. He went around the bar and saw his uncle lying on the boards. The ambulance attendants had turned him on his back so they could give him oxygen. Carl's shirt was ripped open and his face was pale, but the look on his face was peaceful. In the years to come, that peaceful expression would comfort Tilson some, but there on that day, Tilson's thoughts and emotions roiled turbulently. He ran his hand down his face and left it covering his chin and mouth, stifling a sob.

Several of the regulars shuffled around talking. One of them said, "Wonder when they're gonna open." Tilson wheeled on the group and hissed, "Just get out." Then he stomped to the sign in the window and turned it from *OPEN* to *CLOSED*.

From that day on, Tilson Mandrake became the owner of the Top Cat Tavern, and the sole support for his mom. He drank heavily most days, but he never missed work, not once.

"So, what *is* in that shed, anyway Tilly?" Milky asked again.

"When the kitchen was up and running, the pearl diver washed the dishes in there."

Tilson knew where this conversation was going, and he tried to change the subject by talking baseball. Milky was persistent and maneuvered the chat back to the shed. "Let me think about it for a day or two, Milky," Tilson replied when Milky asked him if he could use the shed as his digs.

"Just till I get back on my feet," Milky promised.

Tilson fumbled with his ring of keys and had trouble with the corroded padlock on the door to the corrugated steel shed behind the Top Cat Tavern. Inside, the dust glistened in the sunlight that shone in from the widow. He had forgotten that there was a toilet, sink, and shower adjacent to the main room. Then he remembered a story about a gypsy woman who ran girls out of there for a time after the kitchen closed down. His uncle was paid in cash by the woman every week. He called it his foxy pocket money.

"Do you mean it, Tilly? You sure?" Milky was jostling around looking into the shed over first one of Tilson's shoulder, then the other, like a kid at Christmas who couldn't sit still waiting to get to the gifts under the tree.

"Jesus, Milky, quit yer yapping before I change my mind." He dropped the ring of keys back in his trousers' pocket and stood aside to allow Milky into his new digs.

Milky went right in and looked around with a big boyish grin on his face. "Hey, this is the break I need! Oh boy! How much rent do you want?"

Tilson knew that the pension Milky received was barely enough to get by on. "Let's see how it goes. Maybe you could do some work around the bar to earn your keep." Milky's shoulders slumped and there was an audible intake of air. When he looked up his eyes were glistening. "Thanks so much, Tilly, you're a good man."

"Just don't screw me on this deal." Tilson came up right in front of Milky and looked him in the eye square on. "This ain't charity. You're gonna have to perform, Milky. You need to cut back on the drinking and get some pride back in yourself. You're a war hero, for Christ's sake, start acting like one." This last comment was made as Tilson turned on his heels and strode to the back door of the bar. Milky stood there soaking in Tilson's words.

The remainder of the spring, Milky earned his keep by cleaning the barroom and the facilities every morning. In the beginning Tilson was unsettled at the loss of his solitude in the mornings before the Top Cat Tavern opened. But he grew to enjoy Milky's company and came to the realization that isolating himself was not doing anybody any good.

One morning after Milky had finished cleaning, he sat down next to Tilson. "How do you think things are going, Tilly?"

"What do you mean?" Tilson asked absently as he scribbled another word into his crossword puzzle.

"With me staying in the back and working it off. That's what I mean."

Tilson looked up over the paper. "Why, I'm happy with the arrangement, Milky. I'm glad you cut back on your drinking. You're starting to look healthy again. The customers like you, and when you talk about the war, man, you hold the room."

"How did *you* do it, Tilly? How did you stop the drinking and still work in a bar? That must've been hard."

"This bar is my livelihood, it is all I have. But I was losing it, you know? Not taking care of the bills, forgetting to make liquor orders, being obnoxious to customers and the employees. Booze was running me. My mother kept telling me that Uncle Carl would be very disappointed in me. I just gave her lip service. I kept right on doing the same thing. And guess what? You keep doing what you're doing, you keep getting the same results. Nothing changes. By the time I realized my life was unmanageable it was almost too late. My health was deteriorating, and my business was in the tank."

While they were talking, a regular, a guy everybody called the piano player, came in and sat on a barstool. He was always dressed in a sport coat and tie. As far as anybody knew he hadn't had many jobs since the theaters stopped playing organs and pianos to accompany the silent movies. "Gimme a draft, will ya, Tilly."

Tilson tilted the pilsner glass under the tap and placed the glass on a cocktail napkin in front of the customer. Tilson went and stood behind the bar in front of Milky. "Anyhow, I quit drinking, and business got better."

The piano player gave a snort of disdain. "You still listen to the Bible thumpers at those damned meetings, Tilson?"

Tilson rolled his eyes and replied, "Do you mean do I still go to Alcoholics Anonymous? The answer is yes. And just for your edification, they are not Bible thumpers."

"I used to go. Too much mumbo jumbo and God stuff if you ask me."

"Nobody did ask you, pal," Milky said. "But maybe you ought to give it another try."

"Look who's talking. Ha! A rummy GI," he said just before taking a swig of his beer.

Tilson walked to the customer and said, "Finish up and leave."

"You kicking me out?"

"Just for the time being." He shrugged as he picked up a dishtowel and started polishing imaginary spots off glasses. "It's really just for your own protection." Tilson paused and held the glass up to the dim light. "Look at that, a crack." He tossed it carelessly into a waste bin, where it shattered noisily in the metal can. He turned back to the piano man. "You ain't done yet? You're a braver man than I. Milky may not look like it, but he's pissed off. You hurt his feelings." The piano man looked at Milky, who glared back as if on cue. The piano man huffed and pushed back from the bar. He started to leave even though he had half a beer left.

"And before you come back," Tilson called after him as he made his way to the door, "keep in mind that while you were playing piano in lounges during World War II, he was in a prison camp in the

South Pacific, watching his buddies get their heads chopped off. So think about that, and remember he's a goddamned hero, so cut him a little slack."

The piano player hung his head a little and walked awkwardly the rest of the way to the door. Just before he opened it, he turned and said in a soft voice, "Sorry, Milky."

The door banged shut on a dead silence in the tavern. Then all at once they both busted up laughing. "Nice job with the glare, Milky. Thought I was about to mess myself a bit just standing so close!"

"Yeah, I thought that might be a nice touch." The laughter petered off, and Tilson sighed. "You know, I see a difference in you, Mr. Tolliver."

"Yeah?" said Milky, his face relaxing from his last laugh. "What might that be?"

"A month ago you would've taken that guy and mopped the floor with him. You're a little less aggressive, and that's good."

He doffed an imaginary hat and inclined his head. "Thanks, Mr. Mandrake."

Tilson smiled, but didn't speak to fill up the silence. That wasn't unusual since they often worked in quiet comradery, but something must have cued Milky that this was a different kind of gap in the conversation. "What is it, Tilly?"

"Just wondering if you are up for a suggestion, Milky?"

"S'pose it depends on the suggestion."

Tilson took a deep breath before he went on. "There's a group of us that meet in the basement of the town hall every Monday night."

Milky pursed his lips. "What kinda group?"

"I won't lie to you," Tilson said. "It's an AA meeting."

Milky looked away and gnawed on his bottom lip. "Come on, Milky, come with me. You've nothing to lose, and it may be what's needed to stop drinking."

<hr />

The Top Cat Tavern softball team was meeting in the game room adjacent to the barroom. Pitchers of beer were getting drained on a regular basis. The meeting was to decide who would or could play on the team. Tilson put up the money to sponsor the team and provided them with uniforms, bats, and baseballs plus the fee to the recreation department. The Top Cat had had a team every year since 1928. Tilson had even convinced his uncle to give him enough time off to play on the team one year. As the trophies above the back bar indicated, some years they were champs. The last four or five years they placed in the cellar.

"We need to practice more."

"We need to quit drinking before games."

"We need a good pitcher."

The comments during this preseason ritual never changed.

"Did somebody say pitcher?" Milky asked as he brought two full pitchers of beer for the team.

Milky Tolliver became a regular at AA meetings. He got a sponsor and worked the steps. Abstinence was not easy for him, and sometimes he slipped. But one thing he realized was that no matter how far he fell, he was always greeted with open arms at the meetings. Never in his adult life had he been accepted unconditionally. He learned that drinking was optional. If he surrendered to the impulse, he wouldn't die, and, perhaps more important, he wouldn't lose the acceptance he found in the group. At the first meeting he attended, he was amazed at the number of people he recognized. The initial embarrassment he felt diminished rather quickly when people greeted him. "You're taking the right step," they told him.

When Milky walked away after setting the pitchers down, Willy, the shortstop for the past two seasons, asked Tilson, "What's with Milky? Something's changed about him?"

"He quit drinking and is exercising regularly. You shoulda seen him doing layups on the basketball court the other day. The school boys watched in awe," Tilson said as he gestured to the rear door. "He even had foot races with the kids. He didn't beat 'em all, but he beat some."

Willy nodded slowly with a faraway look in his eye as he watched after Milky as Milky went back behind the bar. "Wasn't he a ballplayer once? A good one as I recall."

"That's right," said one of the others. "I think he was called up to the minors, wasn't he? Had a shot at the big league, some folks used to say."

Willy looked back at Tilson. "So how come he isn't on the team?"

Tilson shrugged. "Don't know. Why don't you ask him?"

"Man, you should a seen it, Tilly. Milky was fantastic. The first two pitches thrown to him? Why he clobbered 'em into the orchard," Sullivan, one of the team members, announced when he stopped in at the Top Cat after the first practice. "Me and Willy looked at one another. I think Willy got fertilizer on his lower lip when his jaw hit the grass," Sullivan added with a chuckle.

The noise level in the barroom increased when the rest of the team arrived, as did the beer consumption. Milky stepped behind the bar and pitched in to help Tilly. "I got this, Milky," Tilson said.

"No sweat, Tilly. I'd rather be here than on that side," he said with a grin while pointing to the imbibers.

"Hey, Tilson, are you ever gonna come to a game?" one of the guys asked.

"Yeah, old man Swanson shows up and so does Templeman from the hardware store," another player chimed in.

"Maybe if I owned a car lot or the hardware store, instead of this joint I could go. Besides, Thursdays are a busy night for me. If you saps were better, maybe you could move to a better bracket and play Tuesdays," he said holding his hands out to his sides. As a few sneers and jeers started, he stepped up onto a case of beer to make an announcement: "Hold on! Hold it! I'll tell you what; if you mugs make it to the championship, I'll throw you the best steak dinner ever! All the trimmings."

"By God, we'll hold ya to that, Tilly," somebody declared from a dark corner of the barroom.

As Tilson stepped off his perch, Sullivan asked, slightly drunk, "If we get to the championship, will you *then* come and watch us?"

"Sully, I got this place to run. I made a promise to myself after my Uncle Carl died that I would show up and work every day." Tilson put his hands on his hips and looked at the guys looking up at him through the ever present haze of cigarette smoke in the dark bar. "And that is what I do," he said as he ran his hand over his face and hair.

———◆———

Before the season started, the Top Cat Tavern team practiced at least every week or two. In previous seasons they just showed up when there was a game. Milky convinced them to put into practice some of the things they'd been griping about when the team met at the bar. He suggested they practice regularly. And he recommended no drinking before practice or games. Not all the players appreciated the routine, but before long the infielders were a firm group and even turned double plays.

"You're like watching a well-oiled machine, boys!" Milky kept yelling from his position at buck short. "Let's keep 'er going during the season! Hum babe!" He then thought to himself, *The defense is tight, I hope we can get some runs.*

———◆———

"Goddamn it, Milky. I only had a couple a bottles of suds. What's the big deal?" Jerry, one of the players, complained after Milky chewed him out for drinking before their next practice.

"The big deal is that we agreed to not drink before we played," Milky explained. "We only got two weeks before the season starts."

"That's your idea, not mine!" Jerry said as he stormed up the trail.

"C'mon Jerry, stick around," somebody yelled from the outfield. Jerry gave a wave over his head and continued on.

Since the first practice where Milky showed up, the players turned to him for direction, sort of an unofficial captain. He had thrust enthusiasm into the team, and he reveled in the role. However, the incident with Jerry gave him doubt in his ability to be the leader. He could see it in their eyes when he called them to the bench just as Jerry crossed the footbridge behind the grammar school.

"Mr. Welch delivered the schedule to Tilson this morning," Milky announced. "We play the Mystery Men the first game. We're home team." He looked into the eyes of his teammates and saw that there was no shine. "What's the matter?" He asked, knowing full well the answer. He was opening himself up, but was ready for it. "C'mon, what gives?"

He could hear their cleats scraping the ground and sensed that several of them wanted to say something, but were reluctant to do so. Sullivan finally looked up and said, "Don't think for one second that we don't appreciate what you've done for the team," he said sweeping his hand around the circle of players. "Before you showed up, we were just bunch of guys playing ball. Now we're a ball team, and we thank you for that," he said stepping back.

"Yeah, you bet!" Willy said. "But keep in mind, Milky. This is supposed to be fun for us. What just happened with Jerry ain't fun, okay."

———•—•———

"Where is everybody?" Tilson asked as Milky walked into the bar.

"They stopped at Reggie's," he replied.

"Oh," Tilson said. "How come?"

"They're pissed off at me," Milky said as he put some ice in a glass and held it under the tap. "We agreed that we wouldn't drink before we played, and Jerry had some beers then showed up for practice."

Tilson stood looking at Milky with a posture that said, *And?*

Milky continued, "So I called off practice until next week."

"And because you called off practice and made them mad, they're drinking at another bar. Is that what you're telling me?"

"Yeah. That's what I'm saying."

"Well, ain't that just grand," Tilson whispered as he paced on the floorboards behind the bar. "Reggie benefits because those guys didn't do it *your* way. That sounds like ego to me, Milky. What do you think?"

"Ah, nuts to the whole outfit. I don't need this," Milky said under his breath as he strode to the back door. Tilson heard the clang of the door on the shed. He looked out at the empty barroom and said aloud, "In my drinking days I would've had two shots of Four Roses by now."

———•—•———

The next morning when Tilson opened the Top Cat Tavern and started his routine, he noticed a five-dollar bill held in place on the bar top by a shot glass. With concern he looked at the back door and sensed that Milky came in after he shut the place for the night to get a bottle. "I ain't gonna check on him. I got my own sobriety to care about. Hell, he's an adult," Tilson said as he emptied ashtrays. When he emptied the trash he made sure he gave the garbage cans a good rattle and clanged the lids extra loudly. *I hope his hangover is a real head banger.*

At ten o'clock Milky opened the back door and walked in ready to start his shift. Tilson was sitting at a table doing the crossword. When Milky passed he looked up and noticed that Milky's hand was steady as he poured his coffee. Milky turned around to face Tilson, and before he sipped the hot coffee, he nodded slightly. He walked behind the bar and noticed that everything was set up.

"I didn't think you were gonna come in, so I did the setup," Tilson commented as he erased an entry in the puzzle.

"Thanks. Why didn't you think I was going to show?" Milky asked.

"I dunno. Guess because of the fin you left on the bar."

"Oh, that," Milky replied. "I didn't crack it. It's out in the shack."

"Whatever. Bring it back and I'll give you your money back," Tilson answered unemotionally.

After the lunch crowd subsided Tilson asked Milky, "What compelled you to come and get a bottle last night?"

Milky took his time before he replied as he wiped an imaginary spot on the bar top. "Feeling sorry for myself I guess." He looked Tilson in the eye and continued, "I saw disillusion in their eyes. Made me think, you know? But the reasons not to drink outweighed the reason to."

Tilson nodded and said, "I'm glad you didn't open the bottle, Milky."

"Yeah, me too, Tilly. Thanks."

Milky was in turmoil as he crossed the footbridge toward the ball field. He had no idea what he was going to say to the team. He shifted the olive green army duffle bag with balls and bats to his other shoulder. "Maybe I'll just let them do it the way they always did. They're right; it *is* supposed to be fun. That's what we'll do, we'll have fun."

"Where is everybody, Sully?" Milky asked as he emptied the stuff out of the duffle.

"They'll be here, I'm sure, Milky."

One by one they shuffled onto the field and started playing catch. Some were playing pepper and others were doing jumping jacks.

A voice from the footpath yelled, "Get the lead out and start looking like a team!" They all turned in unison and saw their sponsor, Tilson Mandrake, walking toward them carrying two cardboard boxes.

"Gather 'round, men. I got uniforms for ya," Tilson said as he pulled a long sleeved collarless shirt out. The shirts were black with bright orange sleeves. On the front were the words Top Cat Tavern in orange and orange numbers on the back. He tossed a shirt to each player, opened the other box, and tossed black baseball caps to them. Milky grabbed his cap and looked at the orange stitching of a forlorn-looking cat on the front and grinned.

Tilson looked at them with pride and said as he turned to walk away, "You *look* like a team, now bring a trophy home, boys."

This was the perfect ice breaker for Milky to speak to the team. He told them that they were, in fact, there to have fun. "And that is exactly what we will do, by God, have fun!"

The team won their first three games, and then lost the next game by one run when it went into extra innings. Milky knew from experience that losing *could* be helpful for the team esprit de corps. At the Top Cat after the loss, some of the players were analyzing their play. Nobody was mad at anybody; they all shared in the loss.

"Hell, I didn't think we would go undefeated. I did think we would have beaten those bums, though," Milky said with a jerk of his thumb in the direction of the field. "When we play Western Gravel again," Milky said, speaking louder with every word as he tried to keep his voice above the team's thunderous cheering and clapping, "vengeance will be ours!"

⎯⎯◆⎯⎯

That loss to Western Gravel was the only one for the Top Cat Tavern, and Western Gravel lost only one game, also. Thus the title game was set: Top Cats versus Western Gravel.

Every night before the championship game the Top Cat team had a practice. Not all the players could make it each night, but they tried. The more avid players tried to instill their competitive spirit in the others.

Jerry showed up late for the last practice before the big game. He went directly to the outfield and started shagging fly balls. He was animated as he talked with another player.

"Jesus Christ! You show up late and you start playing grab ass. Knock it off, will ya?" Milky yelled at Jerry as he tossed a ball back to the third baseman.

"Up yours. You ain't my father!" Jerry yelled back.

Silence fell over the playing field. Not a breeze was felt. No wisp of dust was seen and even the birds in the oak and sycamore trees stopped chirping. The player standing next to Jerry took two steps away from him. The others stood stock-still watching with baited breath.

"I've had enough of your guff!" Jerry said as he lumbered toward Milky. "Expecting us to show up every night, not allowing us to unwind from work with even one bottle of suds beforehand. Who do you think you are, anyway? Connie Mack?" Jerry threw the ball at Milky's feet. "Well I ain't gonna take anymore from you." With that he took off his cap and his glove, tucked it under his arm, and stormed off.

"Fine. Leave," Milky answered back, and he turned away from the retreating Jerry. As he leaned over to grab the ball from the grass, he suddenly felt all the eyes of the team, like those stares were ants just crawling all over him. He straightened without getting the ball and looked around at the group of silent men clustered around. "What?"

No one spoke; they just looked at each other and shuffled.

"Don't mind Jerry, boys. He'll be back. So let's get down to business, time's not running backward."

A few "I don't knows" and "I'm not so sures" rambled through the team. No one made any move to resume practice.

"Come on boys, we got a shot at the championship. Don't let a little tiff between me and Jerry get in the way."

Sully finally spoke out. "Some of us take it more seriously than others, but at the end of the day, Milky, it's about hanging out and having a little fun playing ball."

Several heads nodded. Will, the second baseman, spoke up next. "We all wanna win, Milky, but not like this."

"Come on, fellows, it's hot, and I think maybe that's enough for one night, let's go get a cold one and wash this all away," said Ernie, the catcher.

"Sounds good."

"Yeah."

"Uh huh, I could use one, too."

As the last of them shuffled away off the field, Sully picked up the duffle of equipment. He handed it to Milky and commented, "Don't sweat it, too much, there, Milkman. We'll be okay tomorrow. The guys just need to blow a little steam. You did dress down a guy in front of his friends, twice. I'd a given ya one, but the second time I'd a pasted ya in the snot locker." He gave Milky a quick pat to the back as he followed after the others. Milky just stood there, unmoving, until he was the only man left on the field—and even for a while after that.

Tilson Mandrake stood behind the bar, one foot up on the cooler box. He was scraping his teeth with a flat wooden toothpick listening to Milky's account of the evenings events. When he finished, Tilson asked him, "What does winning mean to you?"

"From where I've been? It means everything—it means I'm part of something good," he replied.

"So if the team loses, your life's no good. Is that what you're saying?" Tilson pressed.

Milky sighed in frustration. "No, Tilly. That's not what I'm saying. I'm saying that I'm part of something. And winning is better than losing. And they're happy I'm on the team."

"Sounds to me you think winning equates to acceptance," Tilson said as he tossed the toothpick in the trash can.

"Jesus, Tilson. You're starting to sound like the head doctors at the VA. Knock it off," Milky said as he got off the stool and stomped off to the door.

"Walking the boards behind a bar is kinda like that, Milky. You got that figured out, don't ya?" Tilson said as the back door slammed shut.

"Hey, Milky. You in there?" Tilson asked as he rapped on the door.

"Go away. I'm sick," Milky answered.

Milky had been awake all night. He tried to sleep but he just tossed and turned. He got out of bed about five, put on his uniform, and sat at his tiny table with a drink of booze. He was going to skip the game; the team didn't need him.

"What's a matter with ya?" Tilson asked as he opened the door. He was shocked to see Milky sitting at his table with his uniform on and a bottle of bourbon and a glass half full in front of him. "You gonna drink that?"

"Thinkin' about it for quite some time," Milky replied, staring at the glass. "Will you take the equipment over for me?"

"Well, ain't that swell. Championship game and the star got drunk. Is that what I'm supposed to tell the fellas? Huh? Is it? You sound like a whiney pedigree bitch."

Milky winced at each of the last three words. "Don't ya get it, Tilly? I'm scared."

"Scared of what?"

"Letting everybody down. Don't you see? If we lose, I'll be to blame."

"We got a little too much melodrama going on here, Milky. It's just a ball game, fer Christ's sake. I'll call Sullivan and have him come and take the gear. But you sit here and get snockered because you're scared." Tilson went over to Milky; he put one hand on the back of Milky's chair and another on the table between Milky and the bottle. Then he got right up in front of his face. "Man, you looked death head on and spit in its face when you were captured. This is *just* baseball."

Milky gnawed on his bottom lip as he dropped his gaze to the back of Tilson's hand.

Tilson slapped the table. "Look at me, Harry!"

Milky's brown eyes met Tilson's steel eyes. "Do you think sitting here *isn't* letting everybody down?"

For a moment it was almost enough, Harry Tolliver almost got off that chair, but then he remembered the stares of the team, crawling over him, he remembered their backs as they left him alone on the field. He sank down in the chair, his head rolling forward, his eyes closing. "I just can't Tilly," he whispered, "I just can't go out there alone."

"The team will—"

Milky shook his head. "Not the team I'm talkin' about." Then he lifted his head, and he found the courage to meet Tilson's eyes. "Will you go over to the game with me, Tilly?" He asked with a plea and a catch in his throat.

Tilson stood up, "Me? You know I haven't closed down the bar since—since Uncle Carl died."

"I know, Tilly, but if I walk out that door alone, I'll stop at Reggie's, and I won't sober up again. I'll be down for the ten count."

The two men stared at each other, dust swirling in a mote of sun slanting between them. Then with a firm-set mouth and one quick nod, Tilson removed his apron. He left the shack and went into the back door of the Top Cat Tavern, leaving both doors between him and Milky open. Then he said in a good loud voice, "C'mon, everyone. I'm taking you guys to a ball game." Then he shouted, "Milky, what's taking you so long?"

Milky, wide eyed, scrambled to his feet, knocking over the tiny table in the process, along with the bottle and shot glass, but he didn't even notice. He grabbed the gear and dashed into the tavern. Tilson was turning off the OPEN sign and looked at the two old codgers still sitting at the bar. "Let's go, I'm closing."

As the group walked across Santa Cruz Avenue, one of the men said, "I'm going to Reggie's. I'll catch up to ya."

The trio made their way down Elm Street after crossing the railroad tracks that ran behind the lumberyard.

"Look," Tilson said pointing down into one of the backyards. Jerry was mowing his mother's lawn. He was still dressed in the uniform he wore at the filling station where he worked.

Milky looked at Tilson. Tilson nodded.

"I'll catch up with you, Tilly. Tell the others we're coming," Milky said as he handed Tilson the equipment and veered off to the left.

<hr />

For the first time in six years, a trophy was brought to the Top Cat Tavern. It wasn't the championship trophy, but it was more gold than the joint had seen in a long, long time. And true to his word, Tilson Mandrake had New York–style steaks for the feed. And the beer was brought out by the pitcher. Borrowed tables and chairs from the parish hall were set up in the back parking lot of the bar. The fire horn even sounded when the barbeque wagon started up— somebody saw the smoke and thought the Top Cat was on fire. Volunteer firemen parked the engine in the alley and stayed to enjoy the revelry. Several hours later a very peeved fire chief showed up and drove the engine back to the fire house.

Milky and Tilson sat on the back porch steps looking at the people partying; wives and kids having a grand time with their husbands and fathers. Tilson was grinning from ear to ear. He stood up and yelled over the crowd for quiet.

Holding a coke bottle in his hand, he announced, "Here's to the 1947 Los Gatos Open League runners-up. I am so proud of all of you. Thank you for bringing a trophy home to the Top Cat Tavern!"

Somebody from the crowd raised a glass in a toast. "Here's to Tilson and Milky. They made it possible. Hip hip hooray!"

Tilson sat back down and said, "Poor souls are gonna be hungover in the morning."

"I think you're right, Tilly," Milky said with a snort.

"I'm glad you're not among them."

"Thanks," Milky said as he clinked soda pop bottles with Tilson and looked over to the spot on the porch where he once spent the night. "Me too."

The Butcher's Scale

At 2:30 on a Thursday afternoon, she walked into the Top Cat Tavern. All heads turned toward her, not because she was female, not because she had never been in the place before, but because that was what the regulars did any time the door opened: they turned to see who was entering their sanctuary. Conversations resumed, cigarettes were inhaled, and ice in cocktail glasses rattled, but quite a few eyes lingered on her at least for a few moments, including Milky Tolliver's. Milky was the bartender, and he watched her as she made her way across the room, drying the same beer glass for longer than it needed. Every part of her moved in some fashion or another when she walked. Her red hair was done in a ponytail that sashayed back and forth rhythmically. The tight turquoise toreador pants she wore accented the sway of her hips. And the white blouse, with the top two buttons undone, accentuated her ample bosom—as did each step she took. The lady had an air about her. It was as if she knew all eyes would be on her, no matter what room she entered.

As she approached Milky, the click of her high-heeled shoes on the wood floor grew louder. She hefted her derriere onto the bar stool and placed her dark glasses on top of her head. She smiled demurely at Milky as he placed a cocktail napkin down on the bar in front of her.

"Welcome to the Top Cat Tavern; what can I get for you?"

"I know it's early, but I think I'll have a Manhattan, please," she said in a sweet-as-apple-pie voice. Before Milky walked away she exclaimed loudly, "Make sure you put a cherry in it. I haven't had one in a long time." She giggled at her statement.

Tilson Mandrake, the owner of the Top Cat Tavern, came in from the back, carrying a case of whiskey bottles just in time to hear that last comment. He stopped short and raised an eyebrow at Milky. Milky came over and took the case from his boss. "Am I the only guy in here that got that?" he whispered as he looked around at the subdued clientele huddled around the tables of his establishment.

Milky shrugged. A couple of bottles rattled in the crate. "They looked when she came in, but no one is paying her any mind now, Tilly. It's all about the booze for them."

Tilson nodded and patted Milky on the back, "We were there once, buddy, don't forget that."

"Right you are, sir."

Tilson gave one last lingering look at her and then went back to the work of running a bar. That left her and Milky to chat as he unloaded the crate.

He learned that she was from Los Angeles and was on her way to San Francisco for a photo shoot. When she said *photo shoot,* she stuck her chest out and smiled. Milky grinned and moved down the bar to refill drink orders. She stopped in Los Gatos because her sister lived in the Santa Cruz Mountains in a place called Lupin Lodge.

"You ever hear of Lupin Lodge, Milky?" she asked with a wry grin.

"Yeah, I've heard of it, but haven't been there."

———•◆•———

Every day at 4:30 PM, the regulars started to filter out, and the business people started to arrive. Employees of the Top Cat called this the shift change. Every once in awhile the regulars and business people overlapped, which the bartenders liked because tips were better. On this Thursday, the shift change was clean.

For fifteen very long minutes, the two were alone in the bar. The lady was nursing her second Manhattan, and Milky was getting the bar set up for Lawrence, the night bartender. He was washing glasses and cleaning ashtrays and getting more ice when the phone rang. It was Lawrence calling in sick.

"Damn it," Milky muttered as he put the phone down just a little too hard. Then he sighed, "I got no life, anyway," he grumbled under his breath.

"What's the matter, Milky?" the lady asked. When he told her she replied, "That is too bad."

Before he could ask her what she meant, the front door burst open startling the two of them. "Hey, Chris the cop is giving parking tickets. Looks like that red convertible is next!" Clancy, the realtor, announced.

"Oops, that would be me," the lady whispered as she slid off the stool.

Clancy was flabbergasted at the sight that trotted past him as he held the door. His mouth was agape as he turned to Milky.

"You better shut your yap before flies get in, Clancy."

"What and who is that?" Clancy queried still leaning to look out the door.

"I don't know who she is, but she's a model of some sort on her way to 'Frisco. She has a sister that lives at Lupin Lodge, so she stopped in Los Gatos to see her, I guess."

"Lupin Lodge, eh? The nudist camp?"

"One and the same, Clancy."

"Jeezus. I wonder what her sister looks like."

The door opened again, and she sauntered in every bit as gracefully as she had the first time.

"Did he give you a ticket?" Milky asked her as she made her way back to her bar stool. Clancy's eyes never left her caboose as she parked it.

"No. He was very kind. He tipped his cap and welcomed me. There is nothing like small-town hospitality."

—◆—

The business cliental was starting to fill the place. Each man and a few women stopped in their tracks when they saw her sitting at the bar with her long legs tucked neatly to one side as she casually leaned on one arm. She nodded her head and smiled when eye contact was made. Sometime into the evening, she told someone her name was Lorna. It was apparent that Lorna enjoyed attention. A few of the men made crude comments and were given the air by her.

At the dinner hour, most of the business people left to have supper. Tilson was out front now, lending a hand with the evening rush. The few guys that remained had called home to tell their wives to eat without them.

Sitting at the bar was Johnny, who owned the Tidewater Filling Station, Clancy the realtor, Emile, the butcher, Bill, the insurance man, and, of course, Lorna. Lorna was getting louder and more giggly and wiggly. Milky and Tilson watched the scene with amusement. The men at the bar were starry eyed; each thought himself charming.

"They haven't got a chance with her. She's too sophisticated for them," Tilson whispered to Milky.

"I do love a well-built woman," Clancy said to Johnny in a soft voice.

"Thank you, Clancy. The Lord has been kind to me," Lorna answered back with a wink.

Clancy looked away, mumbling something that might have been "Sorry, Ma'am." On the other side of her, Emile and Bill had their heads together. Milky thought he overheard something about a bet. He must have been right, for a moment later he heard Lorna ask in her singsong voice. "What are you betting on, boys?"

"Oh, nothing," Bill answered sheepishly with a blush.

"Riiiight," Lorna replied, elongating the word as she stared at Bill, a quirk of a smile tugging at her lips. "Milky, I think it is high time I bought the bar a round of drinks. Set 'em up wall-to-wall," she announced.

There were cheers and claps.

"Please excuse me, but I need to use the ladies room." All eyes were on her as she strutted to the bathroom. Halfway there she looked back over her shoulder and said, "And don't forget to set up another one for me, Milky." She winked and with a sassy flip of her ponytail was on her way again.

Everyone was quiet as all eyes lingered on the space that had last held Lorna in their view. Emile whistled a long low tone. "Listen, I know hams, and those babies are at least eight pounds plus."

"How much do you want to bet?" Bill asked.

Johnny said, "Follow my lead on this, fellas. Let's each of us put a dollar on the bar." Just then the door to the restroom opened and closed and Lorna came back to take her stool. She had undone her ponytail and her tresses flowed freely about her shoulders.

"This is nothing but a row of fools on a row of stools, Tilly," Milky said as the two stood at the other end of the bar.

"Oh. You are naughty, aren't you?" Lorna squealed. After much cajoling and close-in talking, she had finally convinced Emile to tell her what they were scheming. "Is that what that money is for? Bets on how much my breasts weigh? Shame on you," Lorna said with a sly smile. "Most men want to know how big they are." When nobody asked what her breast size was she offered, "Forty-fours if you want to know."

Milky walked down the boards to check on drinks. He put some dimes down in front of Lorna and asked her to play the juke box. "Let me play one first," Johnny yelled, grabbing a dime. He put the dime in the slot, punched in the letter and number, and the Modernaires vocal "It Must be Jelly ('Cause Jam Don't Shake Like That)" filled the room.

Everyone laughed out loud.

"How will you weigh them, boys?"

"Are you sure you are game for this, Lorna?" Milky asked.

"Hell, honey," she said with an exaggerated seductive look, "I'm up for anything that's fun." With a wink, she hopped off the stool and walked across the room. Everyone was frozen in place like they were waiting for someone to paint a portrait of them. Two-thirds the way to the door, Lorna turned. She glanced around and then cocked her head. "Well?"

That was all it took. Bar stools scraped the floor, one even fell over, and the place cleared out, leaving Milky all alone, still posing behind the bar for that picture.

When the group returned from the butcher shop, the gaiety level resumed. While she was in the bathroom tucking her shirt in, Tilson related to Milky what had happened. "I'll tell you one thing, she is not shy. She took her blouse and brassiere off without hesitation. Emile got her a footstool; she stood up on it and hefted her knockers onto Emile's scale." Tilson shook his head as if he could not believe he wasn't dreaming.

"How were they?"

Tilson looked up at his old friend with an impish smile playing across his lips, "Milky, they were breathtaking!"

"So," prompted Milky when Tilson didn't show any sign of continuing, "What was the verdict?"

Tilson wagged his finger, "Patience, Milky, you wouldn't rush a fine wine, now would you?"

Milky rolled his eyes, "We don't drink anymore, Tilly!"

"All the more reason to savor this, my friend." Tilson grinned, irritating Milky just enough to make him sigh. Evidently, that was enough, Tilson resumed his tale. "Emile's scale reads side to side, and that scale kept moving like one of those cat kitchen clocks: the tail ticking, eyes moving back and forth with each tick." Tilly moved his hand back and forth in a tick-tock motion. "It seemed like minutes before it settled."

Milky leaned forward, resting on the bar. "Well, what did they weigh?"

"Twelve pounds, six ounces."

Milky gave a long low whistle. "Whew, that's some set!"

Banter continued well into the evening, but one by one the men left. Each took his shot, and each realized at his own pace that there was no future in a tryst with Lorna. Thus, each man made his excuses and said his goodbyes, then headed home to square things with the wife, taking a vivid memory with him.

Finally it was just Lorna and Tilson, with Milky closing up the bar. Lorna made a phone call to her sister to come and get her, only to discover that she had retired for the evening. The man who answered the phone offered to go to her cabin and wake her, but Lorna told him no. She would call her back in the morning.

That was when Tilson yawned and told Milky he, too, was heading home. He tossed the bartender his keys and told him to do the lockup.

———◆———

On Friday morning, Tilson Mandrake arrived at the Top Cat Tavern at 8:30. Stale cigarettes and spilled booze wafted to his nostrils. A cocktail glass with a little green stir stick and a cherry stem sat on top of the bar. Tilson grinned from ear to ear as he thought about the previous night's events. "See, you can still have fun and be sober," he said aloud. He opened the back door to take the garbage out and saw a little red sports car parked jauntily next to Milky's room behind the bar. "Son of a gun," Tilson thought.

Milky and Lorna came in the back door of the Top Cat and sat with Tilly. Lorna's hair was wet from her recent shower, and she smelled like Yardley lavender soap. Conversation was light. She finished her coffee and gave Tilly a peck on the cheek and Milky a hug and kiss. As she drove out of the parking lot and down the alley, she turned and waved at the two men standing by Milky's room.

"Well?"

"Well, what?"

Tilson gave Milky a playful punch on his shoulder. "You know what."

"Oh, you mean Lorna."

"Yes, I mean Lorna."

"Amigo, in the end-o, it was all innuendo," Milky said as he turned and walked back into the Top Cat Tavern. He said over his shoulder, "I slept in her car, Tilly." Tilson looked where Lorna's car had been parked and saw a red woolen Polar King blanket draped over the garden hose hanger next to Milky's front door.

Six months later, Johnny from the filling station burst into the bar with the December 1948 edition of *Stag Magazine*. Page twenty-seven had a photo layout shot around the Golden Gate Bridge; it was entitled "Lorna's Dunes."

The men who were present that night in the butcher shop would be telling that story for years to come. The magazine became a well-thumbed relic enshrined in a dented old steel case stashed under the bar. Any time someone asked one of the men there that night, out would come the magazine, and they would talk for hours...all except Milky. If anyone asked Milky about Lorna or that night, he just smiled.

The Day Dude Martin
Came to Town

Tilson Mandrake was driving north on California State Highway 101. His light brown 1938 Plymouth two door shimmied badly as he reached 45 mph. He either needed to go over 55 mph or under 30 to stop the shimmy. Neither option appealed to him so he lived with the shimmy. Traffic on the tree-lined, two-lane road was light this early October Saturday morning. Tilson had spent the night in Gilroy with a lady he often kept company with.

The orchards and fields were freshly disked and the white painted trunks of the apricot, cherry, and prune trees were vividly bright. The fertile aroma of damp earth appealed to Tilson.

A smile crept onto his face as he recalled the previous night, and before he knew it, he was whistling a frisky tune.

Just south of the Capri Restaurant, he waited at the Southern Pacific Railroad crossing; the southbound freight was slow moving as it made a wide curve to continue toward Southern California. Tilson stopped counting the cars at sixty. Finally the red caboose came in sight, and Tilson put the car in gear and crossed the tracks.

A mile or so up the road he noticed a shiny maroon Mercury Touring Sedan with its hood up. The sun reflected off of the chrome spotlight on the driver's side. Tilson pulled in behind and got out. A tall rawboned man wearing a wide-brimmed beige cowboy hat looked up from under the hood, squinted as the dust settled, and gave Tilson an exasperated look.

"Can I help with anything? You want a ride or something?" Tilson asked the man.

"I could use a ride to the next town," the man drawled. "My fan belt came loose, and when I tried to tighten 'er, she broke."

Tilson recognized the man but couldn't put a name to a face. That happened frequently to Tilson. Being in the bar business, lots of people pass through the doors. *I probably served him before,* Tilson surmised.

"It sure is a pretty car, mister," Tilson told the man.

"Well thanks kindly, friend. She's a 1948 model. Only a year old and the dern fan belt breaks. But you are right, she is pretty."

The man put his tool kit in the trunk and retrieved a guitar case and suitcase from the back seat and set them in the trunk also. Tilson noted that the man was wearing a western style shirt and what appeared to be handmade cowboy boots.

"You're a western singer, aren't you?"

"Yes, friend, I am. My name is Dude Martin."

"I thought I recognized you! My name is Tilson Mandrake. It is an honor to meet you," Tilson said as the two men shook hands.

On the drive north to the little town of Coyote, Dude Martin told Tilson Mandrake that he was in this part of the state to do a radio promotion for his next gig that was going to be at Napredak Hall in San Jose.

"Well, you're real close to Los Gatos. That's where I live. You should stop by; it's a real friendly town."

The mechanic retrieved the correct replacement fan belt from high on the repair garage wall with a hook on a long pole. Dude paid the man and accepted Tilson's offer of a ride back to his car.

The Mercury was idling after the fan belt replacement as the two men talked.

"I want to pay you for your time, friend."

When Tilson refused the man said, "I have to give you something."

"Maybe you could give me an autograph?"

Dude Martin got a twinkle in his eye and strode to the trunk of his car. He pulled out a promotional poster depicting Dude Martin and his RCA Recording Roundup Gang and wrote with a fountain pen: *To my pal, Tilson Mandrake, Thanks for all your help, Yours truly, "Dude" Martin, Oct. 18, 1949.*

Tilson gave Dude a matchbook with the face of a hopeless looking cat on the front. Over the cat face was the name *Top Cat Tavern* and under the face was *Los Gatos Calif. Phone 08-0660*.

"This is my place. If you ever need anything call me." The two men energetically shook hands and entered their vehicles to continue on their sojourns north. At the Almaden Crossing, Tilson honked his horn and saw Dude Martin give a vigorous wave as the maroon Mercury continued on Highway 101.

———•◦•———

"You're telling me that you met Dude Martin?" Milky Tolliver said incredulously as Tilson was putting up the poster that was given to him by Dude Martin.

"I most certainly did. And guess what? He's real nice."

Milky asked Tilson to repeat the Dude Martin tale any time a customer came in the tavern and asked about the new poster taped to the mirror behind the bar.

That afternoon the Philco table radio on the shelf of the back bar was tuned to KEEN. The radio announcer said in a western twang, "Folks this is Big Jim DeNoon, and we're visiting with the legendary recording artist Dude Martin. Dude, thanks for stopping by."

"My pleasure, Big Jim. Thanks for having me."

The interview continued for about fifteen minutes and was coming to a close when Big Jim asked Dude if he had any parting words for his fans. Dude said, "I hope everybody comes and sees me and the Roundup Gang at the next show at Napredak Hall. I would also like to say hello to my friend, Tilson Mandrake, out in Los Gatos at the Top Cat Tavern. Thanks again, Tilson. See you soon, buddy."

Everybody present at the Top Cat Tavern whooped and hollered when they heard Dude Martin mention their bar and Tilson's name on the air waves. Tilson received back slaps and handshakes all afternoon. Los Gatos' own celebrity. Nobody could ever remember anybody from Los Gatos ever being mentioned on the radio. Frankie Crosetti and Hal Chase, pro baseball players, author John Steinbeck, actress Olivia de Havilland, and violinist Yehudi Menuhin had all been mentioned in the newspapers and magazines. Never over the air though. Furthermore, Los Gatos had never been mentioned before either. It was indeed a big day.

On a December afternoon, Tilson Mandrake entered the bar from the rear. Milky Tolliver was washing glasses and several regulars were talking politics. Tilson, with a smug look on his face, tossed a Christmas postcard on the bar in front of Milky. Wiping his hands on the apron he wore, Milky picked up the card and saw the postmark was Los Angeles. Before he read the note he looked up to Tilson, who still had a smug look. The note read:

Dear Friend Tilson, the Roundup Gang and I will be in your town the first week of May, 1950. We will be staying at the El Gato Hotel. If it is convenient, I would enjoy seeing you. Have happy holidays.

Your Pal,
Dude Martin

The winters in Los Gatos have a wide assortment of weather conditions, from drought to torrential rains with flooding and sometimes snow. The winter of 1950 was predominantly rainy. Some of the smaller creeks that dumped into the larger Los Gatos Creek crested their banks. Most of the fruit farmers would exclaim, "This is a good rain. We need it. It's about dammed time." The nonfarmers were happy to see the creeks flowing and the surrounding reservoirs filling up, but after awhile they would say, "enough is enough."

In March, Almendra Creek flooded and wiped out several out buildings and tar paper shacks on the east side of University Avenue and ruined the high school's lighted baseball field to the south. The newly formed recreation department and the Los Gatos High School District didn't have enough funds to repair the field in time for the Men's Open Softball League season. The Los Gatos High Wildcats had to change their season to all away games. Softball team sponsors and the recreation department board decided that an alternate location for the games was a better proposal than canceling the season. The West Corral was chosen for the temporary site. The West Corral was on the North side of town. The family that owned it was named West, and they were happy to oblige. After a few Saturdays with dry weather, the corral-turned-baseball-field was ready to go. The second week of April, practices started and by May 1, the teams were geared up. The baseball season was considered the most important and wholesome activity for the entire year. Since the inception of the recreation department, many activities were offered to the citizens. Swimming lessons were given at the town pool, and arts and crafts were offered at the youth center, and of course there was baseball. Each year, it seemed, a new league was added, and soon Little League would be available. The department charged a fee for activities, which was a major source of funding.

Mr. Welch, the recreation department manager, received a formal letter from the Jefferson Baseball Association that hailed from San Francisco. The gist of the letter stated that scouts for Jefferson visited the town and reported that the regular field was flooded and that games would be held in a pasture. It further said that because they were a semipro team, they didn't want any of their players to be injured because of an inferior field.

"Inferior field! Who in the hell do they think they are?" one of the merchant sponsors chimed up at a special meeting. "Hell, we've trounced their supposed pro players six of the last seven years. They just don't want to get beat again," he concluded as he shook his head and sat down, puffing on a fat cigar.

"I did the best I could to make the ground good enough to play on," Melvyn West said in an almost whine. "Sure, there are a few rocks, but it's playable, I think."

Murmurs could be heard throughout the small room in the basement of the Methodist church.

Mr. Welch held up his hand in a gesture begging for quiet. When the men present did quiet down, Welch announced, "We have options. We could visit them at their fields for all the games." The two baseball clubs alternated games, giving each club the chance to be home team.

Somebody from the back of the room boomed out, "I ain't goin' to Frisco eight Sundays in a row!"

"Yeah, and what about playoffs? Where will they be played?" Tilson Mandrake asked.

"Another option is to cancel the season," Welch said, bringing a pall over the room. "We need to decide what we're going to do, and I mean soon."

Dude Martin and his band just finished an extensive show schedule in Monterey and Santa Cruz counties and were stopping off in Los Gatos for some fun and relaxation. They were due to start a six-week stint in Emeryville at the Peek-a-Boo Club on May 20.

Tilson borrowed a brand new 1950 Ford convertible from Swanson's Ford Dealership. The top was down, as he maneuvered the car into the taxi cab parking space in front of the El Gato Hotel.

Dude and band members Davie Smith and Carolina Cotton were sitting in fan-back wicker chairs on the veranda drinking lemonade.

When Tilson walked up the pink cement front steps and onto the porch, Dude Martin stood up and greeted him with a hearty handshake and a jovial slap on the shoulder.

As they were sitting and talking, John Baggerly, the editor of the *Los Gatos Times*, tentatively approached the assembly. He looked relieved when he saw Tilson among them.

"Hello, Scoop. I'd like to introduce you to Dude Martin," Tilson announced. John shook hands with all and sat down for an interview. Dude Martin was comfortable and extremely gracious.

After the interview Tilson was driving Dude Martin around town showing him points of interest. They visited Memorial Park, the high school, and the small gauge Billy Jones Railroad.

As they passed through numerous orchards and fields, Tilson piped up and said, "This is probably pretty boring for you, Dude. Is there anything you want to see in particular?" Dude's eyes darted quickly to Tilson's face. For a moment Tilson thought he had upset Dude. With a quick smile, much to the relief of Tilson, Dude Martin said, "Friend, anything that reminds me of home is square with me." It was Tilson's turn to give a darting glance.

"You didn't know I was born in California, did you?" Dude Martin said with a sly grin.

"I thought with the Texas-like accent that you were from a southern state," Tilson answered.

"Hell, I was born in Merced County and grew up in Oakland and Berkeley," he replied. Tilson realized that the accent was missing, and had been since they started their tour.

"The drawl is just an act. My manager says its part of the mystique of show business. Keep it quiet, will ya? I have an image to uphold," Dude snorted with a slight chuckle.

Tilson was pleased that Dude Martin felt comfortable and could be himself.

As they were passing the West Corral, Dude asked Tilson to stop so they could watch a couple of innings.

The sound of the West's blacksmith pounding his hammer on an anvil resonated from the barn adjacent to the field. Several pony carts were lined up waiting for service.

"You mean to tell me that the town teams play ball in a cow pasture?" Dude asked unbelievably. Tilson explained about the flood and the lack of funds for repairs.

Dude was silent on the ride up Santa Cruz Avenue. They stopped in front of the Top Cat Tavern.

"So this is the world-famous Top Cat Tavern? I've heard about it and always wanted to see it," Dude said in a jokingly enthusiastic tone.

"Well, come on in. I know the owner," Tilson answered back with the same joking manner.

Dude was friendly with all the well-wishers and those who just wanted to say they met Dude Martin. After an hour or so Dude gave Tilson a look that said *I need to leave.*

"Dude, remember we need to see Scoop for that interview."

"Oh, that's right. Thanks for reminding me, Partner."

Nobody in the bar caught on to the ruse, and they bid farewell. On the block walk up Santa Cruz Avenue, Dude told Tilson that he wanted to do something for the town.

"Just you being here is enough, Dude. The town is buzzing with excitement. You're the talk of the town."

"Can you call that newspaper guy? I have an idea," Dude told Tilson.

In a meeting room off of the dining room at the El Gato Hotel, were Dude Martin, John Baggerly, Hugh Welch, and Jim DeNoon along with Cottonseed Clark from Radio KEEN.

"So it's settled then. We'll do the show on the third Sunday in May," Dude Martin said.

Welch announced that he would need to get approval from his board of directors before anything was firm.

"Leave that to me," Baggerly replied. "I've got their ear. With KEEN blasting over the airwaves and publicity in the papers, they can't refuse."

"Why would they say no?" Cottonseed Clark asked.

John Baggerly stood in front of the recreation department board and told them that Dude Martin and the Roundup Gang were willing to put on a benefit show to help with the costs of the field repairs. He also told them that professional disc jockeys from KEEN would be the masters of ceremonies. "They will bring with them other recording stars from the area. Just the advertisement on the radio will bring in loads of people to see the show."

"And they're willing to match the total gate receipts. Gentlemen, these are major recording stars who are willing to put on a show for free to benefit Los Gatos. And they'll match whatever we take in. You cannot afford to pass this up. We need to act quickly."

Mr. Welch was sitting and squirming in his seat. The windfall from the benefit show would bolster the wilting budget, especially since the baseball season was cancelled. This was a major plume in the town's cap.

Memorial Park was jam-packed on a Sunday afternoon in mid-May. Families were sitting on the lawns and along the banks of the Los Gatos Creek. The smell of hot dogs and burgers being grilled permeated the sycamore trees. Near the fence that surrounded the swimming pool, several hay bales were scattered forming a barricade between the band and the crowd.

When Dude Martin stood at the microphone and started to sing in a deep baritone, the throng went wild. Those who knew his songs sang along. Those who didn't swayed to the melody. When Carolina Cotton, the "Yodeling Blonde Bombshell," started to sing and yodel, all movement stopped. Couples stopped dancing; children quit running around. All there listened.

It was a genuine community event that was created by a benevolent nonresident. Each adult paid one dollar and children were admitted free. Volunteers prepared food and sold it to attendees. The receipts for the day totaled $1,100.

Dude Martin donated $1,400 making the total $2,500.

There was enough money to repair the playing field and create a mound along the creek to prevent flooding.

In future years, Dude Martin sent checks to Los Gatos for various charitable causes. One cause in particular was the March of Dimes campaign. Los Gatos was recognized nationally, and Dude Martin sent Tilson Mandrake a letter with a check for $2,000 and a copy of a *Los Angeles Times* article about Los Gatos's effort to fight polio. In the letter Dude told Tilson to use the money as he saw fit to further combat polio.

———◆———

Tilson was reading an article in *Country Western Times*, a periodical about western music, musicians, and upcoming and past shows. The article made reference to a Dude Martin show that was held recently in the town of Firebaugh, California, that benefited that town's volunteer fire department. Dude was quoted in the piece:

> I'm glad that the Roundup Gang and I could sing our songs and help the fire laddies. We've been doing shows up and down the Golden State for the past year or so, ya know? Helpin' out where we can. We were inspired by a town up north— Los Gatos. San Jose is near there.

Tilson smiled when he read the reference that San Jose was near Los Gatos, making Los Gatos sound like it was the bigger city.

Tilson Mandrake's most prized possession was a black and white photograph of himself and Dude Martin with their arms around each others shoulders at the microphone during the benefit show at Memorial Park in mid-May, 1950. That photo, the poster of Dude Martin, his Christmas postcard, and the newspaper articles are still taped to the mirror on the back bar of the Top Cat Tavern.

Chief Spearmint

Smoke from cooking fires could be seen in the midst of the domed huts of the Indian village. The midmorning breeze whistled through the cottonwoods and sycamores. Women picked wild onions, carrots, and mushrooms among the vivid purple lupine and orange poppies in the fields next to the corral. Others washed clothes down by the stream. Younger girls ground corn to make bread, or helped their mothers clean and cook the vegetables. The able menfolk hunted for rabbit and deer in the nearby foothills, while older men sharpened tools for use in the corn rows.

Four young children, cousins, ran through the tall wind-bent cornstalks. The girls wore buckskin dresses and bright cloth slip-on shirts. The boys had buckskin pants and no shirts. An old brave gave them a shout to get out, but smiled toothlessly as they passed by, their footfalls stirring dust. "Play while you can, young ones," he said under his breath.

The four ran up the gentle slope, darting between boulders standing on each side of the path that led to the forest behind the camp. Whatever lay beyond the forest was a great unknown to them. All they knew was that the trail through the brush was the path into the taller trees and darkness, which the men took to go hunting. They left that way, and they came home that way.

Visitors to the camp used the wagon road that ran along the creek and ended at the corral where there was a hitch to tie up horses and a trough for water. The horses were kept away from the hut area of the camp.

The people of the camp held firmly to their traditions: they greeted each day with words of hope. They thanked the animals that fed them for their sacrifice. They praised the trees that offered acorns and other nuts for nourishment.

Weather conditions were looked upon as blessings; the sun nurtured growing and the rain watered the soil.

Knowledge about many mysterious issues was imparted after children reached certain ages. One such tradition was about what lay down the wagon road. Another was the forest. The men knew what was beyond the forest and down the road; their women knew also. The older boys were told, at times, tales of the forest and beyond. Maidens learned after they were married. But the tales were kept from the young. They labored with meaningful chores, which the children deemed insignificant, before they earned the right to sit by their father's side and hear of the land beyond the forest or any other grownup subject. First, the young ones must feed and groom the animals or help the grandfathers in the fields. Some older boys prepared arrow heads from obsidian or bones, while others made shafts from yew sticks. These were very important tasks. Gathering water and helping wash clothes were chores that maidens did.

Addie Bird, the oldest cousin, stood next to the path her father, uncle, and other men had taken two days before.

"One of these days I am going to go in there," she said with determination scanning the darkness of the forest's interior. Her dark braids hung to the middle of her back. She was tall for her age and was very quick when she ran. She could beat most of the boys her age in races.

"You can't go in there. You're just a girl!" Easy Eagle replied with a snort.

"We shall see about that, Cousin," Addie Bird said boldly with flashing dark eyes. She turned swiftly away, causing her braids to swing and hang over the front of her blue shirt.

Jake Bird pulled a sling from his buckskin pants pocket and twirled it on his finger.

His frame was sturdy and his hair was growing longer after it was cut off because of a lice infestation. His temper was short and sometimes he fought other boys. The time spent with his sister and cousins, however, was the most fun for him.

"Where did you get that?" Easy Eagle asked.

"By the horses. I found it on the ground."

"Can I see it?" Easy Eagle asked.

Easy Eagle was taller than the others. His lone braid hung just above his shoulder blades.

Several years earlier he was hit in the face with a thrown rock that left a small scar under his right eye, which accentuated his already prominent cheekbones.

Jake handed him the sling. Easy picked up a smooth stone, loaded it, wound it over his head, and released it. The stone flew only a few feet.

Addie went over and sat next to the youngest member of the foursome, Sea Eagle, to watch the boys using the sling.

"We might be girls, Sea Eagle, but I feel we can do boy things just as good as any boy. Don't you?"

"Yes!" She retorted with a kick of her moccasin-clad foot toward her brother, Easy, and Cousin Jake. "Better!" she said, her dark eyes flickering and her nostrils flaring as she twirled the ties to her red shirt.

———◆———

The four cousins finished their midday meal of dried beef strips and berries, and were lying on the bank of the gurgling stream looking at the puffy white clouds scudding across the blue sky. Seagulls cawed as they flew overhead.

"That cloud looks like a man's face," Jake Bird said.

The others followed his pointing finger. Seconds later the formation curled into another shape.

"Have any of you seen Hefe lately?" Sea Eagle asked. All replied at once that they hadn't.

"Did he go on the hunting trip?" Addie asked of nobody in particular.

Their Hefe, or grandfather, was Chief Spearmint, the chief of the village. He had lived many years and had seen many things, some good and some bad. His skill as a hunter was behind him. His bravery, however, was legendary and was the subject of many fireside tales. Respect was still shown to him and would be until the day he died.

Chiefs were not expected to do any chores around the camp. To do so would be beneath the stature of a chief. Chief Spearmint was without a wife, so his daughter and daughter-in-law did his wash and cooking. Fresh vegetables and bread and cleaned and skinned game ready for cooking were left at his hut each morning, which he gave to whomever cooked for him that day.

"Come on. Let's find Hefe!" Addie said excitedly as she got up and started running toward the village, her cousins following her. They stopped at Hefe's hut. Sea Eagle looked inside.

"Nope, not here."

"Easy, you and Sea Eagle go ask your mother if she knows where Hefe is. Jake and I will do the same!" Addie said in an authoritative manner.

"We will meet at the fire circle in just a few minutes!" Easy Eagle yelled over his shoulder as he and his sister ran toward home.

Chief Spearmint was sitting on the bank of the stream in a secluded spot far away from his camp. His back was resting on a felled sycamore tree trunk and his bare feet dangled in the meandering current. His eyes took very long blinks as the warm sun shone down on his seamed and angular face. The smell of moss soothed him, and soon he was asleep and dreaming. His unbraided gray hair wisped in the gentle wind.

The dream was almost always the same; the solitude of his carefree childhood is interrupted when white men on wagons pulled by mules arrive in his camp. The menfolk from the camp are away hunting, rendering the camp practically unguarded. The visitors are friendly at first, but then the situation turns bad in the early evening. They give whiskey and wine to the male population left in camp, making them woozy. Then the guests start chasing the maidens around. The young braves try their best to protect their women, but some girls are taken away. Spearmint watched his sister in her calico dress and four other maidens sitting with tear-streaked faces in the cargo area of the wagon as it raced away over a dusty rutted road. He ran after the wagon until he was too fatigued to run another step. The wagon tore along the dirt road that bisected the grassy land.

Spearmint headed back to camp feeling like a failure. His long raven hair was dusty from the chase and his high cheekbones smeared with dirt, sweat, and tears. Before he showed up at the camp, he stopped at a stream to wash. His large hands dipped cool water onto his face.

He always woke up at this point in the dream, rubbing his neck and right shoulder. The wound healed, but the scar always reminded him of the fight.

"Hefe, we have been looking all over for you. What are you doing sitting by yourself?" Easy Eagle asked as he approached his grandfather.

The others heard the conversation and came running. They stopped when they saw the great Chief Spearmint sitting by himself, barefoot with his feet in the creek and his hair hanging around his face. He saw his grandchildren looking at him strangely, and he said, "Children, get shed of your moccasins, and put your feet in the water. It feels very nice," he exclaimed as he took a rawhide strip from a pocket and tied his hair back.

So they did, and the five of them sat there in the late afternoon heat talking.

"You know, children, we can swim in this stream any time we want. We bathe here. We clean our clothes here. We catch fish here every day. But, how nice is it to put your feet in it for just awhile," he told them in a wise and authoritative voice.

"Do you have any leaves, Hefe?" Jake Bird asked.

From a leather sack, Chief Spearmint brought out fresh spearmint leaves for all. They sat savoring the treat, gently biting into the leaves to release the flavor.

At an early age the young Indian boy, Great Eagle, always ate spearmint leaves. His mother started giving them to him when he was a baby. Any time anyone asked for a leaf, he produced some from his sack, always willing to share. He refreshed his supply regularly from the cool interior of the forest where spearmint grew abundantly. His friends started calling him Spearmint, and the name stuck.

After a good long time in the warm sun, listening to his grandchildren chatting away like busy squirrels, the chief sent them on home.

"You children head back to the village. I will follow later," he said, then added, "Addie and Jake Bird, I will be eating with you this night."

The quartet ran off toward home. Chief Spearmint sat on the sycamore log and let his feet dry in the fading sun before he put his moccasins on. The thought of his grandchildren brought a smile to his face. But their very youth turned his thoughts to his own life, mostly gone. The smile quickly vanished as he thought about his years. *I have nothing to do. All my friends are dead, dying, or don't know who I am anymore,* he thought to himself.

He was chief, that was true, but his duties were humdrum. *I tell them when and where to plant. I tell them when to thatch their huts and when to burn the fields. A child can figure all that out just by looking at the sun and moon.*

The chief of the village was respected, but sometimes it felt more like...well, like he was tolerated, he thought to himself. *My son and daughter are busy with their families. When the grandchildren get older they will have more important things to do than dangle their feet in the water with some old man.* Chief Spearmint gave a big sigh and absentmindedly popped a leaf into his mouth.

The hunting party returned while the cousins were at the water's edge with their grandfather. The camp was teeming with activity. The hunters strutted around boasting about the game they brought back, and the women were getting the carcasses ready for butchering in the morning. The cousins picked up their pace so they could join the revelry. They knew that after dinner, there would be festivities.

After hasty meals, families left their huts and gathered at the fire ring. Drums were rhythmically beating, calling for attendance. Dancing and chanting and the drum beats, rattles, and whistle noise lasted late into the evening.

Chief Spearmint's son, Brave Bird, gave him a fresh bag of spearmint earlier in the evening, which he passed around among his family.

When Chief Spearmint rose, all sound stopped as he left the fire ring area. As he walked toward his hut, he waved his hand in a back and forth motion over his shoulder, never looking back, to let the camp know that the festivities could continue without him.

Inside, Chief Spearmint lay down on his blanket and stared at the framework of his hut. He thought about his mother and father, dead for many years, and about his wife, also dead a long time.

He gazed at an old piece of calico hanging from one of the pine branches that made up part of the structure of the hut. His thoughts turned to his sister. Soon the rhythmic beating of the drums lulled him to sleep, and he was dreaming about his sister's kidnap.

Three days after his sister's abduction, Spearmint's father and the other men returned from hunting. They dropped off the game, mounted fresh horses, and lit off after the wagons. Spearmint waited around for the riders to get out of sight and for the women to prepare the game before he snuck in the corral and selected a swift pinto pony.

He flanked his father's search party so they could not see him. Spearmint knew his father and the others would be angry if he showed up to ride along. They felt he was just a boy. But he had let the visitors take his sister, and he needed to get her back. *Some day Father will understand,* he thought to himself.

Spearmint was gazing at a beautiful vivid purple and orange sunset, the brown grass plain waved in the gentle wind. Crickets chirping lulled him toward slumber. Suddenly he stiffened when he realized he'd let his guard down. Sensing danger, he unsheathed his long knife.

"Your instincts are good, my son. But you should have been facing the other way, toward the canyon. That is the direction an attack on you would come," his father whispered in his ear.

After Spearmint's heart stopped chattering in his chest, he looked at his father and said, "I want to go along with you. I couldn't stop them. Now I need to get Sister back."

Slowly, the search party entered the settlement surrounding Mission San Jose, down the only road in or out. People stood on the wooden walks in front of the brightly painted stores and observed the proud looking group. To see Indians in town was not all that unusual.

It was rare, though, to see them on horses. Usually they tethered their mounts at the edge of town and came in on foot.

Several wagons were parked at the livery stable, and mules were in the corral. "Do you recognize any wagons, Son?"

Spearmint looked at his father and just shook his head from side to side.

"I will check with the brown robe, there," Spearmint's father said with a nod in the direction of the mission. "Go with the others, and water the horses."

Spearmint stopped in his tracks when he saw a man leave the corral area of the livery. The man was wearing a shirt made out of the same calico pattern as his sister wore when she was taken.

Spearmint took his knife out, ready to attack the white man. Before he could act, though, one of the braves grabbed his shoulder and spun him around. He silently admonished Spearmint for what he was about to do.

"He's wearing Sister's dress as a shirt. He must have…"

"They will kill you if you attack him. We will follow him, and he will tell us where your sister is," the brave said matter-of-factly.

From the other side of the street, Spearmint's father indicated with sign language that he and the brown robe were going to the lawman's office and that the search party was to move into the mission yard.

The sheriff told the padre that he didn't get involved in Indian matters, and they should seek help from the government.

With his head hung low, Spearmint's father walked back to the search party. The brown robe arranged for them to have food before they went ahead to find the government agent for Indian matters the next morning.

Spearmint was sitting on the ground eating something he had never had before and hoped he would never have again. A glint of sunlight flashed in his eyes. It was coming from an upstairs window in a building across the street.

After the others were fast asleep, Spearmint rolled out of his blanket and walked in silence to the rear of the building where the flash had come from. With determination he stepped onto the top of a water barrel and scaled up the side of the building on the rain water pipe. He moved the cloth aside and scanned the interior with a flicker of fear before he crawled inside. It was so strange for him; he had never been inside a building before. A long passage stretched out in front of him. His instinct told him that the spaces with boards in them on each side of the route were like flaps on a hut and led to another area. Light shimmered from lantern-like items on the wall. The man in the calico shirt was asleep in a chair snoring next to one of the spaces. An empty bottle of whiskey lay by him. Spearmint quietly approached; the odor from the man made him retch. The man's whisker-stubbled cheeks puffed in and out as he snored. Food or some other substance was visible in the man's full mustache.

Spearmint could hear talking coming from the area on the other side of the board. He stood staring from the man to the opening and back again. He was startled when the board moved inward. He stepped back and was instantly relieved when he saw his sister peek out at him. Her black eyes darted from Spearmint to the man. Sister turned and whispered something to others in the space.

The man in the chair woke up as the maidens, clad in shiny colored dresses, were heading for the opening Spearmint used to get in. When the man got up, the maidens scrambled to get to the outside where some scaled down and others jumped.

Spearmint followed them and was last out the window. The calico man grabbed for Spearmint as he started out to the roof and pulled him to the floor of the passage. Quick as a flash, Spearmint was on his feet facing the man. They grappled, and Spearmint hit the man in his flabby stomach, causing him to grunt and bend over in pain. Spearmint spun the man around and pushed him into one of the boards head first. The man was dazed as he turned around to sit, legs sprawled out in front of him, only to see Spearmint standing over him with a piece of the calico shirt in his hand. The man pulled a pistol from his holster, and Spearmint kicked it out of his hand. The calico man lunged for Spearmint's legs, but he just danced away. That gave the man time to stand up, and he pulled a long knife as he did so; Spearmint pulled his knife too. Swiftly, the man lunged at Spearmint and sliced him deeply in the area between his neck and collar bone, making the hand that he, himself, was holding his knife in, useless. The pain was terrible, but Spearmint came back and knocked the knife out of the man's hand, Then he hit the calico man in the throat with his good fist. The man fell back gasping for air.

Spearmint leapt through the window and fell to the ground just as his people rode up. His father alit his horse and helped his son get astride the pinto pony. His eyes lingered on Spearmint's bloody wounds, but they both knew there was no time to fix the injury now, so the search party thundered out of town with the rescued maidens.

A few miles down the road, Spearmint's father reigned in his horse. "Ho!" he called, holding up his hand. The party stopped.

"We cannot have the white men following us back to camp."

The group dismounted and ran the horses behind the boulders, where the animals could wade in the shallow stream. The braves set up among the rocks to prepare for ambush, should a party be following them.

This also allowed time to treat Spearmint's wound. He felt lightheaded because of the loss of blood. His father placed him on a blanket and administered to him. Sister kneeled by him and soothed him with a damp cloth to his forehead. She kept whispering how brave he was to come and rescue her.

"I'm so thankful that you are my brother," she said before she leaned over and kissed his forehead.

"Yes, my son, you have done well. Any father would be proud to call you son." With that, his father wiped a stray sweaty tousle of hair from Spearmint's brow just before he fell asleep.

The white men never did follow, and the rescue party returned to their camp with much jubilation.

———— ❖ ————

Chief Spearmint awoke with a start. His grandchildren's dog was sniffing around his face. "Ugh, get out you yellow mongrel!" he said as he wiped at the cold damp spot left behind by the dog's nose. The mutt just stood there wagging his tail. He sat up on his blanket, rubbing his neck and shoulder. From outside, a stream of bubbling giggles flowed into his tent. Quietly getting up, he grabbed a wildcat skin, complete with head, from the floor, put it over his head, and got ready to pull the flap back.

The yellow dog growled and barked loudly at the wildcat-bedecked chief, startling Chief Spearmint, who stumbled outside, which in turn startled his grandchildren.

Grandfather and grandchildren frolicked on the ground; all the while, the yellow dog was barking and wagging its tail as he circled the wrestling match. "I'll teach you to send in your dog to wake me," Spearmint said in a phony angry voice.

—◆—

Jake Bird was by the creek practicing with the sling. No matter how hard he tried, he could not get a stone to fly to the other side of the creek. All his attempts fell short of imaginary targets. The blue jays squawked at him like they were laughing. His grandfather watched him from behind some reeds.

Jake threw the sling down disgustedly and sat by the creek pouting.

"Why such a long face, Grandson?"

"Oh Hefe, no matter how hard I try, I can't get these stones to fly as far as I want them to," he said as he pointed to the sling on the ground.

"Have you tried everything?"

"Yes, I have. Easy Eagle told me to use larger rocks. Addie told me to just throw rocks, because the sling is no good."

"Let me see you use it, Jake Bird."

Jake retrieved the sling from the sand, picked up a stone and twirled the sling a few times before letting it fly. "See, Hefe," he said as the rock splashed in the water.

"I don't think you have tried everything, Jake Bird."

"I have, too, Hefe. I am just no good at this."

"You have not tried everything, Jake," his grandfather said sternly.

"What do you mean, Hefe?"

"You haven't asked me to help you."

A look of understanding crossed Jake's face. "Will you help me with the sling, Hefe?" he asked.

Chief Spearmint sat on the bank of the creek and patted the ground next to him for Jake Bird to sit. He plopped down on the ground and took the spearmint leaf his grandfather offered him.

"The sling is a very old weapon, Jake. It has been used to kill game and enemies for ages. It is easy to use once you understand the parts of it. This leather sac in the middle is the cradle. Find stones that are not too large for it. The lengths of rawhide on either side of the cradle are the same distance end to end. Place the stone in the cradle; twirl the sling over your head before you release one length. If your target is far away, more twirling is needed. Remember the older you get the farther you can sling a stone."

Chief Spearmint had Jake repeat what he was told about the sling. Then Chief Spearmint showed him how the sling was used.

"Pick a target for me to aim at, Jake Bird."

"That rock formation on the other side, Hefe, by that felled sapling."

Chief Spearmint got to his feet and smoothed his plaid shirt, slapped at his buckskin pants, which raised dust, and picked up a stone, placing it in the cradle. He twirled the sling over his head about six or seven times and then released one side of the sling and the stone hurled just over the rock formation.

"Wow wee, Hefe! That was very far!"

"You try it now, Jake Bird."

"What do you want me to hit, Hefe?"

"How about the other side of the creek?" Chief Spearmint replied with a chuckle.

Jake stood up and did as his grandfather instructed. The stone landed on the other side.

He jumped and cried out, "Hey, it worked! That was so much easier!"

Jake Bird looked in amazement where the stone landed on the far bank. He kept looking at the sling and to where the stone fell. Then he looked at his grandfather and grinned.

"Very good, Jake," Chief Spearmint said to his grandson proudly.

As he and his Hefe walked away, Jake was beaming from ear to ear. "Grandfather, you know how to do so many things! You are the smartest grandfather ever!"

As they walked down the path toward camp, Chief Spearmint looked over at his grandson. Joy played across the lad's face as he turned the sling over in his hands and excitement put a bounce in his step. The chief felt a swelling in his chest: pride, happiness, and great satisfaction. *That*, he thought to himself, *is what I am supposed to do with the rest of my life. Impart whatever knowledge I have left to my grandchildren.*

His gait became more purposeful, and he felt magnificent, better than he had in a long, long time.

———◆———

From that day on, Chief Spearmint and his grandchildren spent every morning together, walking, looking, and listening to what nature had to offer.

To begin, the children learned about taking care of the land, because the land would take care of them: where to build fires for cooking; when to burn off the land for new gardens; what to plant and when.

He also taught them that their parents were to be respected and that they also had wisdom that must be learned.

The grandchildren were not the only ones learning lessons. Chief Spearmint was learning that each of his grandchildren was unique. The girls were competitive and just as anxious to learn how to hunt and trap as the boys. The boys, on the other hand, resented the girls learning a man's type of work. The two older ones, Addie Bird and Easy Eagle, jockeyed for dominance and numerous arguments would erupt that took all of Chief Spearmint's negotiating skills to resolve. He would not favor one side or the other.

At the edge of the forest on a fine summer's day filled with the laziness of a warm sun and chirping birds, the children sat with their Hefe. The boys and girls had been arguing about who should go on an overnight campout in the forest with Hefe. Of course, the boys said that the girls should stay home, and the girls said that it was not fair if they couldn't go.

"Sea Eagle, I want you and Jake Bird to go and get a bundle of reeds from the pile we keep for thatching roofs, and bring them back up here. Now go. And do this together," their Hefe instructed with a finger pointed to the sky.

Sea Eagle dashed off immediately, but Jake Bird shuffled along behind her.

Chief Spearmint, Easy Eagle, and Addie Bird watched when they returned. Jake was struggling with a bundle as he came back up the slope. Sea Eagle repeatedly tried to help her cousin. "I can do it!" Jake Bird snapped at her more than once.

"What do you see?" Chief Spearmint asked.

"If they worked together it would be easier," Addie Bird replied.

"What do you think, Easy Eagle?"

"I think that Jake is able to bring that bundle up here, Hefe."

"That is true, Easy Eagle. But if he let Sea Eagle help him it would be easier," Addie Bird chimed in.

When Jake dropped the bundle at the feet of his Hefe, he sat down and huffed, out of breath.

"Are you tired Jake Bird?"

"Yes, Hefe, I am. That is heavy," he answered as he pointed to the bundle.

"Why didn't you let your cousin help? It would have been much easier."

Jake just shrugged his shoulders and scratched at the marks the reeds left on the flesh of his stomach and chest.

"Addie Bird, bring me one of those reeds from the bundle."

Addie got up and brought a reed to her grandfather.

"Break it in half, Addie Bird."

The reed snapped easily in two.

"Easy Eagle, would you please bring me the entire bundle?"

He placed the bundle down in front of his grandfather, and all the cousins kneeled in front of their Hefe.

"Can you break it? Can you break the bundle?" Go ahead each of you try."

After each had tried, Chief Spearmint said, "A reed taken from the bundle and broken represents somebody alone. But if the reed remains part of the bundle, it can't be broken. You see children, the bundle represents the family. And a family that stays together will not be broken."

He looked into the eyes of each of his grandchildren and said, "This is your most important lesson so far. You are family, and families are made of men and women, girls and boys. Help each other when help is needed."

He brushed his hands off, and stood up from the reed bundle. "All of us will go on the overnight campout."

The looks of understanding that he got back filled him with pride.

"My family," he said as he pounded his fist over his heart.

———————

"Father, you are the Elder, and I respect you. So what I am going to say is going to sound bad-mannered, but I am just repeating words from others."

Chief Spearmint and his son, Brave Bird, were sitting on a log in front of Brave Bird's hut. A draft cooled the air.

"You have a look of distress, Son. It is best to get it out."

"Others in the camp are saying that you do not act like the great chief you once were."

"It is true; I am not the chief I was once. I will be dead soon and another will become chief."

"It is not because you are old. Men are saying that Chief Spearmint plays with children and shouldn't be chief."

"What do you think, Son?" Chief Spearmint looked at his son waiting for an answer.

Brave Bird had high cheek bones and shiny black hair, just like his mother. Sometimes when Chief Spearmint looked in his son's dark eyes, he felt he was looking into the spirit of his dead wife. *He is wise like his mother. She always deliberated before she spoke,* he thought to himself.

"That is a difficult question, Father. I know that you are teaching the children lessons, and that is important. They love you very much. But you are losing the respect of the village."

"As long as my mind is able, I will impart wisdom to my grandchildren, and I don't care one grain of sand what others are saying. Being chief is thorny. At this time of my life I have nothing to do. I never thought I would live this long but being with my grandchildren inspires me to go on."

Father and son sat silently watching the sun set. The clouds were a vivid orange and started to thin out. Something continued to trouble Brave Bird, something he hadn't been able to say.

"What is it, Son? Is there more you wish to say?"

Brave Bird turned those deep eyes on him and nodded once. Still he took a few more moments in the remnants of the lingering sunlight before he finally spoke.

"A tribunal has been called for. We are meeting in the morning at the lodge. I was asked to invite you, so you can explain yourself to the council."

Chief Spearmint nodded back. "I will come." He turned back to the deepening crimson along the horizon. He shared the rest of the sunset in quiet peace with his son.

When Chief Spearmint entered the lodge, the smell of tobacco greeted him, and a gray haze hung over the heads of the men sitting in a circle. All heads turned, and all talking stopped as Chief Spearmint sat in his spot.

"Brave Bird has relayed to me your concerns about my loss of respect," Chief Spearmint announced in a strong but cordial voice as he sat cross-legged. "So I have come up with a solution; I will step down from my place as chief. We shall select a new chief this very morning."

There were murmurs and whispers exchanged for several minutes. Finally one of the older braves said, "Chief Spearmint, do you not wish to hear about our concerns regarding your loss of our respect?"

"No, I don't. I think I already know, and I care not about your concerns. But know this," he said with a raised finger, "as long as I can, I will spend time with my grandchildren, or any other children, imparting knowledge and legend about our people and the wonders of nature. That is the last decision I make as your chief."

After many hours of arguing and discussing qualified candidates, the tribunal selected Brave Bird as the new chief, succeeding his father. When all was done, Brave Bird stood and ended the tribunal with only a few words. "I shall reach down deep inside myself to find all the Great Spirit has granted me, and I shall lead you with all my heart and all my cunning. I shall strive to lead as well as my honored father," he said with reverence. "But I can only hope to come close. I beg you, Father, to aid and advise me until I can fill the mantle of chief you so deftly wore."

Chief Spearmint smiled such a smile that it split his weathered wrinkled face from ear to ear.

"A chief is always there for his people, and a father for his son," Spearmint said in a soft voice.

When Chief Spearmint walked from the lodge he felt like a huge stone was removed from his back. His son was walking with him. Both men had smiles on their faces, each for a different reason.

"Son, I know you will do well as chief, and you will receive the respect you deserve from me and all the other members of the tribe. Now we must prepare for your ceremony."

That evening, braves were dressed in all their finest costumes, and the beat of the drums played rhythmically. Deer and rabbit were cooked on an open spit, and wild onions and carrots made up the remainder of the meal. Brave Bird, in a ceremonial war bonnet, along with his wife, White Sparrow, and their children, Addie Bird and Jake Bird, sat in the place of honor at the fire ring.

Chief Spearmint rose and stood in front of his son. He removed a rawhide neck piece with an ancient bear's fang on the end. He lifted it up in the firelight and turned so all could see. "This necklace was given to me by my father when I was young," he sang out in a voice he raised so all could hear. "He told me it was a reward for my bravery, and I have cherished it since I got it, both as a gift from my father, and because it signifies that all ended well for Sister and her friends on a day that could have gone very wrong." He strode to Brave Bird. "Stand, my son."

And Brave Bird did as he was asked. Chief Spearmint took the two ends of the thong and reached behind Brave Bird's neck where he tied off the leather ends.

Brave Bird lifted the fang from his breast and looked at it. Then he engulfed it with his hand.

"Father, I shall honor you every time I see this, every time I feel it, just as you honor me with this gift." He leaned forward and kissed his father on the cheek.

Then he strode over to where his sister, Smiling Eagle, and her husband, Moon Eagle, sat with their children, Easy Eagle and Sea Eagle. Brave Bird stood in front of them, extended both hands and had them rise. He led them back to where his family was, including Chief Spearmint. Both families stood together, and the camp cheered and whooped. Chief Spearmint looked down and saw that all four of his grandchildren were gazing at him and smiling. A small tear formed in Chief Spearmint's eye as he grinned back at them, and he pumped his fist over his heart. His grandchildren, in unison pumped their chests, which only brought more tears making a visible trail down his leathery face.

— • —

The four cousins' hearts thumped in their chests as they trudged up the slope from the camp toward the trail that led to the forest. Each had not been able to sleep the night before, but was nonetheless excited and alert. They each carried a rolled blanket under their arms and a leather pack with supplies over their shoulders. All were wearing buckskin blouses and pants. Their Hefe walked behind them. At the entrance to the forest trail the four stopped and waited for their grandfather.

"Well, what are you waiting for?" Chief Spearmint asked in a false cantankerous tone.

"Maybe you should lead, Hefe," Addie Bird replied in an uneasy voice.

The temperature was markedly cooler only a few steps into the forest, and the smells were strange and appealing to them. There was no cooking aroma or smell from the corral. Instead the aroma was a cool and refreshing odor of bay and oak trees, which was very pleasing. The light changed also. Sunlight shone down in slashes through the tree canopy. Songbirds ceased warbling as the group continued farther into the depths of the forest. Each child grinned as they looked up the trail toward unknown discoveries with ever alert eyes.

At each different species of tree, Chief Spearmint told his grandchildren what the wood was good for. They learned that one tree was better for the bow and another was better for the arrow. The boys had learned this before, but listened to their Hefe as if it was new.

"What is off the trail, Hefe?" Jake Bird asked after a couple of hours walking.

"Let's take a look, children," Chief Spearmint replied.

The ground cover of leaves crackled under each footfall, creating a noise that interrupted the serenity of the forest. A large buck bolted from behind an outcropping of rocks, startling the group.

"We would starve if we were hunting," Chief Spearmint said. "We must walk softly to sneak up on prey. Let's try and walk silently, but swiftly around the rocks and back here. If the birds start singing again, we will know that we were quiet enough. I will lead." He walked around the rocks with the lightness of a feather, which impressed the children.

"Now you go, Addie Bird," Chief Spearmint whispered.

She was around the rock quietly and rapidly. The last to go was Easy Eagle. When he took off, Chief Spearmint signaled to the others to hide behind trees, and he followed Easy Eagle around the rocks. When Easy got back to his starting point he was startled to find the others gone. Before he became too anxious, he heard a twig snap behind him and spun around to see his grandfather.

"Hefe, that is not funny."

"It wasn't meant to be funny, grandson. It was a lesson. You went around the tree, and we snuck off without you knowing it. It was like you were lost. What would you do? Stay here or go back the way you came?"

Easy Eagle said he didn't know.

"Well, if you are positive you headed in the right direction, stay where you are. The others might be lost."

"I still think it was a bad trick, Hefe," he said sadly.

"You are the oldest boy, and I thought you would understand, I'm sorry," he said in a conspiratorial tone.

"Come out, the rest of you."

All ran back with laughter, not because they were part of a trick, but because they had completed a mission successfully. Sea Eagle was not with the group, however. She had snuck, quietly and quickly, around to the rear of the assembly standing at the rock outcropping.

She stopped when she heard them yelling for her. She could not be seen and enjoyed the trick *she* was playing. Silently she walked up and stood next to her grandfather.

After several seconds she said, "Are you looking for me?" This startled Chief Spearmint. When he started to admonish her, she exclaimed in a perfect imitation of her beloved Hefe, "It wasn't meant to be funny, Hefe. It was a lesson." All laughed because the youngest cousin had, in fact, played a trick on all of them.

Back on the trail they walked single file deeper and deeper into the woods. The extra tugging at the back of their calves told them they were walking uphill, though with all the trees, it was hard to see that. They walked hour after hour; resting every so often. It was getting darker as the sunlight faded. They stopped at a clearing along a river that appeared to have been used as a campsite before. It was flat and there was a small fire ring.

"Tonight we will eat the food you brought with you, and tomorrow we will need to hunt to eat."

Each child looked perplexed. "Hefe, we didn't bring anything to eat," Jake Bird whined.

"We didn't know we were supposed to bring food," Addie Bird said worriedly.

Chief Spearmint knew that the grandchildren would not bring food. Beforehand, he told their parents to purposely not mention meals or food.

"Well, it is a good thing I was hungry when I packed, and brought enough. Addie, I want you and Easy to gather wood for a fire. Make sure you bring small pieces for starting and larger ones for sustaining the fire. Sea Eagle, I want you and Jake to take these vegetables to the river and wash them." He gave them bundles of carrots and onions, and I have enough pemmican for everyone."

When all had returned from their assignments, he showed them how to light a fire using a flint and knife. He gathered dry leaves and placed them in the fire ring. Using the flint and knife, he successfully sparked a fire in the leaves. When they were aflame, he placed smaller twigs on the leaves, and when the twigs flamed, larger pieces were put on the fire.

Chief Spearmint knew that his grandchildren could start a fire and had done so at their huts. But doing it in the forest was different and the lesson seemed important.

"How are we going to cook the food, Hefe?"

"We aren't going to cook them, Sea Eagle. We are going to eat them raw. We are not home now, and don't have the nice things like a spit to roast meats or pots to boil things. But we will make do."

The fire was roaring nicely, and all were sitting staring at the flames with their own thoughts, sucking on spearmint leaves. The forest was quiet except for an occasional hoot from an owl.

"The next time we take a trip, I want all of you to remember to bring food. Plan for meals," Chief Spearmint explained.

As the fire started to go down, Easy Eagle picked up another log and placed it in the coals.

"Hefe, when you were a boy, which hut was yours"? Jake asked.

"I didn't live in our village. I grew up about four days ride away," he said in a sleepy voice.

"Father told us you saved your sister at the mission. Isn't the mission just over our hills?" Addie asked.

"I did save my sister, but not at the mission over the hill. There are lots of missions. The place I'm from is near Mission San Jose."

"We have a long walk ahead of us in the morning, so we should sleep now."

"I want to sleep next to Hefe!" Addie Bird and Sea Eagle exclaimed in unison.

"Go ahead," Easy Eagle chimed. "Jake Bird and I will be over there," he indicated with a toss of his head.

As they lay on their blankets, each reflecting on the day, the forest came alive with unfamiliar noises; birds squawked and varmints chattered. Before he fell asleep, Chief Spearmint placed two large logs on the fire. An owl screeched hauntingly, and Sea Eagle and Addie Bird snuggled closer to their Hefe. Sometime in the middle of the night, mountain lions could be heard fighting and hissing in the distance. Chief Spearmint sensed movement on the other side of the fire and noticed Easy and Jake scrambling with their blankets around them to the safety of their Hefe's area.

———◦•◦———

In the morning the hike was definitely harder as the trail got even steeper. The trees, too, were different and had a unique fragrance to them. They were a type of pine that could be used to build things.

"If you look at the frame of the lodge and the sweat house you will notice they are made from this type of tree.

Rock formations were more frequent higher up the hill, and there were fewer trees.

"How much farther, Hefe?" Sea Eagle asked.

"We will stop for a meal soon. There is a nice camp just ahead."

<hr />

Sunlight was abundant at the crest of the hill. It was as if the forest stopped. Just before the children reached the peak, Chief Spearmint stopped them and had them stand still while he moved ahead of them.

"I want you to close your eyes and not open them until I tell you to. I will take the first of you by the hand and you will take the hand of the one behind you. I will not let you fall or trip, so don't be scared."

Chief Spearmint's grandchildren stood in full sunshine for the first time in a day and a half. Their eyes were closed and stayed closed while their Hefe positioned them side by side.

"Now you may open your eyes."

The view before them was something completely unexpected. Their eyes grew wide and their mouths hung open. From the top of the hill, the other side swept dramatically down to a meadow with tall, light brown grass that swayed in the gentle breeze. Wildflowers of many colors nodded weakly, but vividly with the current of air. Beyond the meadow lay a huge expanse of bright blue water. The water was moving toward the land with large silent waves, which stopped after turning white with foam and moving back away from the land, only to repeat the cycle over and over.

Chief Spearmint gazed at his grandchildren and enjoyed the astonishment in their eyes, which were as round as river rocks. When he was brought here for the first time, he was much older than these children, but his amazement was just as real.

"Great Spirit, Hefe. That is a wide river. I can't see the other side," Jake Bird said in a whisper.

"It is a sea, not a river," Sea Eagle said. "My father's tribe is from the sea area. That's how I got my name, isn't it Hefe?"

"That is right, Sea Eagle," Chief Spearmint answered as he gazed into her dark and flashing eyes.

"All rivers and streams flow to it. It is full of fish and shells. Some of the shells have food inside," their Hefe explained.

"Can we go to the sea, Hefe?" Addie Bird asked.

"We will be there very soon."

The path led down to a creek that flowed through the meadow toward the sea. After crossing a rutted road they stopped.

"This road is the road that wagons take to get to our village," Chief Spearmint explained as he pointed down the road.

"It looks like it drops off into the water," Easy Eagle replied.

"It leads back around and in the direction of the trail."

In the dirt Chief Spearmint used a twig and drew a map that showed their camp, the trail, the road, and the sea. All the children gave a nod of understanding.

The creek to the sea widened, and large sandy banks sat on each side. As the group got closer to the sea, the noise of water hitting land was deafening. The ground was all sand as they approached the sea. They were shocked at how cold the water was.

Jake Bird dipped his hands into the water and brought some to his mouth to take a sip. He quickly spit it out with a look of distaste.

"I know that it tastes bad, but, although you can't drink it, the salt water is very good for your health." As he was talking, Chief Spearmint removed his clothes. With arms stretched out as if to greet the rolling waves that left foamy trails across the beach, he ran into the ocean. His grandchildren did the same, and soon all were bobbing in the sea laughing heartily.

Refreshed, the group sat in the warm sand looking and listening to the sea.

"Can we sleep here tonight, Hefe?" Sea Eagle asked.

"No child, there is no food here. We need to catch some fish in the river."

"What about the food in the shells, Hefe?" Addie asked.

"They are called clams, and they are under the sand too far out. The fish in the sea are out far, too."

Halfway back up the meadow, they stopped for the day under a stand of sycamore trees along the creek. They created a fire ring and gathered wood for a fire. Chief Spearmint showed the children how to make a basket out of twigs. He wove the wood into a cone shaped container. Where the creek slowly made a turn to the sea, Chief Spearmint stood throwing stones into the current, steering fish over to a small pool on the other side where Easy Eagle was waiting for fish to retreat near some rocks. The fish swam over the basket and Easy quickly raised the basket with a rawhide tether. Gleefully he handed the basket with two large trout inside to Addie Bird on shore. By the time the fire was ready, there were enough fish for all to eat their fill.

Chief Spearmint had the children use their own knives to sharpen the ends of sticks to spear the fish to cook over the fire.

Before they returned to their home, they visited the sea one more time. After a morning swim, they were reluctantly on their way home. On top of the hill above the meadow, they stopped to take one last look at the sea. The children drank in the image, and each slowly turned and descended into the forest.

<hr />

"Did the children behave, Father-in-Law?" White Sparrow asked after the return from the journey.

"They were perfect. We had a wonderful time. I would like to take them again," he answered with a rhythm in his voice.

As Chief Spearmint walked to his hut, he noticed his grandchildren talking with their friends. He saw their trip to the sea unfold with the gestures his grandchildren used. Addie was mimicking their walk around the huge boulder. Jake moved his hand back and forth, like the sea. Sea Eagle showed off a large shell she brought with her, and Easy Eagle pointed up to the path. The other children sat in awe as they were told about the adventures and the wonders of the forest and sea.

Before he raised the flap to his hut, Hefe turned toward his grandchildren again and saw them looking at him. His grandchildren stepped from the crowd they were talking with, and each pumped their fists over their hearts. Chief Spearmint did the same with a grin from ear to ear.

Once inside his hut he collapsed from exhaustion.

"I am getting too old for this," he mumbled as he fell into a dreamless slumber.

<hr />

When the leaves began to change Chief Spearmint was getting ready to take his grandchildren on another excursion into the forest. It was to be a shorter trip this time; they would not visit the sea. Hunting for small game was the lesson he planned to teach this time. When he was explaining his plans to his children and their spouses, the women looked at each other.

Chief Spearmint could feel the weight of unsaid words settling on his shoulders. "What is it?" he asked.

His daughter-in-law, White Sparrow, said, "Smiling Eagle and I think that the girls will stay home. They need to learn things that women need to know."

Chief Spearmint scratched his chin thoughtfully and looked to his son and son-in-law. Both diverted their eyes and he realized there was to be no more discussion. Their wives had spoken. And a wife's word carried much weight in family matters.

"They need to know how to make bread and cook and clean, Father," Smiling Eagle added.

"They are going to be very sad when they find out they cannot go," Chief Brave Bird said. "But they do need to learn woman things," he further stated as he arose.

"I will tell them the bad news then," Chief Spearmint said as he exited his son's hut.

⸺•⸺

"Oh, Hefe, you can't leave us home!" Addie Bird wailed. Sea Eagle sat on the bank of the creek next to her cousin, sniffling.

"Do you remember when I told you that we are family? And that family sticks together?" They both nodded in unity. "Well, this is the same thing. The mother has spoken and wants her daughter to learn how to do woman things. This doesn't mean that we won't go on a trip together. It means just not this time."

"How can this help the family stick together, Hefe?" Sea Eagle asked.

"Being obedient is part of being family. Comply with your parent's wishes and demands. They know what is best for you. Your father and uncle and most of the men are going to Mission San Juan Bautista to do business, and your mothers need extra help."

"Yes, Hefe," the girls mumbled together, though they didn't lift their disappointed eyes from staring at their own feet.

The boys started up the path with their grandfather. Just before the trio entered the forest, they turned. Addie Bird and Sea Eagle still

227

stood below them near the huts. All three pumped their fists over their hearts. The two girls half-heartedly did the same and then turned to shuffle off.

—•—•—

Chief Spearmint and his grandsons' sensed trouble before they exited the forest trail to head down to the village. The smoke smell was different, and as they came into the sunlight, they heard screams. All three stopped dead in their tracks and gazed with the intensity of a hunting cat. It took a moment to understand what was going on, but then Easy Eagle cried out "No!" and started to run down the slope toward the melee. Chief Spearmint sprinted a few steps after him and grabbed his shoulder roughly. Easy Eagle fell to the ground. Before he could say anything, his Hefe put a finger to his mouth and motioned for them to retreat to the cover of the forest.

"Hefe, we have to go down and save them," Easy Eagle hissed.

"The first thing we need to do is figure out who or what the enemy is. Then we can know better what to plan."

—•—•—

The white men had entered the camp at a gallop, causing dogs and chickens to scurry out of danger. They got off the wagons and started taking hostages right away. Whiskey bottles were passed around, and as the day wore on, the white men got drunker. Woman and maidens were beaten and raped. Young braves tried to rescue the females, but were beaten, and some shot.

From a vantage point several hundred yards lateral to the forest trail, Chief Spearmint, Easy Eagle, and Jake Bird observed the events taking place in the community. Several bodies were lying prone near the corral. Two covered wagons were parked and the horses that pulled the wagons stood calmly swishing their tails, despite the slaughter happening nearby.

"Jake, count how many men in hats you see. Easy, can you see any saddled horses? I am going to sneak down to that boulder for a better look. Once I am there and you have the numbers of men in hats and saddled horses, come down one by one. Go quietly and quickly, just like we did in the forest the first time. Remember the birds?"

The two grandsons watched their grandfather descend the slope with the tenacity of a much younger man. Jake and Easy looked at each other and each gave his chest a pump. Their cheeks were flushed, and their black eyes surveyed the best route to take to fulfill the instructions their Hefe had given them.

Chief Spearmint watched his grandsons take off on their missions and knew he was putting them in harm's way, but needed to have some sort of reconnaissance so he could come up with counterattack measures. "This is the only way," he said under his breath. "My, but they are speedy."

"As near as I can tell, Hefe, there are six men," Jake said in a rapid whisper.

"I don't see any saddled horses, Hefe. They must have all rode in on the wagons," Easy Eagle reported after the two caught up with their Hefe.

The crack of a rifle shot sent the three farther down behind their hiding spot. Jake's and Easy's eyes were as wide as the sky. It was the first time they had experienced that sound. Chief Spearmint motioned for them to stay down as he peeked over the top of the boulder. He saw another body, an old woman, lying dead by the fire ring, a tomahawk still in her hand. "Shrewd Owl, you cantankerous old woman, I hope the forest spirits guided your hand to strike as truly as your tongue ever could!" Chief Spearmint whispered under his breath.

Maidens—daughters, and granddaughters of his friends—were running from the attackers, a few were more than half naked. Their screams rang in his ears and raised ghosts of another time he'd heard maidens screaming, seen them running for their lives. His sister's face haunted his memory, made more vivid by the screams and clash below. But this time was different; the fight was on his territory, not in some hallway of a hotel.

——◆——

The screaming ended first, only to be replaced by wailing and weeping, but that, too, ceased as dusk started to fall. It was strange to look at the camp and not see cooking fires. The attackers tied the captured near the fire ring. Men in hats dragged bodies toward the pile of debris from the corral. Red Kite, Falcon Song, River Raven…Chief

Spearmint watched as they dragged these good men and four more through the dirt. Chief Spearmint looked for his own son. His heart felt a short relief that his was not among the bodies, but that relief was sunk by guilt at that momentary flutter; he'd been chief many years. Were those seven not all his sons, too?

Chief Spearmint kept the boys busy with spying and other tasks to keep their minds off the horror below.

Just before complete darkness, Chief Spearmint sent Jake Bird to survey the camp.

When he returned, he said, "Hefe, I saw movement by the creek. I think someone was trying to signal to me. Maybe some of our people are hiding along the creek."

<hr />

White Sparrow, Addie Bird, Smiling Eagle, and Sea Eagle had been bathing in the creek when the attack started. It wasn't long before the mothers wished their daughter's had gone with their grandfather.

Just after the start of the assault, the two mothers whisked their daughters away from the village and hid them downstream.

After night started to fall, White Sparrow announced, "We are going to see if we can find out what is going on. You stay right here. Do you understand?" Both young girls nodded.

"What if you don't come back?" Sea Eagle asked her mother.

"Child, you stay under cover," Smiling Eagle replied as she hugged her daughter.

The screams off in the distance seemed to go on forever. The blood-curdling cries caused them to hunch down further as if in an attempt to get under the ground and away from the agony going on in their camp.

"Hurry, Sea Eagle. We need to find my father and the other men that went to the mission. I don't think our mothers are coming back."

"You don't think…" Sea Eagle started to say.

"Hush! We need to get away from here," Addie said with hard eyes.

"How will we find our way?"

"We will follow the wagon road until we get there," Addie Bird replied with hesitation.

The two started down the wagon road to get help. They traveled until it was so dark that they couldn't see to go any farther. At first light they started off again. About midmorning, they came to a fork in the road.

"I think that way leads to the sea, don't you, Sea Eagle?"

Shrugging, Sea Eagle said, "Are we sure that our fathers would take the road to the mission instead of a trail?"

Addie Bird stopped and thought for a moment. "You are probably right, Sea Eagle. They would take a shorter route."

At the top of the hill, above the wagon road, they saw a trail and ran down to it. Relatively fresh horse droppings encouraged the two and inspired them to go on.

An hour before the sun broke over the hills on the horizon, Chief Spearmint, Easy Eagle, and Jake Bird skirted the camp, crossed the wagon road, and silently entered the creek bed. Walking in the creek, they came upon Smiling Eagle and White Sparrow. With hushed whispers and hugs, they reunited.

"We hid the girls away for their safety," White Sparrow told them when the trio looked around.

"Where are they?" Easy Eagle asked.

Their anguished looks said they didn't know where their daughters were.

"The cries and screams coming from the camp..." Smiling Eagle said with faltering voice, "They will haunt me forever. I just can't get it out of my mind. I think each scream is Sea Eagle calling for me."

Chief Spearmint took control and in an authoritative voice said, "All of you listen to me. We are going to cause a diversion. Jake, I want you to follow the creek past the corral and approach the wagons from the other side. Cut the reins on their horses, but don't scare them right away. Go back and let our horses out. Scare the spirit out of them. Our horses will start running and their horses will follow. While the men try to get their horses, the rest of us will free the hostages. Does everybody understand?"

The thundering of the hooves aroused the sleeping men, some of them still groggy from too much whiskey. The stampede ran right through the camp, knocking huts down and creating clouds of dust. The white men ran around in the dust storm, tripping over each other, waving their arms, and shouting. Their gruff cursing voices, echoed off the hillsides surrounding the camp.

As the dust settled, they did indeed take off down the road chasing the horses. Chief Spearmint and his family were ready to go in as soon as the last man had turned his back. The boys, the women, and Chief Spearmint loosed the captives and motioned them to head for the creek.

But it wasn't over. When the white men got back with some of their horses, they found the camp deserted. With cries of fury, they lit torches and burned the huts.

Chief Brave Bird and his group saw the thick dark smoke and galloped faster toward home. Addie Bird rode on the back of her father's pony and Sea Eagle was astride with her father. When they raced into camp, they found that the white men in hats had left, leaving the village—or what was left of it—vacant. The dead by the corral gave the returning braves an indication of what a night of terror their families had endured. It was even worse than Addie and Sea Eagle had described.

An assessment of the dead and those missing was tallied. Brave Bird gave the order for seven riders, led by his brother-in-law, Moon Eagle, to go after the wagons and bring back any captives they may have taken. With knowing nods, the braves mounted fresh horses and went after the wagons.

Smoke was starting to wane when Chief Spearmint gave a bird's whistle from the creek. Chief Brave Bird answered back and met his father and wife there. The glassy-eyed look of unshed tears in Chief Spearmint's eyes told him there was more trouble. "It's Jake Bird—he was taken by the men."

Brave Bird's sinewy arms flexed, and his fists clenched and unclenched repeatedly. Chief Spearmint told him, with pride, about the distraction and the role Jake Bird played in it.

"Why do they take our people, Mother?" Addie asked as the two of them rummaged through their burned out hut.

Delicately she told her daughter, "Some of them are sold as slaves to work on big farms. Others are kept by the white men and travel with them, taking them far from home."

Addie shuddered as she thought about her little brother all alone with strangers.

By midafternoon, the braves returned with four captives, Jake Bird included. Some of the braves had fresh scalps on their reins as they slowly rode into the camp.

All those preparing new huts stopped working to observe the group. Chief Brave Bird nodded to each man as they rode by. Moon Eagle stopped and dropped Jake Bird off at his father's feet. Brave Bird nodded to his brother-in-law and gave him a grateful pat on his arm. White Sparrow came running and scooped her son in her arms and hugged and kissed him. Addie was dancing around him in delight. Father and son locked eyes, and Brave Bird knew that his young son had seen some things he shouldn't have at such an early age.

―――― • ――――

That evening the departed were honored as their bodies were put on an elevated funeral pyre. The slow melodic beating of drums sounded throughout the night and until daylight.

The next evening, the heroism of Chief Spearmint and his family was honored. All in camp showed their gratitude by bestowing any goods they had left, to Chief Spearmint, which he graciously declined. He told the donors to keep their belongings and rebuild.

A young girl tried to hand her doll to Chief Spearmint. He told her, "Bring me some leaves from time to time. You keep your doll. And always obey your parents."

The little girl started to cry, and Sea Eagle said, "Hefe, her father and mother were killed."

Chief Spearmint hugged the girl and looked to Brave Bird.

"This child will be raised by all in this camp. She is *our* child," Brave Bird announced. "You will be taken care of. That is a promise, child."

Chief Spearmint was busy sifting through the ashes, found the scrap of calico from his hut, and put it in his pocket.

He sensed that people were looking at him. He turned around, and his four grandchildren were standing at the edge of his burned hut. Their faces showed pain that would remain for quite some time.

They have the look of old people. They need to be young again, he thought to himself.

He sat on a log, the two younger grandchildren on each knee and the two older ones standing at his legs.

Words weren't spoken, but long-lasting embraces took place. The tears on all their faces said many things and steeled their love.

The quartet walked away from their grandfather's side. Spearmint turned to continue his chores, when Addie said in a loud voice, "Hefe?"

"Yes," he replied as he turned around. All his grandchildren pumped their hearts.

Spearmint fell to his knees, raised his arms to the heavens and wept.

———◆———

"When will you come back, Hefe?" Addie asked with a catch in her throat.

He was tightening his gear onto a brown pack horse. The horse he was going to ride stood snorting and swishing its tail.

"In the spring, child. Maybe sooner. If I can't find Sister, then I'll be home before the rains.

"Well, where does she live, Hefe?" Easy Eagle asked.

"The last I heard, she is near the mission in Santa Clara along a creek called Los Gatos."

The children were standing and looking miserable.

"Please don't be sad; I'll miss you. But like I said, I'll be home before you know it."

As he descended the hill to get on the trail, he looked back and saw his four grandchildren standing arm in arm. They separated and in unison pumped their chests. Spearmint stopped and from his horse he pumped his own chest. Then he wheeled his horse around and continued on with a wide grin and tears streaming down his tan and creased face.

Il Vapore (The Vapor)

The hausfrau sat in the kitchen of her apartment in Hamburg eating a breakfast of sausage, potatoes, and eggs. Her worn house coat hung open exposing her plump body. The pale blue walls looked dull to her. Lately her life was faded, too. She mindlessly swished a forkful of sausage through the remainder of egg yolk coagulating on the Quimper plate on the chipped two-person table in front of her. When she heard a noise outside, she pulled the robe closed and moved her wooden chair nearer to the table. A picture of her husband, in his dress uniform, sat in a pearl frame on the drain board. The thick eye glasses she wore magnified her blue eyes—and a rim of unshed tears welled up on her bottom lid as she stared unblinking at the photograph.

"God, Willy, I wish you were home," she said aloud pushing her coffee cup away as she continued looking at his portrait. Some mornings she was so depressed she could hardly move. To get dressed and go to market were insurmountable tasks. The life of a German army officer's wife wasn't easy. The letters she received were full of tales about *his* exploits during battle and all the medals, awards, and commendations he'd earned. Conversely, her letters to her husband were very mundane, and she never ever mentioned her depression. It would only upset him. She knew he was someplace in Italy. "Holed up in an old hotel" is how he described his accommodations in one of his letters.

The high-low wail from an ambulance siren headed for the hospital around the corner roused her. She got up from the table and looked out the window just in time to see the emergency vehicle scoot down the rain-slick narrow street of multistory apartments that led to the hospital. The gloomy skies paralleled her mood.

"Maybe today I will go to the hospital and volunteer," she said with an audible sigh. Some of her friends were doing that. Their husbands were also away and they seemed to occupy their time by doing something.

——◆——

The rhythmic clicking of the hard heels on the black boots of the goose-stepping Nazi's brought townspeople to the doors of the shops and cafés along the cobblestone streets of Cernobbio, Italy. As the parade passed, some folks gave half-hearted waves. Others turned their heads in shame and disgust. Pigeons fluttered to shelter in the nooks of the ancient buildings and seagulls headed across the lake, out of harm's way.

"The kraut bastards are here to free *Il Dookie*," Arturo Galliano hissed as he spat in the direction of the marchers. "Him and his whore."

He was standing in the alley behind his café wearing a waiter's apron tied around his waist. He wiped his hands on a dish towel draped over his right shoulder as if he were trying to clean himself after the foul display passed. The midmorning sunshine radiated off his thinning black hair.

"Hush, Papa. They will hear you," the man's daughter, Angela, whispered. A glistening of sweat appeared on her upper lip as she anxiously twisted her white cook's apron and looked behind her to see if anybody heard her father's comments. She became aware of an odd smell, possibly body odor. *I wonder if Papa forgot to bathe,* she thought to herself. The smell wasn't that unpleasant, it was just disconcerting; a familiar mix that Angela couldn't quite recognize.

"What do I care, Daughter? Let them hear," he snorted.

"The Nazis won't be very happy with you if they heard you say *Il Dookie*, Papa," she chided. Locals knew that Il Dookie meant "crap" and was a corruption of *Il Duce*, "The Leader."

Why did they exile him to our region? He sits in a mountaintop villa with his mistress as prisoners of the state, she thought to herself and shuddered. "I wish he was somewhere else," she said in a whisper, shaking her head. "Then the Nazis might leave too."

"You better get started on the risotto, Angela. Lunch will be served soon," her father barked.

The smell lingered, and Angela realized it was coming from her. It always came from her, but she constantly looked to somebody else as the source.

"Yes, Papa, right away." As she moved from the rear to the interior of the restaurant, that smell was overpowered by cooking aromas emanating from the kitchen of Galliano's.

Angela was only too happy to flee to the kitchen of the small ristoranté her family owned; it was her sanctuary. As the door banged shut behind her, she heard the ever-present opera music and took a deep breath and let the rich scent and sounds of an Italian kitchen steady and invigorate her.

"The pesto smells wonderful, Mama!" she sang out.

Sophia Galliano smiled and immediately covered her mouth, hiding her crooked and discolored front teeth. Several cooks were preparing large portions of food, hoping for a decent lunch crowd. Waiters were going over the menu. The noise of the pots and pans clanging was deafening and the heat from the stoves almost unbearable.

Angela's father told her at an early age, "The noise and heat from that kitchen is our way of life. When the kitchen is quiet and cool, there are no lira coming in. So, keep it noisy and hot!"

Angela smiled, and her eyes sparkled. She'd been raised here—this is what home felt like. And it had been the same for her father, and his grandfather. Galliano's had been a popular establishment for generations of the Galliano family. Shopkeepers and businessmen and ladies out for lunch frequented the place. The outside seating was sought after the most. Its location along the shore of Lake Como was unsurpassed. The brightly colored umbrellas over the tables rippled in the breezes against the deep blue backdrop of the lake's sapphire waters.

Angela was setting tableware on the outside tables and spotted several sailboats scudding across the surface toward Bellagio. The boat launch for Como blew its loud whistle, and several people ran from the hotel across from Galliano's to catch it.

"Angela!" called her mother.

"What is it, Mama?" Angela answered as she entered the warm kitchen.

Sophia, who was flushed with the heat coming off the pot she stirred on the big old stove, brushed an errant lock of damp hair from her forehead with the back of her wrist and said, "Go remind your Papa that there is plenty to look at and do inside his restaurant. Hurry up, now."

"Yes, Mama." Angela opened the back door of the kitchen. But it hadn't been long enough. She still caught a glimpse of the last of the German soldiers' procession up constricted Via Regina heading for Villa d'Este. She froze with one foot out the door and trembled. The body odor smell wafted momentarily, then diminished. She shook her head and shut her eyes tight, but it didn't help. Sometimes the memory of...of...it...just plagued her. Sometimes she couldn't chase that horrible night from her mind, and she stood helpless as the memory washed over her.

Stella Bolsano and she had been walking in the early evening, after just leaving the cinema, when a Nazi staff car screeched to a halt next to them. It had kicked up a spray of water stagnating in the gutter, but both girls had been quick enough to jump and keep the floral skirts of their dresses clean. If only they had kept up the retreat when the corporal exited the car and ordered the two into the back seat.

Stella tried to make small talk for a few minutes, and inquired where they were going, but the corporal not only wouldn't answer them, he wouldn't even make eye contact. Angela could feel her heart beating in her throat the entire trip as the car bounced along the cobbles. When the car stopped, they were led into the lobby of the hotel. The ceilings were extremely high and the hallways were wider than most streets in the village. The corporal shoved them up the elaborate stairway to the offices of the commandant inside the Villa d'Este. For both girls, it was the first time they had ever been inside the grounds of the villa. They were too petrified to take in any lasting memories of their surroundings.

They were shepherded through double, carved oak doors, blackened with age. On the other side sat a large man, pushing his middle-aged years. He didn't look up from the letter he was reading when the corporal announced them to Colonel Kneckles. He waved for them to wait just a moment and muttered something about finishing up with the boring letter from his wife. Stella and Angela huddled together. Both girls pulled the lightweight cardigans they wore tightly around them.

Then he put the letter down. The gray haze from his cigar hung heavily in the room. For a moment longer than Angela thought she could bear, he sat staring at the girls chewing the spit-darkened end of the cigar. His eyes were squinted and his lips fat, almost feminine. He nodded to the corporal who ushered the pair in, and the solider gave the two a shove toward Kneckles, clicked his heels, and exited.

Stella tripped and clung to Angela. By some miracle, she kept them both on their feet. Angela's heart was thumping, and Stella was murmuring softly the Act of Contrition. Angela, too, began to pray.

The townspeople had heard stories about abductions and…and worse by the Krauts. Angela prayed that they were untrue. *What will I tell Papa?* she thought to herself. She got a whiff of the Colonel's body odor, and she gagged.

Colonel Wilhelm Kneckles had a ruddy complexion and short cropped rusty hair. His sideburns were barbered above the tops of his ears, and purple veins webbed across his cheeks. His fat neck folded over his high uniform shirt collar. He motioned Stella to come closer. In an almost shy manner, he tilted his head to give the impression that he was friendly. As Stella shuffled one foot forward, Angela reached out to stop her. Kneckles face turned to granite as his eyes shot to Angela. Once he had petrified Angela in her tracks with his piercing and murderous gaze, he turned a friendly smile on Stella as he beckoned her with his index finger

He allowed Stella to stop only when she was right next to him behind the massive ornate desk. He swiveled his chair to her but didn't get up. Angela could not see what he was doing to Stella below the desk level, but she could guess. Her sharp intake of air and soft protestations did not leave much to the imagination. Then she heard the sounds of a belt buckle undoing as Colonel Kneckles fiddled briefly with his uniform pants. Stella started to sob, quietly begging, "No, please, sir, no, no…" But in one lightning move he swung her off balance and yanked her down in front of him. Stella cried out sharply as she ended up sitting on the colonel's lap as he thrust into her. The tears and pleading on Stella's face was more than Angela could take and she turned away. She was aware of noises outside the office and concentrated on them. The click-clack of a typewriter, muffled voices, and drawers being opened and shut occupied her mind.

It seemed like forever, and then suddenly Stella was lying on a couch whimpering. She was nude from the waste down. A trickle of blood was evident on her inner thigh. Colonel Kneckles stood up, walked toward Angela, and hissed in a sinister tone, "I can see you are a defiant one, but I will break you." Then in one movement he tore open her blouse, grabbed a stiletto off the desktop that he used as a letter opener, and cut her brassiere at the front. Angela tried to cover herself, but Kneckles slapped her brutally across the face. She fell to the floor and sobbed. The man picked her up by her hair and held her upright. He reached over into the ashtray, retrieved his cigar, and repeatedly puffed on it until the tip was a bright and glowing ember. Angela tried not to scream but the pain was more than she could stand as the tip was thrust onto the nipple of her left breast.

"Angela! Is the risotto ready?"

"Almost, Papa," she replied. She was still aware of the pain, months after her wound scarred over. Angela looked out the back door toward the villa and shook her head.

Since the Germans had come to town, business had dropped severely. Most people chose to go home for lunch rather than risk the wrath of the Nazis. Young men were beaten if they didn't step aside quickly enough to let the officers pass. Customers in lunch rooms were kicked out of their seats to make room for the soldiers. Plates of uneaten food were thrown onto the floor if service seemed to lag. The menace was real.

News from the south was encouraging. It was rumored that the Allies were gaining the upper hand on the Axis.

"We can only hope that the Allies get here before the thugs completely ruin our town," Arturo Galliano announced vehemently to several fellow merchants seated in the living room of his apartment above the restaurant.

"Our town? What about our country, Galliano?" Luigi Rinaldi, the banker, exclaimed.

"Call me a traitor if you want, Luigi, but I can only worry about my family, my business, and my hometown."

"I am not calling you a traitor," Luigi Rinaldi replied with a hint of apology in his voice. "We all know you are very loyal, and no one speaks his mind more than you."

"That is what scares me," Sophia Galliano whispered to her daughter. Mother and daughter were in the apartment dining room listening to the men talk. They sat at an old cypress table that had been Sophia's grandmother's, eating dessert cookies and sipping tea. The ticking of a wall clock was all that could be heard for several seconds.

"What, Mama? What scares you?" Angela asked as she put her elbows on the hard table top.

"That your father is so vocal, dear."

"Let me get one of those Nazi bastards alone. I'll show him what combat is about," Arturo Galliano said loud enough to be heard outside.

Angela and her mother exchanged knowing looks. Sophia raised her eyebrows and motioned with her hand toward the next room in a *see-what-I-mean?* gesture.

As Angela readied herself for bed she exposed her left breast in the mirror to monitor the healing process. It had been several months since she and Stella were abducted. The scar was blending in, but her left nipple now looked slightly larger than the right.

When Stella and Angela had stumbled out of the Villa d'Este that night, they sobbed for hours, not knowing how they would go home or what to do next. Finally, shivering with cold and emotions that they had never felt before, they made a vow never to talk about the event again. When they parted company that night, little did they know that would be the last time they saw one another. A few months later, Angela heard that Stella was sent to a convent by her parents. It was rumored that she was expecting a child.

The week after Angela heard that rumor, Angela was dicing up an eggplant when her father said, "That one is like a vapor. He comes and goes like a wispy fog." Arturo Galliano indicated with a nod of his head. Angela followed her father's nod across the counter to the table by the window—right smack into the eyes of Colonel Wilhelm Kneckles. Her grip on the knife turned her fists white and her nipple ached.

"You better go see what *Il Vapore* wants for lunch. Remind him we don't have any Schnitzel today," her father said with a snort.

She fingered the handle of the blade still clutched in her hand. The thought of his blood spurting from the artery in his neck and spilling on the café floor was appealing to Angela. She looked at her Papa and around the little restaurant that had taken care of so many generations of Gallianos. She gritted her teeth and set the blade down. It was one of the hardest things she ever did—to force her steps to carry her from the kitchen to that table—but if she didn't, she might have to tell her Papa why. So she put one foot in front of the other until she stood across the table from Colonel Kneckles. Despite her brave efforts, she couldn't keep from quivering. But if Kneckles recognized Angela, he didn't let on. Nor did Angela concede that she recognized him. He ordered his luncheon, paid for it, and left. The tip he gave was tossed on the table for the busboy. After Angela gave the cook Kneckles's order, she went to her mother's side and whispered, "Mama, do I smell? Do you smell anything odd?"

"No, child. You smell just fine."

Still, the odor of stale tobacco combined with a sickly sweet and feminine talcum powder plagued her.

Young girls were still being abducted and taken to Kneckles and his staff for sexual gratification. Several fathers of girls complained to the polizia. They, in turn, were told to keep their daughters in at night. One father was beaten severely and thrown down the steps of the Villa d'Este when he went to defend his daughter's honor.

Benito Mussolini and his mistress were rescued from their villa in Milan where they were held hostage. Adolph Hitler installed Il Duce as dictator of a puppet state, the Italian Social Republic. Mussolini established his headquarters in a mountaintop villa in the Lakes region of Northern Italy. The Nazis continued to punish the partisans and send Jews to concentration camps. The Allies were still coming. "Any day, now," the men would say sarcastically.

Mr. and Mrs. Bolsano, Stella's parents, were in the living room of the Galliano's apartment, weeping. Angela heard the noise from her bedroom and came out to see what was wrong. Not only were Stella's parents crying, her parents were crying also.

"Mama, what is wrong?"

"Oh, child. There is bad news," Sophia Galliano moaned.

"What is the matter?"

Mr. Bolsano spoke up, "Stella is dead. She threw herself off the belfry of the chapel at the convent," he announced as he hung his head and continually wrung his hands.

Angela started to sob and tried to give condolences, but couldn't stop convulsing.

Her parents were by her side in an instant holding their daughter closer than ever before.

It was learned that Stella gave birth to a boy with fair complexion, who was offered for adoption. When Mr. and Mrs. Bolsano asked about the child, the nuns told them Stella said, "The child is of the devil. Keep him from me."

Late that night Angela lay awake, staring at the cracked plaster ceiling over her soft bed. Her mind wouldn't stop playing the image of Stella sobbing and pleading on the devil's lap.

Rage stirred her blood until she couldn't lie still any longer. Quietly she crept down the stairs of the apartment and into the restaurant. The dark kitchen was still warm from the stoves, and the aftermath of freshly caught lake trout, the day's special, still remained. She picked up two knives; a paring knife and an eight-inch chef's knife. Inverting them, she put a knife up each sleeve. Her plan was not well thought out. *Just try to take me, you sons of bitches, I'll stab your eyes out,* she swore to herself. She exited the kitchen from the backdoor. The cool night air revitalized her as she took a back alley to Villa d'Este. As silent as cat paws on powdered snow, she inched herself along the buildings until she reached the gate of the Villa. She stared past the elaborate wrought-iron scrollwork, up at a lit window that might have been the very room where she and Stella were assaulted. She sniffled as she thought of Stella.

"Well, you're here now. What are you going to do?" she said under her breath, each syllable exhausted steam in the cold air. *Go home!* a voice in her head shouted. But then she thought about Stella and felt the knives up her sleeves, which galvanized her courage to continue.

Villa d'Este was one of Europe's leading hotels since 1873. It was without doubt a showcase for Italy and Cernobbio. To have the Nazis take over the establishment was an enormous outrage to Italians.

The gate was locked and Angela could see a guard walking with a huge black shepherd dog around the perimeter of the renaissance main building, their breath visible also. Angela watched him make his rounds for twenty minutes. The soldier's routine never varied as he patrolled through the manicured gardens with Italianate grottoes and ancient cypress trees.

An automobile pulled up in front of the steps, the brakes grinding metal to metal. The headlights played on Angela momentarily before she ducked behind some foliage. The figure of a man strode down the steps and got in the backseat of the car. The driver followed the guard as he walked with the dog to the gate. The guard's boot squeaked with each step.

The hinges of the iron gate moaned as it scraped along the cobbles. Angela laid unnoticed flat on her back, smashing geraniums and other flowers. The dog growled, sensing something was wrong. The guard yanked on the leather leash leading the dog back to their appointed rounds. Angela was certain the dog was getting a whiff of her.

Angela looked into the backseat as the sedan passed; all she could see was the glowing tip of a long cigar. Her prey had left the hunting ground.

She was horrified as she watched the car head toward town. When the taillights finally disappeared, as the car went over a hump in the road, relief and frustration washed over her in waves: Frustration, because she didn't get to slit his throat. Relief, because she didn't have to slit his throat.

That was when she realized no one had shut the gate. *You can't get him,* she told herself, *but maybe you can make it so he can't get anyone else so easily, either.* She crawled along the cobbles and down the driveway toward the main building. She hardly noticed her knees scraping along the slimy damp stones. The click of the sentry's boots faded as he walked around the side of the villa.

———•◦•———

The paring knife entered the tire with more ease than she expected. The cars were parked in a parking area removed from the buildings.

In thirty minutes, all the tires of seven staff cars were flattened. The five autos parked in front of the crippled seven, kept them from being noticed.

Headlights bathed the driveway; Angela ducked behind a jeep whose tires she was trying to puncture. The hard rubber of the jeep's tire would not give, and the knife tip bent. The car stopped in front of the building, and Il Vapore exited. Angela's heart was hammering; she was sure the driver and guard could hear the beating. The driver pulled straight toward the front line of cars and turned sharply, reversing the auto into a parking spot. After she finished puncturing the tires on the last car, she looked up at the darkened room of Colonel Kneckles and said, "I may not have been able to deflate you with my little paring knife, you pig. But see just how easy it is to force girls into cars that have no tires! Buona fortuna finding any, you Kraut bastard!"

The gate was now closed. Angela looked around like a cornered animal. The lights from Isola Comacina were shimmering on the water. If she could make her way to the water's edge, she could walk along the promenade toward home. The growl from the guard's dog startled her. She saw the sentry as he approached. He stopped no more that twenty yards from the palm tree Angela hid behind.

"Hush, Rex!" the guard whispered as he yanked on the leash. The dog sat whining and squirming. The guard lit a cigarette and stood looking at the water and back at the villa. The dog didn't take his eyes off of the palm tree. An owl screeched, and the dog started to bark. Angela silently reached for a stone and tossed it in the direction of the automobiles. The guard and his dog went in the direction of where the rock landed.

Silently she moved to the walkway along the beach and smugly headed for home. She was surprised at how calm she was. The fresh smell of the lake and night blooming flowers accompanied her along the way.

When the kitchen started to heat up later that morning, the prep cook held up his paring knife and stared at the curled tip. Suddenly, Angela found his quizzical look extremely funny. When he looked at her, she grinned. As he tried to straighten the tip, Angela laughed harder. All present in the kitchen gawked at her. The more they stared, the harder she laughed.

"Mama Mia! What a morning I have had, Galliano."

"How so, pisan?" Arturo Galliano asked as he poured coffee for his friend, Fredo Graziano.

"The head Kraut came to my filling station to buy tires. I don't know where this babau has been. Doesn't he know there is a war going on?" Graziano said with a shrug of his shoulders and outstretched hands. All present in the dining room laughed.

"It seems that all the tires on the cars at the Villa d'Este got flattened." Graziano explained further, "Tells me he wants me to call Esso to deliver tires. When I told him all the rubber was being used to put tires on the Allies' vehicles, he glared at me and spit formed on the corners of his fat mouth. I almost messed myself. He spun like a ballerina and walked out. If I hadn't been so scared, I might have laughed," he said as he did a pirouette, mimicking the colonel.

At that moment Colonel Kneckles and a captain entered Galliano's, and all noise stopped.

Arturo grabbed a menu and indicated with a gesture to a table by the front door.

Pointing at the table Fredo Graziano occupied, Kneckles hissed, "No, I want that table."

"But Colonel, that table is taken. The one by the door is much nicer."

Kneckles strode over to Fredo and said in a whisper, "You are in my seat, now get out." Fredo started to move, and patrons headed for the exit.

The captain had unslung his rifle when he heard chairs sliding on the floor.

"Please, take another seat. There are plenty available now," Galliano pleaded.

Kneckles grabbed Graziano by the shirt collar and stood him up. His face paled and his eyes widened with fear. Arturo Galliano tried to intervene, and said, "Come on, Fredo, I'll put you over by the window." Kneckles looked at the captain, who raised his rifle and clubbed Arturo savagely on the temple with the butt. Arturo dropped to the floor and started convulsing.

Sophia, who had been watching from the kitchen door, grabbed a knife and flew like a mad woman at the colonel. Kneckles removed his Luger from its holster and shot her in the chest.

"Mama!" Angela screamed. She grabbed a knife and ran for the dining room. The cook grabbed her and pinned her arms against her body in a bear hug. She struggled mightily, but the cook held her tightly. He crooned in her ear for her to calm down, that it would only dishonor her mother if she got herself killed. "Let me go!" she sobbed, going limp in the cook's arms. "Let me go to her, please…" she whispered as tear-stained eyes met her mother's. Dark blood seeped from under Sophia's body. Her mouth was open and her teeth were exposed. The only thing Angela could think of as her mother died was, *Mama doesn't have to be embarrassed by her front teeth anymore.*

The two Nazis were backing out of the restaurant with weapons still drawn. Nobody moved until after the Nazi jeep sped up the narrow road next to Hotel Regina Olga.

Remo Visconti, the Galliano's doctor was sitting in the living room of the upstairs apartment administering a sedative to Angela. The last thing she remembered as she slipped into sleep was his gentle whisper: "You rest now, my dear. We will talk in the morning."

Angela woke with a start, sat up, and lay back down. Then she remembered the events of the day before and began to wail. In an instant, Mrs. Bolsano and Mrs. Graziano were by her side trying to calm her.

"Papa?" she asked weakly. Before they responded, she knew the answer; her father was dead also.

"I am so sorry, Angela," Mrs. Bolsano said with a solemn tone. "Your father never woke up. He died several hours ago. We have notified your Aunt Louisa in Genoa. She should be here soon." She pronounced *Genoa* as *Genova.*

Angela lay in bed looking from face to face seeking answers. Mrs. Bolsano and Mrs. Graziano looked at each other for a clue of what to do or say next. The silence between the three of them weighed on Angela, so she said the only thing that came to mind, "Funeral arrangements need to be made. The sooner, the better."

The two women agreed and said they would call the undertaker right away. They hustled out together, passing the doctor as he entered the room. Angela refused another dose of sedative and got out of bed to help with arrangements.

The entire town turned out for the double funeral and the gathering afterward. When they were alone, Angela asked her aunt if she could be by herself for a while. Her aunt complied and went to the cathedral to pray for her sister and her brother-in-law.

Angela Galliano sat on a wooden chair in the dining room of the family restaurant looking intently at the scene where her parents died. She wondered if she could work and walk on those hallowed places. She stood up, moved her chair aside, and lay down on her back. She stretched her arms out and touched both places where she had last seen her parents. She stared at the ceiling and vowed to keep the restaurant open. She lay there for several hours soaking in her parents' auras. Before she got off the floor she became aware of the coolness in the ristoranté, and vowed to keep it hot and loud.

Galliano's opened every day and Angela greeted each customer with grace and charm. She kept making the traditional Italian foods that her family had passed down parent to child for generations, but her mother's recipe for pesto was the featured entrée. She served it over pastas and sausage or with lasagna and cheese, sometimes on brochette. Each patron was served olives, almonds, and peppers. Meats and melons were passed from table to table, in *famiglia* style. At least one day a week, a bone-in ham was put on a side table, and patrons could slice off a helping. After a meal, chunks of Parmesan cheese and a small jar of honey were put on each table. Many times Angela would say, "Just try the cheese and honey. It is like candy." The opera music her father played was replaced with more modern tunes. Mario Lanza records could be heard. Italian-American singers' songs were played along with big band music.

The Nazis were rarely seen around town, and their presence in the dining establishments became less and less. The Axis power was waning and *Il Dookie* and his whore were on the run. The Allied forces were taking Anzio with a vengeance. Somebody said they saw Colonel Wilhelm Kneckles headed for the Swiss Alps, but it was just an unsubstantiated rumor. Then the rumor was confirmed; the Nazi stronghold at Villa d'Este was abandoned on a Sunday morning. The pilfering of art work and antiques from Villa d'Este by the departing Germans was extensive, but they were gone, on the run. And the citizens of Cernobbio sighed with relief. Then the parade of jeeps and transports loaded with GIs showed up Monday to great fanfare and frivolity, and the citizens sensed liberation.

<hr />

Late one afternoon Angela was making a food supply order when the door opened. An American GI stood in the doorway and asked if he could see a menu.

"The kitchen is closed. But have a seat," Angela replied as she put her clipboard and order sheets down on the wine bar. "I'll see what I can find."

She noticed the name in black stencil on his olive army coat. It read RAPALLO.

"You are Italian, eh?" she asked in broken English.

"Yes ma'am I am. Born in America, though." He said sheepishly in Italian. "My name is Dante Rapallo."

Angela introduced herself and went to the kitchen to get Dante something to eat. She snuck looks at him from between the hanging pots and pans. She liked the look of him right away. Brown hair cut short and dark brown eyes that revealed he had seen too much of what a young man should not have seen. He had an angular jaw and a nose slightly too large for his face. His smile came easily, and Angela was intrigued.

She sat at his table watching him eat a plate of risotto and mushrooms as he talked about the battle in Cassino. She wept with him when he talked about the buddies he lost in combat. He wept with her as she related the murder of her parents.

Each day after that, Sergeant Dante Rapallo took a meal at Galliano's, sometimes lunch, sometimes supper. Angela enjoyed it when he ate his evening meal because he would always stay after closing and talk with her and help her with her English. The staff of the ristoranté was pleased for Angela. They had not seen her happy and giddy in quite some time.

"Hey, Rapallo, you seeing your girlfriend again tonight?" one of Dante's pals asked.

He was embarrassed but said that he indeed was.

"You better watch out, that dago food will make you fat."

"We don't get fat from eating Italian food, you stupid mick. We get fat from eating Irish stew and soda bread." All in the barracks laughed.

"Are you serious about this girl, Dante?" one of his closer companions asked as they lay on their bunks.

"Yeah, Ron, I am. My heart flutters every single time I see her. She is so darn nice and pretty. And smart. She is very smart. She's a good cook, too."

"She is pretty, that's for sure, Dante. She reminds me of Rita Hayworth."

Dante Rapallo smiled as his chest swelled with pride.

"Tell me about your family," Angela asked of Dante as they walked along the path beside the water's edge. Their feet crunched on the pea gravel. A slight breeze blew in off the lake with a scent of cypress and olives, and seagulls seemed to accompany them on their stroll.

"Well, my family lives in Los Gatos. That's in California, about fifty miles south of San Francisco. My father, my older brother, my brother-in-law, and I build houses. My sister lives next door to my family home. My brother lives across the street."

"Where do you live?"

"I live with my mother and father. When I get home, I am gonna build a house on a lot my grandparents gave me on the street behind my family home."

"What is your mother like?"

"She's real nice. There isn't anybody that doesn't like her, and nobody she doesn't like. She's clean, very clean. And a good cook. She is always cooking and cleaning. If somebody stops by the house they better be ready to have something to eat," Dante explained as he tossed a stone into Lake Como.

"Do you think she would like me?"

"You? Probably not," Dante replied turning his head away to hide his grin.

"Hey!" Angela replied as she hit his shoulder. "What do you mean she wouldn't like me, eh?"

"Of course she'll like you. What's not to like?" Dante replied as he gave her a hearty hug and took in her delicate scent of roses. He could feel her heart beating and held her tighter. The breeze rattled the mast on an old sailboat that was tied to an ancient and rusted ring cemented into the archaic seawall. The clanging of the mast and the crunch of their footfalls as they went along were the only sounds they were aware of. Every time he turned to look at Angela, she was looking up at him. "What are you looking at?" he asked with a song.

The two sat on a dark green park bench adjacent to the boat launch with heads together, vowing their love to one another.

*

"What will I do if he asks me to marry him, Tia?" Angela asked her aunt as the two sat in the apartment above the restaurant.

Do you love him, child?" Angela's aunt asked as she put down her crocheting.

"With all my heart, Tia."

"Do you trust him?"

"With my life."

"How can you be so sure? You have only known him for a short time."

"Every time I see him, I feel that Papa is smiling."

"Well, child, if he is half the man your father was, then you better hold on to him."

"I know, Tia. But what about this?" she said with a sweep of her hand.

"What *about* this?" her aunt replied.

"Well, what if he wants to live in *his* town? What will happen to Galliano's?"

"Do you want to be a cook all your life," her Tia Louisa said with a squinted eye and the point of an arthritic index finger at her niece.

For several minutes the only sound was the tick-tick of the wall clock. The squeal of brakes on a delivery truck at Hotel Regina Olga broke the moment.

"And you, what about you, Tia?"

"Forget about me. I'm old. I've lived my life. If I was your age and a handsome American asked me to go with him to California? Mama Mia, I would be on the next boat over."

———◆———

Angela sat at a vacant table in the restaurant reading the newspaper about Mussolini's capture. A few lunch patrons were finishing up, and the kitchen was closed. The clanging of pots being washed echoed in the dining room.

The Germans convinced Benito Mussolini that it was time for him to flee Italy. Near Tyrol, the partisans had blocked the road. They agreed to let the Germans pass, but not Italians. The Germans persuaded Mussolini to put on a German soldier's great coat and hide in the back of a transport truck. That is where the partisans found Il Duce, hiding in a truck with a German's coat on over his striped general's trousers.

When the Liberation Committee was informed of Mussolini's capture, strict orders were given for fair treatment.

Angela's hands were trembling, and it was difficult for her to breathe as she continued to read.

Mussolini and his mistress, Clara Petacci, spent their last night together in a farm house in the country.

Vice-Premier Togliatti countermanded the fair treatment proclamation and ordered the execution of Benito Mussolini and others. The bedroom that Clara and Benito shared was broken into. The company commander told the pair that he was there to rescue them. They hurriedly went to a waiting car and were driven about a mile down the road, pulled from the car, and placed against a stone wall and shot.

The bodies were transported, along with thirteen others to Milan and hung by their feet with piano wire from the canopy of an Esso filling station.

With a raucous intake of air, Angela Galliano stood up and lifted her arms skyward and exclaimed loudly, "How about that, Papa!"

The cathedral in Cernobbio was filled to capacity with towns-people and soldiers to witness the nuptials of Angela Marie Galliano and Dante Luigi Rapallo. The head chef from the restaurant gave the bride away. Angela's Aunt Louisa was bridesmaid, and Dante's friend and fellow soldier, Ron, stood in proxy as best man for Dante's father, Giuseppe.

"Are there really two bathrooms?" Angela asked her husband as they lay in their honeymoon bed in a suite at the Hotel Regina Olga. She was looking at photographs his parents sent showing the house that G. Rapallo and Sons Construction Company were building for Dante and his bride.

"Yes, for the millionth time, there are two, count 'em, two bathrooms."

"Don't be cross with me. It is just that I have lived all my life in that apartment..."

"Honey, I'm not cross. It's like you don't think this is real. It is real. You're my wife, and we're going to live in a nice new home in Los Gatos, California. A house that has three bedrooms and two bathrooms."

"The bathrooms are inside?" Angela asked as she removed her nightgown.

He gazed at her and marveled at her beauty. Earlier she had tried to keep her left breast from him, but realized it was no use. She told him the story about the German colonel and her night in his office. Dante held her and told her she was beautiful and perfect in every way. They were in each others' arms when the chimes from the church woke them.

"Oh, Dante, it is absolutely perfect," Angela squealed as she ran from room to room. The smell of fresh paint and sawdust filled the dwelling. Dante's heart was overflowing with joy and his eyes with tears at the delight his stunning wife was experiencing.

"The construction is almost completed," Dante proclaimed as he looked over the floor plans. Angela stood at the kitchen sink staring out the window at the front yard.

A yard in front. Mama Mia, she thought to herself.

"Where is everybody? It is so quiet here."

"They're still asleep. It's only seven. People sleep in on Saturdays around here."

They had honeymooned in Scandinavia for a month before getting on a ship for San Francisco. The taxi ride to Los Gatos was costly, but their anxiousness outweighed the fare.

Husband and wife stood together in a warm embrace and kissed long and passionately. They heard giggling, and Dante announced in a sing-song voice, "I hear monsters."

Angela and Dante turned and saw two little girls in nightgowns standing at the back door. Their hair was tousled, and they appeared to have just awoken. The girls sprinted toward them screaming, "Uncle Dante, you're home!" Dante bent and scooped them up in his arms. They hugged his neck and kissed him repeatedly. Angela stepped away to give more room for the twirling that was taking place.

"Is that your new wife?" the older girl asked breaking the hug and looking at Angela.

"Yes it is. Isn't she pretty?" Both girls nodded.

"Would you like to meet her?" he asked as he put them on the floor. He held their hands and walked with them to where Angela was standing.

"Sally and Victoria, I would like you to meet your Aunt Angela." Both children grabbed her and embraced her. Angela's eyes welled up as she caressed the soft hair of the two beautiful children.

The reception was crowded with relatives, neighbors, and friends. Dante's Nona was taking Angela around and introducing her to people, some more than once. The Rapallo family home was used to parties. "It's company friendly," Rachel Rapallo, Dante's mother, always said.

The parties at the Rapallo's home always ended the same; women in the kitchen and men outside by the brick barbeque pit.

Dante was learning who made it home from combat and who didn't. Mentally he took notes on the families he needed to see so he could offer condolences.

"You better go and rescue your bride, Son. Before the sharks get her," Dante's father, Giuseppe said with a laugh.

"I was thinking the same thing, Pop."

"Hey, Son, before you go in…"

"What is it, Pop?"

His father hesitated, then started to speak and stopped, and then burst into tears and said, "I am so relieved you're home safe. And I'm so damn proud of you." The two hugged long and tearfully.

"I know I don't say it enough, but I love you."

"I love you too, Pop. More than once over there, when I was up against it, I'd say to my self, *What would Pop do?* And I got through it."

———————

Angela stood at an intersection with grocery bags in a wire basket on two wheels. She noticed the silt and leaves caked around the storm sewer in the curb and gutter. The recent floods had played havoc with the drainage system, and back yards along the creeks were still muddy. Daily she walked to town to shop. "You have a beautiful new station wagon to drive. Why don't you use it?" Dante asked her often. "I enjoy the walk. I can talk to neighbors and be outside," she would explain. She had reluctantly sold the restaurant business in Cernobbio to the head chef, but still owned the building and got a nice rent check every month. Her aunt convinced Angela that moving to America was the right thing to do and gave her blessing. Aunt Louisa moved from Genoa into the upstairs apartment where Angela had lived with her parents. She lived rent free and kept an eye on the property for Angela.

"That is your money, Angie. You do what you want with it," Dante told his wife on more than one occasion. But all Angela did was deposit it in the bank.

"We will go on vacation to Italy with the money. Maybe visit Mama and Papa's grave. Take the boys. That's what I'll spend the money on."

———————

The pleasures she derived from walking in town were unsurpassed, except maybe for the strolls she took along the promenade along Lake Como. *Another time and another place,* she reminded herself. The climate and quite a few Italian immigrants, especially those at the bocce ball courts, kept her birthright alive.

Surveying the town when she first arrived gave her pause. There was no lake, but the Pacific Ocean was a short drive through the Santa Cruz Mountains. The greenness of the hills reminded her of the Alpines. The streets of the town were wide and gave a sense of serenity. The traffic was heavier in Los Gatos, but seemed calmer than on the narrow cobbled roads of Italian villages. And everything was new. The native Los Gatans thought that a one-hundred-year-old building was ancient. "They have no idea," Angela would say.

As she started to cross the street, a 1955 beige Chevrolet passed her. She just got a glimpse of the driver and was horrified. She stood motionless for a long time. Angela became aware of *the* odor again, and her mind reverted back to Cernobbio and 1943 as if she were watching an old news reel at the movies.

She wobbled to a bus stop bench and sat down. She realized she left her grocery basket at the curb, but couldn't bring herself to get up and get it.

She didn't hear the whoosh of the bus door as it opened, or the driver ask her if she were getting on. Only when the driver laid on the horn did she come back to the present. She waved off the driver, who gave her a harrumph, and left her in a cloud of diesel exhaust.

Lots of people have red hair. What would that kraut stugatz be doing driving in Los Gatos, California, for Christ's sake? she thought to herself. After two blocks, she had convinced herself she was mistaken. She clung to pleasant thoughts about her children, husband, and her new town to escape darker memories.

New town? She'd been living here for over ten years. Every time she walked the two blocks from her neighborhood, lovingly called Ravioli Ridge, to town, she marveled at the convenience. The grocery, post office, bank, and pharmacy were on the same block. The five-and-dime store was just another block up. Coffee shops and restaurants were close, too. The elementary school lay just two blocks away on the other side of her house. "This is just a great town," she often wrote to her aunt, pleading with her to visit.

As Angela was putting groceries away she had a sense of foreboding she couldn't shake. "It just can't be Kneckles," she said out loud.

And then the smell. She looked at the clock and realized that her two boys would be home from school soon and would want something to eat. Dinner needed to be prepared also.

She was putting the last bit of oregano into the tomato sauce when the door chime sounded. On her porch was her friend Brenda Sullivan, and she was in tears.

"Brenda, for goodness sakes, what's wrong?" Angela asked as she opened the screen door so her guest could enter.

"Hank got drunk again last night and came home looking for love," Brenda answered as she sat on the maroon brocade couch in the Rapallo living room.

"All he got was a fight," Brenda continued through sniffles. "I'm thinking about leaving him."

"What about your kids, Brenda?"

"That is a problem, Angie."

"Where would you go?"

She just stared at Angela for a second, then burst into a new round of sobs. "I don't know," she wailed and collapsed against her friend's shoulder.

———————

"Brenda came by this afternoon. She was in tears again," Angela announced to Dante as they lay in bed that evening.

"What's the matter? Hank get tight again?"

"As a matter of fact, he did."

"I don't see the big deal. So a guy ties one on once in a while. You women hack on the poor guy…" He sensed her stiffen and realized he crossed a boundary.

"Listen, Honey, all I'm saying is Hank has a good job at the winery, a nice home, and, as far as I know, he doesn't hit her."

"No, she would tell me if he hit her."

"So maybe she should look at herself. Maybe she should get out of the house. Get a job."

Angela lay next to her husband, wide awake, listening to him breathe. She got out of bed and went down the hall and checked on her boys. She then went outside and sat in a wooden chair under the pepper tree in the backyard thinking about Brenda for a bit. Something else other than Brenda was bothering her. She couldn't quite put her finger on it. She then realized that her nemesis from Italy, Kneckles, was the problem. Il Vapore!

Back in her bed she felt safe and secure. But sleep still eluded her. She watched the streetlight out her window, glowing in the night, and saw it go out at daylight.

———————

Angela couldn't quite shake the cloud that followed her everywhere now. Even when things were going well, she felt restless. Sometimes she felt like she didn't fit in her own skin quite right. She had told Brenda what Dante had said about getting a job, and to her surprise, Brenda did. She started work at the local hospital. But the idea she had planted in Brenda's head had also taken root in hers. Maybe she could get a job. Maybe that would help her feel like she fit again.

So here she was, sitting in the cocktail lounge of the Live Oak Inn.

"Why should I hire you?" Buster, the owner, asked. He was a large man with a head of thick blond hair. He always wore slacks and square-cut shirt.

"I have been around the restaurant business all my life. I know the kitchen, the dining room, and the bar," she answered confidently.

"Lots of people know those things," Buster said smugly as he snubbed out his cigarette in a glass amber ashtray.

Angela had a feeling he was not taking her seriously, so she said, "I also know how to order, and if I was doing the ordering you wouldn't have run out of veal last Saturday night."

"We ran out of veal?"

"Yes, and way too early, I might add."

"You're Eye-talian, aren't you?"

Angela cringed every time someone mispronounced Italian. Still not thinking she had a chance for the job, she said, "Yes I am. I'm from Cernobbio, Eyetaly."

If he got the jibe, he didn't show it.

"What will your husband think about you working here?"

Feeling a glimmer of hope, Angela backed off a little.

"My husband supports me in all my endeavors," she said with her fingers crossed.

"Do you know good Eye-talian dishes?"

"Anything your heart desires."

"Okay, you can begin on Wednesday for lunch. We get here between 9:30 and 10:00 AM."

"Thank you. You won't be sorry you hired me."

"You sure your husband won't mind?"

"You let me worry about my husband. You worry about the veal, eh," she replied with a grin.

After a long discussion, Dante relented to his wife working outside the home when Angela explained to him that she would not go to work until he and the boys were gone in the morning and would be home when they returned in the afternoons. She also assured him that his masculinity or ability to provide was not an issue. In the end, he just put his arms around her and said, "When could I ever deny you anything?" He ended the conversation with a kiss on her forehead.

After a few weeks at the Live Oak Inn, Angela sat in the kitchen talking with her boss, Buster. She offered him a few suggestions about making the kitchen more efficient by rearranging a few items. Slowly he took her proposals, and the staff agreed that the kitchen was indeed better.

Over time Buster could go on vacation and not worry because his manager, Angela Rapallo, was on the job. She was running the kitchen, the waitstaff, and the bar. She ordered the food and liquor. She did it all except hire and fire.

Most days would find her as the hostess for the lunch crowd.

On a Tuesday, she was chatting with one of the waitresses when she sensed people behind her.

"My name is Jim Stoddard, and we're from Cottage Grove Cannery. We have a reservation for sixteen for lunch," a balding man said to Angela as he stood at the hostess stand.

"Right this way," she replied as she grabbed a handful of menus and led the party through a long hallway back to the banquet room.

"The room has been set up just for you, and David will be your waiter."

"Thank you. Our foreman is not here yet. This is a surprise birthday party for him. Could you make sure somebody shows him back when he arrives, please? His name is Rusty." A banner on the wall above the head table had large letters that said HAPPY BIRTHDAY RUSTY KNUCKLES.

Angela was busy taking drink orders when she heard the crowd yell, "Surprise! Surprise!" She turned around and was met face to face with Wilhelm Kneckles, wearing a Bogart-like fedora, being led to Angela by Stoddard.

Instantaneously a black and white newsreel flickered to life in her head. The film flashed from Galliano's to Villa d'Este. A bumpy ride in a German army command car and Stella Bolsano's corpse sprawled on pavement below a bell tower. Her parent's gravestones ended the movie, and she became aware of the current situation. She felt trapped, as if in a cave that was collapsing. She wanted to run, but couldn't. She was choking on cigar smoke and after-bath dusting powder. She tried to shake off the feelings, but suddenly her face stung from a slap and her nipple ached from a burn.

Stoddard said to Angela, "Meet the guest of honor, Bill Nettles, fondly known as Rusty Knuckles."

Angela rocked on her heels and became mindful of her rubbery legs. When Kneckles spoke, his German accent was almost nonexistent. He took Angela's hand and attempted to kiss it with his fat lips. Before he could do so, Angela pointed toward the head table. Kneckles handed her his hat and turned to his coworkers and gave waves and hellos. Angela promptly dropped the hat on a chair and fled the dining room. She barely made it to the restroom before she vomited.

He didn't recognize me, Angela thought. "Is that a good thing or a bad thing?" she asked aloud. In Italian she said, "The son-of-a-whore gives me his hat. I should have *shit* in it!"

She had another sleepless night. Dante knew something was wrong. Every time Angela brought home food from the Live Oak Inn for dinner, she had a bad day and was not interested in cooking.

Apparently Rusty Knuckles liked the food at the Live Oak Inn because much to Angela's anxiety, he had lunch there once a week. One time he brought in a woman with thick eye glasses, whom he introduced as his wife, Waltrude.

Kneckles and his wife fled Germany and, after several years traveling around Europe and the states, settled in Monte Sereno, an area of upscale houses on large pieces of property. Monte Sereno was established by a retired Navy Admiral and several other retired military officers. *I wonder what Kneckles's neighbors would think if they knew a Nazi guilty of war-time atrocities lived just down the lane. What nerve.*

At first she would shudder with fear whenever she couldn't get a waitress to cover his table, but he never recognized her. She had never been anything to him. Why should he remember a girl whose young life he'd ruined. She, her father, her mother—they were nothing to him. She spat in his food every time she served him, but it only felt childish and impotent.

She increasingly found it harder to talk to people, to laugh with her customers, or to banter with her banker. Even at home she found herself withdrawing.

"What's the matter with you, Angie? You seem so far away most of the time," Dante asked his wife as they put dishes away.

"Just work, Honey," she replied with a caress to his cheek.

"Why don't you quit? Let's go on a vacation. Go back to Cernobbio. Just the two of us. My brother and sister can watch the boys. C'mon what do ya say?"

"Soon, my love. Soon."

———◆———

Brenda Sullivan sat in her living room with Angela Rapallo. The two had hugged and exchanged pleasantries, but when it got time to get down to the purpose of the visit, the room fell silent. Brenda fingered a small brown vial the size of her thumb. "What could you possibly need with this?" she finally asked.

Angela held out her hand. "Don't ask me what I am going to do with it."

Brenda pursed her lips and her brow furrowed. "You know, I could lose my job at the hospital, and things are going great with Hank and me since I've been working."

Angela reached out and clasped Brenda's hands between her own. The bottle was a cold hard lump between them. "Don't worry, Brenda. If anyone asks, I don't even know you." With that she gently plied the vial from Brenda.

263

Brenda sank back into the overstuffed back of the sofa and ran her hands over her face. She looked back to her friend. "You haven't been yourself much recently. What's wrong? Are you going to be okay, Angie?"

Angela opened the clasp of her clutch and dropped the little bottle in. "Yes," she said, glancing down into her purse. Then she snapped the silver catch shut. "Everything is fine, now."

Still Brenda pushed for more. "Is Dante okay, your boys?"

Angie leaned over and gave Brenda's shoulder a little squeeze. "Everybody is going to be fine, really."

<hr />

Rusty Knuckles hadn't been in for lunch in three weeks. *Maybe he gave up his charade and moved back to the fatherland,* Angela thought.

But no such luck. Well after the lunch rush one afternoon, he walked into the lounge and ordered a glass of white dinner wine. Angela heard the order and told the cocktail waitress that she would get the wine. She looked over her shoulder to be sure no one was paying her any attention before she pulled out the vial. *Chloral Hydrate* it said on the label. She opened it and with a flick of her wrist, up ended it into the glass of wine for Rusty Knuckles.

He started to slur his words as he talked with coworkers. He even almost fell asleep. What Angela hoped would happen was that he would walk out the door and into traffic. He argued with his friends when they said he was drunk. He drove out of the parking lot and side-swiped a creamery truck delivering milk to the 5 Spot Drive-In next door to the Live Oak Inn and continued on Saratoga Avenue toward Monte Sereno.

The next morning the buzz around the Live Oak was that one of their customers was in a terrible automobile accident.

"Was anybody hurt?" Angela asked nonchalantly.

"That Rusty guy went off the road," someone replied.

"Well, was he hurt badly?"

"My friend that drives the ambulance says he's paralyzed from the neck down. He's on a machine that helps him breathe. He is sometimes alert," a busboy announced with importance.

Damn! The son of a bitch is still alive, Angela reflected. "This calls for more drastic measures," she said under her breath.

The walk down the corridor of the hospital was a long one for Angela Rapallo.

She entered the room and saw the tufts of red hair on the pillow.

He saw her enter and his eyes softened.

"I bet you think I'm here because you are a customer at the Live Oak Inn, eh. Isn't that right—Colonel Kneckles?"

His eyes widened when he heard her speak his real name.

"You're an outstanding actor, Colonel. Everybody is taken in by your charm. You don't remember me do you? Arturo and Sophia Galliano. Do they ring a bell? Galliano's Restaurant in Cernobbio. Remember that place? How about Stella Bolsano? No? Well maybe this will be familiar."

As she walked toward him, his face screwed up around the oxygen mask over his nose and mouth. His eyes showed fear and vulnerability. She smiled at him, not a friendly smile like the townspeople sported as they walked down the sunny streets, but a cold wicked smile that she would have never expected to find within her. Slowly, she unbuttoned her blouse and removed her left breast from her brassier. She showed him the scar on her nipple.

"Do you see that? Is it coming back now?" she rasped in a voice hoarse with anger. "You did that to me, Il Vapore!"

He closed his eyes only to open them when he sensed Angela coming closer. Just before Angela turned the oxygen tank off, she whispered in his ear, "Say hello to Mussolini and Hitler, you son of a bitch."

After driving away from the hospital Angela pulled off the road, exited the car, and went and stood by the passenger side. When there were no cars passing she raised her hands to the sky and yelled, "How about that, Papa!"

Later she went home and made her mother's pesto lasagna.

"What's the occasion, dear?" Dante asked.

"I just felt like celebrating, that's all." She leaned over and kissed Dante before placing his plate down in front of him.

She found herself humming without knowing it off and on throughout dinner. Dante, shook his head, but smiled right back at her. "You know you look as beautiful as the day I met you."

"You old flatterer! But truth be told, I do feel young again. And I feel freer than I have since I was a girl in Mama and Papa's restaurant."

"You can take the girl out of Italy, but you can't take Italy out of the girl, eh?"

She giggled. "Something like that. But you know, you've given me an idea. Why not bring Italy to the girl?"

Dante paused with his fork hovering over his floral rimmed plate. "What do you mean?"

"Galliano's. I know what I want to do with the money I've been saving. I'm going to open a restaurant."

Dante put the fork down and rested his hands on the table. "Yeah?"

"I think Los Gatos needs a Galliano's. I think I am strong enough to pick up the responsibility of my family tradition."

Dante looked stunned. "I never knew you missed it so much, but if that's what you want…"

She nodded vigorously. "Oh, it is."

Angela jumped up from the table and threw herself in Dante's lap. She really did feel like a girl again. She threw her arms around his neck and plastered his face with kisses.

"I love you, Dante. You are and have always been my salvation." With that she took his hand and started to lead him away from the table.

Dante hesitated, looking at his plate.

"What about the lasagna?"

———◆———

Six months later Angela and Dante Rapallo stood in front of the converted Little Village Market looking at the red, green, and white awning that said *Galliano's*. The grand opening had been a success, and the diners were pleased with the menu and service. But the food was what everybody raved about.

Dante was taking a picture of their two sons standing in front of the entry wearing bright white aprons, each holding a tray of food. A

Dean Martin record could be heard over the early evening traffic on Santa Cruz Avenue.

"It's beautiful, dear," an old lady said as she sat in a wheelchair under a huge oak tree in front. Your Mama and Papa would be proud of you."

"Thank you, Aunt Louisa," Angela said with a thinly stretched voice as a tear rolled down her cheek. "Yes, I think they can truly rest now, Tia. And so can I."

Author's Notes

Gallivanting in the Gem City is an assortment of original short stories about Los Gatos, California, and some of the inhabitants who have resided there. Most characters in the stories are fictional, so for the most part, if you recognize people living or dead, it's purely coincidental. There are, however, actual people in some of the stories (as is listed hereafter). I do hope you can recognize composites of people, places, and events from your past, and that you let me know about it. Nostalgia can be a wonderful thing.

Actual Places in My Stories

Los Gatos is my hometown. It was my father's hometown, also. Many of the locations that are long gone may be familiar to you senior-grade citizens.

I've taken liberties with some sites and features. For example Los Gatos has no Water Street or Waterside Bar and Grill. They're made up. Verduci's Boat Works doesn't exist; the building, however, is Forbes Mill. "Forbes Mill? Where is that?" some might ask. Well, that's the present location of the History Museum of Los Gatos behind Old Town. If you've never been there, you are missing a real chance to soak up the ambiance of Los Gatos and its history.

Oak Meadow Middle School is a fictional name. The school building is the site where University Avenue School once stood. That's where Old Town sits today. The footbridge behind Old Town is described as a wooden bridge that leads to the other side of the creek behind the McKeever home. It's nice to write fiction and move or remove things so they adapt to the story, don't you think? For instance I don't mention Highway 17 by name, and I put back the railroad tracks.

The fictional El Gato Hotel is patterned after the Lyndon Hotel. Lyndon Plaza stands on the actual old hotel location.

The Top Cat Tavern is a fictional name for a long-gone watering hole on Santa Cruz Avenue. Years ago, it was called Club Gato and the last drinking and dining establishment in that place was Mesa's Saloon. CB's of course, is CB Hannegan's, a long-established enterprise that has become an institution. You can learn a lot there if you listen.

The gravel quarry was real and was situated where Vasona Country Park is today. There was a hobo jungle there, too.

The municipal park described on Los Gatos Creek was real. It had a swimming pool and sand playgrounds with swings. The sand led to the creek, which for a lot of us was more fun to play in than the swings and slides. Highway 17 runs right through it today.

The Plunge on the Boardwalk in Santa Cruz is long gone. The museum described does not exist.

Boo-Gang was real also. My brothers Doug and Bert and I fished there. My father swam there. Take a walk up the Los Gatos Creek Trail toward Lexington Dam to a spot where the cement channel no longer lines the creek and the banks become more natural. Around that location, give or take a few yards, might be where Boo-Gang was. *In 1933 there was an actual kidnapping, murder and lynching that took place in St. James Park in San Jose, California.*

Napredak Hall is still in operation. I have not heard of any country and western singers performing there in years. Saratoga Springs is still in operation and is located above Saratoga, California.

The Butcher's Scale is based on a true story out of Greenfield, California, and told to me by my friend Bill Cotton.

The Gem City Gypsys did not exist. They were made up by me. I don't know if the Nazis invaded Cernobbio, Italy, or not. I visited Cernobbio and conjured the image that they did. The Hotel Regina Olga and Villa d'Este exist.

The Live Oak Inn and the 5 Spot were actual places. Double D's now occupies the building where the Live Oak was, and the intersection of Santa Cruz Avenue and Saratoga Avenue is where the 5 Spot stood.

Swanson's Ford Dealership and Templeman's Hardware existed.

Actual People in My Stories

Chris Benson and Johnny Hannegan are the proprietors of CB Hannegan's.

John Baggerly was the editor of the *Los Gatos Times Observer* and a fantastic Los Gatos character. Rest easy, Scoop.

Hugh Welch was the first director of the recreation department in Los Gatos.

The character described as Buster was patterned after Bus Benson who owned the Live Oak Inn.

The baker Ray Robertson owned the Polly Prim Bakery.

Dude Martin was an actual cowboy singer. He and his band may have come to the area to do a show. Where or when, I can't be sure. Jim DeNoon was an actual radio personality in San Jose.

Adolph Hitler and Benito Mussolini, unfortunately, were real.

If you have any questions about any of this, let me know and we can talk. I'd love it!

Steve Sporleder

losgatos.stevesporleder@gmail.com

276302BV00001B/11/P

BV0W071334171111
Printed in the USA
CPSIA information can be obtained at www.ICGtesting.com